UNCLE TARGET

It wasn't just a tank, it was the next generation
Main Battle Tank with a radically new gun –
and the Ministry of Defence had lost it. Or
rather the Jordanian Army had. Major Harry
Maxim's former secondment to the Jordanian
Army draws him into a problem that from the
start goes bloodily wrong.

How the mission changes from a simple
demolition job of the tank before it falls into
Russian hands, and turns into an epic run for
freedom – or cover, is the nerve-jarring core of
UNCLE TARGET.

Uncle Target

Gavin Lyall

CORONET BOOKS
Hodder and Stoughton

First published in Great Britain in 1988 by Hodder and Stoughton Limited
Open market edition 1988
Coronet edition 1989

Printed and bound in Great Britain for Hodder and Stoughton Paperbacks, a division of Hodder and Stoughton Ltd., Mill Road, Dunton Green, Sevenoaks, Kent TN13 2YA. (Editorial Office: 47 Bedford Square, London WC1B 3DP) by Cox & Wyman Ltd., Reading, Berks. Photoset by Rowland Phototypesetting Ltd, Bury St Edmunds, Suffolk.

British Library C.I.P.

Lyall, Gavin, *1932–*
Uncle target.
I. Title
823'.914[F]

ISBN 0-340-48841-7

Uncle Target

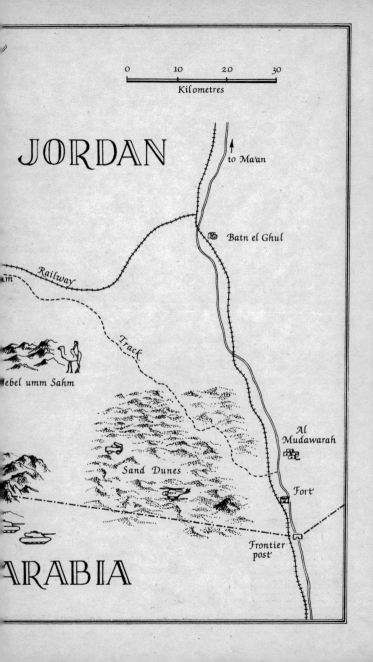

1

Since terrorism had become normal, there were police No Parking cones along the streets outside every London barracks, but a guard sergeant who recognised Agnes Algar let her drive in and wait on the edge of the square itself. When it was past midnight, he brought her a mug of tea and chatted, in a confident but stilted way, because she was an officer's girl-friend, not a wife.

At last a Land-Rover drove in followed by a Bedford truck, and parked neatly side-by-side some yards away. Two soldiers got out of the Land-Rover, carrying an array of haversacks and weapons, and she knew one of them must be Major Harry Maxim yet for a moment couldn't tell which.

That brought a little twinge of isolation, realising that she had never seen him in his camouflaged uniform, slung about with packs and webbing that he would wear if he ever went to the war he had spent his life training for.

Then she saw him stretch, cat-like, within the baggy combat clothing, recognised the gesture and saw, or thought she saw in the lamplight, the lean concave face with its uncommitted smile, and then another gesture as he checked the set of his beret, one he must have done thousands of times and she had never seen before, and she felt isolated again.

Other soldiers were clambering stiffly out of the back of the Bedford, and the sergeant who had been with Maxim began giving orders in a roaring whisper.

'Don't stamp about, lads, your mates are trying to get

11

some kip. Forester, organise the signals kit. The rest of you . . .'

When he had finished, a voice asked: 'How did we do, sir?'

'Terrible,' she heard Maxim answer. 'I'd rather have a troop of Girl Guides.'

'So would I,' another voice said. 'Just bring 'em to me, one by –'

'Knock it off,' the sergeant growled. He turned to Maxim, saluted, asked: 'Carry on, sir?'

'Carry on, sergeant.'

'Good night, sir.'

'Good night, sergeant.'

How dreadfully *formal*, she thought; surely they can't fight wars – even exercises – with such rank-conscious politeness. Then she remembered that she knew nothing about fighting anything but a secret war, and that the sergeant was just pulling them together in their weariness, reminding them that two days of 'playing soldiers' was over and they were back in the Real Army of a London barracks.

The group tramped away towards the still bright-lit barrack blocks and she lost sight of Maxim again, until he became the one heading towards the officers' quarters. It annoyed her once more not to recognise instantly the man who so happily shared her bed, and she glowered at the barracks that was the Army she shared him with. And swore slightly that she would never marry him and It. If he ever asked her, damn him.

Then she felt childish and got out of the car to wait

Underneath the lamplight
By the barrack gate . . .

and grinned because she had never seen herself in the Lili Marlene role, though her life in the Security Service had brought odder ones.

Maxim came out wearing plain clothes and carrying a

12

tote bag of, probably, dirty shirts and underclothes that he would insist on running through her machine himself and then even ironing himself.

He grinned at her, hugged her, and said: 'You shouldn't have waited. But thanks. How are you? Did you hear anything about Jordan?'

One day, one night, she might get in her own query about his day before he asked his own questions. Good old Harry: don't ask about me, I'm all right, just tell me about yourself and the world . . . she had come prepared.

She drove off. 'I'm fine, Jordan isn't. There's still growlings on their frontier with Syria and the 17th, I think it was the 17th, armoured brigade –'

'It would be. They should never have formed that one.'

'It's revolted and declared the Aqaba district an independent republic.'

'Have they got the town itself?'

'They seem to have got it cut off. I honestly don't know more than that.' There were things in both their lives they couldn't tell each other, but in an odd way that made them closer, because they were both keepers of certain keys. But this time, Agnes was out of her depth; Maxim had far more inside knowledge of the military situations in the Middle East than she had.

'Rumour by radio,' he said. 'Start broadcasting that something's happened and it has happened . . . Oh well, I'm running an HQ unit in London District.'

'And how did it run on Salisbury Plain these last two days?'

'We ran the Land-Rover into a ditch and had to sort out its steering, that's why we're late, sorry about that. But they're good, they're bloody good.'

'I heard you tell them so.'

In the passing flicker of street lamps, she saw his quiet smile. 'They кnew what I meant.'

'If you say so . . . When you all got out you all looked, well, tired but terribly tough, and all the same. At first I couldn't pick you out.'

Another glance showed him nodding, not displeased. 'Neither can enemy snipers, then.'

'That's not what I meant, you self-centred yobbo . . . Then I saw how young they all are, just boys, really.'

'But not me? They always are young. Look at the ages on war graves sometime.'

Then, when she didn't say anything more, he went to sleep, cat-like both in its suddenness and its trust in her. She was a good driver, very good, but she had never had a man before who would fall asleep beside her in a car. *I don't understand this man, so how can I love him?*

Let's just say I won't let him go until I understand him.

2

Not much work was done in Maxim's office next morning: perhaps not much was being done in any Army office where two or more officers had managed to get hold of a map of the Middle East and were plotting – from scraps of information and inspired guesswork – just what was happening in Jordan. Those who had been attached to the Jordanian Army – and there were quite a number, Maxim included – were kept answering questions or, if they chose, giving impromptu lectures that began: 'One thing I'm quite certain of . . .'

News that somebody had been shot in a London hotel and that police were surrounding a room where there were gunmen and hostages passed almost unnoticed until it was reported that the hostages were Jordanian. Then there was a pause while they agreed that it was probably all part of the same affair, but a siege in a London hotel wasn't as interesting as the mobilisation state of an armoured brigade, so . . .

In other offices, which were actually supposed to be worrying about Jordan, the name of one of the hostages was fed into a computer which ruminated upon it and flickered back a file number. Somebody dug out the file, but most of it was ten years old. The most recent item was a single-page report dated four years before and signed by Major H. R. Maxim.

It took Maxim a good quarter of an hour to identify himself and talk his way past the police checkpoints at the hotel entrance, at the lift, coming out of the lift at the third floor, and then at the top of the stairs onto the fourth floor. Nobody seemed to know why he was there and he wasn't sure himself.

The gunmen and hostages were in suite 421, which was luckily at the back of the hotel, not overlooking the street, and the police had cleared the whole floor and probably parts of the third and fifth as well. There was an incomplete barricade of tables, desks and chairs just at the top of the stairs, manned by police marksmen with pistols and shotguns; no rifles, Maxim was glad to see. A modern rifle would probably shoot through half a dozen of the hotel's internal walls. Police listeners were in 419 and 423, bracketing the gunmen, and a forward command post had been set up in 415, a safe distance away. It was rather sad how efficient the police had had to become about tackling sieges.

He was explaining himself yet once more at the open door of 415 when George Harbinger's voice called: 'Is that you, Harry? Come on in. Let him in, for God's sake,' and Maxim went in.

It was the drawing-room of the suite, tall and spacious and kept furnished and decorated in the style of the hotel's opening day before the First World War. It would have cost an arm and a leg to rent, but the hotel's guests were, financially, octopuses.

Now, the elegance was rather spoiled by a clump of small tables pushed together in the middle and with a street map and an architectural plan of the hotel spread over them, surrounded by policemen, wires, field telephones, radios, Norman Sprague from the Home Office, and George: tubby, slightly frog-faced and wearing his usual checked grey suit, rumpled but never shabby.

But it was Sprague, never daring to look rumpled, let alone shabby, who reached to display his firm, cool handshake. 'Major Maxim! How delightful to see you again – although the circumstances could be more congenial. I understand you knew Colonel –'

'Let me, Norman,' George cut in. He introduced Maxim

to two high-ranking policemen, one of them in uniform, who didn't smile at the idea of an Army presence. 'You knew Colonel Katbah in Jordan, right? Anyway, you wrote a report on him.'

Maxim nodded.

'He's held hostage in 421 by at least three gunmen. We don't –'

'Hostage for what?'

Nobody knew. George said: 'I may have been speaking loosely. The point is, they've got him and they've put him on the phone twice already, just saying what they told him to. To wit: if we barge in there, he gets killed along with his wife. Yes, she's there, too. The next time he comes on, we wanted somebody he recognised to do the talking. All right?'

'What about the Jordanian embassy? There must be somebody there who –'

'They should be sending somebody over, but they're in a state of chaos since the Aqaba district revolt.'

'Have the gunmen asked for anything?'

One of the policemen said: 'Nothing except to be left alone.'

A junior policeman, having decided that Maxim belonged, offered him a mug of tea. A crisis in Britain wouldn't be complete without constant mugs of tea. Maxim took it automatically.

'Do you think this is a show siege, lots of TV coverage, publicity for the cause and so on?'

'We don't think so,' the other senior policeman said. 'We think they just intended to kidnap the Colonel and take him somewhere else. They got surprised by a security guard in the corridor and shot him. We think that was panic; he wasn't armed, of course. Then they holed up in the Colonel's room.'

'No diplomatic squad guard?' Maxim queried.

'We weren't –'

Sprague said: 'There was the *tiny* breakdown in communications between Defence and my Office over the

Colonel's visit.' He smiled at George, who shrugged.

'He was hoping to keep his visit fairly incognito; he was going down to Coventry today to visit the GTL works – you know we've been testing the prototype of the new MBT in Jordan?'

'I heard something.' In fact, Maxim's ears now automatically shut off when the lunchtime or coffee break conversation turned yet again to what design the Army would choose (or have forced on them) for the next generation of Main Battle Tank.

'We're hoping the Jordanians will buy it as well, and Katbah wanted to have a look at the factory. It seems he didn't make his visit incognito enough and somebody . . . so here we are.' He nodded in the direction of suite 421.

Maxim considered. 'If they'd wanted to kill him, they'd just have killed him. If they wanted to get him away somewhere, they either wanted him as a hostage or to get some information out of him.'

'Or both,' Sprague said smoothly. 'Our thinking *had* got that far.'

Maxim flickered his quick defensive smile. 'But either way, they planned on getting away themselves, so presumably still do. They aren't on a suicide mission if they want to get some information out. Do they have an outside phone in there?'

'It's been cut off at the hotel switchboard,' one of the policemen said.

'So the next move is theirs.'

'That's right.'

Maxim settled down beside the telephone; Sprague went to find another phone to call his office, the policemen started giving orders on the field telephones and radios. George looked at his watch and took a flask from his briefcase and poured something into his tea, then offered the flask to Maxim, who shook his head. It wasn't quite eleven o'clock.

'How well do you know Katbah?' George asked.

'So-so. He'd been at Sandhurst . . .' Most senior Jordanian officers had been trained in Britain; '. . . so we had something to talk about, but he's a tank man. Mad about them. I thought he'd probably get to the top, that's why I tried to understand what he was talking about and did a report on him.'

'And you're not mad about tanks?'

'Nothing wrong with them except they're big and noisy and smoky and smelly and cramped and attract a lot of attention.'

'But the queen of the modern battlefield.'

'You can capture ground with anything, even helicopters,' Maxim quoted, 'but you can only hold it with men.'

It was an old argument: George's two years of Army service had been with a cavalry regiment (whose senior officers shared Maxim's opinion of tanks, but reluctantly accepted that they were more practical nowadays than horses), while Maxim's career had been with a light infantry battalion and in two tours with the even more man-orientated Special Air Service.

At that moment, his SAS past caught up with him. One of the senior policemen came away from a field telephone with his face looking sour. 'Major, there's somebody from the Special Air Service at Hereford wants to talk to you. He says his name's Barney, won't give any rank.'

Maxim grinned and took the phone; the SAS went in for a lot of highly personalised anonymity. 'Harry here.'

'Me old chum, nice to have you on the spot. We're setting up a little exercise here in case we have to come in and Save The Day. We've got the floor plan, but what sort of windows?'

Maxim glanced at those in their own suite. 'Double glazed.'

'Ouch. Rather a lot of glass whizzing around. How about the walls?'

'Can't tell by looking. I'll call you back.'

The senior policeman got even more sour when Maxim opened a penknife and started poking through the rich wallpaper.

'But,' Maxim asked, 'aren't you poking microphones into the walls yourself?'

'Of course we are, so why don't you go along and ask the chaps in 419 what the walls are like?'

Shamefacedly, Maxim got permission from George to desert his post. As he went out, Sprague came back. 'COBRA meeting at half past,' he told George. 'I'm away to brief my Minister.'

Sinister though it sounded, COBRA meant merely the Cabinet Office Briefing Room, where emergencies of this sort were discussed by ministers and others involved. The Defence minister would be there; George hurried, insofar as his figure allowed of hurry, to find the next-door phone.

A look at the floor plan had shown Maxim that the suites along the corridor were each a mirror image of the one next along. Drawing-room (with the only door onto the corridor), bedroom, bathroom, then bathroom, bedroom, drawing-room and so on. 419's drawing-room was next to 421's, so that was where the team of lower-rank police and technicians had gently peeled off the flock wallpaper and picked out the plaster and mortar to set probe microphones into the brickwork.

Maxim was surprised to hear rock music, muffled but obviously strong at its source. An inspector led Maxim back into the bedroom, away from the earphoned listeners.

'Why,' Maxim asked, 'have we got a sound-track with this epic?'

'Because they've read enough books and newspapers about us poking mikes through walls on other sieges,' the inspector said evenly, 'and they've got a battery radio in there. Not the usual piped hotel stuff, we got that cut off, but independent. It screws us up something splendid. Not that we'd get much from here. We've pin-pointed one person in the drawing-room, just through the wall, but he's probably just there to watch the corridor door. They've got the hostages in the bedroom, in the middle. We're trying to put mikes in from above and below, but it takes a while to get a floorboard up quietly. If they start shooting through the ceiling . . .'

Maxim's glance at the plaster mouldings on the high ceiling told him nothing, but he guessed that, unless it hit a joist, even a pistol bullet would go straight through. He didn't envy the policemen working above 421, knowing that one creak might bring gunfire. It was a nasty direction from which to be shot.

He and the inspector offered each other cigarettes at the same time, decided to stick to their own, and sat down on chairs beside the big double bed. It was unmade, with pyjamas and a nightgown mixed up in the sheets, and the wardrobe doors hung open, showing suits and dresses. He wondered briefly who the occupants had been and where they had gone once the police had turfed them out; probably there was a refugee camp of the rich and famous somewhere in the hotel getting a free champagne breakfast . . . in the end, would the hotel profit or suffer from the publicity?

It wasn't his concern, nor the inspector's. 'The walls between the bathroom and bedroom are just lath-and-plaster, the others are single brick. The corridors are the supporting walls, double brick, no cavities. The plaster's pretty thick, they didn't take all the old stuff off when they redid it, probably ten years ago; the inside stuff close to the brickwork, it's pretty crumbly. Ask me, it's only the heavy wallpaper that's holding it on in places. Some contractor saved a few bob and didn't tell the management.'

'I never realised how much of a siege was architecture.'

The inspector smiled lopsidedly. 'A few more years in this job and I'll be able to design my retirement cottage single-handed.' He was about Maxim's age, late thirties. 'But aren't you one of the Hereford Heroes?'

Maxim controlled his wince. 'I was for a time, but mostly abroad; never a siege. Now I'm OC a desk.'

'But your lads are getting all kitted up, got that special

21

building arranged with partitions just like next door, fill the place with smoke and go charging in firing blanks? Or do they use live?'

The only answer he got was Maxim's polite smile. Very likely that was just what Barney was organising at this moment, but it was Barney's business, not his.

'And knitting themselves more little black ski masks?' the inspector suggested. 'They'll have time to finish them. These things take time.'

He sounded tired already, as if the days and nights ahead had crept back on him. Maxim stubbed out his cigarette, stood up – and then, without any help from the probe microphones, and through three single-brick walls, they heard Colonel Katbah scream. So perhaps there now wasn't so much time.

George was at one of the field phones which was patched through to COBRA. He put his hand over the mouthpiece and turned to the policemen and Maxim. 'The Home Sec won't agree to Army action yet. There's a helicopter just landed at Hereford to bring a team down . . . How long?'

'About an hour's flight,' Maxim estimated. 'Loading and unloading won't take long, but even if we put them into Hyde Park with transport waiting . . . hour and a half minimum before they're here. Probably half an hour to set up charges, I'd like a whole hour to get things properly sorted out. If you just barge in, you may get everybody killed, and that isn't the objective.'

'Two and a half hours, not allowing for hitches.' George looked at the policemen.

The senior plainclothes policeman shook his head firmly. 'We just aren't equipped or trained for this sort of thing. We can go in through doors, but that's a last resort. We prefer to talk such people out. We aren't the Army.'

'Harry: how fast could you go in there?'

'By myself?'

George took a deep breath. 'Such modesty. No, *not* by yourself, but with what you can collect around London.'

Sergeant Travers from my own unit, Maxim thought, and Corporal Delaney from the Famish support party, he's a cold-hearted bastard who can think with a gun, and . . . and plastic explosive from the Duke of York's HQ, an X-frame . . .

'Hour and a half from the word Go. Less with luck. I can start clearing a place for the charges now – if somebody'll cover me.'

'How would you go in?'

'Through the corridor wall straight into the bedroom.'

The policeman sucked in his breath. 'What'll that do to the hostages?'

'Not much good to their eardrums, but not much else. The windows'll blow outwards, there won't be a problem with glass.'

The policeman looked at Maxim, curiously, as if he were something new in an aquarium. George started talking rapidly into the field telephone.

'Why not,' the policeman asked Maxim, 'go in through the drawing room wall? There's only one of the gunmen in there, and if he gets –'

'The blast could jam the door into the bedroom and we'd have to shoot it open and God knows what we'd hit on the other side. Same with the bathroom on the other end. I want to arrive in the middle of the party.'

The senior policeman said quietly: 'I hope to hell there's still a party left.'

George turned from the telephone: 'Harry – you've got the go-ahead for everything up to the word Go.'

3

That morning Agnes had taken up a long-standing invitation to coffee with Annette Harbinger in Albany. They made How-Dreadful-Quite-Terrible noises about the hotel siege, neither having any idea that both their menfolk were involved, and left it at that.

'Am I allowed to ask how you like your new job?' Annette asked. 'Or is that an offence under the Official Secrets Acts?'

'More likely an incitement to the use of language liable to cause a breach of the peace.' Agnes put her cup down with more of a clang than she had intended.

'Oh dear. You never did get on with the Gentleman Attached To The Foreign Office, did you? Why did they do it?'

'After my goings-on in America and what that did to our Director-General's reputation (incompetent old fart) they reckoned it would be tactful to have me out of the way for a while. So they did a swap with some goon at Six and here I am in the Secret Bloody Intelligence Service! I don't know anything about spying abroad. I've spent my life catching spies *here*. The thinking's different.'

'And after all you've said about them. Well, you'll just have to learn to love them.'

'If I ever feel it coming on, I'll take a cold shower. They aren't nasty to me, they're infuriatingly polite. But they just don't know what to do with me. They've got me working on some report on the future status of women in Islam. File fodder.'

Annette, small and dark with a comfortable figure, cocked her head and smiled at Agnes with more sympathy than she felt. She herself had been married into government service for twenty years and had learnt to take each day as it came. Maybe this will make Agnes grow up, she thought – and maybe somebody long-sighted in Security had had the same thought.

Then she felt guilty, because Agnes's commitment was rare enough in the service, and she herself had no intention of letting George stay until retiring age. The moment he inherited the Gloucestershire estate, she was going to have him in green gumboots, bouncing through the mud in a Land-Rover with a collie dog sitting in the passenger seat. Half French, Annette had a very clear idea of what sort of Englishwoman she wanted to be before she died.

Agnes said: 'How's George keeping? – I haven't seen much of him recently.' It couldn't be pure coincidence that she was gazing at the tray of bottles in the corner when she said that.

'George is fine,' Annette said firmly. 'And Harry? I haven't seen so much of him since he and George left doing whatever-it-was at Downing Street.'

'Oh, he's fine. He's running some HQ unit for London District and he had them out charging over Salisbury Plain for a couple of days. Came home last night happy as a sandboy and with his ears full of camouflage cream.'

'George told me you'd been to France.'

'Yes, they gave me some leave before . . . So we took a car over for ten days.'

'A sort of honeymoon,' Annette risked.

Agnes's face blanked. 'A sort of.' Then her expression flickered through memories of joy and anger. 'He wanted to look at battlefields and forts and I thought he'd better look at some cathedrals as well. I tell you, Annette, I *swear* to you, that he spent his whole time in Chartres Cathedral wondering where to set up machine-gun nests. He didn't say a thing, but I just *knew*.'

Annette laughed aloud. 'You really shouldn't try to

improve your men. I'm beginning to think it doesn't work with children, either. Just try and enjoy them.'

Agnes sipped her cooling coffee. 'I suppose so . . . but I don't know where we go from here . . . I don't understand his work –'

'My dear girl, I don't understand half of what George does at Defence. I'm not supposed to.'

'Yes, but this is the *Army*. I just don't see myself as an Army wife – or camp-follower. How his first wife, Jenny –'

'She's been dead some time, now.'

'He was very much in love with her.'

'He's in love with you, now. I can see that.'

'But can he really –?'

'He's changed. I remember when George first brought him here for dinner, scrupulously polite and quite, quite untouchable. Now time's gone by, he's had new postings, things have happened to him – mostly you. You've been good for him – and he for you.'

Agnes looked at her suspiciously.

Annette said: 'My dear Agnes, hadn't you noticed that you're happy? Never mind your new job, you're happier now than I've ever known you. You really ought to admit it to yourself.'

Agnes felt tears starting in her eyes and said: 'Oh bugger it!' because she hated women who cried easily.

'How do you get on with his boy, Chris?'

'Scrupulously polite and quite, quite untouchable. I can't tell if he likes me . . .'

'He may not want to know himself. He doesn't know how permanent a fixture you are.'

4

They grouped in suite 417, an exact duplicate of 421 except for the furniture, and nobody knew how that might have been re-arranged in 421 anyway. They were a mixed bunch – two of them, plus Maxim himself, weren't even in uniform – but all except one were NCOs and men he had worked with in the past six months. The one was an SAS captain stationed at the Duke of York's HQ in Sloane Square, who had supplied the weaponry and wanted 'to see if it works' but was torn, Maxim guessed, between wanting the Hereford group to arrive in time to take over and the knowledge that, if they did, he would be squeezed out.

The bedroom of 417 was their map, its bed their armoury. Captain 'David' had laid on both Sterling and Heckler & Koch submachine-guns, standard Browning pistols and shortened pump-action shotguns – even a few grenades. Maxim ruled those out immediately.

'One bang only, and that's the mousehole charge. It's on a three-by-two X-frame blowing through here.' He indicated the planned gap in the bedroom/corridor wall.

'We've got something a little more advanced than that –' David began.

'I know you have, but I haven't. An X-frame is the best I could do in the time. We seem to be getting ahead of ourselves. Okay; intention: to break into suite 421, kill three terrorists and rescue two hostages. I'll give more information on them later, descriptions, whatever the police listeners have picked up . . .' He was giving himself time to look around their faces after that 'kill three terrorists', because this wasn't 'capture that hill', it *was* just 'kill three terrorists'. Then it would be over. No consolidation, setting up a defence against counter-attack, lines of communication . . . kill three people and we can go home. And it had to be spelled out in the old 'O Group' format, because this wasn't a shopping list where you could say 'I forgot the cabbage, I'll pop down later and see if the corner shop . . .' If it took more than ten seconds from the firing of the charge to the last shot then he would likely have failed, and have taken casualties as well.

No, he told himself, I won't have 'taken casualties': I'll have got some of these, my people, killed or crippled. They must know exactly what I intend and I must be sure they know. State the obvious and restate it. The alternative is a bullet in the guts.

The passive or nodding faces reassured him. A spiral of trust: the more he told them, the more they trusted him, the more he trusted them to do the right thing when the unforeseen happened.

'Method: we blow in the corridor wall and immediately afterwards shoot out the lock of the suite door. I'm not bothering with diversions, it would simply alert the terrorists. Our forces: two groups, David and Corporal Cox; Travers and Delaney with me. David, you wait just inside 419 and tackle the door, with Cox as backup. My group in 422 across the corridor, I'll fire the charge from there. When we go through the wall fan out sideways and stay close to the wall. The same thing with you, David, if you go into the drawing-room; don't go deep in. If the chap in there runs back into the bedroom I want to be able to shoot without worrying about you on the far side.'

David nodded; he wasn't going to be part of the main action but at least he was in charge of his own part.

'Gentlemen, choose your weapons.' The chuckle lightened the atmosphere. The distant music and an occasional scream were getting them too tensed, too much of a hurry to get stuck in. 'Everybody takes a pistol as backup, you can pick your personal weapon yourself but don't take a Heckler & Koch or a shotgun unless you know them properly. You all know Sterlings.'

'I've got my own gun, if you don't mind, Major,' Corporal Delaney said. It was a fat American revolver, a Magnum something-or-other, and almost certainly illegally owned, but Delaney would be good with it. There were, God help us, times for people like Corporal Delaney. Perhaps times for people like Major Maxim, too. Am I actually *enjoying* this? he wondered. I like it better than my desk, but please God, not the way Delaney likes it.

'I do mind,' he said. 'This is going to end up at an inquest and a lot of coppers with nothing better to do than dig bullets out of walls and people. They're all going to be standard issue bullets – okay?'

Reluctantly, Delaney accepted that his own career was at stake and chose a Browning pistol instead. David prompted: 'Enemy forces?'

'I'm going next door to get the latest gen. Will you run through it again and handle any questions?'

He left Captain David looking distinctly happy.

Suite 415 was even fuller. Sprague had returned, with another Home Office man, a Colonel from London District and a mixed Army-civilian medical team with their kit, and at last somebody from the Jordanian embassy. There was a hush as Maxim came in, then everybody started asking or telling him things.

'We're ready once we've got the latest gen on where everybody is in their suite,' Maxim announced. One of the policemen picked up a radio, George reached for a field phone.

The Colonel said softly: 'The SAS team's held up, their helicopter had to put down at Benson. Bloody helicopters. So if we're asked to go in in the next hour and a half, you're it, Harry.'

Maxim nodded.

'Pity you couldn't be in *some* sort of uniform,' the

Colonel added, and Maxim realised why they had hushed when he came in. From the waist down he was in his blue pinstripe suit and black shoes, around his waist was a webbing belt with holster, but above that he was naked except for a police flak jacket he had borrowed whilst placing the X-frame in the corridor. Flak jacket and shoes apart, he would be happy to go into action stark naked. It was fragments of clothing rotting in the body that made wounds medically interesting.

The inspector from 419 appeared beside them and, with a nod from his seniors, began speaking quietly and methodically. 'There are three of them. We think one is a woman, from what we can make out from the voices through the music, and footsteps. We call them Alpha – the woman – Bravo and Charlie. Charlie stays in the drawing-room and doesn't move around much, mostly he's by the door to the bedroom, probably watching the corridor door. Bravo stays mostly by the window at the head of the bed. We think Colonel Katbah is at the foot of the bed, probably tied to a chair. Alpha's with him, doing the torturing. Mrs Katbah is over in the corner, by the window, the other end from Bravo.'

He hesitated and consulted his notebook. 'At 12.17 Bravo and Mrs Katbah went into the drawing-room. There was what appeared to be angry talk in Arabic and then she screamed. They returned to the bedroom at 12.31, to their old positions.'

The Colonel said: 'They – Bravo – raped her?'

'I don't know, sir.'

'Weapons?' Maxim asked.

'No useful idea, except that they must be the size you could get into a suitcase. They shot the guard with a 9 mm., but . . .' He shrugged; that could be either pistol or submachine-gun, since both used the same cartridge.

The inspector shut his notebook.

'Does any of that change your plans, Harry?' the Colonel asked.

'No, sir.'

A senior policeman asked: 'What guarantees can you give, Major?'

'That the terrorists get killed. Nothing else.'

'The safety of the hostages? Your own men?'

'No guarantee.'

The policeman took a deep breath. 'That spells it out for us. I'd like to wait it out until we know more.'

George said: 'If they're torturing Katbah it's because they want something out of him. When they've got it, they can walk out alive, facing charges of murder, kidnapping, probably rape and . . . you know the menu better than I do, but there is no way, no way at all, that we can stop them passing that information on, soon, if they're alive.'

'What information?' Norman Sprague asked.

'*I* don't know,' George said irritably. 'I'm just trying to frustrate their intentions.'

'I only asked because Defence seems to be surprisingly eager to take this out of the hands of the civil power. I confess to the unworthy thought that you knew something we didn't.'

George said nothing. The senior policeman said: 'Personally, I wouldn't mind having these people dead and finished. If they end up in jail there'll be more hijackings and hostages to blackmail us into letting them go – I know all that. But I can't recommend an assault at this time . . .' He considered; 'Well, if it's at COBRA level it's out of my hands anyway, thank God. I'm just obeying orders and I can't get hurt.'

'Just cogs in the great machine,' George said, 'and for once the great machine is going to have to take a decision without green papers and white papers and debates in the House . . . The one person here who could get hurt is Harry. What d'you think?'

'Ring them up,' Maxim said promptly.

'*What?*'

'If they can get through to us, we can get through to them. Tell them we're coming in to kill them if they don't walk out right now.'

Sprague asked: 'What would that achieve, Major?'

'If they want to get information out, they might settle for coming out alive with what they've got so far.' He was watching George, not Sprague.

George didn't look him in the eye. 'How well will Katbah have held out?'

'He's tough, they haven't got him in the place they planned, they haven't got the time they planned for; they're improvising. They may not have got much, yet.'

Sprague said: 'They appear – sound – to be trying hard enough.'

'He'll talk in the end, if we give them the time. And they won't bother to leave him alive at the end of it. They've got one murder charge to face, why not two?'

There was a moment of everybody looking at everybody else, hoping to see a decision in another face. Then George said: 'If I've got anything to say about it, go ahead. But make sure you speak to Katbah.'

One of the senior policemen waved at the phone. 'If you call the switchboard, they'll put you through. But . . . who are you going to be?'

'I have to be myself. He's got to recognise me.'

'Will *they*?' George said.

'Doubt it. It was some time ago, there's been a lot of British officers through Jordan since then.'

The policeman said: 'If you say *Major* Maxim, it tips them off that you could be going for a break-in. Army presence and all that.'

Maxim looked around. 'They must be expecting that anyway, the thing they most fear, that's why they're doing a fast job on Katbah.'

The policeman said: 'You might put more pressure on them, to speed it up even more.'

Maxim wished he'd thought this through better. 'All right . . . is it okay if I'm Superintendent Maxim?'

'You can be a commander as far as I'm concerned.' With a cool little smile.

32

Maxim picked up the phone. He felt, rather than saw, the audience gather behind him, breathing softly.

The blast of rock music at the other end of the telephone was deafening. 'What?' he yelled. 'I can't hear. Turn it down, turn it down.'

It cut off completely. A guttural Arab voice said: 'Who is that?'

'Superintendent Harry Maxim. I want to talk to Colonel Katbah.'

'Why?'

'To make sure he and his wife are still alive.'

'We are not making deals. We will come out when we come out.'

'Are they still alive?' There was a threat behind that, and the voice on the telephone recognised it. With nobody left to rescue, you could sort the whole thing out with a handful of grenades.

'He is here. Go, speak.'

A drained, strained voice said: 'I am Colonel Katbah.'

'Superintendent Harry Maxim. We met once at a –'

'Yes. Yes, I remember . . .' Then he suddenly switched into German, taking Maxim very much by surprise. His mind switched gears, trying to catch up. '*Verfechter*,' Katbah said, then the phone cut off. They heard the music start again down the corridor.

Maxim put the hard-clenched phone down slowly.

'What did he say?' the real police superintendent asked. 'Well, at least we'll have that clean on the tapes.'

'He said they were castrating him.' Maxim's German had caught up with the numbing words. 'Then he said *Verfechter* and was cut off.'

'What does that mean?' the Superintendent asked.

'Oh, sort of master, boss, champion.'

'What did he mean?'

'I suppose the head of the terrorist group. He was using German as a code, he knew I knew a bit.' He stood up. 'If we're going in, we've got to go before he bleeds to death.'

George was on one field phone, Sprague on another. Maxim looked at the Jordanian embassy man – in his thirties and dressed in a better pinstripe suit than Maxim's was or ever had been. 'Do you know the Colonel and his wife?'

'I have met the Colonel once, not his wife. We were not informed he was coming to England.'

'Yes.' Too much damned secrecy. All the wrong people ended up knowing what the right ones didn't.

George called: 'The Cabinet agrees. You go, Harry. Colonel?'

The Colonel from District nodded. 'Is there anything else you want, Harry? All right, you'll be backstopped. Good luck.'

'Three terrorists,' Maxim told them in 417, 'one a woman. All –' he had been going to say 'young', but the men around him were 'young' by his standards; '– in their twenties. Not Arab dress, as far as we know. Colonel Katbah's around fifty, short and squat, grey hair. He may be half dressed or even naked – if he's tied to a chair, you'll know him anyway. His wife's about the same age, I don't know how she'll be dressed, she's . . . I wouldn't call her pretty. A rather dumpy lady. They come out alive, the rest come out dead – okay? Any questions?'

He checked the X-frame one last time as he, Sergeant Travers and Corporal Delaney tiptoed along to 422. The frame was simply two lengths of wood nailed in the middle so that the ends were two feet apart at the top and bottom. The four tips each had four ounces of plastic explosive moulded around detonators and detonator cord and taped into the holes Maxim had carefully picked in the plaster. Plaster absorbs explosions; brickwork tries to resist, and loses.

The det cord ran back into 422, which now had all its windows open to save them from the blast, and hung over the back of a chair. He wasn't using an electric initiator; fire would run down that cord as fast as a pistol bullet, but explosions remained a tricky thing, at least for him. It was only into the ear of a true Engineer that God had whispered The Word about demolition charges, as Engineers had told him often. Maybe the hole wouldn't be complete, or the whole wall would collapse, or . . . life is maybe, maybe even for Engineers.

'Ready.' Their weapons clacked into the cocked position, they pulled down the ear protectors, leaving one hand on them to wrench them off once the explosion had passed.

He leant into the corridor and spread five fingers at David, peeking round the door of 419. David nodded and ducked back.

He flicked his lighter; lucky he'd taken up smoking again. '. . . four, three, two . . .' he touched the flame to the cord; '. . . one . . .' The cord fizzed, the building shook under his feet and a shock-wave punched him in the stomach. He tore off the protectors and charged into the gust of warm dusty air coming from the corridor, Delaney hustling him. It was dark – the lights had blown out – but there was a near-perfect rectangle of dust-hazy light in the wall; he'd got it right.

Other figures – David and Cox – moving to his left, the boom and flash as they blew open the drawing-room door, then he was through the hole and back against the wall. The room was full of settling dust but not as dark as he'd feared; one set of curtains had blown out with the window behind them. Beside him, Delaney fired a Sterling, tearing the bed into sudden waves of silk, and a man crashed back against the wall beyond. More shots, shotgun and submachine, and where was Katbah? – lying on the floor, yes, tied to a chair and half naked, covered in blood and dust, and Mrs Katbah? –

'Cease fire!' It wasn't exactly silence, with the ringing in the ears, the patter of falling plaster, somebody moaning . . .

'Which was her?' Delaney demanded. 'Mrs Katbah? You said she was old.'

The dust faded. There were two women, both thirtyish and both, as far as he could see, fully dressed. The one in the far corner by the shattered window was doing the moaning. At least one bullet had hit her in the chest.

'Which *was* she?' Delaney was shouting. 'You said she was *old*!'

'Get the medics. *Move!*' Maxim knelt beside the wreck that had been Colonel Katbah. He was still alive, too. But he died in the ambulance, with Maxim still holding his hand.

5

'It was my fault,' Maxim said. 'I didn't know he'd divorced and married a younger woman. But I should have checked with the hotel desk to find somebody who'd seen her when they arrived. I made an assumption and I was wrong . . . How is she?'

'Critical,' Sprague said, fluttering his hand elegantly, 'in intensive care . . . She may or may not. Do you know who actually shot her?'

'My unit. I was in command of it.'

'I'm afraid a British court wouldn't accept that, if it should ever come to court –'

George said: 'I don't think this is going to court, Norman.' He gave Sprague an intense if rather bleary stare and poured himself another whisky. It was his office, and they – including a police Superintendent from suite 415 – were sitting around a small conference table in front of the desk.

'One never knows,' Sprague said, 'what an inquest may decide – if it comes to an inquest. The underlying principle of British law is individual responsibility, that's why we can never get convictions in fraud cases –'

Maxim said: 'I'm individual and I'm responsible.'

'But,' George put in, 'acting on orders from COBRA, effectively the Cabinet itself – so are they *individually* responsible as well, and in danger of prosecution? All Harry guaranteed was that the terrorists would end up dead, and I'll testify that you heard that as clearly as I did.'

Sprague's expression clicked into a jovial smile. 'My dear

George, we aren't trying to *create* blame, only preparing to fend it off. The clear intention of the operation – in the simple public mind, if not elsewhere – was to bring the hostages out alive. It clearly failed, unless there was some other intention . . .'

The Superintendent was looking at George questioningly, without asking the questions. Maxim was curious, too; he believed he had been told to do the right thing, but he wasn't sure he knew the reasons. However, he said: 'They'd castrated Katbah by the time I talked to him on the phone. By the time we got in, they'd cut off his prick. He bled to death.'

Sprague's smile had become rather rigid. 'When that comes out at the inquest it will obviously help our cause . . . However,' he lifted a copy of Maxim's report from the table, 'a suggestion that Mrs Katbah was trying to defend herself – from whom? – by reaching for a weapon. Did you see this yourself?'

'No.'

'Ah. Then it must have been Sergeant Travers or Corporal Delaney, presumably the one that shot her. Do you believe this, ah, person?'

Do I believe Delaney? Maxim wondered. He's a killer, but not a berserker. He has no doubts to overcome when he touches a trigger, and that gives him the tiny advantage in time, time to see what's going on. Maybe he saw something I didn't, and maybe somebody who's just been knocked down by an explosion does inexplicable things, reaches for anything . . .

'It was mentioned,' Maxim said stolidly. 'That was why I put it in my report.'

'Well . . .' Sprague said, and again: 'Well . . . we can only hope that Mrs Katbah recovers so that we can show some profit from the operation. Unless Defence think it's already been profitable enough.'

Sprague suspected something, but Sprague always suspected something.

George shrugged. 'It's now clear we couldn't have saved

38

Katbah's life, no matter what. At least we killed off three terrorists, so there'll be no trial, no more terrorism to get them free from jail – and we've passed the word that we'll fight firepower with firepower. Cutting future losses is also a profit, or so my banker brother-in-law assures me.'

'Unpredictable though it may be. However, we did not find out what they wanted Katbah to tell them or what he did tell them. Unless Mrs Katbah recovers to tell us.'

'It doesn't matter, not now, what he told them,' George said. 'The point is that the information didn't get out of suite 421.'

'But we don't know just what information that was,' Sprague pointed out. 'Unless the Colonel said something before he died.' He looked at Maxim. 'You were with him in the room, and in the ambulance.'

'He said something which might be an address,' Maxim said.

'*That* isn't in your report.'

'For security reasons,' George said. 'Special Branch has got it.'

'At the Home Office we have some *slight* connection with security matters.' Sprague was happily back in the saddle of indignation.

'We're pretty sure,' the Superintendent said, 'there was a fourth person involved. A Mr Al-Warid took a large third-floor room in the hotel yesterday afternoon and we think the terrorists spent the night there. But we haven't been able to trace him yet. Perhaps he went to get the car, they must have been planning to get the Katbahs away by car to some safe house. He probably scarpered the moment the first patrol cars arrived.'

'The house would be outside London,' Maxim suggested, 'if they were planning to interrogate him in the way they did.'

'Or some embassy,' George said. 'There'll be more than one around London with nice sound-proofed basements for just such a social event as they planned.'

'I'm afraid you're probably right,' the Superintendent

said, 'if any other country but Jordan is involved. And quite possibly Mr Al-Warid is there now. But we can't kick down embassy doors.'

'Quite.' George looked at Sprague. 'Anything further, Norman? You probably want to hurry back and prepare a comforting statement for your Minister to issue. And I think Harry ought to get a good night's kip; probably be a long day for him tomorrow.'

The evening was quickly forgetting the fragile spring warmth of the day when Maxim reached Agnes's flat. He had tried ringing her there earlier but had got no answer, and he was shy of calling her new workplace.

'Where have you been?' she demanded, and then saw the state of his clothes: 'Where *have* you been? My God, you didn't get mixed up in the hotel siege, did you? I thought it was the SAS.'

'We're keeping that thought going. But the rubber band on their helicopter broke and we had to patch together a group from District.' He flopped into a chair, and caught her looking at his hands. He held them out. 'No blood. I washed.'

It had been Katbah's blood, anyway, and still was, on one knee of his trousers.

'The funny thing is,' he remembered, 'that I didn't fire a shot.'

'You?'

'The others were younger and quicker, but I was in command, so . . .'

'Did it go . . . all right?'

There was an evening paper on the table, its headline glaring at him. 'I don't know, we didn't save Katbah but I don't think we ever could have . . . Mrs Katbah, yes, she shouldn't have got hit . . . No, I could have done better.'

'Have a drink and a shower. What d'you want to eat?'

'Not much.'

She knew him well by now; 'not much' meant he would hardly touch the Parma ham and delicate sole fillets she had

40

planned, but would munch his way through a fifteen-inch pizza. There was a place just round the corner. 'I'll get you something.'

He did just about eat his way through the pizza, too, leaving Agnes feeling smug about anticipating his wishes, annoyed about the Parma ham and sole fillets and worried about his day (why can't I get all my feelings about this man onto my own pizza, gulp it down, and then have him digested? she thought. No, I'm not a female spider. At Security I took time building up files on people, not jumping to conclusions. But they had secrets to hide; this man has no secrets from me. I think).

Over coffee, she asked as casually as she could: 'Did you volunteer for this?'

'No, they hauled me in because I'd known Katbah in Jordan, years ago. After that, I was Joe-on-the-Spot.'

'Did the Colonel tell you anything before he died?'

He looked wary, and she went on: 'My people – my *new* people – were in a fair old tizz this afternoon, about Jordan generally and if Katbah had said anything new.'

'They should have got the telephone tapes, or transcripts of them, by now. He spoke German to me, mostly.'

'Why?'

'I suppose he knew I knew some, and assumed the terrorists didn't. You don't get much German spoken out there, just English and French. Then he said something to me as he was dying, it didn't get taped. That's in a special report that'll go to your new mob.'

'What did he say?'

Oh well, she might have no immediate Need To Know, but she belonged to the secret world. And there certainly was a Need To Know what Katbah had been whispering about as he died.

'Something about the master in the house of the two winds.'

'It sounds like a John Buchan title.'

'Well, he said that in German, too. Don't know why,

41

there wasn't anybody left to overhear him by then . . .
maybe he'd just got it worked out in case I got him on the
phone again.'

'What exactly did he say?'

'I think it was "*Der Verfechter bei der Zweiwindburg.*"
Special Branch think it might be some place around London or the home counties where the terrorist leader was
based.'

'It doesn't sound a very London or home counties name.
Could it be somewhere in Jordan?'

'Could be; I haven't heard of it.' He finished his coffee.

'Do you want some more? Or a drink?'

'I'll have one when I go to bed.'

'You must be tired, I don't have to –'

'No.' He smiled wearily, but he didn't want to try to
sleep yet. The memory of Katbah was still too fresh. He
didn't want to forget, but he wanted it filed away, not lying
on his mental desk staring up at him.

Agnes poured herself more coffee. '*Burg* means more a
castle or fort . . . and *Verfechter* is defender or champion.
He didn't say *Meister*?'

'No, I'm pretty sure . . .'

'How good was his German?'

'Probably not as good as mine.'

Agnes gave a grunt that she tried immediately to turn
into a cough. She had read Modern Languages at Oxford;
Maxim had been through an Army cram course in German,
supplemented by some years of chattering in German
taverns. "Defenders of burgs of two winds' hadn't come
into such chatter much.

'I'm sorry,' she said. 'You'll probably have to go through
this with some of my new mob tomorrow anyway. There's
a lot of heat coming down from our clientele at Defence
about Jordan.' She must have seen something in his face,
because she asked quickly: 'Was there heat from Defence
at the hotel?'

'George was there, if he counts.'

'He usually manages to be at Ground Zero on such

42

occasions. Was it him who pushed you into going through that wall?'

'I was the only person on the spot who could organise it.'

'You could have got yourself killed.'

'I could have got some of my men killed.'

6

Maxim was shunting papers around his desk – already they included a demand that he account for a quantity of plastic explosive and detonator cord he had drawn yesterday and who had authorised its use, if it had been used, and why it hadn't been returned if it had not been used, and if it had been used in part but not in whole . . . when his Colonel came in.

'Your chum George Harbinger requests the pleasure of your company over at Defence. I gather you're going to be kidnapped for a while.' He picked up the paper Maxim was studying. 'I'll sign or stall all this for you . . . Good God, anybody would think you'd indented for a nuke. Pure cover-my-arse. Well, everybody thinks his own arse is important. Go on, get moving.'

The Foreign Secretary had fallen off a horse a couple of weeks before and cracked his right leg, leaving Fleet Street cartoonists desperate to draw the scene with the horse labelled 'France', 'South Africa' or now, though hopes were fading along with public memory of the accident, even 'Jordan'. But the Foreign Office had made no public bloomers in the fortnight – which, as Opposition spokesmen happily explained, was simply because Lord Purslane hadn't been near the Office in that time.

Instead, he was holding court stretched on a sofa in his weekend retreat, a well-preserved country house set in umpteen hundreds of landscaped acres that had been pre-sented to the nation by the original family for some such official use. You drove up to it through a small village that must once have made most of its living from the great house itself, although far less now with the house only intermittently used and a police checkpoint barring the main gate.

A man who could hardly be called a butler, since he wore a dark blue military jersey (and was, Maxim guessed, a retired sergeant-major) let them in. A younger man in plain clothes smiled and said: 'Good afternoon, Mr Harbinger, Major Maxim.' It was the final check on their identity, and Maxim glanced around for the walkie-talkie that must connect to the check-point.

'The drawing-room is this way,' the older man said, but Maxim had stopped to stare around. The high ceiling and walls were almost covered with flintlock rifles and pistols; not a true collection but an armoury of the same types, arranged in sprays, concentric circles and echelons, enough to equip a regiment. As indeed they had, one long since disbanded but originally raised and equipped by the family of the house.

'Come on, Harry,' George growled, and they went through into the house-width drawing-room. Long and light were Maxim's first impressions, with family portraits round the walls and moderately antique furniture arranged in areas so that half a dozen private conversations could go on simultaneously. But there was only one at the moment, centring not so much on Purslane himself, stretched out in his dressing-gown, as on his plastered leg. Its bulging white incongruity dominated even that big room, although the clutch of Foreign Office officials gathered reverently around it also helped.

'Afternoon, George.' Purslane leant to stretch out a hand. 'Don't you be another to tell me I'm too old to go falling off horses. Major Maxim? Very glad to meet you, heard quite a bit about you. We want you to go to Jordan.'

'Yes, sir,' Maxim said automatically, forgetting to say My Lord.

Purslane smiled. He had a long head, slightly jowly, a

beak of a nose and was almost bald except for a stubble of white hair over his drooping ears. His eyes, well supported by pouches of flesh, were big, light and clear.

'I know the Office can't send an Army man anywhere,' he went on, 'so it's being cleared right up your chain of command – *if* you agree to go. It's nothing world-shaking, but it could help diplomatically.'

'Yes, sir,' Maxim said again, wondering what on his record suggested any talent for diplomacy.

'You were the only person – on our side – who spoke to Colonel Katbah before he died. That's right, I believe?'

'It's all in the transcripts and my report, sir.'

'Yes, I've seen those, got them here . . .' he fumbled in a despatch box on the floor beside him and knocked over a glass. 'Bugger it. Somebody get me another brandy and soda. Better get one for George, too; he looks as bad as I feel. Here it is . . . We've sent a long cable through our ambassador regretting Katbah's death, Mrs Katbah's injury, the whole affair, assuring them of our co-operation, the usual blah-blah . . . Now we want you to back him up by giving them the tapes the police recorded and explain the details. I gather the tapes are mostly rock music, but if you're there as well it shows we're trying. I hope we're not taking you off something vital?'

'Filling in a few forms, sir.'

'Fine. Thank you.' He took the glass that the youngest of the Foreign Office squad had fetched from the sideboard; a second glass went to George, who sipped it quickly and sank into a chair.

'Now,' Purslane said, 'Scottie's going to give us a bit of background on the situation over there. Have you met Scott-Scobie?'

He had. Maxim smiled politely; Scott-Scobie grinned and said 'Hello, Harry. In medias res, as usual?' and helped put up a map board. He was chubby and tubby, but compensated by bouncing around brisk and birdlike, a robin whose waistline is all feathers really. The map didn't convince Maxim, either. Why can't the FO ever get decent maps of an area? – I want proper contours and spot heights, not just the arbitrary straight-line frontiers scratched out by the British and French in the 1920s, probably in some drawing-room just like this . . . But foreign policy *is* frontiers, not observation posts on high ground and whether a pass can be used by tanks . . . Perhaps it takes 2,000 years of warfare to establish realistic frontiers as in Europe, and even there . . .

He had missed Scottie's opening words and, in that company, daren't ask for them again.

'. . . After thirty-five years in charge, King Hussein is probably the most experienced statesman in the world and nobody knows whether Jordan can hold together without him. If it does hold together, it'll be because of the army. Traditionally, it's been recruited from the Bedouin: desert Arabs, born warriors, strong loyalty to the Hashemite royal line, but not so hot on handling laser ranging equipment and computerised gunsights. In fact, about 60 per cent of Jordan's population is what you might call Palestinian: refugees from Israel and the West Bank or their descendants. Townees, better educated than the Bedouin and more politicised. But most of them have blended into the population, and without them Jordan wouldn't have its new road network, airports and airline, its potash works and . . . er, whatever else it's now got.

'The same goes for the army. It needs such people, what with increased mechanisation and electronification – if there is such a word.'

'There's always such a word nowadays,' Lord Purslane growled.

'I'm afraid so, Minister. Apart from one mistake, when they formed units that were mostly Palestinian and had to disband them when they proved unreliable, such people have been carefully vetted and spread thin among existing units. However, they may have made much the same sort of mistake in forming 17th Armoured Brigade.'

Scott-Scobie caught Maxim's eye and grinned quickly;

Maxim realised he must have been nodding agreement.

'Just to clear up one small point,' Scott-Scobie went on, 'Jordan does not have seventeen armoured brigades, it has seven. But the numbering is done on the usual confusion-to-the-enemy principle. The 17th itself is not, I'm informed, a true fighting unit and wasn't intended to be. On paper it was an experimental unit directed by the Central Armour School to practise new formations and tactics. Politically, it was a catch-all for men suspected of less than total loyalty to the King: PLO sympathisers, pro-Syrian republicans, Shi'ite Fundamentalists and so on. I don't know how long it would have taken the Brigade to realise it was just that . . . Harry?'

'About five minutes,' Maxim said. The room chuckled appreciatively.

'You're probably right. For the Jordanian Army it may have seemed the least bad solution, grouping all the potential trouble in one unit. I gather it took other precautions: the Brigade was understrength and equipped with Jordan's oldest tanks, except for a troop of Khalids – that's the updated British Chieftain and, I'm told, the best tank in the Middle East – attached at Headquarters level. It had no more than a battery of artillery. The commander, Brigadier Kawar, was supposedly of unquestioned loyalty to the King.

'And finally, the Brigade was stationed out in the desert well away from any of Jordan's cities and frontiers. It only moved to the Aqaba district a few weeks ago when the troubles started on the Syrian frontier and the units normally around Aqaba went north to strengthen that region. There is no doubt in my Department that the revolt was Syrian inspired, although so far Syria has done no more to support it than send messages of congratulations and increase its growlings on the northern frontier.'

'What d'you think Syria's trying to achieve, then?' Purslane asked.

'Ultimately, long or short term, toppling the Hashemite dynasty and getting rid of the royalist officer class; after that, Jordan is virtually certain to become a Syrian satellite. We are assuming there are no coincidences involved, that Syria started trouble on the border to get 17th Armoured moved to its alert position down near Aqaba. If it had revolted in its normal position out in the desert it would have had far less effect; now it virtually controls Jordan's second biggest city.

'We assume Syria expected the next move to come from King Hussein. If it tried direct intervention – an invasion – it would probably just unite Jordan behind the King. They probably hoped the King would suppress the revolt with loyal army units which might create a civil war and force people to take sides. To say nothing of all the casualties, loss of equipment, the destruction in Aqaba *and* having to withdraw a lot of its forces from the Syrian frontier to do the suppressing. So what we have at the moment is a stalemate. The revolt may collapse if it can't be seen to achieve anything more than it has – the 17th Armoured Brigade isn't strong enough, I'm told, to move north. But while it stays where it is, it cuts Jordan's sole sea supply route – which is possibly even more important to Iraq. I believe Iraq paid for most of the improvements to the Desert Highway coming up through Jordan' – his stubby finger traced it on the map – 'and on east to Baghdad. As long as the revolt lasts, Jordan is landlocked and Iraq nearly so.'

Scott-Scobie planted a finger on Aqaba itself, Jordan's only port. It lay in the far south, at the tip of one branch of the Red Sea. Saudi Arabia held one side of the branch, Egypt the other, with Jordan and Israel shouldering in to occupy a few miles of coastline between them. Maxim remembered how the lights of Elat in Israel blended into those of Aqaba at night – but there was a very real frontier between them. Indeed, Jordan virtually sealed Aqaba off from the rest of the country with roadblocks and tough baggage searches for anybody driving down from the north. They didn't want anybody cutting the barbed wire and heaving grenades around: it needed only a slight nudge from Israel to put Aqaba out of action. And now the 17th Armoured had done that anyway.

Scott-Scobie explained: 'As far as we can tell, they haven't occupied Aqaba itself apart from the airport and the radio relay station. They've simply cut the roads and the railway north of the city, although they've proclaimed the whole place an independent republican state of free Jordan under Brigadier Kawar. The Friends' – that was Foreign Office jargon for the Secret Intelligence Service – 'say there's no evidence of his actual commitment, so the rebels may just be using his name to attract loyal Jordanian support and holding him hostage. Or he may well be dead. The same goes for any of the other unit commanders – but pretty obviously the revolt was staged at headquarters level. It couldn't have been so effective so quickly otherwise. So somebody or bodies among the senior officers are behind it.'

'Who's the Brigade Major?' George asked, twisting his empty glass in his hands.

Scott-Scobie consulted a piece of paper. 'Ah . . . Major Mahmoud Zyadine – d'you know him? – or Kawar? Harry, do you know either of them?'

'Kawar, no. I met Zyadine, he was a captain then, in their Special Brigade. Paratrooper. He . . .' A tall, ascetic man with a rather square face and cheek muscles that bulged as if he was always clenching his teeth. Seemed a committed soldier, one to have on your side, if you knew he was on your side. It was easy to be a British soldier, compared to some armies. '. . . I met him,' he repeated feebly, and their interest shifted.

But George had been right to pinpoint the Brigade Major. Loyal or false, he was the man at the Brigadier's elbow, the man whose job it was to know what was going on in the brigade.

Purslane wriggled and stretched on his sofa, muttered something rude to his leg, and said: 'So Jordan isn't likely to blitz its second largest city – and through difficult country, too, isn't it, Major?'

Maxim nodded. 'You can only attack from the north, on two roads. One's flat and open and right alongside the Israeli border, the other comes down through a steep gorge. I'd rather defend than attack there, though you don't have a line of retreat.'

'People who start revolutions don't usually have a line of retreat anyway,' Purslane said grimly. 'All right, Scottie: other countries. You've dealt with Syria. Israel?'

'High blood pressure, as usual. They've reinforced their border in the last couple of days and flown a number of reconnaissance sorties over southern Jordan. Syria could be hoping that Israel will react aggressively, but Israel probably assumes Syria is hoping that, so . . .' He shrugged.

'Saudi Arabia?'

'Backing the Jordan government but can't do anything practical. Militarily too weak to risk any clash with Syria, and the same goes for Egypt. Iraq's got its own problems.'

'Washington?'

'Again backing Jordan, of course, and willing to supply arms – but for once, lack of arms isn't the problem. If it did come to a civil war, it's a difficult place to intervene without using Israeli bases as a springboard and that could give Syria an excuse to intervene and behind Syria . . .' his finger drifted up off the map northwards, then closed into a clenched-fist salute.

There was a silence. Purslane cranked his head around to look at the group one by one. 'So there we have it, gentlemen. A normal morning in the everyday life of the Near East. At one end of the scale a revolt that may simply peter out, at the other end a possible clash of American and Russian forces. Syria is totally dependent on Moscow for military equipment, I think –'

'Four thousand Russian tanks, 500 jet fighters, 600 surface-to-air missiles.' Scott-Scobie had done his home-work and wanted teacher to know it. George glowered at him.

'Thank you, Scottie. When Moscow gives somebody

that big a stick, it attaches a big string to it. Question: did Syria get the Kremlin's approval to start this revolt? Second question: what does Moscow stand to gain from it?'

'At the moment,' Scott-Scobie shook his head slowly, 'we just don't know. We have to assume Russian approval, and in the long term the republicanisation (I'm sorry, Minister) of Jordan is in Russia's interest – but we can't see any short-term gain to offset the risks. The timing baffles us: why now? Jordan's politically and economically stable at the moment and the weather won't be reliable for another month – I gather you can still get high winds, storms, even snow on the mountains. Not good campaigning weather. So, why now? We just don't know. And Washington doesn't seem to, either,' he added defensively.

Purslane did another painful survey of his advisors, none of whom had any advice to offer, and ended on Maxim. 'So, Major: you see the somewhat delicate situation we're sending you into. Just hand over the tapes and explain the circumstances of Colonel Katbah's death, assure everybody of our sympathy and goodwill.'

'And,' Scott-Scobie put in, 'see if anybody knows any reason why Katbah was grabbed and tortured. At the moment, we don't have any clue as to how he's involved.'

'And you can thank George,' Purslane wound up, 'for a trip to the sun at this time of year. Unless you get one of Scottie's snowstorms.'

The group broke up and everybody had a drink, especially George, who then led Maxim into Purslane's private den to phone Defence. 'I want Harold Maxim – use that name, no "Major" – on the first flight to Amman tomorrow. There'll be no problem, there'll have been a raft of cancellations the last couple of days.' He turned to Maxim. 'Have you got a Jordanian visa?'

'I think it's expired.'

Back to the phone: 'And get the Jordanian consul to issue a visa, chop-chop, they'll co-operate, you'll need his passport' – to Maxim again – 'is it at, er . . . Agnes's place?'

It was odd how coy men could be about such things, Maxim had noticed. Women were much more blunt.

'It's in the top right-hand drawer of my desk at the office.'

'Get somebody at London District HQ to break open the Major's desk, top right-hand drawer. All clear? Splendid.'

There was no 'sensible' way of driving back to Whitehall, just the alternative grinds through south or south-east London. Having cursed his way down through Croydon, George elected to go north on the M25 and then curse his way in through Bexley and Lewisham.

'The defence attaché will meet you at Amman airport; Roger Jeffreys, colonel from the Grenadiers. D'you know him?'

'I don't think so.'

'We should have a cavalryman out there, at the very least RTR.' George's attitude towards the Royal Tank Regiment was cavalry, not just cavalier. 'Jordan's tank country.'

'There's a fair bit of it that's mountain goat country.'

'You *silly* little man!' It was a moment before Maxim realised that George was addressing a small car that had swung in front of them. They zoomed around it.

'You'll take over copies of the police tapes,' George went on, breathing heavily. 'Apologise for the quality, but they'll see the reason, and say the Yard is getting them cleaned up, getting rid of that rock music. Damned if I know how, but this electronic age leaves me at the bus stop in the rain. So if we get a better transcript we'll send it on. And tell 'em, well, anything they want to hear. I'll be in touch through Jeffreys.'

'Why?' Maxim was mildly surprised, since he appeared to be on a Foreign Office mission.

'Well, something might come up . . . If the police can wipe that sort of music off tapes, we ought to give them powers to wipe it out at source.'

53

7

There was a long arrow-shaped shadow rippling over the cloud that covered most of western Europe and Maxim knew it must be from their own aeroplane, but couldn't think why that shape. After a while he got it: the arrowhead was the aircraft, the long shaft the vapour trail stretching behind them. He had asked for a port-side seat because the sun would be low and dazzling when they reached the Mediterranean. Just like on the old passenger ships: you tried for a cabin Port Out, Starboard Home, supposedly the origin of POSH.

The cloud broke up past Italy. They passed the emerald rings of sea around the Greek islands, then Cyprus and in over Syria, avoiding Lebanon and Israel. South, and turning into a setting sun as they rumbled over dry fields just dusted with green, south of Amman. The new airport building had Islamic windows on the outside and confusion on the inside, tinged with fear; a lot of conspicuously armed soldiers and blue-grey security police; airports were the bastilles of the late twentieth century. If there was anything to be afraid of, an airport was the place to be afraid.

Colonel Jeffreys was very obvious, tall, lean, grey moustache, intensely courteous, grabbing for Maxim's luggage although he was a good ten years older, saying things like: 'Have a good flight? Terrible mess here since the revolt down south, I've got a car and driver, you don't mind spending the night with me? It seemed simpler, but I'm afraid my wife's away, I can knock up an omelette or something, did you eat on the plane?' And they were in the Embassy Jaguar and away to the Defence Ministry.

It was an aeroplane hangar, but one which only dead aeroplanes ever reached. They filled most of the space: four-seaters, helicopters, a thirty-seat airliner and a far bigger one – all battered and often burnt beyond any value save to know what had gone wrong. Propped on metal trestles or piles of old railway sleepers, their shattered stillness gave no feeling of the violence which had brought them to this vast autopsy room.

Yet people died in these machines, Agnes thought, reading the chalked signs which gave the place and date of each crash, and I can't remember reading about any of them except the big one. It gave her an irrational sense of guilt in a place where there was no guilt, because machinery has none. Designers, makers of parts and assemblers of them, maintenance engineers, pilots, they and their guilt were elsewhere; this hangar was warm and quietly busy, no more.

Along one side, what in a normal hangar would be store rooms was a line of small offices and laboratories. She and Davies, the Man From The Home Office, were led to one heavily placarded with No Smoking signs. There were double doors to keep out dust and, inside, stack upon stack of electronic recording equipment. A heavy jovial black-bearded man in a white overall that was presumably intended to show the dirt, and did, shook their hands.

'It's about the hotel siege, isn't it?' he said. 'We very seldom get such stuff, but we've done what we can.'

'Have you got a transcript?' Davies asked. He was an impatient balding man in his late thirties, with heavy spectacles.

'Good Lord, no, man. We've just done our best to isolate the voices. What they're saying – it mostly seems to be Arabic. Do you speak Arabic?'

'No, I'm afraid not.' And Agnes shook her head, too, although she had begun to learn it. Davies went on: 'I don't see quite why it was sent to you in the first place. However –'

'Only because we're the best there are,' Blackbeard said jovially. 'Once they got going with flight-deck voice recorders we had to have some way of interpreting them. They use little open mikes that pick up all sorts of engine noise and whatnot, and this wizardry here' – he waved a hand at the stacks of electronic equipment – 'does its best to wipe out the background noise. We know what frequencies a given engine emits at certain power settings, so we can take that band out. But with your little problem – it was more difficult and easier in some ways. They'd used a . . . a fixed background noise: the pop radio programme. It happened to be Capital. All radio stations have to tape their broadcasts, by law, and keep them for three months . . .'

'Yes, yes,' Davies said, 'but what –'

'Let him go on,' Agnes said. 'I'm interested. Can you superimpose the broadcast on the siege tapes and sort of suck it out?'

'That's it!' Blackbeard splayed a thick-fingered hand at her. 'We re-record through graphic equalisers, cancelling the broadcast music. I stayed up two nights doing that. That's the easy part, in its way.' He looked at Davies, as if challenging him. 'The trouble is that music involves far more frequencies than engine noise. Luckily it was rock music, where they're normally singing at well above conversation frequencies. If they'd tuned to an opera with a good basso profundo we'd have had far worse problems. But – as far as we've got – we've lost a fair bit of the . . . interrogation, where the frequencies matched. The trouble is that in Arabic we don't know what we're missing. Oh, we took out the screams, too, but they were in the high frequencies along with the singing.

'We haven't lost anything,' he finished; 'the original tapes are still there. We can work them over and over.'

'All we want to know,' Davies said, 'is what they were torturing Colonel Katbah about.'

'Well, if you can find somebody who understands Arabic – oh, there's a few words of English and German, during a telephone call – well . . .' He smiled and handed each of them a tape cassette. 'If your Arabists can't find what they want from these, give me a tinkle and we'll put in or take out a few more frequencies. Anything to oblige.'

Davies stared at the cassette in his hand and said reprovingly: 'People were killed on this tape.'

'People are killed on almost all our tapes. That's why we analyse them.' Blackbeard ushered them through the double doors to the hangar, taking a small cigar from his pocket and lighting it next to a No Smoking Within Fifty Feet Of This Notice notice. 'Most tapes end with the pilot saying "shit" or "Christ" when they see what they're going to hit. In the transcript, we put it down as "irrelevant final exclamation" or something like that. I've heard more people die, over and over and over again than I hope you ever will, Mr Davies. I'll show you the way out.'

They handed in their security passes at the main gate and drove off in their own cars. After a few minutes, Agnes couldn't resist the temptation and pushed the cassette into the car's player, wondering if Davies was doing the same. Probably not; he was just being the perfect messenger boy, angry though he was at being given the job. Well, so was she, the new girl in the Secret Service, send Agnes, she's got nothing important to do, and isn't she supposed to be doing some file-fodder on Islamic womanhood, perfect, get her out of our hair for half a day.

The tape wasn't good. The deletions had left it with a jerky unrhythmic quality that gave only patches of words, rather than sentences or remarks, and long blanks where the only sound had been the radio. She fast-forwarded it to the end, back-tracked, and picked up the moment that Maxim and company had blasted in through the hotel wall. The explosion itself had been played down on the tape, but there was the rattle and bang of weapons after that, and maybe some 'final irrelevant exclamations' and unmistakably Maxim's voice shouting: 'Cease fire!'

She snapped off the player. It had been a very odd feeling, although she had been braced for it, hearing her man in the middle of a killing party he had organised himself. No, that was wrong, he was just reacting, the terrorists had set it up, if it hadn't been him it might have been somebody less competent, getting his own men killed. Only, why had Mrs Katbah got shot?

She found she was driving very fast, slowed down, and wound back the tape. God help me if this player turns the tape into spaghetti, she thought, but started it again, trying to pick out any Arabic words she knew.

8

Jeffreys' bungalow was up off the Third Circle near the Embassy, white painted and with a lot of outside lighting – perhaps a security measure – snuggling down behind a high ornamental wall. The gate was fancy ironwork, the lock was serious.

His wife was back in Britain trying to persuade the headmaster of their son's boarding-school to keep the lad on even if he had got drunk on his birthday and told the senior classics master where to put his Greek texts; they had the place to themselves.

'Anything to drink?' Jeffreys asked.

'Something long, if . . .'

'I know, Fawzi's been plying you with whisky. He has set ideas about how Englishmen behave and you can't hurt his feelings.' He went through a doorless arch to a bright kitchen.

At some time he must have had an African posting, because there were zebra-skin rugs on the floor and a couple of horned heads on the white walls. The only other decorations were silver-framed pictures of his wife and children in that carefully-lit and over-posed style of a photographer whose prints cost more than any frame you could put round them.

Jeffreys brought back two glasses of lager. 'So you think it went well enough. Cheers.'

'The tapes were pretty bad, I hadn't heard them myself before, but we played a few bits and I promised them something cleaner if we got it. They seemed happy enough, and they didn't make any fuss about Mrs Katbah.'

'No, women don't have the status out here that – well, you know that, of course. And she didn't have to go with him on what was really a military trip. Probably they blame that woman terrorist; when women get into terrorism it puts all women bystanders at risk. But I suppose that argument won't help you back home.'

'I don't think I've heard the last of it.'

Jeffreys sipped his lager thoughtfully. There's something coming up, Maxim realised, some advice, some comment. He stiffened inside.

'And George,' Jeffreys said, 'George Harbinger, he's well and so forth?'

'He seems so.'

More thoughtfulness.

'I just got a long cable from him, obviously backed up by the sixth floor, and what it boiled down to is . . . we've lost our latest tank. Out here.'

'The MBT90? I thought those trials were over.'

'So did I, but apparently not. And now it's lost.'

'Captured? – by 17th Armoured?'

'They don't know, but George thinks possibly not. Not yet. Defence has been in a bit of a bind about it; I can see their problem. At first they hoped it had got clear and up to the loyalist units around Ma'an so they didn't say anything. After they'd started to get worried they still didn't say anything, like asking me to ask Fawzi, for fear of spreading the word that it was still missing. They were scared there might be some supporters of the revolt in the ministries here – and I dare say there could be. But now they don't think 17th Armoured can have caught it or they'd probably have boasted about it.'

'It can't have been alone,' Maxim said. 'There'd be support vehicles . . .'

'Oh yes. We'd actually handed the tank over to Katbah and a crew from the Jordanian Armour School to run their own trials, down near Wadi Rum – d'you know it? Yes, of course. They'd got one of our bowser trucks and a Jordanian Land-Rover with them; the bowser was back in Aqaba filling up again when the revolt started and the crew got out to the support ship. Nobody knows about the Land-Rover, may still be with the tank.'

'What were the Jordanians doing with the tank?'

'Trying it out for size,' Jeffreys seemed surprised at the naivety of the question. 'We hope they'll buy it.'

'Oh. Are *we* buying it?'

'Not as far as I know. It's supposed to be too revolutionary, certainly the one photo I saw of it, it looked very odd from the neck up. But the idea is if the Jordanians buy it then the Saudis might and a few to the Emirates and the unit price'll come down and maybe we'll be able to afford it ourselves. It doesn't usually work that way. It's almost impossible to sell stuff abroad that your own service won't accept, but I'm supposed to say what a wonderful thing it is whenever I see Fawzi or anybody. Damn it, *I* don't know anything about tanks, I'm a foot soldier, same as you; I don't even like personnel carriers. Battalions spend half their time repairing the bloody things and our business is *men*, not machines.'

He looked grumpily fierce for a moment, then gave a bark of laughter. 'Oh well . . . I'm probably getting stir-crazy, sitting here not knowing what's going on. What George wants me to ask you is whether anything Katbah said could be about where the tank is.'

'Me?'

'Katbah did say something before he died, didn't he?'

'Yes, but – would he know? He was in London.'

'George said it was a long shot. But if Katbah smelt trouble coming he might have told the crew that if they couldn't escape up to Ma'an, then to hide out somewhere. Somewhere particular.'

'Oh Lord . . . he did say something about a fort of the two winds. I don't know what that would be in Arabic.' He daren't try his own translation on a man who'd been speaking the language daily for eighteen months. Jeffreys sat moving his lips, tasting different phrases; then he shook his head and went to rummage out a large-scale map and spread it over the dining table.

Maxim found himself at Jeffreys' side without consciously having got there, but no Army officer worth his rank can resist a map. Proper study of a map will win the battle, increase potency, pick a Derby winner and cure warts. A map is The Future – to those who can read. And provided it is the right map: this one showed nothing of any fort of the two winds in any language.

'What did he actually *say*?' Jeffreys asked.

'He was speaking German to me, as a sort of code, I think . . . He said "*Der Verfechter bei dem Zweiwindburg*" I think.'

'That sounds rather poetic. He didn't say "*Burg der zwei Winde*"? Katbah's German was pretty much confined to military phrases, he was always planning to improve it so he could read Hugelmann and the others; it was Katbah who got me interested in archeology.'

'Does the tank have a name?'

'Not an official one. If we buy it, it'll be called C-something. Challenger, Chieftain, Centurian, Comet, Cromwell . . . we're running out of C-names. GTL were calling it the Champion, I believe.'

'And *Verfechter* could translate as Champion.'

'It could.' Jeffrey's mouth set in a tight smile. 'We're on to something here . . . Get yourself another drink.' He sprang at a line of big but unmatching leather-bound old books.

'Is there anything particularly secret about this tank?' Maxim asked.

'Ummm . . . oh yes. The gun's a new type . . . If Syria's backing this revolt and Moscow's backing Syria, they could have that tank on the Kremlin breakfast table in no time.'

'A bit big for the breakfast table.'

'Say dinner table, that looks big enough in the photos of their banquets . . .'

'The ambassador here's only just been told the tank's missing, have I got that right?'

'Hasn't been told yet, as far as I know. The cable was for me personally.'

And there'd been no mention of it at the country house meeting yesterday, yet George must have known the tank was at least unaccounted for then . . . must have known at the hotel siege the day before, been scared Katbah would tell the terrorists. That was why he wanted them all dead and wouldn't tell Sprague or the police why. Nor Maxim himself.

'We're getting close,' Jeffreys said, balancing the heavy book one-handed while he ran a finger down the page. 'Wadi Rum . . . Hugelmann led a small German expedition around there in 1911. Wonder what he was really doing? – that was the time we had T. E. Lawrence snooping around getting to know the tribes and the waterholes, all in the name of scientific inquiry and trying to carve a piece out of Johnny Turk's empire . . . Here we are: he found a small Crusader fort, just an outpost really, there wasn't anything left but the stable under it, he excavated that and didn't find anything so he just named it after the winds that blew either up or down the Wadi and went on his way. Zweiwindburg. There isn't even a sketch, but it's marked on his map.'

He dumped the book to show a hand-drawn map, all careful lines of hatching to indicate the slopes. It was of the south end, where the Wadi Rum broadened into the desert, and a tiny square nestling against the western slope was marked simply Zweiwindburg.

'It doesn't even have an Arabic name, though the local tribes must call it something. Jordan doesn't much bother with Crusader sites unless they're really big ones like Kerak, and they've got Nabatean ruins, Greek, Roman, Byzantine – you can't stick a spade into Jordan without hitting a mosaic floor or Moses' tomb, so who cares about a crummy little Crusader stable? Katbah did: it must be just big enough to hide a tank.'

Maxim was trying to read across the exact location of the stable onto the modern map, but reckoned he could do it only to within a few hundred metres. Even if Hugelmann had got his slopes precise, seventy years of erosions and landslip would have changed the detail of those aged and crumbling cliffs. Yet he was quite sure he could find it on the ground, simply by looking where he himself would place an outpost. Tactical lore weathered far better than mere rock.

'Wadi Rum,' Jeffreys repeated. 'That's where Lawrence had his base in 1917. Thought it was the most beautiful place in the world.'

Maxim gave a non-committal grunt. Like any professional soldier who had been attached to Arab armies, he had read *The Seven Pillars of Wisdom* (modestly subtitled *A Triumph*) with a rather sceptical eye. Jeffreys' smile reinforced military trade unionism about the flamboyant amateur. Then he turned serious: 'Look, I'd better get a signal off to London saying we've solved the riddle for them. And I haven't given you anything to eat, yet. Can you scratch around in the fridge and so on? Anything you like, help yourself.'

It would still be early evening in London, two hours behind Jordan in time, but after an airline lunch Maxim was distinctly hungry. He prowled gingerly in the unfamiliar kitchen of an unfamiliar senior officer (and far more important, the senior officer's wife) and finally decided to eat some of what they had most of. That turned out to be eggs, tinned macaroni cheese and fruit cake.

He got the oil only slightly too hot for the eggs and broke the yolk of only one and ended up quite full but despising his own timidity. Worst of all, he would have to pretend to Jeffreys that it had been his favourite food; it was unthinkable to say he'd been intimidated by the unknown and distant Mrs Jeffreys. So he washed up the evidence, poured another lager, and went back to the main room with its hunting trophies and map.

For a time he stood running a finger over the Wadi Rum area, tracing the tracks that were faint on the map and sometimes invisible on the ground. He had driven through the area in a Land-Rover once, simply as a tourist, but remembered no more than the map showed him now: that it was a jumble of small mountains and flattish patches of desert, utterly without any pattern.

It had grown chilly; warm nights were still some months off. He found an electric fan heater and switched that on and sat staring at it as if it were a fire and thinking of the fake log fire in Agnes's flat and the white goatskin rug in front of it . . .

Jeffreys bustled in, looking serious. 'Harry, look – I'm sorry about this, but London insists. They don't think they can put the exact location of the Zweiwindburg into a signal. So they want to get a copy of Hugelmann's map down to the ship. I'd normally go myself but none of this would be happening if things were normal – I have to get you to the Gulf of Aqaba.'

The track home to the gas log fire, the rug, faded as if it had been a desert trail.

9

A small but at least twin-engined plane lifted Maxim towards the rising sun and stayed on that heading until it was well east of any inhabitation. Then it turned south and began a slow climb above the turbulence set up by the faster-climbing sun until they crossed into Saudi Arabia – always called Saudia, since most Arabs assume they live in Arabia.

He had the plane to himself and two Jordanian pilots, one of whom seemed to do little more than pour coffee, causing them to sway like a small boat whenever he climbed out of his seat. After nearly three hours and two flasks of coffee they rattled down a potholed slope of air into Tabuk air base.

As they taxied in, the coffee pilot emptied a tiny flask of whisky into Maxim's foam-plastic cup. 'It comes with the compliments of the British Embassy and I suggest you drink it before it melts the cup. They thought you would want one last drink before entering Saudia.'

They were rolling to a stop in a very teetotal country, but Maxim wasn't staying there. Then he realised it was a small gesture of security from Jeffreys to suggest he *was* going to stay, and a small price to swallow undiluted luke-warm whisky before they stopped the left-side propeller to let him out. The plastic cup actually had begun to melt by then. That must have been one drink even George hasn't tried, he thought: Scotch and polystyrene.

A Saudia Air Force officer led him – in English, since Maxim's Arabic was so rusty – to the shadow of a hangar.

When the Jordanian plane had restarted its engine and taxied away for refuelling, the hangar doors were cranked open and he met a Royal Navy helicopter.

He shook hands with the pilot and observer, wriggled into a life-jacket, was presented with a headset of earphones, then stowed himself and his luggage on a bench back seat. He never felt much at home in helicopters – it was the vibration rather than the noise that tired him – but they were now as much a part of military life as brown windsor soup. He had learnt not to fall asleep in the soup – and how to do so in helicopters. He pulled out the headset jackplug and dozed until the change in blade noise brought him awake over an ungainly pale grey ship chugging along the Red Sea. Apart from looking like a stretch of Brighton pier that had broken loose, the odd thing was that it said on its side ARMY.

If asked, Maxim would have remembered that the Army operated its own private navy (after all, the Navy had its Marine Commandos) through the Royal Corps of Transport. H.M.A.V. *Alamein* was, indeed 'The most expensive single bit of kit the Army's ever bought,' as the Captain – actually a Major – boasted cheerfully, 'though I've only got the equivalent of a platoon to run it. When you've observed the proper sea-going ceremonies of saluting the arse end and kissing the helipad, we'll offer you a pink gin. Must keep up with the Senior Service.' He grinned at the helicopter pilot who was scratching life back into his hair after an hour and a half inside a flying helmet.

The pilot looked dour, although his very pale eyes and grey-tinged black beard made it difficult for him to seem much else. Or maybe, after a month in the Red Sea, inter-service jokes wore thin and sand rubbed between the personalities of men living very close together.

Maxim put on his quick no-comment smile and said: 'I'll skip the pink gin, if you don't mind, Captain, but if you could spare a sandwich . . .'

'Of course, you've had no bloody lunch!' He did an

attempt at glaring around; his rather boyish face wasn't good for glaring. 'Get Major Maxim a sandwich or something, nicely dried up, curling at the edges . . .' Back to Maxim, 'And please don't call me Captain. Either Skipper or Ronnie. It was all right when I was a Captain Captain, but now I'm a Captain Major or a Major Captain . . . and you're Harry?'

He might have been Maxim's age, but shorter and fatter and with a fair skin that reddened, flaked off, reddened again and flaked in a cycle that left him camouflaged in red and pink blotches while his crew had turned to bronzed godlings around him. His shirt pockets bulged with pens and notebooks.

The ship was shifting course northwards, so Captain Major Ronnie must have given some order that Maxim hadn't noticed. It wallowed awkwardly even in a calm sea and light breeze. They climbed a steep ladder down off the helipad.

'See what they've done to my mighty vessel?' Ronnie waved a hand back at the pad, a metal awning over the middle of the ship. 'Bloody good idea and all that, they had to put helipads over all sorts of ships when they went to the Falklands, ought to have put them on from starters, but the only trouble is it blocks the view from the bridge, can't see where I'm going, not that that matters much, the Navy's paid to miss hitting land, I'm paid to hit it and spew out five tanks, now if we'd got them down below we wouldn't be rolling like a virgin getting her first taste of the good life, five tanks is 250 tons of ballast, but with the topside weight of this helipad *and* the way the wind takes her . . .'

Maxim eventually got his sandwich.

He was still licking mayonnaise off his lips when five of them met at the map table in a small cabin behind the bridge: Ronnie, the helicopter crew, Maxim and a civilian introduced as Alec Timbrell from GTL, the makers of the missing tank.

'I have a signal from London,' Ronnie said, 'which requests that if I'm satisfied that we know where the Champion's got to, I should insert – I love that word – a party to blow it up. So the first point is, *do* we know just where it is, accurately enough to be found at night by helicopter?'

Maxim took a breath. 'Unless it's been captured, we know of only one place it might be: a Crusader stable, all that's left of a small outpost fort, at the south end of the Wadi Rum.'

The pilot and observer pounced at a map. 'It isn't marked,' the pilot said. 'It can't be much of a landmark.'

'It won't be,' Maxim said. 'Just a stable, maybe half-covered in rocks by now.'

'How big?' Timbrell asked. He was perhaps forty-five, lean with thin pale hair and a narrow face that was trying to become mostly nose, and succeeding. He wore rimless glasses.

Maxim found his jacket and notebook. 'A single arch four metres wide, three metres at its highest, twelve metres deep. Could your tank fit into that?'

'Yes, yes it could.'

'Covered from aerial view?' the pilot asked.

'I think it must be,' Maxim said. 'I think the Americans diverted one of their military satellites to photograph the area and couldn't come up with anything.'

The observer was still at the map. 'Take a look at the immediate terrain, boy. It's about three miles from a peak of nearly 6,000 feet; mind you, the ground itself is around 3,000 feet.'

'Well,' the helicopter pilot said, 'we've been expecting something like this, haven't we?'

'Yes,' Ronnie sighed. 'Ever since the revolt and being told to pull out of Aqaba but hang around just over the horizon.' There was a short silence that wasn't really silent with the ship humming as it swayed and occasionally sending ripples of vibration that went through Maxim's bones. Then Ronnie said: 'Are you sure about the location?'

'Mouth of the Wadi, west side, right up against the cliff.'

'London seriously wants it destroyed, particularly the gun. I think we have to go ahead with this *insertion* and if it isn't there, we've done our best. Let's work out who's going. Corporal Crowther to handle the demolition – and Alec, could you go along to tell him just what to blow up?'

Timbrell nodded briefly and not very enthusiastically. I don't blame the poor bugger, Maxim thought; flying in a helicopter at night through mountains into what might be a dicey situation.

'D'you want any sort of escort?' Ronnie asked. 'Just in case.'

'We've got a problem here,' Len said. 'Not fuel, I'll probably take off light anyway, but weight and space. We'll be flying way above our normal levels, it could be as high as 7,000 feet if we can't see that mountain, and any helicopter's load capacity falls off badly with altitude.'

'Will another bod or two make that much difference?'

'No-o, I'll do some proper calculations on temperatures, altitude and load later – but if we find this tank, aren't we going to find the crew as well?'

Maxim wished he'd thought of that; so, clearly, did Ronnie. The two Navy men stared at the Army, Len expressionlessly, the observer slightly smugly.

'We've got enough personal weapons on board to equip everybody,' Ronnie said slowly.

'How's this corporal at ground combat?'

'Damned if I know. Sorry.'

Len looked at Alec Timbrell. 'Is setting the charges going to be a long complicated job?'

'I really don't know; I've never handled explosives.'

Maxim tried to be helpful. 'It doesn't sound too tricky. I assume it's something about the breech that's new, not the barrel. Wrap enough plastic around the breech and maybe some more inside and you'll end up with lumps of welded metal. They'll be able to tell what metal, but not much else.'

They were all looking at him.

Oh *fuck*, he thought.

'It sounds as if you have done a course, Harry,' Ronnie said. 'The signal said you'd been in the SAS.'

'I'm no expert.'

Len said: 'But you don't think it would be too tricky. Have you been in combat?'

'Yes.'

Len might have flashed a quick v-shaped smile within the beard. 'He sounds ideal, doesn't he, skipper?'

Ronnie avoided Maxim's eyes. 'You do, rather . . . I can't compel you to go, any more than I can Alec here . . .' that was blackmail: a civilian had accepted, a serving major hadn't even volunteered. 'But you do seem to fit the bill – and you know this part of the world already, don't you?'

I came to Jordan to deliver the tape, Maxim recalled; now I want to be back at my desk and in bed with Agnes.

But I'm in the Army.

He nodded. 'But on the ground, I'm in command.'

Len said: 'That's all I wanted to hear.'

10

Preparing for an action he hoped wouldn't happen, Maxim prepared them, too. Even with the *Alamein*'s plodding ten knots, they had time in hand, so he got Ronnie to steam (if two 2,000 h.p. diesels can 'steam', unless they're going wrong) a tight circle around some plastic cartons while they blasted off every weapon they might use, mostly Sterling submachine-guns and the bipod version of the 7.62 General Purpose Machine-Gun (GPMG or, almost acronymically, Gimpy) with a belt feed. He hardly bothered with rifles and pistols.

'If anybody feels better carrying a pistol they can have one. We'll take a rifle, but if we get into trouble it's firepower, not accuracy, that counts. If they hear enough bullets coming past or bouncing off the rocks beside them, they'll keep their heads down. At night we probably won't hit anything anyway except by luck; the object is to stop them trying their own luck, stop them firing back.'

The soldier-sailors loved it all. After a month at anchor off Aqaba or hanging around the Gulf of same, somebody knocking over a sauce bottle had become a major event. It ended with a mass assault on the remaining carton, turning it into a thicket of spray and luckily sinking it. The crew cheered wildly and applauded.

'Thank you for that last touch, Harry,' Ronnie said. 'Better than a John Wayne video, and we've worn the only one we've got into shreds. Mind, the chaps have started chanting the dialogue in chorus so the sound-track doesn't matter much.'

'Haven't you got anything else?' Maxim was automatically checking over and half-cleaning the Sterling he'd fired.

'Some stuff, but you can't show *Nights in a Paris Brothel* to chaps stuck on a ship in the Red Sea. John Wayne's a far safer influence. Though you seem to use up almost as much ammunition as he does. I hope you'll help me account for it.'

'I hope we've fired our last shot.'

Maxim sat down in the shade of the helicopter pad to think. He hadn't really wanted to check out their shooting skills, you couldn't do that from the deck of a rolling ship anyway, just make sure they could handle weapons. Beyond that was whether you really wanted to kill somebody, and shooting a plastic carton couldn't tell you or anybody else that. You were trained, selected or discarded; at the end, you knew how to kill, but nobody knew whether you would try. He listed them in his mind.

Len, the pilot. Recently promoted Lieutenant-Commander which made him equal to Maxim except in seniority. Quick-witted, enclosed, maybe a bit touchy that he hadn't been in Operation Corporate, the Falklands, where other helicopter pilots had made names for themselves. Has a gangster-like affinity for a submachine-gun; knows it, seems to enjoy it.

Piers, the observer. Lieutenant, coming up to thirty. Large and blond – despite which, and his name, has the speech rhythms of Wales. He actually was in Corporate, so knows stress and himself under it. Also knows the GP machine-gun perfectly: they sometimes mounted them at the door of Navy Lynxs, when the observer became gunner.

Alec Timbrell, civilian – *but* (and *why* hadn't Maxim found out earlier?) had had an eight-year commission in the Royal Tank Regiment before leaving to try his hand at designing tanks. Quite familiar with all the weapons, if a bit rusty. Why didn't I think of a man who designs tanks having been involved with them operationally? Still, he has been a civilian for nearly twenty years.

He took out his notebook and began to list all the equipment he wanted to take.

'Disaster planning, Major?' Timbrell said, sitting down beside him.

'I'd say in Britain all military planning is disaster planning. It would be a sight easier if we were plotting to invade somebody.'

'I thought we were, tonight.' Timbrell's smile was a little wan. 'Anything I can tell you about the MBT90?'

'Go ahead.' The Red Sea – of which the Gulf of Aqaba is an arm – is always hot, but at that time of year it wasn't stifling. With the ship's speed and a wind almost on the bow, there was a healthy draught funnelled under the helipad. Maxim turned aft to light a cigarette.

'I led the design team, and I hope I'm not boasting when I say it's leading the way in which tank design has to go. But I only got a chance because GTL wanted a design to wrap around their new gun.'

'What's so new about it?'

'It uses liquid propellant. Does that mean anything to you?'

'I think I've read something . . . it seemed years off.'

'They've been firing test rig versions for a long time: General Electric in America, Rheinemetall in Germany, GTL in the UK. And there's a lot of development yet to be done. But GTL reckoned they had something at least as good as the standard 120-mm. tank gun, so they built a few of them and decided to try and break into the tank business as well. Why not sell a complete package? Or at least the Army might buy the gun without the tank or the tank without the gun.'

'Backing yourself both ways.'

'You could say that. Do you know how liquid propellant works?' Timbrell had a slightly high nasal voice – not surprising, with so much nose for it to come through. He poked his glasses back up the slope of it and looked at Maxim through much-magnified blue eyes.

'No – except I suppose you fill the breech with liquid instead of a solid charge, but I'm damned if I see how.'

'It's that "how" that's made it such a long job. There's a lot of different ways been tried, and now you're supposed to make sure nobody knows just how GTL have solved it.'

'I'm not sure I see *why* you want it, either.'

Timbrell pointed at the borrowed Browning pistol Maxim was wearing on the borrowed belt around the borrowed Army clothing. 'With that thing, the assumption is that every cartridge has an identical amount of propellant so that each bullet leaves the barrel at exactly the same speed. Then you adjust for range by pointing the gun higher or lower – and it's the same with the two-ton barrel of a tank gun. But of course it wasn't always that way. In Napoleonic times you could adjust the range of a cannon by putting in a spoonful more or less of gunpowder – and we've come back to that. Except the spoon's a computer reading from a laser rangefinder that puts in a few drops more or less of liquid. Napoleon would have understood it perfectly – he was a gunner, of course. It can make aiming simpler.'

'Except,' Maxim said, bristling at the idea that a British major couldn't understand something Napoleon could, 'for windage and whether you're shooting uphill or downhill.'

'Oh yes, and barrel wear and temperature and trunnion tilt – if the tank's shooting sideways across a slope – and whether the gunner's remembered to change his socks. But all that's been built into tank fire control systems for years: just leave it to the computer. But when you think of the effort it takes to wave a two-ton six-metre tank gun around, anything that reduces that helps a lot. And secondly . . .'

He assembled his thoughts, instinctively taking a metal-stemmed pipe from a shirt pocket that had tobacco stains running down from it like rust on the good ship *Alamein*'s side. Then he looked at the wind and put the pipe away again. 'Secondly, replenishment. You won't have fired off any more propellant than you need. If you want to fire at 400 metres you don't waste a charge that'll send a shell accurately to 3,000 metres. So when you come to replenish, you just pump the stuff on board like fuel. Have you ever seen a loader handling sixty shells and separate charges down his hatch in a hurry? It takes it out of you.'

'I visited a tank regiment once and they kindly let me load on a practice shoot . . .' He remembered vividly hauling ten-kilo shells from a rack, ramming them into a breech, then a nine-kilo charge behind that, something about the firing cartridge magazine, finally holding down a button to make sure the gun was off safe. Six times a minute, they had told him, he should be able to do that, all in a dark jolting little compartment designed to stab him in the shoulders and kidneys whenever he moved. Or when it did, unpredictably. But most of all he remembered the bulk of the breech slapping back just inches from his ear when the gun fired. It wouldn't have noticed if it had taken off his hand – or head – in its recoil.

Timbrell reached for his pipe again, then remembered he'd decided against it. 'I've actually designed out the human loader, given that the machinery has to pump in the propellant anyway, and got down to a three-man crew on Russian/Swedish lines. That's very important in cutting down the size of the tank. You can't go on having Main Battle Tanks that are nearly sixty tons in weight, not when they're going to have to add more armour on top in the next few years, with overhead kinetic-energy missiles . . .' he looked at Maxim sideways, then explained: 'missiles that actually have very high velocity penetrative powers, not just explosive –'

'Like bullets that shoot people,' Maxim suggested.

'Like bullets that shoot people, yes.' It was odd how somebody agreeing with you so often showed his agreement by repeating your own words. 'So, while maintaining the same engine space, we've lopped fifteen tons off the weight, which allows for increased top armour when the time comes without a loss of power/weight ratio over the current MBT's – and made it both smaller and roomier.'

'It sounds like the ideal country cottage,' Maxim said absently, turning to pitch his cigarette butt into the sea. 'Could be good camouflage if Britain ever gets invaded.'

'Thank you, Major. It hasn't been called that before.' Timbrell was watching his clenched hands, the fingertips turning red under the month-old tan.

You prick, Maxim, Maxim thought. Deep in his own problems of the unexpected 'insertion' he had only been listening to the surface of Timbrell's explanations: it was just machinery that he was going to blow up in a few hours anyway. But it was only the wonder-gun he could blow up, not the wonder-tank, and Timbrell's tank design would be on the Moscow breakfast table no matter what. Or so Timbrell thought. And the problems of command are the problems of those you command. You prick, Maxim.

'I'll wrap about two kilos of plastic around the breech,' he said rapidly and unemotionally, 'and when that blows it'll take the whole turret off its ring and into the stable roof and bring down the roof and bury it. It'll take . . . God knows what, but more than 17th Armoured have got, to dig it out. Months at least.'

'The archeologists will love us,' Timbrell said wanly. But he relaxed his hands.

'A hundred years from now they'll all be writing theses on how to untangle a Crusader stable from a late-twentieth-century tank. They'll all become professors.'

'You may not know how right you are,' Timbrell said. 'Learned gentlemen are very inclined to dwell on the difficulties of finding their material. I suppose they think it gives weight to their interpretations.'

Timbrell stood up and went away, perhaps brooding on the next paper he would submit to the RUSI or IISS or maybe even the Royal Society. Anyway, a long way from being a captain in the Tank Regiment. But placated. Maxim lit another cigarette.

*　　*　　*

77

Ronnie waved a hand at the chart-room. 'Help yourself. Len and Piers have marked the route they want to take, and my Nav Officer's put in what he's heard about 17th Armoured's dispositions, but I wouldn't count on 'em.'

The Navigating Officer's marks showed the 17th Armoured occupying a fan-shaped zone running about twenty miles north of its point in Aqaba itself. The west side was the Israeli border, the east the steep mountains running alongside the main highway down to the port, the far top being a line of outposts so obvious that an Army cadet would have placed them there in his first week and not changed his mind when he became a full General.

The easternmost one was at the mouth of the Wadi Rum which cut through the mountains and split into two canyons. One went north-east and held the freight-only railway, the other turned south and had a recent paved roadway as far as a toy fort occupied by the Desert Patrol. After that, Maxim knew, it narrowed to a cowboys-and-indians pass that finally opened onto the desert and where, he hoped, the Zweiwindburg was.

The helicopter route simply cut across the mountains at the Jordan-Saudia border and came up to that end of the pass, keeping the mountains between them and Aqaba. Except for those mountains, and other scattered peaks he hoped the pilot would notice in the moonlight, it was nice and simple; he tried to forget the Army helicopter crews' view of Navy ones – that they could find their way impeccably across the trackless ocean, but got lost immediately they came over land and land-marks.

Captain Major Ronnie came up beside him. 'Does it march? And have you been cheering up Alec Timbrell?'

'Hardly. The trouble is, I can wreck the breech of the gun and probably blow the turret off, but there'll be a lot of his tank left if they're really serious about finding it. I just hope the revolt folds up before they get round to it.'

'I suppose it is rather ironic that he spends years trying to make something indestructible and now his trouble is that he's succeeded. Ah well, into each life . . . Len wants to lift off just after oh one hundred when he's got a reasonably high half-moon. I don't blame him with that terrain, he's not used to climbing mountains in his job.'

'Forgive me asking, but why a *Navy* helicopter?'

'Our chaps aren't used to landing on rolling and pitching ships. And the Navy *is* used to sending single-helicopter units, all complete with crew and servicing crew, anywhere anytime. I believe they've got about fifty of them scattered around the fleet, far easier to get one of them than teach our bods to sit down on a ship without bending a blade, it's good for inter-service co-operation as well. It works.'

There might have been a warning emphasis in that last phrase.

'What's the helicopter been doing, mostly?' Maxim asked.

'Normal ship-to-shore stuff, bods and spares. Once they'd got the tank out in the desert it was the easiest way when they signalled that they'd busted a sprocket on the widget and could they have a new one, we got it there in under an hour.'

'How did you get the tank ashore?'

'Ah, a noble operation that, we beached at first light just down the coast east of the town, sent the tank off first, all wrapped in swaddling bands of tarpaulin to hide the shape of the turret – it does look very different, I hope you'll see – then the tank transporter. I knew that bloody thing would get stuck in the sand and it did, that's why I insisted the tank was loaded last, last in first off. So the tank pulled the transporter up to the road then crawled up onto it and was driven out to the trials area, all the local populace by then going "Ooh cor love a duck, look at that" in Arabic.'

'What happened to the tank transporter?'

'It's in Aqaba somewhere, but the drivers were back on board before the revolt blew.' He looked at his watch. 'Len and Piers are getting a bit of kip, why don't you? You can use my cabin.'

*   *   *

79

They had a late dinner which Ronnie watched with a glass in his hand, chortling: 'I can have a drink but you can't.'

He was just keeping the atmosphere light, but Maxim was tempted to defy him – then didn't because it would be another little separation from the helicopter crew, who certainly daren't take a drink. Instinctively he was trying to blend them into a team.

Timbrell had no such ambitions. 'I'm a civilian and I'm getting a bit old for this sort of thing.' He poured himself a large Scotch. He was dressed in a mixture of his own clothes – which had been chosen for the desert anyway – and Army kit.

After dinner, Maxim got Len the pilot in a corner and asked quietly: 'What about emergency rations?'

Len's face was quite expressionless. 'We've got standard survival packs all round, but they don't have much that'll be useful in the desert except glucose sweets and some water. I've scrounged a ten-litre can of water as well and some tinned stuff. Was something worrying you?'

'No, I was just planning an aerial picnic on the way back.'

Half an hour before take-off, they started loading the Lynx. Maxim was taking two kilos of plastic explosive, Cortex detonating cord, a lot of safety fuse, gun cotton primers and fulminate detonators. Only he and Len took pistols, there were three Sterlings, the GPMG with a hundred-round belt and one rifle. It wasn't easy to stow the weapons securely, so Maxim took the loaded magazines out. They all had torches but there weren't any walkie-talkies, which could have been useful in the dark.

When all that and the emergency supplies were in, the helicopter looked quite full.

Trickling in the heat of an Army pullover, camouflage jacket and life-jacket (but it probably wouldn't be at all warm in the desert) Maxim strapped himself in beside Timbrell on the rear seat. The Lynx was lined with loose-hanging grey quilted soundproofing and it was a bit like being in a rhinoceros that had been turned inside out. Len and Piers muttered a start-up check, the two engines above them whined, and a more urgent checklist was rattled off. Then Len reached for two big levers in the roof, the rotor began to move, wound up to a fluttering throb and they abruptly swayed up off the helipad and into the night.

11

They had launched about thirty miles south of Aqaba, well out of sight of the port itself, but once they got airborne there were faint smudges of land on either horizon: Egypt and Saudia. As they climbed, a few points of light appeared on both coasts, then the little sparkle that was the conjoined lights of Elat and Aqaba dead ahead.

'I'll give you odds we're registering on Israeli radar right now,' Len said on the intercom. 'Let's hope they assume we're none of their business.'

'Has 17th Armoured got any radar?' Maxim asked.

'Nothing with a search range.'

'There's your mountains, boy,' Piers said, and there they were, milk-grey in the moonlight shining over their left shoulders, but hardening as they neared. 'Starboard onto 035 and I suggest a bit of height.'

They swung in towards the coast and slowed into a straining climb. Perhaps Piers was cutting in a bit early, across Saudia territory for a brief while, and Maxim agreed with him.

They crossed the coast with the mountains on their left, now harshly defined in creamy-white and black, the reddish daytime colours bled away, against a star-littered horizon. They swung north again.

'There's a light down there,' Timbrell said on the intercom.

'Bedouin camp-fire,' Maxim suggested. 'Wherever you don't think you'll find them, you'll find them.' The desert was never empty. If they found this Crusader stable, its roof would be blackened by Bedouin cooking fires; why put up a tent when somebody else has put up a stone roof? The Jordanian government had had a hell of a job getting the tribesmen out of places like Petra, which they wanted to parade for the tourists.

Timbrell craned round, watching the light fade out of sight. 'How are you going to do this demolition?'

'Wrap plastic round the breech – does it have grooves and knobs and things to get a grip on?'

'Not too much, but probably enough.'

'This liquid propellant – can you fill the breech with that as well?'

'If there's enough left, yes.'

'That should give a sympathetic detonation. We ought to get an explosion inside and out.'

Piers said: 'I do like that phrase "sympathetic detonation". Personally, I have never felt any sympathy with any detonation.' The helicopter suddenly rocked in a wind gusting round the gaunt peaks, now mostly black shadows on their left.

'Can we have the intercom to ourselves, please?' Len asked. He zigzagged right, running along the moonlit line of lower peaks away from the coast. They talked figures on the intercom until Maxim took off his headset and concentrated on looking out.

The ground began to get less sharp and sloped downwards in front of them; they slid down with it. Then, quite suddenly, the land between the mountains became almost smooth, as if somebody had poured sand and gravel over the landscape, flooding the peaks so that they became islands in a sea of sand. And somebody – time – had done just that, delegating the job to the subordinate commands of wind, rain and earthquake, wearing down the rocks to choke themselves.

Timbrell tapped Maxim's shoulder and pointed forward. Maxim put on his headset, unstrapped himself and stooped a couple of paces forward to look over Piers's shoulder.

'Is that it, do you think?' Piers crackled.

Ahead and slightly left reared the solitary blunt peak of the 5,800-foot Jebel Rum, seeming two-dimensional because it was so sharply two-coloured in moonlight cream and shadow black. They were far below its top, running in towards the ragged steps of cliff that gave it a base. And dead ahead, the bottom step showed a wide fissure that quickly narrowed into the shadows.

'Looks like it.'

'I can't see anything of your Crusader fort.'

'It's on the west side.' That was to the left, in the moon-shadow of the cliff, and nothing is darker than a moon-shadow. 'It's probably further in, where the Wadi narrows.'

'That'll be a thrill,' Len said calmly.

'If they were to put up any sort of defence, they'd want to be able to fire an arrow from one side to another: 200 metres, say.' As if that explanation made things any better.

The helicopter slowed and drifted down. 'I'll do a high recce,' Len said, then explained: '500 feet.'

Piers said: 'I reckon some of those cliffs are 300 feet.'

The Wadi became a canyon as they fluttered over it, the moonlight splitting it in half. In the shadowed half it was almost impossible to see anything, and they didn't. Len turned gently. 'Now for the low one, 200 feet.'

They dipped below the cliffs, slower now, Len edging over until suddenly they were in the moon shadow itself and when their eyes adjusted, the shadow took on shapes and tones. They glared into it.

'Something there,' Piers said, 'something not natural.'

Then Maxim saw it, a squareness below the infinite irregularity of the rock face. Three sides of a square, the middle side broken in its middle.

'A courtyard,' Maxim said. 'They'd have a courtyard outside the stables.'

'What's the ground?' Len asked.

'Stony desert,' Piers reported. 'Looks like the usual thing.'

'Okay. Strap yourself in, Harry. I'm landing in the light, towards the north, zero-zero. NVA please.' His tone had gone formal, which Maxim found reassuring.

Piers clambered back from his seat, slid open the right-hand door – letting in a blast of hurried night air – and aimed a hand-held spotlight on the Wadi floor ahead.

They came in to the 'zero-zero' landing, which Maxim later learnt meant arriving on the ground in a slowing slant, so that height and forward speed were gone at the same moment. Hovering down in the desert meant stirring up dust, blinding the pilot, choking the engines.

Even so, they stirred up a brief cloud while Len yanked at the roof levers to declutch the rotor, then shut down one engine. 'You're in command, Harry.'

But Maxim was already out of the open door with a Sterling, crouching a few yards away. The others followed more slowly, banging home magazines on their weapons. The rotor whiffled to a stop, but with one engine humming (without a ground power unit they needed one engine to start up the second one) there was no silence.

'Len, Piers, set up the machine-gun here,' and when they had, Piers going as number one on the gun: 'Well, if they're there, they know we're here. Alec, you and me. Cover us.'

The helicopter had landed about 400 metres from the stable, diagonally away from it towards the wide south end of the Wadi. Maxim and Timbrell ran straight across into the moon-shadow and up against the tumbled rocks at the base of the cliff, perhaps now 200 metres short of the courtyard. If anybody was going to fire at them, they'd have fired already . . . wouldn't they?

He led the way at a careful walk, staying as close as possible to the rocks but not scrambling over them. In those shadows lay broken ankles.

The courtyard wall must once have been at least high enough to stop a stray horse jumping over it; now it was just an outline, two to three stone blocks high, barely enough to hide a man lying down. It was wider than the stable arch, but not much; above, the stable roof was raggedly flat-topped where the living quarters had been swept away by landslide and wind, leaving drifts of rubble. And the arch seemed to be blocked by dry brush.

'Crawl up to the corner of the wall and cover me,' Maxim murmured. 'I'm going along the wall.' He waited until Timbrell was in position, then flashed NO-NO-NO on his torch towards the helicopter. If the machine-gun fired now, it was more likely to hit them than anybody inside the stable.

He stepped over the wall where it came out from under the fallen rocks, and moved forward, back against the wall, towards the arch. Then he realised the dry spinifex bushes had been piled there, not grown.

'If anybody's there,' he said loudly, 'we're British soldiers and well armed.' Then the same in Arabic.

Something moved inside.

'I'm waiting,' Maxim said. 'And I've got grenades,' although he hadn't.

'Do you promise you are English?' an echoing voice called.

'I promise. How many are there?'

'I am here only. Sergeant Ahmed Al-Hamedi, Central Armour School of Jordan. I will come out slowly.'

'You do that.'

A dark slim figure with hands raised kicked his way through the spinifex camouflage. Maxim waved him into the clear and shone the torch on him. At the same time, he sensed Timbrell getting up from his corner.

'Stay where you bloody are, Alec! Keep covering.' Then, to the Sergeant, who was wearing the Jordanian near-copy of the British Army's 'woollie-pullie' sweater and plain khaki trousers: 'Is the tank in there?'

'Yes, sir, it is there.'

'Tell me what happened.'

That order was too broad, and flummoxed the Sergeant. Maxim tried again. 'Who sent you up here?'

'Colonel Katbah. Is it right he is dead?'

'Who told you that?'

'I have a transistor, I said they must leave that. I can hear some long-wave broadcasting.'

'Who were the others?'

There had been another sergeant and two corporals in the Land-Rover. When the radio had announced the first muddled news of the revolt, they realised the tank hadn't enough fuel to run north to the safety of Ma'an – if indeed Ma'an was safety any longer. A surprise attack – and presumably a surprise revolt – sends a tremor of rumour and fear far beyond its immediate effect. So they had remembered Katbah saying the stable was an almost un-known hiding place and had headed there instead. Then the Land-Rover, with its emergency cans of petrol that were useless for the tank's diesel engine, had gone north for help and . . .

'How long ago?'

The Sergeant hesitated, counting and translating. 'I think almost four days.'

'Stay there. Cover him, Alec.' Maxim walked delicately over the courtyard floor, swinging the torch. It was hard-packed gravel and sand, now scuffed with footprints, but no vehicle tracks. Not even of the tank coming in. Well, in five days the wind can blow such tracks away. No tracks even at the gap in the outward wall, where a gate would once have been, not a gate wide enough for a tank, though, and when Maxim kicked the left-hand side, only a couple of feet high, it fell apart. So the tank had crushed its way in over that and somebody – Sergeant Al-Hamedi? – had reconstructed it and wiped out the tracks and piled up the spinifex . . . Christ, *I'd* have done all that to protect myself if I'd been left alone to hold the fort – literally. And if the 17th Armoured *had* got here, would they have bothered to wipe out their tracks?

He turned to the helicopter and flashed OK-OK-OK, called Alec in and went back to the Sergeant. 'I am Major Maxim, I had to be very careful – you understand?'

87

'Yes, sir.' Al-Hamedi saluted and Maxim returned it, although he was bare-headed. 'Will you take the tank now?'

'No, we've come to blow it up.' *I come to bury Caesar, not to praise him.*

'*Insh'Allah.*' If God pleases, an acceptance of fate.

'What is your job, your work in the tank?'

'I am a tank commander and so I have also done all the jobs. But mostly a gunner, that is why –'

'Good. Is there any of this liquid propellant left?'

'Yes, sir. I think . . . thirty per cent.' Counting in a foreign language is the most difficult thing.

But that was good news anyway; a propellant tank one-third full would fill the breech twenty times over at least, and certainly add to the fireworks party.

Timbrell said: 'Can I rejoin now?' from the wall, and hauled himself stiffly upright. 'They're on their way.'

Len and Piers, two weighed-down figures, were just moving into the moon-shadow but staying as crisp silhouettes against the moonlit far side of the Wadi. *My God, what targets we must have made,* Maxim thought – then: 'Have you got any weapons, Sergeant?'

'A rifle. M-16.'

So my life was in your hands when we ran across the Wadi. Trying to say *Thank You,* and compensating with something he should have said before, with exaggerated formality: 'I hope you will feel free to fly out with us, Sergeant?'

'Yes, sir.'

'Let's have a look at the tank, then.'

In the years since the German excavation, the sand had drifted up into a small ridge across the stable mouth, so there was a slight slope up to the piled spinifex and then a steeper slope down into the stable. Going into the darkness, Maxim reached up to steady himself on a long beam that, oddly, seemed covered in rough cloth. Then he realised he was clutching the tank gun barrel itself, wrapped in a 'thermal sleeve' to even out the temperatures around it. Ten feet on, the tank itself began, surprisingly flat-fronted and no driver's hatch visible in his torchlight. It *is* different, he thought, then realised that they would have driven in forwards, like a car into a garage, with the gun swung to the rear.

I'm not doing too well. 'How do you climb up on it?'

'Any way, sir. It does not break.'

There were two big loops of solid metal sticking out at the bottom of the tank's backside. He got a foot on one, a hand on the barrel again, almost hit his head on the stable roof, and was crouched on the thick grille over the engine. Ahead of him, the 'turret' seemed to be just a long narrow box of armour with angled sides and front that covered no more than the breech of the gun. It was mounted on a convex disc of more armour, like an upturned plate set into the top of the tank, that obviously swivelled round with the gun. On either side of the turret a half-circle-shaped hatch led down through the disc into the tank itself.

'Well, it's different, all right. How do we get in?'

'Wait please. I go through the gunner's hatch.' Al-Hamedi moved easily on hands and feet, swung the thick hatch aside and slithered down out of Maxim's torch beam.

'I think,' his voice came back muffled and metallic, 'the batteries have still enough . . . yes.' Surprisingly bright light shot through the open hatchway and glittered through the row of dusty periscopic windows that formed the hatch rims.

'You go through the other hatch,' Al-Hamedi called. 'You must pull the handle and push to the back.'

Crouching awkwardly, Maxim followed the instructions and the hatch – several inches thick – swung smoothly backwards on a huge hinge mounted on the side of the turret. Indirect light came up to meet him, and he saw below a seat covered in worn khaki material. Without knowing where to put his hands and feet he bruised himself down onto and then into the seat. A chatter of voices started outside: Len and Piers had arrived.

It seemed both smaller and better organised than other tanks he had visited. There was no room to stand upright; just sitting, his head was barely below the hatchway above and his feet were on the floor of the 'turret basket' as they called it. This 'basket' was actually a huge steel can that rotated within the hull of the tank itself. His seat was on the floor of the can, to one side; the roof held the two hatchways and between them, in a narrow slot that formed the actual turret, the silvery and brassy mechanisms of the gun breech. The curve of the can side was virtually lost, being covered with radios and other gear, except for two blank spaces where curved sliding doors led – if the can were properly aligned – fore and aft.

Al-Hamedi sat on his left, side by side except that they were separated by about a couple of feet into which the breech would swing down if the muzzle were raised. Seeing the Jordanian in a proper light, Maxim guessed his age at around thirty, his chin a solid matt of black stubble and his eyes deeply sunken. He had been here a full four days and mostly sleepless nights, all right, but he still had an intent suspicious expression, like a good security guard.

'Well . . .' Maxim said, looking up at the breech. 'I can't wrap explosive round it there. Can you elevate the barrel?'

'Yes, but not in this place.' Of course: it was already almost touching the roof outside.

Footsteps thumped on the engine decking and Timbrell looked in down the hatch. 'How does it look, Major?'

'Very nice. Now can we drive it out of here and elevate the gun so we can set the charges?'

'I don't know. Let me come in and look.'

Maxim stood up and scrambled his way out. He hated doing things ineptly, as he was with getting in and out of the tank. He almost banged his head on the stable roof again, too.

'There's Sergeant Ahmed Al-Hamedi down there, he was with –'

'We've met.' Timbrell slid expertly into his own design, and Maxim scrabbled across the engine grilles and jumped down.

Len asked: 'How long?'

'Don't know yet. If we can, we'll move the thing out so as to elevate the gun to help set the charges.'

'I've got one engine running. I'd like to get back to the helicopter.'

'No. Did you bring the machine-gun? Good. Set it up there' – the left corner of the courtyard, looking down into the dark narrowing Wadi – 'with Piers. Shout before you shoot.'

'If anybody gets at that helicopter we're *buggered*!'

'That's why I'm putting you in a position to pick them off before they get to it.' The Wadi was no more than 200 metres wide – arrow-shot, as Maxim had guessed – at that point. For a machine-gun, it was murderously close range even by moonlight.

Mind, if they brought up a tank . . . No need to mention that.

The helicopter crew went off to position the machine-gun. The tank engine whined, chugged grindingly, then black diesel smoke blew around Maxim and a steady rumble followed. He stepped quickly aside as the tank backed very slowly up the sand slopes, crunching the camouflaging spinifex.

After that, he worked fast but carefully. Not that plastic explosive was dangerous: you could drop it, dance on it, even burn it and it wouldn't explode. But because it was so stable, he had to make sure the pad of it he and Timbrell were wrapping round the breech was all in one piece. A separated lump might not go off just because its neighbour, an inch away, did so.

The breech itself was perhaps eighteen inches in diameter and twice that length, very fat for the 120-millimetre calibre of the gun. This, according to Timbrell who was ready to talk technicalities until the next Ice Age rolled over him, was actually The Secret. It held a reservoir of liquid propellant wrapped around the gun barrel itself with a 'regenerative piston' (what *were* pistons getting up to nowadays?) that moved back – only it was forward in this gun, that was the Clever Thing – so spurting the liquid forward (backward) as a fine inflammable mist through valves in its face until it hit a stop set by the range requirement, having delivered enough bang for that distance.

'All combined mono-propellant regenerative systems work on the same basic principle,' Timbrell explained helpfully. 'The neat thing about this design is wrapping the reservoir around the barrel, to shorten the breech enough to fit into a tank. But I still don't understand quite how they get over flame erosion problems on the obturator when they're turning the pressure through 180 degrees.'

Maxim's dozing surface mind, which had been saying 'Yes?' and 'Uh-huh?' in the right places, was about to say 'You don't?' when he caught it in time. Instead: 'All finished. Can you load up with propellant?'

Timbrell set and pressed a switch and a distant pump whined for a few moments. Maxim checked the explosive sequence: safety cord to Cortex det cord to detonator to primer to plastic. He cut off a short length of safety cord and lit it to check the burning speed – supposedly 7.6 millimetres a second. It seemed to fizz properly, so he cut four and a half metres for the actual fuse: ten minutes.

'Can we block the barrel somehow?' Otherwise some of the explosion would be wasted in whooshing up it.

'I'll put a round in the breech and you try jamming another into the muzzle. You don't have to push it in far: any obstruction will burst the barrel.' Between the seats, just about on a level with the seat backs, there was a vertical rack of shells – just like the magazine in the butt of Maxim's pistol, except that this had two stacks of different shells, and a complicated mechanism at the top because it wasn't attached to the breech of the gun. Timbrell touched more switches; the breech block dropped open, the mechanism lifted the chosen shell, clanged against stops on the block when it had reached the correct height – which could vary, Maxim saw, depending on how the gun was angled – and an arm rammed it home. The breech snapped shut.

There weren't many shells left in the rack and the lifting and ramming machinery had sounded tired, dimming the lights in the tank as it sucked the last from the fading batteries. Oh well, it would all be junk soon.

Then Timbrell half-turned his seat – there must be a catch to unlock it, though Maxim hadn't found it on his own seat – and took another shell from a carousel that ran round the back of the turret basket. He passed it to Maxim; it was heavy but not impossibly so. He raised it above his head and dumped it on the deck outside the hatchway.

'Right: depress the gun and drive back in, will you?' The breech lifted up into its turret slot as Maxim clambered out with the shell, then waited until Timbrell had got out and down to the driver's hatch and set the tank grunting forward into the stable. Maxim managed to jam the shell partway into the muzzle and walked out to the machine-gun. 'We're ready to go. You get the winged chariot wound up, the Sergeant and I'll bring the gun.'

'It's been long enough,' Len said, petulant with nervousness about his helicopter.

'Always seems like it. Flash us an OK and I'll light the blue touch paper.'

Piers and Len loped off towards the helicopter and Maxim sent Timbrell after them when he came out. Then he sat down behind the gun. Al-Hamedi came over, his M-16 rifle slung from his shoulder, and picked the machine-gun belt up to start rubbing sand off the cartridges. 'It will jam the gun. They must have something to lie it on.'

'They're Navy. No sand in the sky.'

'You said you were British Army.'

'And Navy. I wasn't feeling like a long speech then.'

'You said you had grenades, also.'

93

'I wanted to frighten you."

After a pause: 'Yes, I was frightened, with a grenade in that place. Do you think what happened with the Land-Rover . . .?'

'It doesn't look like they got through – and I wouldn't bet on them being alive. If they'd been captured four days ago, you'd have had 17th Armoured patrols in your lap before we got here.'

He let Al-Hamedi absorb that: two comrades probably dead, along with others he'd known. In a way, that and the business of rubbing sand off the cartridges had made him feel closer to the Jordanian Sergeant than to anybody else on the mission.

The distant breath of the helicopter doubled and a torch blinked OK-OK-OK. Maxim flashed an acknowledgement and walked back to the tank.

The internal lights were still on – what did batteries matter now? – but the gunner's hatch was closed and the commander's open just enough to let the fuses dangle out. He draped the safety fuse across the engine decking and lit it. Ten minutes.

Al-Hamedi had the machine-gun cradled in his arms. Maxim supported the dangling cartridge belt and they jogged across to the helicopter.

The moon was going down and its shadow had widened almost to the helicopter itself by now. Maxim slid the door shut behind them and sat beside Al-Hamedi and Timbrell. The engines slid up to a whine, the rotor began to turn, the pilot reached for a roof lever.

Then he said: 'Shit!'

The front seats became a controlled babble.

'Number 1 won't engage.'

'Actuator?'

'Going to ground idle. I'll try it again.'

'We're stirring up dust.'

'I know . . . shit *again*. Actuator failure on number 1. Go for rolling take-off on 2 only. NVA please.'

Piers threw himself over the back of his seat with the

94

portable spotlight and yanked open the door. Dust swirled in. 'Get her moving!'

The rotor thudded, the helicopter strained and began to bobble forward over the uneven ground. The spotlight beam wavered and flared blindingly in the churning dust outside; Len began to yell. Then a wheel hit something, the cabin reared and slewed and the rotor touched the ground with a shuddering crack. There was a vicious snap overhead and the helicopter stopped with Maxim piled on Al-Hamedi and Timbrell in the corner.

I'm alive, Maxim's brain raced on, and not badly hurt, get everybody out of here, might be a fire, do we wait to be rescued or start walking home? – what about the tank? – *the fuse*!

He scrabbled uphill to the open door, set the helicopter rocking as he jumped clear, and ran wildly for the stable. Dark, torch back in the cabin somewhere, feet skidding on loose stones, God let me be in time, if it blows now I'll be torn into total unMaximness . . .

Al-Hamedi was up with him, then past him, crashing through the spinifex to hold up the sputtering eye of the fuse.

'Just pull it loose,' Maxim panted. 'But carefully.'

Al-Hamedi held out the fuse, free, and tossed it aside to burn out. Maxim didn't want to know how much time they'd had. He took out his cigarettes, lit one, then remembered to offer one to Al-Hamedi but let him light it for himself. He didn't want anybody to see how his hand shook.

12

'The helicopter could be salvaged,' Len said, 'but with the rotor smashed up and God-knows-what in the gearbox, it can't be done here.'

'Long walk home,' Piers observed.

'Can you get through a signal?' Maxim asked.

'I tried. I couldn't get any answer. These canyon walls.' Short-wave radio signals had nowhere to go but straight up.

'All right,' Maxim said, 'this is the place they're most likely to look when we don't come back.'

'Come looking with what?' Len snapped. 'There isn't another British helicopter closer than Cyprus or the Gulf.'

'Well, let's get this one unloaded while we think about it.'

There was quite a pile of stuff once they'd finished. Water can, food, weapons, survival packs, life-jackets, medical kit . . . They weren't going to walk far with that lot.

Maxim shone his torch on the helicopter's map. 'If we go north up the Wadi we reach the fort and anything 17th Armoured might send that way. The Land-Rover went that way and hasn't been heard of since. Going south is rougher country and it's about forty miles to the Saudia border, probably more, around the mountains.'

'Do we want to go into Saudia?' Timbrell asked shakily. He had been sick and had apologised profusely, angry at himself. The others had shrugged it off; if you can't be sick after a helicopter crash, when can you be?

'I'd be happier on their side of the border,' Maxim said. '17th Armoured won't chase us over there. I hope.'

'Will they chase us at all?' Len asked.

'I don't see why, unless they want to parade us as hostages or something. And if they want to make an international incident they can do that with just the helicopter here.'

'I'm going to burn that,' Len said.

'Maybe. I'm not too keen on setting bonfires right now. But whatever you do, it'll still be the remains of a British Lynx.'

'Of course,' Piers said, as if remembering something, 'you come from Whitehall, really.'

Perhaps that wasn't the insult that it sounded: a political soldier, not the one who'd made them brush up their personal weapons training, had set the charges, told them where to place the machine-gun. Perhaps – Maxim simmered down – Piers simply meant that Maxim could see the wider implications of their actions because he was in constant contact with Them, the civil servants who pondered every possibility and always ended up deciding the best course was to deny helicopter crews what they really needed. Maxim knew the feeling.

'I'm really,' he said calmly, 'in the middle of the same Wadi that you're stuck in. And in command. We'll sort out the kit and then walk south. I'll re-set the charges in the tank . . . if I'm going to blow that, you may as well fire the helicopter.'

'Them's me orders,' Len said bleakly. A pilot coming home without his helicopter wasn't in a happy situation. The least he could do was say he'd made it useless to the 'enemy'.

Timbrell said: 'We could do the first few miles in the tank.'

'I thought it was just about out of fuel?'

'It is, just about, by tank standards. And you can't trust the gauges when it's as low as that. But if it's got ten

97

gallons, that's ten miles even on this terrain. It's that much less to walk.'

'And then blow it up when it runs dry?'

'We were going to do that anyway.'

Maxim took a series of rapid decisions. 'Sergeant, turn off the lights to save the batteries. I'll strip off the explosive. The rest of you, pick up everything and we'll pile it on board somehow, sort it out when we start walking. Len, you can –'

Al-Hamedi said in his low guttural voice: 'There is light in the Wadi.'

Not direct lights, just a wavering flow on the narrow walls: headlights.

'Get the weapons! Just them! – and back to the stable!'

A minute later they were crouched haphazardly behind the low courtyard walls, breathing hard – particularly the aircrew, in their flying suits. The light still wandered on the rock face down the Wadi. Whoever was coming was coming slowly.

'What'll they send?' Maxim asked, of himself as much as anybody. 'A Land-Rover probably . . . an armoured car?' What armoured cars did Jordan use? – he could only remember they had armoured personnel carriers, British and American. 'They wouldn't send a whole salvage party until they'd located the tank . . .'

'Please listen,' Al-Hamedi said.

With the helicopter's engines dead, the night was very silent. A light breeze, one of the two winds, drifted down the Wadi from the north, bringing a wavering hum of motors – and maybe a faint clanking.

'A tank,' Al-Hamedi said firmly. 'That is diesel and the tracks.'

'That's all we needed. What ammunition does our tank have?'

'You have seen it: practice shell and live shot.'

'What?'

With the polite superiority of soldiers who go into battle

98

sitting down, Al-Hamedi explained to the mere foot-slogger: 'The shell is practice HESH. The live shot is discarding sabot.'

High Explosive Squash Head: really just a blob of plastic explosive that slapped up against a tank like a custard pie as the shell nose crumpled, and then exploded. But the practice version would only have a flash charge, to show where the shell had landed.

'Sergeant, are you prepared to fire at this tank? It belongs to your army.'

'It is a tank of revolutionaries now. I will fire.'

'Get ready to do that. Use the live shot.' That was a daft name, too, because discarding sabot was never 'live': it was just a dart of the heaviest, hardest metal around – tungsten steel or depleted uranium, maybe – wrapped in the sabot of lighter metal that widened it to fit the nearly-five-inch-wide barrel. But the moment it left the muzzle, the sabot flaked off – being 'discarding' – to leave the dart, probably just an inch and a half wide, to fly on with its perfect streamlining until it collided with another piece of metal. It was as primitive as firing stone cannon balls against stone forts, but that had worked, too.

'I'll unblock the muzzle. Len, Piers! – set up the gun by the gate and keep the belt off the sand this time.'

Maxim twisted the half-jammed shell out of the muzzle of the gun while Al-Hamedi climbed aboard. Alec Timbrell was at the mouth of the stable. 'You're not going to fire at that tank, are you?'

'What's it going to do to us?'

'It could be from the rest of the Jordanian Army, coming down to rescue us.'

'I don't think they know we're here and I don't think they care. This whole mission is based on the idea that 17th Armoured does know the tank's somewhere around and wants it. Yes, I'm going to fire if I want to. Pile up the bushes here again.'

He hauled himself onto the tank and crawled to the commander's hatch, bruising his knees and knocking skin off his knuckles and still feeling very incompetent, to begin ripping the explosive off the breech. At least it was easier to get off than put on; he squidged it into a lump and threw it out of the hatch, along with the det cord and primer.

Al-Hamedi was cranking a lever that finally dropped the practice shell out of the breech; he threw that out of his own hatch. Then he sat down, swung a small instrument panel out in front of himself and selected switches. The lights dimmed again, the automatic loader groaned about its negotiated rights and finally rammed a discarding sabot round into the breech, then sagged with a mechanical sigh. Hydraulics powered by electrics, Maxim thought; he knew that much.

'The batteries are running down,' he said. 'Can't we start the engine, or isn't there an auxiliary power unit?' He thought tanks had such things. 'They won't hear over their own engine noise.'

'We are back end towards them. If we start an engine they might see it on their thermal imager. They will know the tank is . . . working.'

'Do we have a thermal imager?'

'I have the sight switched to infra-red, yes.' He sounded very patient compared with how Maxim guessed he himself must sound. 'And it is 200 metres only range.'

He could probably hit a tank with a pistol at 200 metres; using a tank gun six metres long was like putting the pistol to a man's belly before firing it – if Al-Hamedi knew the gun as well as it sounded as if he did.

'And can you do it all yourself?' Maxim persisted.

'Yes, Major.'

Maxim groped his way out of the dark hatch and crawled forward to the arc of bright stars outside the stable. 'Everybody get your heads down!' he yelled. 'Down where you can't see!' It was one of the weirdest orders he'd ever given, but on a thermal imager you can spot the heat of a human head at a thousand metres. The infantry also used imagers.

He snaked his way over the lumpy sharp ground to the

courtyard gateway and poked an eyeball and as little else as possible round the corner. Now the whole Wadi was in shadow, the moonlight starting a few feet up the far cliff. The wrecked helicopter was just a black silhouette of a broken dragonfly. A Land-Rover (or something like that: it was just a shape behind its rocking headlight beams) came into sight. Behind it, the ground glowed with the lights of the clattering, roaring but still invisible tank.

They don't think we're here, Maxim thought, not coming in with headlights full on. But are they going to turn in towards us, or go on to look at the helicopter, out to the right?

'Stay down until I tell you,' he said slowly and loudly. 'Alec . . . Alec?'

There was no sign of Timbrell. Looking back at the stable, the spinifex he'd crawled through had been piled up again half-heartedly, looking very unnatural. How unnatural he realised a moment later when the incoming tank's searchlight slammed a bar of light onto it.

Maxim rolled onto his back, propping his head against the remnant of the gatepost and watched the wobbly beam play over the stable arch. About two out of ten for camouflage this time, but did that matter? In this situation, if you recognised camouflage as camouflage, it didn't necessarily mean there was somebody manning the tank behind it. Then the searchlight beam swivelled away and fixed on the helicopter.

Maxim wriggled back to the stable, tearing his pullover and getting gravel stuffed down his trousers. Just inside, he found Timbrell. 'Get yourself out there with a rifle, shoot for the Land-Rover when we start up.'

'I'm not going out into the muzzle blast of this gun,' Timbrell said firmly.

Oh my God, I'd forgotten that. I've put Len and Piers right under the gun, their eardrums'll be blown in . . . too late now. 'Get in the tank and be ready to start up once we've fired.' Timbrell moved. 'Sergeant?'

'Yes, Major,' from the echoing stomach of the tank.

101

'Can you lay on the target?'

'I have it side-on at only 150 metres, moving slowly.'

'Ready to fire?'

'Yes, Major.'

'Piers, Len!' Maxim called; 'Cover your ears!' Then: 'Fire!' He covered his own ears. Nothing happened. Then the tank jolted beside him, the world went SLAM and turned silent while dust and stones pattered on him from the stable roof. Something like a vast photoflash and just as brief, blinked on the side of the tank in the Wadi. For a moment he thought Al-Hamedi had used an explosive shell, then he realised he'd just seen one lump of metal hit another at something like three times the speed of sound.

The tank in the Wadi had stopped, leaking smoke or steam, and Maxim was vaguely aware of the gun above him creaking round a degree or two, but the second shot took him totally by surprise. The concussion seemed to make his eardrums meet in the middle of his brain. He grabbed the tank for stability, and that was moving, settling back on its suspension, then shouted: 'Cease fire!'

Or thought he had; he couldn't hear himself.

He staggered forward through the spinifex. The tank in the Wadi was dead. 'Machine-gun, target the Land-Rover: fire!' Could they hear him?

The Land-Rover had circled the helicopter and was now tearing back towards the dead tank. A light flickered at him and he recognised rather than heard the bullets come past. Dimly he heard the brrrap-brrrap as Piers fired short controlled bursts. One man toppled out of the Land-Rover, then it darted behind the wrecked tank, doused its headlights and shot out at the other end. Piers fired perhaps two shots and stopped. Gun jammed, Maxim thought, Al-Hamedi was right about sand on the cartridges – but then he saw Piers and Len hastily shifting the gun. The Land-Rover had escaped from their field of fire and was now a scuttling black shadow blending into the blackness up the Wadi. Piers fired one longer burst, then gave up.

Maxim couldn't hear the Land-Rover's engine, but that

didn't mean anything with his ears still in purdah. He didn't hear Al-Hamedi come up behind him; he was just there.

'Why did you fire the second shot?' Maxim demanded.

'A gunner fires until the target is destroyed. That is what a fire order means – to you too, I think.'

Well, yes: soldiers didn't fire only one shot when he said 'Fire' – but somehow he'd expected with a tank gun that it would be different.

'Well, it worked. We'd better go and have a look.' He picked up his Sterling, Al-Hamedi found his M-16. 'Get Alec to move the tank out and start loading it up. Have you got any ammo left?'

Len held up the belt. 'About twenty rounds.'

'Cover us.'

They walked well separated and clear of the machine-gun's line of fire across the Wadi. The tank was a Khalid, the updated desertised version of the Chieftain but without the latest armour. The hatches were all open, so the crew hadn't expected a tank action, and the commander was hanging half out, but that half was all there was. The first shot had gone in just below him, the second a bit further forward: Al-Hamedi had been aiming that at the driver's compartment, Maxim realised. From the outside all he could see were two small cratered holes where the metal had melted and set again, literally, in a flash. Inside was very nasty indeed.

Maxim's torch showed the floor of the tank to be a pink puddle of blood and – there was no diesel smell, so it couldn't be fuel – was it water?

'It is from the charge storage,' Al-Hamedi confirmed. 'They are put in water containers so they will not burn if they are hit.' He muttered a quick prayer in Arabic.

Maxim went across to the man who had fallen from the Land-Rover, hoping he was dead, too. But as he closed, he realised the man was twitching; closer still, he couldn't understand why. The whole back of the skull was shot away.

There was no way they could repair this man, perhaps

103

no hospital in the world could. Why hadn't Piers aimed just an inch or so to the left? Never mind the darkness and return fire, just an inch would have done it.

Al-Hamedi cocked his rifle.

'No,' Maxim said. He was supposed to be in command. He took out his pistol; it seemed more traditional, anyway.

Their own tank rumbled across, headlights full on, with Piers and Len standing up in the hatches. Al-Hamedi stepped forward and directed Timbrell to swing round so that the front faced up the dark narrowing Wadi. The helicopter crew climbed down: Al-Hamedi climbed in and the gun swung round to face the same way.

Timbrell left the engine going. 'We don't need to worry about fuel now.'

'Can you pump from one tank to another?'

'You can't with the Chieftain, sorry, Khalid, but you can with mine. I put in a two-way pump; it seemed damn silly not to be able to suck dry a knocked-out vehicle to keep an operational one going.'

'Get cracking on that, then. D'you need any help?'

'Not yet.'

Like all tanks, the MBT90 was ornamented with external stowage bins and baskets: you didn't crowd the inside with camouflage nets, sleeping bags, tools and whatnot; let them ride on the outside and if they collected a few bullet holes, too bad. There was a basket affair wrapped around the back of the narrow turret, built-in toolboxes alongside the engine grilles and two rails leading a distance forward from them, about a foot above the tank armour and filled in with heavy mesh. Len and Piers had simply piled all the helicopter equipment and weapons into those spaces.

There wasn't a camouflage net anyway, and only Al-Hamedi had a sleeping bag and a kitbag of spare clothing. We may all smell a bit by the time we get out of this, Maxim thought.

'You've got a water tank on board, have you?' he asked

Timbrell, who was getting the cap and filter out of the Khalid's fuel tank.

'Yes. I don't know what's left in it. Pass me that hose, will you? Then tell Al-Hamedi to turn the fuel transfer pump to "intake". It's on the panel up by the right of the commander's position.'

With fuel flowing into the MBT90, Maxim established that there were several gallons of drinkable water left on board, and decided to leave their own supply on the outside. If they had to abandon the tank in a hurry, he wanted a chance to take some water with them. And make sure they distributed the little packets of water from the survival kits so everybody had one . . . but later. The nasty part came first.

'How much ammunition have we got left?' he asked Al-Hamedi.

The Sergeant unlocked his seat and swung it slightly to look back at the carousel. 'Much practice shell and . . . two of shot.'

'Any machine-gun ammo?'

'No.'

'Have we *got* a machine-gun?' He hadn't noticed one.

'There is a place for a commander's machine-gun by the hatch, but it is not with us. There is the co-axial . . .' Maxim could just see the breech embedded in the turret roof beside the main gun breech, up behind the gunner's position.

'7.62?'

'Yes.'

'And is this the same main gun ammunition as the Khalid uses?'

'The same.'

'Right. Throw out as much of the practice shell as you can.' Maxim clambered out again; he still bumped himself, but he was getting quicker at it, and there wasn't the stable roof overhead.

'Len, Piers, I need a hand.' Timbrell was still supervising the fuel hose.

105

As he climbed carefully into the loader's hatch of the Khalid, Maxim reflected that there were advantages to knocking out a British-built tank with another British-built one – commonality of ammunition, at any rate. But to get it, he had to go down and slosh around in the bloodstained water of that sickeningly warm charnel house, shunting the decapitated body of the loader forward in the turret basket so that he could reach the shells stored at the back. He jammed the torch in among some equipment to shine on the ammunition bins, but too much light bounced around. Then he trod on something that crunched with sudden childhood memory of treading on a dead crab; he tried not to look down but did, and it was part of the loader's head.

He passed shells up to Piers, who handed them down to Len. When he had got a dozen each of HESH and discarding sabot he forced himself to search on and find a box of machine-gun ammunition. He passed up two 100-round belts and hauled himself weakly out after them. The cold night punched him in the stomach and he was vomiting before he had tumbled down off the back of the tank.

'Even in the darkness you are shining with paleness,' Piers commented, 'and you have forgotten the torch.'

'Get fucked,' Maxim coughed.

'There is not much immediate opportunity for that out here.' Piers walked off with the cartridge belts. Maxim saw there was another dangling from the free-mounted machine-gun on the turret and wearily climbed back to it – then realised the gun itself might fit onto the MBT90 mount, so took the whole thing.

13

Five minutes later – it was now just after three in the morning – they had 140 gallons in the MBT90's fuel tanks, the fresh shells mounted as Al-Hamedi directed in the autoloader and carousel, and the co-axial machine-gun loaded. Maxim was sucking a glucose sweet from one of the survival packs and feeling better, if emptier.

'Right, Alec,' he said, 'how far can we go now?'

'It all depends on the speed and that depends on the terrain. But I could promise you over a hundred miles. Far more if we're on a road.'

'I don't want to go up the Wadi to the fort. They came looking in exactly the right place; they know where the tank was, and very soon they'll know their own expedition isn't coming back – if they didn't hear our firing anyway.'

Timbrell said: 'They must have picked up the people in the Land-Rover.'

'I don't know . . . if they were caught it would have been within a few hours of leaving here, and that was four days ago. They'd have talked quicker than that. But 17th Armoured sent a tank and a Land-Rover up here at night, in a tricky Wadi . . . they must have been in a hurry. I think they've only just found out about the stable.'

'Perhaps they saw the helicopter?' Timbrell suggested.

Len and Piers collided head-on with their refutations. With the authority of his rank, Len said firmly: 'No. Certainly not after we got in among those mountains, they wouldn't have any idea of where we were going.'

'The point is,' Maxim said, 'they know where we are and they'll be coming back – in force, this time – down the Wadi. We're heading for Saudia. We could save the tank; the Saudis will give it back to us. Mount up, or whatever you say.'

'Who's commanding the tank?' Timbrell asked. 'Both Al-Hamedi and I've been tank commanders. I've handled a troop.'

Maxim considered. 'No, it has to be me. I don't know how to do anything else.'

'A wonderful life you have in the Army,' Piers said, 'where the path to promotion is paved with ignorance of anything technical.'

'We've got to have somebody who knows how to drive driving, and somebody who knows the gun on that. Commanding this isn't a big deal; we're just in a tin lifeboat rowing like hell for the Saudi shore. Unless something goes wrong, we should be there at dawn or soon after. You can elect anybody you like commander once we're there. Now let's just *get* there.'

That still left the helicopter. Maxim could have stuck plastic explosive and fuses all over it and done a very thorough demolition job, but it would take time. Far easier to let Len throw a can of fuel from the wrecked Land-Rover into it and fire it with a flare pistol.

The tank waited fifty metres on to the southward, Timbrell lecturing Maxim on how to give steering orders. Because tanks had traditionally been steered by two hand-brake levers, one to slow each track, commands were still 'left stick' or 'right stick' to make turns – although Timbrell assured him there was nothing as primitive as 'sticks' in his design.

The helicopter lit with a thud of flame that turned into a steady roar, lighting the whole Wadi and silhouetting Len as he backed away, probably savouring the last fun he'd get out of this machine – or maybe just that basic human enjoyment of a good fire. Everybody except

Timbrell, in the driver's seat at the other end of the tank, was watching too.

Spits of dust jumped up between them and the helicopter; at first, Maxim thought it must be debris from the blast of fire. Then, as Len toppled over, an unmistakable bullet howled off the side of the tank and he heard through the blaze the distant rattle of a machine-gun.

He snatched back the cocking handle of his own gun. 'Move off!'

Timbrell may not have realised what was happening, but the sound of Maxim's machine-gun chopped off his questions. The tank jumped forward.

'Left stick! . . . right stick! . . . stop!' Now he had put the blaze between them and the other end of the Wadi. 'Gunner, load shell and fire through the flames.'

"What range?'

'Five hundred. Then a second at 700.'

The turret swivelled a few degrees and the gun lifted. They wouldn't hit anything, but a couple of explosions, probably knocking down a bit of the rock face, would deconcentrate minds. My God, where was Piers, last seen sitting on the engine grilles steadying himself on the barrel? But he was down off the tank and running along the edge of the fire towards Len. Maxim saw him duck as the tank gun threw out its own blast of flame.

Piers dragged Len into the cover of the flames, then towards the tank. Maxim fired the machine-gun and was knocked off his aim (what aim? – in that light and dark) when the main gun fired again. He yanked out his headset jackplug and scrambled down to help Piers. No more bullets seemed to be coming in, although the fire made a great aiming point; that was what had betrayed Len. They hoisted him up behind the stowage rail on the left-hand side, with no idea of how badly he was hit, then Maxim made his most bruising descent into the hatch.

When he had got his headset plugged in: 'Move off . . . left stick . . . on . . . right stick . . . on . . .' in this so

109

newly-learnt language, keeping the fire between them and the narrow dark end of the Wadi.

'Major,' Al-Hamedi's voice through the intercom. 'We could fire smoke launchers.'

'Have we got . . . ?' Yes, he had seen the two bunches of splayed metal tubes either side of the barrel at the very front of the turret. 'Have we got a reload?'

'Yes.'

'Then fire them.'

'I must traverse the turret. Are the airmen safe?'

Piers was kneeling on the jolting deck beside Len, just behind Maxim's hatch, with the gun still pointing back-wards. If the gun swung too far it would wipe him off. You can't argue with a two-ton gun barrel. It was safer to aim the whole tank.

'No. I'll line us up . . . Driver, slow . . . left stick, on. Bit more, on. Gunner, fire the smoke.'

They went off with metallic chunking sounds like light mortars, throwing ten small smoke-bombs in a spray a hundred metres or so back. A wall of smoke bubbled up across the Wadi, dimming the still-bright helicopter fire and – maybe – blurring the thermal imagers and sights that might be beyond that. For a tank to fire smoke was a confession of defeat but a hope of survival.

'Alec, put on your headlights and go as fast as is safe. Aim for the right-hand end of the Wadi.' That wasn't his new-learnt language, but neither was Timbrell a raw recruit to tank driving.

They speeded up, the engine surging like a car on a tricky road with an automatic gearbox – but of course, today's tanks had automatic gearboxes; he'd read that somewhere. Maxim was surprised how agile it was, swerv-ing, speeding up, slowing down; Timbrell might have de-signed it lighter than current operational tanks, but it was still over forty tons, call that twenty Rolls-Royces.

Piers crawled up beside his hatch and shouted: 'I think the Lieutenant-Commander is dead!' In life he was Len, in death the Lieutenant-Commander.

'I'm sorry,' Maxim shouted back.

'Stop the tank!'

'No. Not until we're well clear.'

'If he is not dead, he will die, then!'

'I'm sorry. When we're in cover. Do what you can.'

Piers hesitated, then backed away along the rocking tank.

The shock of action was draining away and leaving Maxim, as usual, concussed with tiredness. Others reacted differently, with hyperactivity and restlessness; this was his way. He just wanted to sleep; ten minutes would do, and then the ripped bodies and the bowel-clenching sound of bullets coming past would be dimmed in an immediate yesterday.

I had to be in command. I don't understand monopropellants and hydraulics and computers and lasers and diesel engines, I've only been trained to understand men. Take the men out of this tank and it would be as dead as a pyramid. And I've been in action before – not that that teaches you much except that only one bullet in a thousand or more actually hits anybody.

Tell Len that: he hadn't heard more than a dozen come past before he felt them tear into him. Unlucky, that's all. And unlucky that I'd let him hang around that fire, hadn't insisted on using a fuse to start it, hadn't had the tank on the other side of the helicopter to take incoming fire? Oh, there were good reasons for those things and I'll be convinced of them tomorrow – after just ten minutes sleep.

But no sleep yet; tomorrow has to wait. I have to get this lifeboat and its lives to shore first. And one thing I don't have to do, Thank God, is try to make it a fighting unit. Just a lifeboat.

Then the Wadi had widened, the flat-topped hills lowering to final cliffs just ahead of them; beyond, they would be in the open and the last of the moonlight. To the right, still in shadow, a landslide had spilled down to make a reef of rocks dwindling out into their path. That would do.

111

'Driver, slow down, right stick, bring us into cover behind those rocks.'

Timbrell curved the tank behind the reef, then backed carefully under Maxim's directions until they were 'hull down', with just the gun showing back up the dark Wadi.

'Shut down.'

'We call it "silent watch".'

'Okay.'

The engine stopped and Piers said, too loud in the silence: 'He *is* dead now. I lost another pilot, in Operation Corporate. We were on *Bellerophon*, she got hit by a bomb that started a fire in the wardroom flat and we were trapped in our ready room above it . . . it took them a long time to get us out. He was too badly burned. But he took longer to die than Len.' Then, quietly and viciously : 'I should have killed them all in that Land-Rover. Or we should have gone after them.'

'We don't know it was them, it could have been somebody else, following up. And I wasn't going up the Wadi.'

'Then you should – ' But Maxim over-rode him: 'We'll bury him here. No point in carrying him further.'

Piers looked around at the drift of sand, gravel and stones that had piled up against the reef; it was just a piece of desert in a desert that stretched hundreds of miles in three directions.

There were a shovel and an axe strapped to the sloping front of the tank near the driver's hatch. The axe came in useful when they had dug out the loose top layer and reached the compacted earth beneath; even so, they got down less than three feet and it was sweat-streaming work. Maxim had dug plenty of fox-holes before, but never a grave. Somebody else had always done that.

When they were exhausted, he asked: 'Have you got all his papers, anything else?'

Piers saw the military sense of it. 'I will get them.'

At Maxim's gentle insistence, they also stripped off the flying suit and its badges, laying Len down half-undressed and quickly scooping the desert back on top. It was almost an Islamic burial, speedy and spartan, with no gesture of carrying anything from this world to the next. Inevitably, there was quite a mound; Maxim did his best to kick it smooth without Piers noticing.

'D'you want to say anything?'

'He was not much of a believer, I think. And I don't have a Bible or . . . Good-bye, Len. You were a good pilot and I will get you out of this blasted place as soon as I can.'

He wanted to put up a marker, maybe a cairn of stones, but Maxim said No. 'They might find him and dig him up. You'll remember where.'

Piers stared up at the dark headland of rock. 'Yes, I will remember.'

14

When they got back to the tank, Timbrell was standing by with a mug of coffee for each of them. A cooking device hadn't occurred to Maxim, but of course a tank must have one if it was to be the much-vaunted '24-hour environment', shut down on a battlefield poisoned by radiation or gas. It turned out to be called a Boiling Vessel, or BV, and Al-Hamedi had turned it on the moment they stopped. A sound instinct.

They gulped the oversweetened coffee down while Maxim flashed a torch over the map. It was a 'Tactical Pilotage Chart' in half-millionth scale which was ridiculously small for ground use and not helped by the lines and figures Piers had scrawled across it for the helicopter flight. The tip of Maxim's little finger could hide the Jebel Rum that lifted a good 2,500 feet above their level and the length of his thumb took them to the Saudi border. He tried to remember the greater detail on Colonel Jeffreys' big map, but he had only been dreaming theoretical journeys over that one. Now he had a real decision to make.

A few miles south, there seemed to be an island of rock maybe a thousand feet high and he thought he could actually see a last glimmer of the moon on its flattened top. They would swerve to the east around that; pursuit would be coming from the north – behind them – or the west, where Aqaba lay behind the coastal mountains and perhaps wadis through them.

He showed Timbrell what he wanted and told him to

hop in and start up. Then he ushered Piers into the hatch ahead of him. Behind the commander's seat there was just room for Piers to sit on the floor of the turret basket with the wadded sleeping-bag as a cushion and his back against the curved ammunition rack. Al-Hamedi warned grimly about the dangers of getting in the way of the automatic loader or the recoiling breech if they should have to fire the gun, then went back to studying a small cathode-ray screen in front of him. Maxim was about to ask what it was when the engine coughed and rumbled to life. 'Commander, can you guide me?' Timbrell asked. 'My infra-red periscope's on the blink and I can't see much without headlights.' Maxim stood up on his seat and started giving directions.

They waddled out over the scattered debris of the land-slide and speeded up on the relatively flat stony desert, Maxim straining his eyes against the cold slipstream. Just when he wanted to go really fast, in the open, they daren't do it without headlights. The desert has none of the man-made logic that is stamped across most of Europe, allowing you to predict ditches, hedges, marshes before you see them. If the desert wants to have an outcrop of rock, a patch of soft sand or a steep dry watercourse, it just has them. You take the desert at its own pace.

After a while, he asked: 'What's that screen you're watching?'

There was a babble on the intercom, finally Timbrell saying austerely: 'Commander, can you be specific in your commands? Always say 'gunner' or 'driver' unless you're giving an obvious string of instructions.'

'Sorry, driver,' Maxim said humbly. 'Gunner, forget that question. I'll ask later.'

Timbrell had a point. Maxim had worked with radios ever since he joined the Army, but always at a distance, acknowledging and later giving orders and situation reports that – he prided himself – had become models of precision and concision. But he had never worked on a closed intercom circuit like a tank or a multi-crewed aeroplane

115

with everybody just a few feet apart yet out of sight in darkness and engine noise. It had been shouts and whispers: 'Jim, get your bloody head down, move left behind that bush,' and 'Jackson, get your section up there, that crest, *move!*' – pointing a finger, waving a hand.

This had to be tea-party manners, formal and disciplined. He had to fit into the tank's ways even to make an efficient lifeboat out of it.

Glancing back, he could see the black shapes of the Wadi Rum cliffs outlined against the stars on either side of the dust that poured up behind them, even as slow as they were going. Maybe they were out of effective range now, certainly any pursuit couldn't be going faster unless it was using headlights. He couldn't see any lights, but the dust . . . even the muzzle of the gun, still pointing backwards, was lost in the cloud.

'Are you – sorry, *gunner*, are you watching backwards on that screen?'

'Commander, yes.'

'Nothing in sight?'

'Commander, no.'

Some sort of remote camera must be feeding into that screen, Maxim realised, but had no idea of where it was or how it worked. As long as Al-Hamedi understood it, and was confident he could watch their trail through the dust, that was all that mattered. Just keep the lifeboat on course.

Ahead and to their right the big tabletop rock, another flat black shape cut out of the infinity of star pinholes, looked a little larger. He was getting used to the rocking motion, although it was never predictable as in a ship, and was holding himself in place more lightly and confidently. The sodden, tired feeling was gone – for the moment; perhaps buried with Len or at least the effort of burying him. But how was Piers taking it? He ought to have something to do, keep his mind busy . . . but what? There wasn't even a seat for him, let alone a job, and he knew less about tanks and army procedures than any of them.

Piers would just have to stick it out. Only a few hours. He still wished he could give Piers something to do. They should at least –

'Stop! Driver! Stop!'

The tank dug in its nose, Maxim banged his stomach on the edge of the hatchway, their dust trail caught up and drifted past them.

'Driver to commander: what is it?'

'A wadi, I think. Advance, slow.'

They crept forward.

'Stop. Gunner, will you take command? I'm getting out. Give me a torch.'

It seldom rains in the desert, that's why it remains a desert. So when it does happen, there are no grass or tree roots, no soft soil, to mop it up. It must have rained recently on the mesa ahead, then poured off down cracks and gullies until it crashed like a dam-break into what had been a shallow watercourse. The sharp unweathered edges, the raw rocks at the bottom of what was now an eight-foot-deep trench showed how new it was.

A man could cross it easily; Maxim would have had a company of infantry across in five minutes. But now he was in a tank, invented originally for crossing trenches – but not this one. He flicked off the torch and walked back to where Timbrell had his head up through the driver's hatchway.

'Alec – how wide a trench can you cross?'

'A plain gap? About six feet. What's it like?'

'About twenty wide and eight deep, sheer sides.'

'No, thank you.'

'Right. It'll spread out and get easier lower down. Tell Al-Hamedi to tell you to turn left and follow me.'

The tank growled round, pivoting on one track, and followed a few metres behind him. It was a bit like leading an untamed bear on a chain: you hoped he kept the length of the chain away, that Timbrell's foot didn't lurch on the accelerator.

The flash flood had torn out a long wadi. He had seen

117

it before in the desert, though never seen it happen, and learned never to camp or park in such places, however enticing as cover. You didn't even have to be very near the thunderstorm that flooded the high ground upstream: a dry watercourse suddenly became a thundering river that battered vehicles into junk. If you were down there with them, at least you didn't drown: the rocks in the torrent and the ones it whacked you against made it quick. It had happened to a party of French schoolgirls at Petra some years ago.

Perhaps the desert has killed as many people with water as lack of water, but who keeps records?

As the gentle slope got gentler, the charging army of water had spread out, slowed by its loot of rocks and stretching supply lines until it had tired and sunk down onto and into the desert. Maxim turned and held up both hands; Timbrell stopped.

'It looks like you can cross here.'

But Timbrell climbed out to see for himself. Satisfied, he got back in, swivelled the tank over the edge, charged the far side and clawed over, the tracks gouging out a shrapnel of stones and impacted earth. Maxim walked across, testing the surface: it was desert dry now, as if the water had never been. In daylight, there would be a spatter of green from the long-lived and optimistic seeds that seemed to lie everywhere in a desert, but by night he could see nothing but the damage the army of water had done.

He caught up with the tank and put on the headset before climbing in and was about to speak when Al-Hamedi said: 'Gunner to commander – perhaps I have seen something behind us.'

Instinctively and uselessly, Maxim jerked his head to peer back across the wadi into the night. 'What sort of something? – lights?'

'I do not think so . . . just on the infra-red perhaps . . . it is not there now.'

'Okay, keep watching. Gunner and driver, I should have thought of this before: can we try the radio?'

118

They chewed it over, then Timbrell said: 'We never managed to reach the ship before. The kit's pretty short-ranged and with all the high ground . . . But you can get some freak ranges at night, when the ionosphere –'

'Yes, fine. Gunner, give Piers a headset and let him have my seat, if he can work the radio from there. I'll stay on top.'

In the dim glow from the whatever-it-was screen, he saw Piers scramble onto the seat below, then heard him come on the intercom and Al-Hamedi briefing him on how to use the radio. Piers would be experienced with radios and procedures anyway, and was the only one who knew the ship's frequency and the callsigns. And if they didn't achieve anything, it was still something for Piers to do. Satisfied, he perched himself on the swung-open hatch, clutching the storage bin behind the turret for support, and told Timbrell to move off.

If anybody *was* following, they couldn't cross the wadi higher up than the tank had crossed. All he had to do was find a dip in the ground where they couldn't be flanked and hit the follower in the side as he floundered across the wadi's banks . . . Hold on, he told himself: lifeboats don't set ambushes. Just keep moving.

'Blackbird, this is Harpoon . . . Blackbird, this is Harpoon . . .' Piers' voice seemed to reach Maxim only through his left ear, and he realised that earphone must be for radio, the other for intercom. Before, he'd just thought the left earphone was dud. So he could go on giving driving commands to Timbrell without cutting in on the radio, or it drowning him out. Clever, that, but confusing until you got used to it.

The radio crackled, then Piers came on intercom: 'Commander, I think that is the ship answering. They have better reception and transmission facilities than we do.'

'Okay, tell them' – this had better be in some sort of code – 'tell them we are in Champion heading for Dixieland. Better say we've lost Len and the helicopter, put that in code somehow.'

119

Piers' rather pedantic Welsh diction was ideal for radio, Maxim reflected; the Welsh with their songs and reading poetry at eisteddfods believed in the voice. God help us if he'd been a Scot – but then the Navy would have worked on his accent before they let him near a transmitter.

He heard Piers repeat the message three times and get a crackle in reply. By then they were almost beside the towering blackness of rock that would cut out any radio anyway, so he called Piers off but let him still sit there, tuned in and listening.

'Driver, left stick . . . on. I want to keep well out from the cliff, there'll be landslips and more wadis.' They rumbled into a slightly deeper darkness that was no more than the blotting out of one segment of the stars above the desert rim. Maxim knew only a handful of stars by name – probably Piers, a navigator, knew far more – but he found their steadiness and infinity comforting. Whatever he did, however many mistakes he made, it wouldn't change the stars in their courses. They would drift on, night after night, aloof and uncaring . . .

No, that wasn't comforting at all. If the bloody stars didn't care about him, be buggered if he'd care about them. 'Piers,' he called down, 'what time's first light?'

15

The room – in fact two rooms, with an ever-open door between them – had the transient look of a church hall, a place with no basic purpose but where something was always about to happen or just had. Trestle tables and folding chairs were scattered around waiting for a new pattern, an empty map-board covered half of one wall, a couple of unplugged telephones sat in a corner.

Since it was a basement room under the Ministry of Defence Main Building, it shouldn't have looked any bleaker at three in the morning than any other time, but to George it did. He slumped soggy and dry-mouthed onto a chair, still wrapped in an overcoat over hastily-thrown-on clothes. The only other person in the room was a Brigadier from Military Operations, but beyond the connecting door a phone rang and was answered, a teletype chattered to itself.

'What the hell has been going on?' George demanded.

'The insertion team that went in by helicopter from the *Alamein* has gone missing and the helicopter's now past its fuel endurance time.'

'Did it knock out the MBT90?'

'There's been no signal from the helicopter at all, but we've had an intercept from Cyprus of 17th Armoured Brigade's signals. It seems . . .' the Brigadier consulted his clipboard. He was a thin man in his late forties wearing a gingery tweed suit which he would never have dared show at Defence during the day. His hair, eyebrows and moustache looked like clippings from the same tweed, and he had very blue eyes. 'Yes, here: a 17th Armoured tank was knocked out in the Wadi Rum area. Other casualties reported. That was about 0100 hours our time."

'God Almighty . . . Has our tank come to life? What's happened to . . . Are we in touch with anybody?'

'The ship, the *Alamein*. They reported the helicopter missing and who's in it. It includes a Major Maxim.'

'Harry? No, they didn't send *him*, we didn't tell them to send him . . . What are we doing about all this?'

The Brigadier waved a hand around the room. 'This. The night shift at the Foreign Office has been on – the Cyprus signal was routed through them, of course – and they sounded very agitated and asked what we were doing; so we started this.'

A Squadron Leader from Defence Intelligence came from the adjoining room, said Good Morning brightly to George and started pinning a map and a batch of teletypes onto the board.

The Brigadier passed George the clipboard. 'I've been jotting down all the departments that might be involved or want to be, but I'd welcome your advice. This seems to have policy overtones, and you know the form and the people better than I do.'

'Who shall we invite to the party?' George murmured. 'Who's been a good boy or a bad boy? And who's not going to invite us to their next party unless . . . All right, let me pop upstairs and find my address book.' There was just half a bottle of vodka in his desk, too. 'And we'd better have somebody from the Cabinet Office: it helps spread the responsibility upwards. Are we a committee or a planning group or what?'

'I haven't the slightest idea, old boy. I imagine they'll dream up some format for us when it's all over and done.'

The Brigadier was right: long after the event, the written record showed that the Snowflake Committee sat in continuous session throughout the next twenty-four hours, chaired by Brigadier T. C. Crowley-Thompson, secretary George Harbinger (Ministry of Defence, Policy), with representatives from the Cabinet Office, Foreign Office, Home Office and Secret Intelligence Service, and a secretariat from Defence Intelligence and Signals. During a wide-ranging discussion the Committee rejected certain possible lines of approach (the things the record-writer knew, by then, had not happened) and pursued other lines (the things which had happened).

None of the 'Committee', not even those who bothered to read the record, objected. It showed the way things ought to have happened, and that was what records are for.

On his way out, George noticed a small handwritten card slotted into a holder on the outside of the door. 'Why "Snowflake"?' he asked.

The Brigadier looked at the Squadron Leader.

'I was thinking of their chances in the desert,' the Squadron Leader said.

In the moonless dark, Maxim could feel rather than see the comforting bulk of the cliff that gave them cover from the right – roughly the west – and relaxed a little, although he still had to guide Timbrell around rocks and over dry wadis. He also had time to feel cold, giving up his handhold on the tank to shove his hands into his armpits under the feeble warmth of his combat jacket. His feet, still wet with the nightmare mixture from the floor of the wrecked Khalid, had already gone through the pain barrier to numbness.

On a winter exercise, he had once asked a tank commander why, whenever a tank stopped, the crew raised the engine covers and sat around the edge staring diligently in; surely tank engines didn't play up that often. No, the commander confessed, they were just warming their feet on a hot engine; the diligent expressions were to impress the untechnical infantry. The thought that a hot engine was only a few feet behind him now made his cold bones ache.

They bounded over a small reef of rock with a thump

that made them ache even more, and Timbrell's too. 'Driver to commander, could Sergeant Al-Hamedi take the driving for a spell? I'm getting a bit stiff down here.'

'You designed it.'

'I didn't design my age.'

'Gunner, did you hear that?'

'Yes, I will drive.'

'We'll stop when I find some cover. Does that Boiling Vessel work on the move?'

'To boil yes, not to pour out.'

'Turn it on.''

A low headland jutting out from the base of the main cliff forced them aside, and when they had passed it Maxim turned them in behind to another hull down position.

'Driver, stop. Silent watch. You can get out. Piers, you hop out, too. Gunner, stay on that screen, I'm coming down.'

Back in the commander's seat, he found he could swing his own keyboard-cum-instrument panel, a duplicate of the one Al-Hamedi was using, to lock in position above his knees. The dead screen was mounted on top of it at the back. 'How do I turn this on?'

Al-Hamedi reached across under the breech and showed him the control. The rest of the keyboard depressed him – if it wasn't a computer, its mother had been very friendly with one – but the screen flickered alive and stabilised to a landscape of dim electronic greens. That wasn't so bad: he had used thermal imagers before.

'What do you call this system?'

'Passive Vision Device; you say PVD. It is also ordinary for day. A video camera.'

'Where is the camera?'

Al-Hamedi seemed surprised. 'On top, at the behind of the turret.'

Riding on top of the tank, Maxim had been vaguely aware of a metal dome at the rear of the turret – the highest point of the tank. Now he realised it must be the armoured casing of the camera unit and of course it would

124

have to be at the highest point. He began to see the thinking behind Timbrell's design: in other tanks, the highest thing was always the commander's hatch – and sticking out above that, the commander's head, getting a good look around. And too often getting a bullet between the eyes. You could have armour a foot thick – the front of this tank certainly had that much – and the commander pokes his head up for a quick shufti and a single sniper – bang. Half the tank's efficiency knocked out by one bullet.

Yes, he could see the point, and the infra-red camera was essential at night, but he didn't like the idea of sitting down there trying to fight a battle by TV screen in broad daylight. Oh well, he wasn't planning to cross-badge to the Armoured Corps anyway.

The Boiling Vessel, set on a bulkhead and reached through one of the sliding doors of the turret basket, was winking a red light. Al-Hamedi started running off hot water into mugs ready prepared with instant coffee and sugar. If you don't like your coffee sweet, don't stir it. If you like it with milk, go somewhere where there's milk.

Maxim took his mug and scalded his mouth, wishing he could simply pour the coffee into his shoes where he really needed the warmth. He hadn't bothered to draw a pair of boots from *Alamein*"s stores, along with his combat clothing, and didn't regret it: breaking in new boots was at least one trouble he didn't have now.

Had something moved on the screen?

Not now, but for a moment, something brighter green. He glared fiercely, willing the thing to move again and it did, fractionally to the right now, vanished again . . .

'Action! Enemy vehicle back the way we came, to the right.' He had no idea of how to give proper commands for a tank, but 'action' seemed to get results. Timbrell crashed down onto the gunner's seat and he heard Al-Hamedi scrambling into the driver's position in front. But wherever Piers was . . .

'Where was it?' Timbrell demanded, staring at his own screen.

'About threequarters right, halfway up the screen –'

'Centre it!'

'I don't know how to turn the thing!'

'Oh shit!'

'There, there it is!'

Again a bright green dot. Under Timbrell's hands the screen jumped to place the dot in the centre, then he reached for another control and the whole turret basket jerked around. The dot on the screen flared briefly and bullets clanged on the tank.

'Return fire?' Timbrell wanted to know.

'Co-axial.'

The machine-gun embedded in the top of the turret chattered in short ranging bursts. Empty cases rattled into a box. The dot on the screen disappeared.

'Cease fire,' Maxim ordered. 'Driver, start up. Gunner, d'you know what you were shooting at?'

'Not a tank, but it had some sort of night vision to see us at all.'

'Fire if you see him again. I'm going to find Piers.'

The engine grumbled and roared as he lifted himself half out of the hatchway, and he had to yell above its noise before Piers bobbed up behind the tank and scrambled forward over the engine grilles. Maxim climbed out, crammed Piers down the hatch and followed him. It was clumsy and risky and . . . and it was all a mess.

'One of these days,' Timbrell said sourly, 'we're really going to have to get organised.'

'Shut up. Driver, reverse, slow . . . stop. Forward, hard right stick . . . on. Speed up.' And they scuttled away from their covering headland of rock.

'Gunner to commander, why are we –'

'Shut *up*. Stay on that screen. Driver . . .' he went on giving driving commands to Al-Hamedi. If Timbrell couldn't see that the one thing they had to do was move and keep moving, Maxim had no time to explain it. Probably it had just been a Land-Rover out there – a tank would surely have fired its main gun, not given itself away first

126

by machine-gun fire – but somewhere behind it would be tanks. Not too close yet, it had told them that much; if tank backup had been near at hand, the Land-Rover would have held its fire and tried to stay hidden while it radioed for help. Instead, it had taken a chance on delaying them: a stopped tank might well have some of its crew standing around outside – as they had been – and vulnerable to machine-gun fire.

Keep moving – but where now?

'Piers, are you plugged in? Pass me up the map and a torch.'

By clasping his hand over the torch lens he got a reddish glow of light coming through his flesh, and red light didn't harm night vision. But it took a long time, between watching the faint starlit ground ahead and the tiny detail on the map, to plot any sort of course. As they gradually cleared the cover of the isolated mount on their right, he turned Al-Hamedi slightly south. Miles ahead on the horizon he could just make out the bulk of the Jebel Umm Sahm, 5,000 feet above sea level, at least 2,000 feet above them. Head for that, then keep it to their east so they were shadowed from the dawn – if they hadn't got past it by then.

Saudià lay to the south, safety from pursuit to the east. Going south-east was a compromise – but most things military were compromises.

Gradually the tension, and probably some of their alertness, seeped away. I haven't been shot at in the last minute, why should it happen in the next? In the last and next five minutes? Or ten? Or half hour? But war is plodding as well as waiting. Past and future faded into an endless present of the surging engine noise, the rocking motion, the muttered driving commands, the Jebel on the horizon that got no closer, the wind that got no warmer.

Tanks are reptiles, he thought with half his mind, they belong in the desert and the mud. The Germans were wrong. They built some of the best tanks in the world but then gave them big-cat names: Panther, Tiger, Leopard. Yet tanks have none of that grace, the stalking flow of a cat. They are thick-skinned, cold-blooded (by God are they cold-blooded) scuttling along, then freezing still as a lizard, only the eyes – the PVD cameras – moving in search of prey or predator.

But where do you find C-names among the reptiles? Crocodiles and chameleon, and there was a wartime Crocodile, a flame-throwing tank, he recalled. Dragon would be a good name, not a C but a logical step forward. Then Dinosaur – no, that was always an insult, although they'd run the Earth for umpty-million years and no other species had chased them out; they'd gone down to disease or some climatic change or a meteor collision . . . what *was* the latest theory that had killed them off? It was the sort of thing Agnes would know . . .

The under edge of the hatch was rimmed with rubber, presumably to make an airtight seal when it was closed against nuclear or gas attack, and he was holding one-handed to that rather than the cold steel. And suddenly his confident grip had become a clench: the engine had stuttered. Just one missed beat and it was as if the tank's armour had turned to thin glass around him. He held his breath and waited. The engine surged as they took a small slope. No problem. No problem at all. One missed heartbeat doesn't send you screaming to the doctor. The engine stuttered again.

This time, they slowed. The engine had picked up to normal again, but he could feel Al-Hamedi was holding back.

'Driver, what's the problem?' His voice sounded crisper than he felt.

'I am not so sure . . . I think fuel is coming okay . . .'

'Gunner to driver: Sergeant, how long have you run on these air filters?'

'I think we have been always with them.'

'That could be it: the air filters clogging.'

'What do we do now?' Maxim asked.

'We can't change them, we haven't got replacements. We can get them out and bang some of the sand out, but . . .'

'How long does that take?'

'Half an hour, an hour.'

'How long can we keep going as we are?'

'I don't know. We won't suddenly stop, we'll just gradually lose power.'

Maxim shaded his watch to bring up the brightness of the luminous dial. In an hour it would be first light. Whatever he did, they were going to get caught by the sun; his only choice was where.

'Gunner, can you see anything on the PVD?'

'I thought I had something a little time ago, but I'm not sure.'

'Okay. Driver, keep going at your own speed. Don't force it.'

They didn't seem to be scuttling any more; now they were a tired old crocodile clumping along far from water. Maxim's momentary empathy with the tank had gone, farted away by the missed beats of its exhaust. Now he loathed it, as he loathed being dominated by any mechanism. To an infantryman, freedom of movement was the true weapon, the gun in his hand merely the last resort. Now this whole damned box of tricks and trickery was his weapon, his mobility; he was only part of its brain – and not the best-educated part.

He stood swaying rigidly, tensed for every hiccup in the engine noise. It was like the first car he had ever owned, and he didn't like the memory. He could also sense an uneven but constant rise in the ground beneath and he didn't like that, either. They were getting close to the tall Jebel which blotted out a whole sector of the eastern stars. It was time to turn more south, to crawl along its 'coastline', as he had planned. But that left him with a wide-open flank to the west, the way they had come, the way the Land-Rover was still – probably – following. But nevertheless it headed them for Saudia . . .

129

'Commander, look back!'

He jerked his head round. A wobbling glow was fading in the open desert some miles back: headlights on a dust cloud. Then it cut out. The Land-Rover had run into a problem that made it flick on its lights for a moment. And it wasn't just west of them, it was south as well; they were being outflanked.

'Driver, left stick . . . on. We should hit a dry wadi soon; I want to follow that.' The wadi had been clearly marked on the map as a broken blue line, an established watercourse whenever there was water. And it led east, around the far side of the Jebel. Saudia would have to wait.

Whether or not the darkest hour is before the dawn, Maxim had never noticed. What he had noticed, time and again, was that it is the coldest. He had switched jobs with Timbrell for a time, learning more about how to control the PVD system, but apart from the tank's self-made wind outside, the inside was no warmer. It might become airtight when the outside world was poisoned, but with all the hatches open it was as draughty as a Scottish castle.

With the engine now growling and stuttering, they were crawling along a snakey dry wadi at the bottom of a shallow v-shaped valley. The bulk of the Jebel and its consort peaks shut out the stars on their right, but there was an irregular outline of cliffs on their left as well, and occasionally the wadi sides grew too steep to climb. Maxim didn't need telling that this was tactically a bad place for a tank, but he was more concerned with hiding than manoeuvring. From behind, even a thermal imager would have to be within 200 metres to see them.

Was it getting lighter? Was their dust trail becoming more obvious? He had been staring too long at the east: the one way not to see a change is to watch constantly where you expect it. The PVD system had thought of this: you could actually freeze the picture and study it at one moment of time, then freeze it again some seconds later.

That way, a slight subtle movement turned into obvious jerky steps.

He looked up. Without his noticing, the stars had quietly been switching off.

'Gunner, take over up here, please.'

With Timbrell in position, he slid down onto his seat, orientated himself quickly with the screen, and picked up the map. The valley stretched for miles ahead, but the high ground was broken and patternless around it – and would be far more so when he could see it in daylight.

There would be plenty of hiding places to nurse the tank back to health, but he wanted the light to pick them out.

He lit a cigarette, not knowing whether it was permitted or not, but there didn't seem much inflammable around him. And when they stopped – what else besides sorting out the filters? Food. They had the tins from the *Alamein*. More coffee, of course. Try the radio? No, he was going to find a niche in the rocks that would block any transmissions. And get himself taught more about this tank; lifeboat it might be, but even a lifeboat needed seamanship to reach the shore.

He finished the cigarette and stamped it out, then stood up on the seat. In the short time he had been below, the sky had become an abstract of dark crude colours, poster-paint red, orange and blue, grainy like an overblown photograph. Against that, the first shadowing of the mountains made them incredibly delicate and detailed, more fragile than the sky. The sun would tell the truth, but he still smiled at the gentle deception of a desert dawn.

Timbrell looked across the top of the turret at him and Maxim held up a hand. 'Stay where you are, Alec, I'm just sightseeing.' He began to scan the cliffs professionally rather than artistically.

16

The silence was immense once the engine had stopped and
died away in ticking and chortling noises. They climbed
stiffly down and stood wriggling their shoulders and listening to nothing. There was no wind yet, no birds or insects,
trains, planes or cars. It was a landscape on which man
had left no mark save their own tracks up to their hide
under an overhanging canopy of rock.

'Piers – take the Gimpy and find a place within shouting
distance where you can cover back up the wadi and still
get back here without being spotted. Is the BV on? Can
you heat some tins in it, too? Good, get on that. How
soon'll the engine be cool enough to work on? Any other
maintenance we have to do that we could do waiting for
that?'

He had to blitz them or they would slump into the silence
– working, but at only half the speed they could and
without knowing it. That was inherent in any command
situation; take a bunch of full generals, lifetime soldiers,
put one of them in command and the rest would instinctively start goofing off. But not entirely a blitz.

He nodded towards the back of the cave and said to
Al-Hamedi: 'Mecca's about that direction, as I reckon.'

Al-Hamedi gave him a brief, grave smile but headed for
the open air to make the dawn prayer – the most important
in the Islamic day – so Maxim took a spade from its clips
on the front of the tank and went in beyond it to inaugurate
the area as a lavatory. He then saw what Al-Hamedi had
assumed: that he wasn't the first by a hundred years or so,

although the dry air had killed any smell. And, of course, the roof was blackened by cooking fires.

After that, he walked back down their tracks. They had climbed out of the watercourse and up a gentle slope of gravel, sand and rock to the base of the first step of cliffs that became the Jebel above. The mountains here were sandstone layers stacked roughly on each other like a random collection of kitchen plates, and at this point a softer layer had worn away, leaving the overhang of harder rock. One day it would collapse, too, but perhaps not today. A cascade of broken rock had spilled down from above the canopy and gave them some cover on both sides. There was no retreat from their position, but they had height and a field of fire right across the wadi.

He tore up one of the seemingly but never quite dead spinifex bushes and walked slowly back, trying to wipe out their track. It didn't really work, but it stopped looking blatantly like a tank trail. Above, the crude sky was paling fast and a lava flow of sunlight was trickling down the east face of the Jebel.

Piers had the machine-gun placed in a sensible enough position along the cliff and slightly higher than they were. Maxim congratulated him more than the choice of site was worth and headed for the tank. This was the first chance he had got to see the beast he had been riding and fighting in. He hadn't even known what colour it was: irregular rectangles of sand, grey, brown and dusty green – not counting the real dust blurring its sides – speckled with bright metal flowers where bullets had flaked off the paint.

As a tank, it looked unnatural, pin-headed with its low narrow turret (though for Heaven's sake, what tank looked 'natural'? – whatever a generation of soldiers was used to seeing, he supposed). Standing in front of it, he realised you would see no more than the gun muzzle and the PVD camera above and behind it if the tank were 'hull down' behind cover – and that, he supposed, was the point of Timbrell's design. But now the gun was swung to the right and a short stout crane had been unfolded from the side

133

of the turret, its chain hooked to an engine grill it was winching up. Like so much of the tank, Maxim had vaguely noticed the crane without bothering about what it was.

He climbed back on the tank and, unnecessarily for the moment, started checking over the weapons and kit in the stowage bins and racks. They had far more weapons than men to handle them, but were down to 250 rounds for the machine-guns – about twenty seconds' firing time for one gun. Hungry things, machine-guns; in the Falklands, he had heard, Scorpion light tank crews had been reduced to bartering food for ammunition with forward infantry units.

The second engine grill was upright, balanced slightly beyond the vertical, and Timbrell had lowered the slab of armour that was the back end of the tank to form a tailgate work platform. The air filters, flat square boxes that took two of them to lift out, lay between the huge radiators.

'And we just *bang* them?' Maxim queried.

'That's right.'

'Can't we replace the fabric or paper or whatever's inside?'

'No, they're sealed throwaway items.'

'In the most modern tank in the world.'

Timbrell's face tightened. 'I didn't design the engine, it's just a version of the one in Challenger. When you're designing for somebody as conservative as the Army you don't change everything at once. You go step by step. They've got a point: they have to retrain people whenever they get a new piece of kit. When the RAF gets a new plane it probably only retrains twenty pilots a year and a hundred ground crew. When the Army gets a new rifle it has to retrain the whole bloody lot – 150,000 of you. A tank comes somewhere in between.'

Al-Hamedi was holding his end of a filter and wearing the wryly bored expression of somebody who had heard it all before and was resigned to banging filters as long as the sun kept rising in the east.

'Sorry, Alec. Okay, we'll bang. Can you check the BV and serve breakfast?'

With his age, Timbrell was probably tireder than any of them. If there was a crack of time into which they could stuff a little moss of sleep, he'd let Timbrell take it. But meanwhile, the military machine had found another heavy, boring and dirty job to do: whacking metal boxes against the bazooka plates that half-hid the tank's wheels. The clangs echoed loudly from the roof of rock and distantly from across the wide valley. If anybody was within earshot . . . Maxim shrugged mentally and banged on, grey dust like cement sifting over his trousers and caking on his still-damp shoes.

The tins were hot well before they had finished the filters, but they kept banging and clanging except for gulps of coffee from a single mug: the others had all got lost in the panic boarding when the Land-Rover had caught them. Maxim tried to remember to hang onto some empty tins to replace them.

'What do you think 17th Armoured will send after us?' he asked Al-Hamedi.

'They have three more Khalids. And Centurions and M60s.'

'Have they got any guided weapons mounted on Land-Rovers?'

'I think yes. TOW, I think.'

Maxim made a face. TOW was one of the biggest anti-tank missiles, too big to be really man-portable so that it was usually mounted on helicopters or small vehicles. TOW on Land-Rovers were just the weapons Maxim would have chosen to hunt a lone tank, like dogs baiting a bear and delaying it until the real hunters caught up – except that one TOW missile could wreck them if it hit in the right place. And 17th Armoured wouldn't mind a wrecked tank as long as the gun breech survived for a Moscow breakfast.

But they'd probably send tanks as well. More than one, though the more they sent, the longer it would take to collect them up.

135

'If the Land-Rover,' Maxim panted between clangs, 'was the same one as at the Wadi, it's got somebody senior in it. Taking his own decisions. When he turned south to flank us, he deliberately abandoned our trail. You don't decide to do that without authority.'

Al-Hamedi just nodded, saving his breath. Timbrell, standing by and chewing his empty pipe, said: 'Or getting orders by radio.'

'They'd still have sent somebody with some rank to pick up this tank at the Wadi even if they weren't expecting trouble. And he'd have been in the Land-Rover, not the Khalid.' He paused and stared at the shadowed rampart of rocks that hid their back trail. 'There could be a mind out there, as well as a Land-Rover. Maybe we should have fired the main gun at him.'

'I could have tried it.'

'I know, and I didn't know how to give the proper fire orders. Or fire it – *can* the commander fire the gun?'

'He can do anything the gunner can,' Timbrell said. 'All controls are duplicated. Only it isn't encouraged: a commander shouldn't have anything to do except give commands. If he gets absorbed in handling some aspect of the tank he can be distracted from the bigger picture.'

Al-Hamedi nodded again, but so did Maxim, because it was fundamental military doctrine. It was why he had been too busy to fire a shot when they broke the hotel siege.

'The commander sees a target,' Timbrell said, 'and says "Action" then the type of projectile, "Sabot" or "HESH", and he lays the gun roughly on the target and identifies it with a rough range, such as "2000, Tank" and says "On". The gunner takes over and aims precisely and says "On", the commander says "Fire", the gunner says "Firing now", and fires and reloads until he gets a hit and says "Target" or the commander stops him by saying "Target stop".'

Timbrell had a way of explaining things that made Maxim want to shut his eyes and try to see the explanation in slow, separate steps. But he couldn't shut them now, so he nodded; he'd get Al-Hamedi to run him through it later.

They fitted the filters back in place and Maxim stood off while Timbrell started the auxiliary generator for power to reassemble the rest of the engine compartment. He tried to rub some of the gritty grease off his hands, but it was going to stay with him until he met soap and hot water again. In fact, he was gritty all over, from between his toes to his scalp via everywhere in between.

Al-Hamedi was looking at him with quiet dark eyes. 'Shall I bang you on the side of the tank, Major?'

He grinned lopsidely. 'Not until I start making the same noises the engine did. When this is finished, traverse the gun to cover the wadi, check the water on board and put some more in from the can if we need it, and get some food.' He opened two of the hot tins – one curried chicken, one beef and veg – and plodded over the rocks to Piers' outpost.

The far side of the valley was in sunlight already, all the dawn delicacy turned to vivid horizontal strips of red-orange, brown and grey, slashed with long black shadows. It didn't look as if the sun would touch their own hide until it was considerably higher, which was pure luck.

'I am glad that noise has stopped,' Piers said, choosing the beef and veg. 'It has a better range than the radio in that thing.'

Maxim sat down on a cold rock just uphill from the machine-gun. 'It's a quiet place, the desert. Only nobody remembers it that way, because they're never there unless they've got some sort of engine running.'

'How long – now?'

'Don't know. We'll have to keep going east until we're clear of this stuff –' he jerked his head at the mountain behind them; '– then if nobody seems to be following, we'll turn south.'

'How did they find us last night? It was *not* the helicopter.'

'I don't know, but they knew where to come. It doesn't matter now. Hang on here until I give you a shout. We'll move in a few minutes.'

But it was Piers who shouted first. Maxim was almost back at the tank when he heard the yell through the chugging of the auxiliary, and looked round to see Piers scrambling down the rocks after him, the cartridge belt flapping from the cradled machine-gun.

Al-Hamedi and Timbrell had heard it, too, and were moving to climb aboard. Maxim stopped to wait for Piers, but why in hell was he abandoning his post just because something was coming after them? He was there for that.

Then he heard what Piers was actually shouting: 'Helicopter!'

It was small, bubble-nosed and with a rear fuselage like a bit of girder work. An Alouette, Piers said, one pilot and up to four passengers, cruise at 100 knots, maximum range about 250 miles –

'Is it *armed*?' Maxim growled.

'It might have a machine-gun, nothing more. Probably it is just communications and reconnaissance.'

'It's damn sure recce.' The helicopter buzzed a wandering trail down the middle of the valley, the sun flaring off its perspex cockpit. But it stayed higher than they were so the rock canopy still hid them, and their side of the valley was still mostly in shadow – and so was the sunken watercourse below, where their tracks would still be showing. There must be dozens of other hiding-places, too, even if the helicopter was already looking for hiding-places.

Al-Hamedi was sitting up on the hatchway by the commander's machine-gun. 'There are two helicopters at the airport,' he called down, 'attached to 17th Armoured but do not belong to it. I do not know if they have joined the revolution.'

'It looks like it to me.'

'But if the pilot is flying with a gun at his head,' Piers said, 'he may not be helping as much as they hope.'

'Or twice as much.' He pressed himself back into the shadows of the already shadowed rocks as the helicopter drew level and then passed without hesitation.

'Did he spot us?' Timbrell called from the driver's hatch, out of sight of the helicopter.

'I don't think so. But they don't know we've had to stop. He could be doing a fast run down the valley, then come back slow when he hasn't seen us in the open. Piers, how long can a thing like that stay airborne?'

'Two hours or more, but if he has first come from the airport and then has put down to consult with the ground forces, perhaps back at the Wadi, and then has not been following a straight course, all that takes fuel and he must get back again, so . . .' There obviously wasn't a useful answer, but Piers was enjoying the pure theory of it as a change from the grease and grit of life in a hunted tank, so Maxim heard him out.

'Well, it sounds as if we'd better give him another twenty minutes rather than get caught in the open. Alec, find the sleeping bag and see if you can get a few minutes kip. Piers, you're on stag again – on guard, I mean. Stay in the shadows. Sergeant, I want the fastest course you've ever given on tank gunnery.'

Nearly twenty minutes later he lifted his sweating forehead from the padded eyepiece of the gunsight, let go of the pistol grip below it and reached for the half-empty pack of cigarettes. Al-Hamedi accepted one, then Maxim tried to pick one out with his lips, bypassing his greasy fingers. 'We'd better get to Saudia soon: we're running out.'

Al-Hamedi reached across with a match. 'Perhaps it will make us more healthy, Major.'

The smoke just hung in the thick still air around the gunsight. So now he could fire a tank gun – well, this one, anyway. One more tiny drawer in the Army's vast cabinet of knowledge had been opened to him. He could skin a rabbit, too, and jump by parachute and balance an accounts book – if he had a rabbit, a parachute and an accounts book. It was comforting to have so many tiny skills, but sobering to think how few were ever needed. Probably he'd never touch a tank gun again. He climbed out.

Timbrell was awake already, leaning against the front of the tank and writing in a small notebook. 'Keeping up your diary?' Maxim asked.

'No, just design factors wrong with the tank.' Maxim raised his eyebrows, walked past and called Piers in. 'Small things,' Timbrell explained, 'that only show up in situations like this. The seat-locking mechanism isn't right yet. The sights are a bit too obstructive when we're closed down. It makes me feel better: I'm a better designer today than I was yesterday.'

It made sense, in a misplaced sort of way. 'Did you get any rest?'

'Yes. And . . . thank you. You're doing all right.'

'Thank *you*.' Confidence was always welcome. 'Will you take the driving for a spell?'

Piers came up and dumped the machine-gun beside the two rifles behind the retaining rail on one side of the tank deck. 'There is nothing moving out there at all.'

'Okay. Hop in.'

'Can I ride on the top?'

'It's going to be windy and dusty and bumpy up there. And how the hell you'll get in when there's a panic . . .'

'I can try it.'

Maxim opened his mouth to argue, then just nodded. The cramped space behind his own seat couldn't be much fun for somebody with no job to do, particularly for somebody who'd once been trapped in a burning ship. And Piers was old enough to make his own decisions . . . the only nagging doubt was that Maxim wanted to get him across the border alive, cramped, distressed, frightened and whatever but alive. He didn't want another casualty on the bill.

'Start up.' He took a last breath of the soft fresh desert air before it turned to dust and diesel fumes. 'Driver, move off. Turn right along the wadi and then as fast as you can.'

17

Now their sheer speed gave Maxim a sense of temporary safety. With a clear view for himself, and driving his own design, Timbrell took them down the rambling wadi like a one-horse cavalry charge. Tank suspension systems had finally caught up with other aspects of design, and the MBT90 flattened humps of sand or gravel, small rocks and rain-made ditches down to a ride that was no more than an erratic trembling.

The price was a dust trail that started halfway along the tank, billowed almost house-high and probably stretched half a kilometre behind them. There was no point in looking back, although Maxim did so to rest his eyes, protected only by Al-Hamedi's sunglasses; Timbrell wore the only pair of tank goggles they had. Al-Hamedi himself sat inside watching rearward through the infra-red camera, which could see through thin dust or smoke, and for all the good he was doing Maxim could have been below as well. But his years as an infantryman trusting only his own eyes inhibited him.

'You're old-fashioned,' Timbrell grunted over the intercom. 'In fact, you're just old.'

'Thank you.'

'Literally that. Think about it: most tank commanders are ten or fifteen years younger than you are. They met their first computers in primary schools and spent their evenings watching TV or playing Pac-Man. They don't believe anything they *can't* see on a screen – believe me, Harry, I see these kids coming into industry. If you showed

142

one a slide rule, he'd think you'd bought it in a sex shop.'

A little nettled, Maxim passed the sunglasses to Piers, sitting on the hatch behind him, and slid down into his seat, resolved to trust the PVD screen. He could watch through the normal 'daylight' TV camera independent of Al-Hamedi watching through infra-red, could turn it, zoom in and out, adjust the brightness and colour, almost anything except tilt up beyond a certain degree; directly overhead was out of sight.

Gradually he began to feel confident (though no younger) that he could glance electronically over his own shoulder whenever he wanted to. He was even more reassured when he, rather than Timbrell or Piers, spotted the lone Bedou ahead.

The Jebel Umm Sahm was well behind them now, with only its last foothills flanking them to the right; on the left, the lower hills had dwindled and retreated and the whole valley was opening out into a gently rolling desert of gravel, spinifex and grey dust that compacted like a layer of cement. A single rider on a camel, thin and tall as a minaret when seen head-on, had come over a small rise nearly half a kilometre ahead. A pack donkey followed.

'Driver, slow. Stop before you get to him.'

Al-Hamedi flicked his screen to the daylight camera to see what they were talking about, then asked: 'Do you wish me to talk with him?'

'Please. My Arabic would take a week.'

'If he keeps going where we have been,' Piers said gloomily, 'he'll be talking to 17th Armoured in half an hour.'

Maxim said nothing. They stopped and were briefly washed by their own dust cloud, drifting away northwards. The rider ambled on towards them; elderly, with a short grey beard and looking, as usual, like a comfortable bundle of old faded clothing. Ten years before, he would have had a rifle slung on his back, as his people had carried for centuries, but the government had got tough with such conspicuously unofficial firearms.

A few yards away, the Bedou raised a hand in greeting

and reined in the camel, who took a few more steps to show who was boss, then stopped and sneered at the tank. The donkey, covered in shapeless bundles, drifted on like a dinghy towed by a launch until stopped by the rope, then began to nibble a bush.

Maxim and Al-Hamedi jumped down and walked across. After a round of polite greetings, Al-Hamedi passed around Maxim's cigarettes, they all lit up, and the Bedou hung onto the remainder.

'I feel healthier already,' Maxim murmured. 'Where's he come from?' It turned out to be Al Mudawarah, a village on the north-south road – and railway – some thirty kilometres ahead. He was heading for the Wadi Rum, had heard of the revolt, but didn't know if it had affected the Huwaitat tribe that pitched its tents there. Al-Hamedi translated this in short muttered bursts as the old man rambled on and puffed his cigarette in elegant gestures. He had dignity and style, but a sense of unease beneath it; he couldn't see how a mixed Jordanian–European crew and the tank fitted into events.

'Tell him the rebels are in Wadi Rum: we've seen them. Say we're loyal to the King and trying to escape, and has he seen anything?'

The declaration of loyalty was obviously welcome; as to the rebels, a scrawny hand went up as if screwing a light-bulb into the sky: he had obviously seen the helicopter. The hand landed: so had the helicopter. Hand on breast, hand towards tank: they had asked him if he had seen the tank . . .

Al-Hamedi's normally puzzled-serious expression got more intense, he gave up any pretence at interpreting and smothered the Bedou with questions. Maxim had lost track of the flickering gestures, but waited patiently.

Al-Hamedi nodded abruptly and turned to him. 'The helicopter landed – yes, you understood. A man in it was a major – he understands badges – with parachute wings. He looked not Bedouin, but . . .' he puffed and lifted his cheeks.

'A bit Chinese?'

'Yes, like that. I think it is Major Zyadine, he is brigade major to –'

Maxim was nodding.

'You know him?' Al-Hamedi asked.

'Met him. And you?'

'I have seen him, yes. They say he is a clever man.'

'He could have been in the Land-Rover,' Maxim mused. 'And got the helicopter to pick him up at dawn. I'd have done that.'

'Yes. But this man wants to go to Wadi Rum still.'

'Ask him if he's got a spare kefiyah he'll trade with me.' Al-Hamedi looked surprised, but passed it on.

The Bedou did indeed have a spare head-dress and could see Maxim needed one, but unfortunately did not have a spare circlet of ornamental rope (originally a camel hobble) used to hold it on the head and – even more unfortunately – suppose Maxim got caught and told who had given it to him?

Maxim had wondered if the old boy's thinking would go along that line: it showed he was taking the revolt seriously and was also expecting to run into it soon. Maxim unbuckled his pistol belt.

'Please tell him that when he meets a rebel patrol, he will be in far more trouble if he is found to have a British Army pistol on him. So, most unfortunately, we had better not trade.'

Maxim's gesture had puzzled the Bedou, but now his eyes flicked to assess the gun: a well-respected Browning automatic, easily hidden from Government officials, cartridges simple to come by . . . the thoughts were almost in neon lights. Then the camel was forced to its knees and the old man stepped off to begin rummaging at the donkey's load. In moments, Maxim had a plain off-white kefiyah and a scrap of ordinary rope to hold it in place.

Once back inside the tank, Al-Hamedi began laughing aloud.

'What was all that about?' Timbrell asked.

'You saw: the Major bought a kefiyah, a most expensive kefiyah, but not with his own money.'

They moved off gently, so as not to startle the still-kneeling camel, with Timbrell still puzzled. 'He'll be picked up by 17th Armoured and talk his head off. He can even tell them who we are, now.'

Al-Hamedi was still chuckling. 'No, he will not meet 17th Armoured now, he does not wish to meet them. He wishes to find a cave to sit for a day, two days, to look at his new pistol. Major, will you help me to trade in the bazaar when we are free again?'

Scratch an Arab and you find a wheeler-dealer; that trade had impressed Al-Hamedi far more than any military skills Maxim had shown.

18

When the car picked Agnes up from her flat it was still dark, as dark as it ever got under central London's street lighting, but the roads were still empty and the car went very fast. Is this very urgent or is he trying to impress me? she wondered, not liking to be driven fast by somebody she didn't know.

But all the driver said was: 'Looks as if it could be a nice day, Miss,' which was as good as any television forecaster ever got.

Agnes just grunted. Brought up in the country, she didn't regard London as having any weather. She had once met an elderly writer who said that it was only when his cat jumped on his lap in the middle of the morning that he knew what was happening outside: if the cat was wet, it was raining.

They ran along the side of the Thames, then up past the Palace of Westminster into Whitehall and the back entrance to the Main Building. The car zoomed – the driver was definitely a zoomer – away to some unknown car pool (she had never been important enough before to use a Service car) leaving Agnes at the zoo-type turnstile at the security desk.

'What sort of day does it look like, Miss?' the guard asked as they waited for somebody to escort her inside.

'The driver said it could be a nice one.'

'Ah.' Then Edwin Giles and somebody – the Squadron Leader from Defence Intelligence – appeared to sign her in. As she walked away, the guard turned up his transistor radio again.

'Listen to me,' Giles said, 'and don't waste time reacting.' He was head of the Near East Department of the Intelligence Service and her more-or-less immediate boss; they had first met when both had Washington postings.

'Your . . . major is part of a crew apparently trying to get our new tank prototype out of the rebel area of Jordan. We understand they've shot up one rebel tank already and are probably heading south for Saudia.'

Agnes's knees quite literally gave way and she grabbed at the corridor wall. 'But he told me . . .' she babbled, '. . . he was only supposed to take the tapes to . . .'

'I know. We don't know exactly how he got involved, except that he and the military attaché out there worked out where Zweiwindburg was, and he went with a helicopter mission to blow the tank up. The helicopter went wrong somehow and they must have decided to drive the tank out. All we've got is one garbled message from them via an Army ship in the Gulf of Aqaba.'

'Did the rebels find out where the tank was, too?'

'Somehow. Here we are.'

He ushered her in through the Snowflake door. By now, it was beginning to look intended. The map of Jordan had coloured pins in it and a clip of teletype messages hung beside it; several people sat around a trestle table littered with paperwork and coffee cups, and the Brigadier had a smaller table against the wall and a scrambler telephone. He got up to introduce himself and shake hands; the Squadron Leader brought her a cup of coffee, then sat down at the Brigadier's table.

'We're delighted to have you with us.' In company, the Brigadier adopted a penetrating, almost yappy voice, softened by frequent smiles. 'You've briefed Miss Algar, have you, Edwin?'

'In outline.' He was a bulky tall man, almost bald, and with an indefinably well-bred face that looked more sympathetic and less clever than he was. It was a useful face for a career in Intelligence.

'Is it daylight out there?' Agnes asked.

The Squadron Leader said: 'It has been for over an hour.'

'Then they'll get caught, won't they?'

'It's a faster tank than anything 17th Armoured's got,' George said. 'Better armed and armoured, too.'

'But Harry doesn't know anything about tanks.'

'He, they, whoever,' the Brigadier said, 'knew enough to knock out another tank.' He obviously disliked sitting, or the chairs the room offered; he had propped his backside on the back of a chair just outside their circle. 'They've got the chap Timbrell who led the design team, it could be him, I suppose. He was eight years in the Royal Tank Regiment. The other character seems to be the helicopter observer. Navy, of course.'

'It's not even a real tank crew?' Agnes was appalled. But perhaps this Timbrell is in charge, she thought with a sense of relief that immediately reversed itself. No, if something as lunatic as this is going on, at least I want Harry in charge of it. And I bet he is. If he gets out of this alive, I'll kill him.

Scott-Scobie, representing the Foreign Office, rocked pudgily and precariously on his folding chair. 'I can assure you, Agnes, that it was no doing of ours. We simply wanted him to deliver the tapes to Amman and show goodwill. While he was there, Defence realised the tank wasn't present or accounted for and signalled the military attaché to ask Major Maxim if anything Katbah had said gave a clue. Then, it seems –'

'With the greatest possible respect, Scottie,' Giles said urbanely, 'that is pure balls. Somebody at Defence knew right from the start of the revolt that the tank was missing. That was why they pressed so hard for a direct assault on the hotel room, to kill off anybody who'd learned anything from Katbah. Yes, George, I have heard about what happened there. You hoped to find where the tank was from American reconnaissance, and when that failed you fell back on what Katbah had said.'

Scott-Scobie let his chair bang down on the floor and glared across the table at George. Then he turned and glared at the Brigadier and Squadron-Leader as well. Finally he said: 'I'm not sure what I'm doing here, since the foreign policy aspects seem to have been taken care of for us – and for the last several days, too.'

'Government policy as a whole,' added Sir Anthony Sladen, tall, aristocratic, nervous and better dressed than anybody else there. 'Really, George, it might have been better to consult us before, ah, taking any irreversible steps –'

'We had to move quickly once we'd located the tank,' George growled. 'If we'd managed to get it blown up, policy wouldn't have come into it.'

'But you didn't get it blown up,' Scott-Scobie pointed out. 'You got a Jordanian tank blown up –'

'A rebel tank.'

'It belonged to the Jordanian government! They hoped to get it back in one piece, now we'll have to pay for it. *And* a Navy helicopter. And God knows what else by the time we're through; Harry Maxim isn't the sort to go down without a fight . . . Sorry, Agnes, you really shouldn't be here.'

The Brigadier said crisply: 'Mr Giles thought Miss Algar might be able to help on a different aspect, you may recall. Namely, how did the rebel 17th Armoured find out themselves where the tank was?'

'Well, I didn't tell them,' Agnes said.

'Let's take the time-scale first,' Giles put in. 'The revolt started five days ago. At the time, the rebels believed the tank was somewhere within reach but evidently didn't know where. The cleaned-up tapes confirm that.'

'Do they?' Agnes asked.

'I'm sorry, of course you didn't know. The torture was directed at getting Katbah to tell where the tank would be, since he'd planned the Jordanian trials before he came to London. In the end, close to the end, Katbah told them it could be at Zweiwindburg.'

'So he only told Harry what he'd already told them in the hotel.'

'Yes. But what he told them never got out of the hotel room. It was shot dead in there. The word *Zweiwindburg* only came out of the room in Major Maxim's head and on the police tape.'

'He told me what he remembered Katbah saying,' Agnes said slowly. 'It was in German . . . I couldn't make anything of it. I asked you the next day.'

'You did,' Giles agreed. 'I'm sorry to say I'd never heard of Zweiwindburg before. Did you mention it to anybody else?'

'No. I didn't know it was important, anyway.'

'Did he mention it to anybody?'

'I have no idea.'

There was a moment's silence. Giles looked down at a pad on which he had drawn a rough grid of days. 'You brought the cleaned-up tape back from the aeronautical lab at about noon, is that right?'

'A bit after.'

'And we can assume the Home Office got their copy at much the same time . . . Is anybody joining us from the Home Office?'

'Norman,' Scott-Scobie said.

'Ah.'

The Brigadier asked: 'Who?'

'Norman Sprague.'

'I don't think I know him.'

'I suppose anybody who rises to Brigadier must have a certain amount of luck. Go on, Edwin.'

'We started getting a translation a couple of hours later.' Giles was an Arabist himself, but nowadays he didn't spend his own time winding and rewinding poor-quality tape recordings. 'It came to me in dribs and drabs . . .'

'And you passed it to Defence the same way?' suggested Scott-Scobie.

'We told Defence – they being our main client in this – as soon as we were certain the torture was directed to locating the tank. But we didn't hit on Zweiwindburg until virtually the end of the translation. After six o'clock the day before yesterday.'

'It wasn't much later that we got a signal from Amman saying Colonel Jeffreys and Harry had solved it themselves,' George said.

'So,' Giles summed up, 'after 1800 hours the day before yesterday – about thirty-six hours ago – the probable location of the missing tank was known to my Department, to the Home Office and whoever they told, and to Colonel Jeffreys and Major Maxim in Amman.'

A lot of people, Agnes thought. It always is a lot of people.

'But the rebels,' the Brigadier said, 'didn't know until late last night.'

'How do we know that?' Sladen asked, perplexed.

The military men and George exchanged looks. The Brigadier, who was more impressed by a Second Permanent Secretary to the Cabinet than the rest of them, lowered his voice a little. 'Well, sir, the rebels sent their own tank up there at night. It's a messy business shunting tanks around at night. To me, that suggests both that capturing our tank was a prime objective and that they'd only just heard where to find it.'

'Ah,' said Sladen. 'Ah yes, I do see. Thank you.'

'And they didn't know that we might know,' George said, 'or they'd have gone in with more force.'

Does he know that I know that he knows that I know? Agnes recited the old intelligence school song to herself, hunching her shoulders for warmth. She had thrown on a thin black sweater and a fawn denim suit that were too cold for the room (it was far easier to sit and take decisions which could cause men to die and nations to squabble than to get Ministerial central heating turned on early).

Just then, Norman Sprague was led in by a messenger.

He had not thrown on his clothes; his dark woollen suit and waistcoat, fresh shirt and club tie had all been carefully chosen, and his chin shone from a fresh shave.

'Good morning,' he smiled all round. 'I hope I'm not the last, too humiliating. What a splendid gathering. Scottie, George, Edwin. I don't think we've met' – he shook hands with the Brigadier – 'and dear Agnes. Now will somebody explain to me what all this is about?'

'*No,*' Scott-Scobie said rudely. 'Just sit down and listen . . . Edwin, can we backtrack from 17th Armoured? How did they get the news?'

'Radio. They're cut off from anything else. But with the civilian relay station they've got a powerful receiver as well as transmitter, so it could have come through from Syria. Or Amman – I think we ought to assume that the revolt has some sympathisers in Amman, possibly quite highly placed.'

Everybody nodded wisely; yes, they were quite ready to assume that. Scott-Scobie said: 'All right, then one step back from *that*?'

'On the other hand, I find it difficult to assume that 17th Armoured, or even Syria, has somebody well-placed in any of the departments or services represented here. But if we accept the popular view that we are all riddled with *Soviet* agents . . .'

This time, everybody groaned. 'Oh no,' Scott-Scobie said miserably, 'not another bloody mole hunt. My nerves won't stand it.'

'The country won't stand for it,' Sladen said. 'The constant undermining of trust in the civil service . . .'

'You asked me,' Giles said urbanely. 'I say the possibility is there, no more.'

'London to Moscow to Damascus to Aqaba,' Agnes said. 'It would take time.'

'A full day,' said the Squadron Leader from Signals. 'It would have to be decoded and encoded at each step and somewhere it would have to be translated, too. Certainly a day.'

153

Gloomily, they recalled that it was a day's delay they were trying to account for.

'But what are you doing to try and help Harry?' Agnes demanded.

'Nothing we can do,' George said. 'Not until we've established communications with them.'

'How are you going to do that?'

'The best hope is relaying messages through the ship, we've had one brief contact that way, but the tank radio's short-ranged, there's 5,000-foot mountains around there and high-frequency reception is usually better at night.'

'Have you worked out what to tell him when you do get in touch?'

George looked around for support. 'Umm, not yet; that's what this meeting is roughly about.'

'The trouble is,' the Brigadier added, 'that we don't know where they are, don't know what the situation is. Until we can get some recce coverage –'

'When will you have that?' Agnes asked.

'The Americans have promised us satellite pictures as soon as possible, and should put over a recce flight tonight.'

'*Tonight?* By then they could be –'

The Squadron Leader chimed in from behind the side table. 'It'll be one of their new Stealth aircraft, invisible to radar and all that. We're actually rather privileged: they flew one into Cyprus the other day just to help us. But because it's so secret they won't let it take off or land there except at night. They're scared the native Cypriots would take snapshots and sell them to the KGB. Or the Japanese model aircraft kit makers. As they probably would.'

The Brigadier looked at him a little severely, but nobody had anything else to offer.

'And when you know where he is,' Agnes persisted, 'and you're in touch, what will you do? Send in proper troops?'

'No,' Scott-Scobie said. 'No we bloody well won't – not even if we had them within reach. We've trodden on

154

enough Jordanian toes already. I'm sorry, Agnes, but Harry is on his own.'

She looked around helplessly. Sprague gave her a sympathetic smile that she didn't believe in, and said: 'So *now* will somebody tell me what's going on?'

Agnes saw no sense in going back home for a quick breakfast before turning round and getting herself caught in the rush hour. She signed out and walked through the streets, now lit by the shadowless sunless big-city dawn but still almost empty, across the river to Waterloo station. The only thing open there was a tea-and-coffee stand on the concourse, so she sipped instant black coffee from the plastic mug, leaning against the metal cattle-pen that defined a few square yards for customers only.

So Harry had done it again.

Three evenings ago, their last night, she had said: 'You aren't going to get *involved* in anything, are you?'

'Like what?' He had seemed honestly surprised, then amused. 'Suppressing 17th Armoured Brigade single-handed? There's a few Hollywood types that specialise in that sort of thing, but I never got the right training. I'm just a messenger boy: tell the tale, show willing, give them the tape . . .'

'That tape's a mess. We're trying to get it cleaned up, but –'

'We? I thought it was police, Home Office, your old mob.'

'With Jordan involved, we have to be, peripherally.'

'We,' he mused, smiling quietly to himself in the way that either enchanted or infuriated her. She decided to be infuriated.

'Yes, *we*. I belong to that bunch of middle-aged peder-asts now and I'm trying to make the best of it I can. *You* said that if you're loyal to the main thing it can be transferrable among the smaller things. From your battalion to the SAS to your London unit. Now I'm trying to do the same thing so don't you start criticising *me*.'

'I'm not criticising, I'm admir –'

'And don't you admire me, either! I'm just doing my job!'

And why am I going on like this? she had thought, trawling her emotions back inside herself. Perhaps because I'm afraid for him, because he's a cat, warm and loving at home, but Lord help any other tom who wanders into his garden. But the other toms are getting younger and he's getting older; there could come a day – God, it could have been at the hotel if one of the terrorists had got off a few shots . . . once a bullet's fired, it has to go somewhere (something else he'd pointed out to her), and how many lives has my cat got left?

'Whatdoyouwantfordinner?' One fast command.

'Anything except lamb, where I'm going.' Then he had taken an airline ticket from his pocket and flapped it at her. 'It's return. How can they *involve* me?'

'It's not them . . . it's you.'

And also George Harbinger, she thought now, drinking her coffee while it was still hot enough to suppress the taste. I shall have words with Master George when we meet alone, since he'd known about the tank being lost right from the start . . . had he deliberately sent Harry out there to . . . ? No, it was the Foreign Office which had asked for him. After years of investigating conspiracies, Agnes had settled firmly for the cock-up, not conspiracy, theory of history. And in any case, George would just say he was doing his job, as she had said to Harry, as he would say to her when – *if* – he got back. And Katbah and the terrorists and 17th Armoured, everybody just doing their job.

She bought a packet of ham sandwiches and a newspaper and walked out of the station.

19

The sun was very bright now and the tank had reached a comfortable midpoint between being untouchable either because of the night chill or the noonday heat. The raw rock of the foothills ended with an abrupt plunge into the desert, opening their flank to the south. Maxim grasped the pistol grip of the main gun.

'Traversing right. Piers, hang on.' Their seats swung with the gun so that now they sat crosswise in the tank: it was still a disorientating feeling that the direction he faced could be quite different to the way the tank was heading – and the PVD screen could show a third direction as well. But right now he kept it lined up with the gun, watching the end of the cliff 800 metres away, where trouble might be waiting.

For the same reason he kept the tank going east until they were a kilometre beyond the cliff, before swinging south. Then, with the distance between them and any ambush increasing fast, he relaxed, handed over the PVD to Al-Hamedi, and stood up.

One thing the PVD could never do was give a sense and feel of the landscape. It was like a bore at a cocktail party (probably somebody who worked in television, from recent experience of Agnes's friends) who could talk of nothing but the detail of his or her professional world. Fair enough: if the PVD wanted to be a military bore, obsessed with tactical detail, that was what it was for. But you had to carry the broad picture in your mind to interpret the screen; clever as it was, it couldn't solve the oldest military problem of all: seeing what was on the other side of the hill.

He had actually wanted that kefiyah; it was a vastly more practical use than a pistol in a desert situation. He already had it on over his headset: now he wrapped it loosely across his nose, mouth and microphone to keep the dust out (could a pistol do that?) and scanned around the whole horizon except for the bit blocked by Piers, still perched on the hatch behind him.

Eastwards, the horizon was a lumpy orange of real sand desert that seemed to be edging closer as they went south. But ahead, the vivid blue of the sky ended in a milky blur: perhaps the last south wind of winter beginning to stir the dust, though it was impossible to distinguish the wind from the tank's own speed. But out to the side, he thought he could see nervous ripples over the ground. Did he want wind? – it would flatten their dust trail, already not boiling as high as in the windless valley, but what about the engine air filters?

'Commander, aircraft, west!' Al-Hamedi yelled. He jerked his head to see the dark shape almost head-on, then it sliced past, low and fast and trailing thin dirty smoke. He got a frozen glimpse of the long drooping nose, down-slanted tailplane and a blue star on white. Then the noise hit like a thunderclap.

He dropped into his seat. 'Close the hatches!' – but he couldn't close his own: Piers was sitting on it – 'Driver, slow, right stick. Gunner, track the aircraft on PVD . . . It was an Israeli Phantom.' He began rattling commands, keeping them turning to face the Phantom. If it came back shooting, he wanted it to see the smallest target and the toughest armour.

'Traversing left!' Al-Hamedi called, and as the tank swung one way and their sets another, Maxim grabbed for support in a moment of dizziness. Then he settled to concentrate on the screen.

The Phantom was a jiggling shape at full magnification, but side-on: it must be circling them. Gradually their turn

158

slowed and the aircraft became more end-on. The screen flared as it tried to see below the sun, but the Phantom was now just a stretched dot, blurred by its own smoke. Maxim hauled himself up.

They were facing south-east and the distant wings flashed in the sun over the sand-dunes; it was circling again.

'It is an RF-4E – reconnaissance,' Piers said in a shaky, breathless voice; he must have had a rough few moments up there as the tank and turret swerved around separately. 'It has side-looking radar and cameras.'

'We're getting popular,' Maxim said sourly. 'And one thing the bastard's done is give away our position, circling like that.' But what was it circling in the dunes?

Whatever it might be, the Phantom abandoned it abruptly and reared up into the dazzling blue. Maxim watched it out of sight, then called Timbrell to stop.

'Okay, Piers: you ride inside now.'

'No, I'll stay up here.'

'I'm not giving you a choice. You're inside from now on. I want to be able to button the tank and everybody up tight.' He climbed out as Piers climbed in, and stood smelling the wind. It was warmer and stronger than when they had stopped with the Bedou, and the milkiness was creeping up the sky. Beside them, dust and sand crawled in a gentle northward tide. It was always a spooky feeling, seeing the ground move.

He climbed back inside. 'Driver, move off. Steer about 160. Piers, try the ship on the radio. We're well clear of any mountains now.'

It gave Piers something to do, but that was all; they were probably a hundred kilometres from the *Alamein*, and had had the radio on 'receive' all the time except when stopped to clear the filters. The ship must have been trying to reach them all morning and they'd heard nothing. It didn't matter now: the Saudi border was perhaps only half an hour off.

What had the Israeli Phantom been up to, a general snoop, or looking for them specifically? Israel was twitchy about the revolt, as Scott-Scobie had told them, and would

159

be monitoring 17th Armoured's movements, but they were well away from the Israeli frontier here. Yet it would also be interested in any new tank Jordan might buy, and he had no doubt the Israeli secret service had reported about the trials. But interested enough to send out that Phantom to violate Jordanian airspace? And what good would knowing where the tank was be?

They might tell London, of course. But what could London do?

Piers was still mouthing the 'Blackbird, this is Harpoon,' routine. Maxim cut him off. 'Sergeant, can you try the radio and see if you can pick up any 17th Armoured chatter? I'll take the PVD.'

He found he had turned the screen to the sandhills ahead and left of them, where the Phantom had also circled. It was the least likely place for any pursuer. Behind, yes, to their right, yes – but not left, to their east. How could they have got there?

He tilted the map to catch the daylight from the hatchway overhead. There was a faint track swinging round from the north fork of the Wadi Rum to meet the motor road near Al Mudawara, the village the Bedou had been coming from. He had ignored it until now; the desert was covered in 'tracks' which meant nothing more than routes from hither to yon that didn't actually lead over sheer cliffs, but this one did pass some ten kilometres north of them. A patrol, driving hard from Wadi Rum, could by now have got down here and turned off into the sand-dunes – but all it did was herd him towards the Saudi border where he wanted to go anyway.

It made him uneasy, nonetheless, since he had been thinking of the east as safe: he could always edge a bit further in that direction before dashing south for Saudia. But now . . . The PVD gave him no idea of how far off the sand dunes were, and even when he stood up to look he could only guess vaguely. Range estimation was always difficult in the desert; ironically, if a Land-Rover or tank showed itself, his guess would become far more accurate.

Indeed, he could pinpoint it with the rangefinder. But the laser wouldn't work on something as indefinite as sand dunes.

Call it about 2,000 metres – extreme range for most anti-tank guided weapons. 'Driver, right stick . . . on. I want to keep well clear of the sand. And keep your foot down.' He regretted that immediately: his nervousness was showing. He reached for a cigarette, then blasted the old Bedou; he might at least have given the packet back when he got that pistol.

Irritably, he snapped the screen to infra-red, hoping to see any pinpoint that was different from the ghostly-green outline of the dunes. Hotter or colder didn't matter, it was difference that showed up on IR – but 2,000 metres was a bit much for it. So he switched back to the TV camera, alternating an all-round scan with a careful search of the sand, again and again.

The clicking and crackling on the radio abruptly changed to a loud burst of unintelligible speech. He glanced over at Al-Hamedi, suddenly hunched forward in concentration. More speech, faint this time, then another loud chatter. Then a hum.

Al-Hamedi licked his stubbled upper lip, arranging his translation. 'A callsign I do not know reports he is in position with a map reference' – he looked at Maxim and spread his hands: they didn't have the right map – 'and he is told to attack. He must be close.'

The volume of the transmission had told Maxim that: in the dunes, all right. 'D'you know if it was tank or Land-Rover?' It wasn't long ago that the British Army had been using callsigns that clearly gave away whether they came from armoured or 'soft' units.

'No.' So the Jordanian Army had learned that lesson, too.

Back to the screen, now just searching a 90-degree arc on their left. Silently, he mouthed the commands he would have to give to turn the tank (but turn to meet the attack, or away from it, spinning round to hide in their own dust trail?) then switching on the gun system, switching off the stabiliser, loading – shot for armour, shell for soft – aiming, range . . .

They must be only minutes from the border – although he wasn't expecting any marker, let alone a fence, to show where it lay; borders were just an idea down here. And 17th Armoured wouldn't be too finicky, either: he'd keep going flat out until they were well into Saudia.

He couldn't just sit there. 'Gunner, watch the sand.' He stood up again, staring fiercely at the dunes. They must be outrunning anything ploughing its way through that sand. And minutes, only minutes . . . come on, Time, *move* yourself!

He heard the *crack* as a shell went past, knowing exactly what it was although he had never been under shellfire before, and utterly bewildered because he had no idea where it had come from. Nothing in the dunes, nothing to their right . . .

'Tanks ahead!' Al-Hamedi shouted. 'Traversing right!' The gun whipped round to point forward, throwing Maxim against the hatch coaming as he slithered down into his seat.

'Gun kit on,' he croaked, but that was all done. 'Action, shot. Fire smoke!' He knew of the autoloader cranking up a round and of Piers scrabbling out of the way, Al-Hamedi's hands darting like striking snakes at the controls, and a world-filling *Clang* that checked the tank in its charge and blinded him with smoke. Smoke – fire – My God, they had to get out of this thing! 'Driver, stop!'

They pitched forward, he jammed his hands down to lift himself – but the smoke was clearing, no flames, no smell . . . it was just dust, shaken from every pore of the tank.

But they had been hit.

'Did we fire smoke?'

'Yes.' A glance at the screen showed the bubbling tide of smoke rising ahead.

'Driver, reverse.' Nothing. '*Reverse!*'

The tank jolted into gear and Timbrell said breathlessly: 'Sorry, bit . . . shaken . . .'

'Gunner, look forward and steer us backwards. Keep us behind the smoke.' He had his own screen on infra-red, impervious to the smoke, and two bright shapes showed clearly in front; he tried to aim the jolting gun – no stabilisation system is perfect – and kept his thumb on the rangefinder until a figure of 192-something jiggled at the bottom of the sight.

The tank abruptly tilted backwards, the stabilisers fought to keep the gun and PVD aimed, and Maxim yelled; 'Stop!'

The tanks had gone from the screen; the MBT90 must have crashed blindly into a dip that hid them from frontal view. He went on staring at the empty screen for a moment, then switched to TV. Ahead was a rim of sand with their tracks plainly visible on it, beyond was the ragged horizon of their smoke. They hadn't so much gone into a dip as over a stray dune of blown sand.

And all the time, he realised from the light around him, his own hatch had been open. He reached up and dragged it closed.

Piers muttered: 'Oh Jesus, no . . .'

'Shut up. Driver – are you okay?' The hit had been on the front somewhere, nearer Timbrell than anybody.

'I think I'm . . . got just a nick . . . I think I'm all right.'

'Is all the engine and steering okay? Gunner, can you spot any damage?' In the rumbling silence, he looked around at his own keyboard and controls, but all he could tell was that the usual lights were on. The PVD still worked, anyway, and showed the smoke fading towards them, blown by the south wind. The rim of sand was almost clear.

'Driver to commander . . . I think we're okay in my department.'

'Good. Forward, dead slow.' They inched back up the slope, until . . . 'Stop!' The two tanks were back on-screen, still head-on and unmoving. Maxim zoomed in on them, pale and blurry in the blown dust, then flicked back and forth with the IR camera.

'Gunner, what d'you make of those two?'

The first thing Al-Hamedi said was: 'Bad position. Not hull down and not moving . . . now we are ready, we can kill them from cover.' Even in the fear and anger of battle, a soldier could still be professionally offended by an enemy's incompetence. Al-Hamedi looked across to Maxim, eyebrows raised and waiting for the command.

'What type of tank?' Maxim demanded. 'Take a close look.'

All they themselves were showing above the dune was maybe a foot of the armoured dome holding the cameras, and it would need a lifetime's luck to hit that through dust at two kilometres. It was exactly the situation Timbrell's design had envisaged.

Al-Hamedi was switching between the blurred daylight vision and the sharper infra-red. 'I do not know,' he said slowly. 'It is not Khalids, I do not think Centurions . . . perhaps . . .'

'What tanks does Saudia own?'

Al-Hamedi looked up, surprised. 'French, and American. They are not M60s . . . perhaps AMX-30s.'

'Would you expect 17th Armoured to behave a bit more sensibly than these tanks are?'

'I think, yes.'

'And we're probably into Saudia by now . . . Well, we can't start a war with Saudia. What the hell are they up to?' But it wasn't really a question. Scott-Scobie had said the Saudis had stiffened the border in this sector, nervous about 17th Armoured's anti-Royalist revolt. And they'd seen a tank charging at them, so . . . 'But why should they be waiting just here? We could have crossed anywhere.'

'AWACS.'

'What? Oh, yes.' It had sounded like an Arabic word; in fact it was Airborne Warning and Control System. The Saudis might not have the world's most skilful warriors – the two tank commanders out in front certainly weren't –

but they had more than their share of the world's spare cash. And a big bite of it had gone on 5 Boeing AWACS – basically airliners with huge radar discs rotating on top – that could spot a moving target as small as a tank at something like a hundred miles. Maxim remembered the squawk the Israelis had sent up when America sold an Arab state such aircraft. He glumly added his own squawk.

'We could try a white flag,' Timbrell suggested.

At that range? But the tank gunsights would see it, of course, though Maxim very much doubted those tank commanders would have the authority to accept it. They'd probably been told to stop anything crossing the border – and that was all. Still . . .

'I'll try it. Driver, reverse, right stick . . .' He brought them to the bottom of the dune, swung to face the threat of the main dunes to the east, and opened his hatch.

'Gunner, you're in command. If anything happens, forget about me.' He climbed off the front of the tank. The impact of the shell – it must have been solid shot, like their own Sabot – was very clear. It had gone through the right-hand headlight, which had stood up above the shallow-sloping frontal armour, torn a bright silver groove up the slope and ripped through the top of the righthand track guard, just missing the track itself. Where the metal was curled and broken, the edges were melted smooth by heat.

Timbrell opened his hatch – it slid forward – and half-raised his head behind it. He was holding a bloodsoaked handkerchief just above his right eye, then took it away for Maxim to see.

'How does it look?' He sounded more anxious than he had on the intercom. The cut was about two inches long, a slash from a metal splinter, and still bleeding freely. His face and glasses were smeared with blood, which made it all look more serious than it was – unless his skull was cracked as well.

'Not too bad,' Maxim reassured him. 'Get Piers to bring

you some water and any first-aid we've got.' He unwound his kefiyah and tramped up the steep slope of the dune into the gritty blast of the wind tearing sand off the crest like spume from a wave.

The two distant tanks came in sight again just as shadows through the haze of dust sweeping towards him. He held up the fluttering kefiyah two-handed, hoping enough of it showed sideways, and reflecting that it was the first time he'd ever tried to surrender except on exercises. Using a white flag was doing it in style.

He then wondered how the Saudi tank commander could acknowledge it – and how he, without binoculars, could see any acknowledgement. Then he learned: one of the shadows blinked a pink-white flash and he dropped off the crest and rolled down, still clutching the kefiyah. The shell went past with a *zipp-bang*, throwing a small puff of dust maybe 200 metres beyond the MBT90. Against a hidden target they had used an explosive shell with its slower speed and higher trajectory. He trudged back, shaking sand out of the kefiyah, and clambered into the tank.

'So we've tried surrendering,' he said when he had the headset on again.

'That means we cannot get into Saudia?' Piers asked.

'Not in one piece.'

'I do not know of any other countries in easy reach.'

'Nor me. Alec, how are you feeling?'

'All right, commander. I hate to say anything so corny, but I think it was just a scratch. I got a plaster on it.'

'Good.' He was about to say Tell me if you get a headache, but that was the quickest way to give a man a headache. 'Good.'

Al-Hamedi said: 'On the radio, the callsign said he could not catch us. I think I have seen him, also.'

'Where?'

'On the PVD.'

The camera was at full zoom, showing one small arc of the dunes to their northeast, the blown sand giving the impression of a thin layer of water washing across the screen. Maxim switched to IR and the little bright dot was obvious.

'It is not a tank,' Al-Hamedi said firmly. 'Not so wide as a turret.'

'Okay. That's the way we'll have to go.'

'Commander,' Piers said, 'we could blow the gun up now and surrender to the Saudis on foot. They would not shoot at us then.'

The common sense of it was tempting, and Maxim tried to work out why he didn't like it. It wasn't just that the tank was security – perhaps even more so, now it had taken a hit without any real damage – it was control. If they got out and walked, whatever happened next was completely out of their hands. He would have abdicated all vestige of command, even over himself. Yet sometimes the wisest command decision was to give up, save your men and forget your pride. God grant he would never put his pride before his men. And the gun would be destroyed: mission accomplished – except that he couldn't be sure he would have saved his men.

'What does everybody think?' he asked (and was that abdication? he asked himself. But this wasn't exactly the sort of unit he was used to leading; it wasn't even a unit).

'Driver to commander: leave it to you.'

'Sergeant?'

Al-Hamedi, expressionless, looked across at him. 'How you like, Major.'

'Piers?'

'You know what I think.'

'All right – I'm going to go on. I think we can get through. We're in a good tough tank, we're well up on fuel – and if it comes to it, we can blow the gun later.' If we're still alive to do it, his nagging second thought said. 'Driver –'

'Harry,' Piers cut in, 'I want to get out. Just out. I cannot take any more down here. I have –'

'Right, out.' Maxim stripped off his headset and

scrambled up to let Piers past. Crouched on top of the tank, he could talk through the engine noise without being overheard on the intercom. 'Look, Piers, out there you're on your own and a long way from anywhere.'

'I will take the chance. Anything is better than this damned steel box. Boy, I have been wanting to scream and cry ever since we got hit. I tell you, I am not any good for anybody's morale.'

That was honest enough. But: 'We agreed before we started that I was in command on the ground –'

'What use am I? If I had a job to do I would not be walking out on you, do you think that? I am just a piece of live meat getting in everybody's way. You are better off without me.'

Maxim looked at him; was it pride that made him want to bring home a full contingent, all under his mothering wing? Pride hurt by losing Len already?

He nodded resignedly. 'All right. Take the packets of water from the survival kits, any food – don't take any arms, they could give the wrong impression.' Piers was already rummaging in the stowage bin. 'Wait until we're clear, there'll probably be more shooting. Then if they don't pick you up, head for the motor road about thirty kilometres east.' He was going to add a lecture about desert survival, but Piers would have had that before he came out here. 'And take care. When the Saudis find you, tell 'em what we're trying to do.'

Piers nodded, raised a hand, and dropped off the back of the tank. Maxim slid down through the hatchway, closed it above him and put on the headset. 'Driver, gunner: I plan to break through the dunes and reach the motor road. The Saudis will have some sort of command post where that crosses the border, some senior officer we might be able to contact. They've got the range of this dune, so we'll reverse away using it as cover as long as possible, then . . .'

He spelled it carefully out for them, knowing, as they did, there would have to be sudden changes of plan and direction, but feeling – as he hoped they felt – a lean stripped-for-action sense now they carried no passenger. The idea of being a lifeboat was fading fast.

20

They had all been on crisis committees before and they all knew the signs, although no one wanted to point them out. The basement room was now tidy and well organised. The signals – and there were already dozens of them, from the *Alamein*, Amman, Washington and Cyprus, together with other bits of paper from Whitehall departments just getting into the act – were neatly clipped to the big board; the telephones were properly distributed around the tables; the girl at the teletype next door made fresh coffee and washed the cups every hour; the Squadron-Leader had started and kept up a proper log of their proceedings.

In short, nothing was happening.

Now that their own offices were beginning to be staffed, most of them had started to peck at the telephones, trying to pick up grains of other affairs that might be going on, while George and the Brigadier were discussing some photographs of the MBT90 somebody had sent down and which they hadn't yet let the Squadron-Leader pin up to make his board look fuller.

'How much does this chap Maxim know about tanks?' the Brigadier asked.

'Bugger all, as far as I know. He's always taken the regulation infantry attitude that they're highly effective in enemy hands and your own are never there when you need them. God knows how he's getting on now he's having to command one.'

'Is he?' The Brigadier was surprised. 'How do you know?'

George looked blank for a moment, wondering himself. 'He just would be, in a situation like this.'

'He's got a reputation as a bit of a loner, hasn't he? Of course, a lot of these people who've been in SAS are a bit that way.'

'That's not quite it . . . he just decides something's the best thing to do and anybody standing too close finds himself doing it as well. You might call it leadership.'

'Well, of a sort . . .'

The teletype girl brought in another signal, passed it to the Squadron-Leader, and started collecting the cups. The Squadron-Leader read it and passed it to the Brigadier with a murmured: 'Ouch.'

Everybody was looking. The Brigadier stood up, coughed, and announced: 'Something rather odd: the Cyprus listeners have picked up a plain-language broadcast from the rebel radio that they are going to, and I quote the translation, "protect Jordanian territory by repulsing and driving off Royalist Saudi forces massing on the border". Ends.'

There was a puzzled silence while everybody looked at each other and the virgin map.

'Are they massing – the Saudis?' Scott-Scobie asked.

'We haven't heard anything more than strengthened border patrols and aerial activity,' the Squadron-Leader said. 'And they've been doing that since the revolt started.'

Giles said: '*We've* had no vibrations from Jedda about them taking an active stance.' The news seemed to affront him.

'Not their style,' Scott-Scobie agreed. 'And Jordan hasn't asked for help. Is 17th Armoured trying to make *more* enemies? – it can't be short of them.'

The Brigadier was staring across at the map. 'But if they can stir up the Saudis to try and close the border, perhaps shoot up any tank that tries to cross it . . .'

'Oh bloody hell,' Scott-Scobie said. 'All we need is for some poor Saudi to take a pot-shot at Maxim and . . . Oh God.'

'Can you "close a border",' Sprague asked, 'when it's just a piece of desert like that? It would seem to me –'

'They've got the patrols in place,' the Brigadier pointed out. 'All they have to do is tell 'em to shoot at anything they see. And you can see for miles in the desert; it isn't like your back garden in Pinner.'

Sprague, who would sooner have had smallpox than a back garden in Pinner, stared at the Brigadier as if he had exposed himself.

'Can you get the Minister to get the Saudis to *un*close the border?' Giles asked Scott-Scobie. 'Their embassy here, our embassy there . . .'

'I'll try.' He stood up abruptly, then hitched up his trousers, which didn't always follow their master. 'Except it takes a week to get any thought through to the Saudis unless it's the price of oil or an insult to their national pride. That's the trouble' – he picked up a phone – 'somebody barging across their frontier *is* an insult. And we'd better get another signal off to that boat, try and get them to keep Maxim laying waste only one country at a time.'

At that time, Maxim had no clear idea of which country he was in. Strictly, the Saudi tanks should not have tried to blow him apart until he was in Saudia. But if they were ignoring diplomatic protocol on account of being trigger-happy and probably a bit lost themselves, he could still be in Jordan. He didn't care either way: what mattered was that the MBT90 was halfway to the dunes on a roaring zigzag course and they hadn't been hit again.

He didn't even know if the Saudis had fired again: there was no point in watching that way since they couldn't dodge a shell. A slower missile, which had to be guided onto its target by an operator in sight of that target, gave them more chance. They had the screen wide on the dunes ahead, the gun aimed north-east, a HESH round in the breech and Al-Hamedi scaling the range down in 100-metre steps as they closed in.

The sand began as an orangeness scattered patchily

across the yellow-grey desert, a smoothing of the trembling rush as they left the rocks behind. In front, the dunes rose in low terraced waves, each higher than the last, each leaving hidden gulleys in between. A good place to hide, and just as good for somebody to creep up on you unseen. And now only half a kilometre –

He and Al-Hamedi yelped at the same time, both seeing the flare of the missile launch.

'Slow!' That was in the plan; so was Al-Hamedi doing all the gun-handling. The turret twitched, the breech lifted fractionally, then slammed back and forth with a gigantic bang and the tank seemed to skip in its rush.

'Left stick!' and they swerved downwind into their own dust trail, Maxim twirling the screen, Al-Hamedi twirling the whole turret, the world spinning in every direction. Sand flashed and jumped near the top of a dune, a black streak haloed by its own fire slashed across the screen, there was a muffled crack and a far louder clang on the tank itself. But it was only noise: some lump of missile had bounced off them, but the warhead had detonated on the desert.

'Right stick! On. Flat out.' They slewed back clear of their dust as the Gun Ready light came on again. 'Target stop.' There was no point in firing again; it took far longer to reload a TOW missile tube than it did their own gun, and the opposition probably wasn't sticking around to reload anyway. The one shot had done all they'd hoped: by aiming deliberately low, Al-Hamedi had exploded the shell in front of the missile operator, throwing sand in his eyes and fear in his belly. Now the Land-Rover would be bugging out.

For a moment, Maxim was tempted to follow it and what would be its clear trail in the sand, but it was a bit too far to their left. And there were probably two of them.

The noise as well as the ride changed as they began to pitch and roll over the pure sand, and the dunes rose up on either side to hide and blind them.

21

Back at her desk, Agnes sifted through the morning's batch of internal memoranda. Car mileage allowances were going up but would personnel please note that this was expected to cover all maintenance and repairs and only in exceptional circumstances would . . . A talk by the recently returned head of Far Eastern station would be given in conference room B on Tuesday . . . Those wishing to attend any of the following courses should apply in writing by . . .

She ate her sandwiches and read the newspaper, listening subconsciously to the building waking up around her. A messenger knocked on her door with a trolley of battered files, nominally sealed, the service's equivalent of the leather-bound and locked 'boxes' delivered to government ministers. She signed for her box, agreed it could be a nice day, and the trolley trundled off on its day-long postman's round, safe at least from rain and dogs.

There wasn't much in the box; there never was. She was the outsider at Christmas: 'Did anybody remember to get a present for Agnes? Round up a few little things, just to make her feel part of it.' Today's little things were two low-grade files, with her name hand-written at the end of a long printed distribution list, a day-old MI5 briefing on the movements of London diplomats who were under surveillance, and a police report. She started with that.

The first account of the hotel shoot-out had come through as, you might say, a pencil sketch. Since then a police team had been inking in the lines and filling in the colours, painting by numbers, interview by interview, statement by statement – although the report was a condensation of all that leg- and penwork, thank God. But it added little to the two previous days' reports in her office safe. She got them out and read through the whole lot again.

Fingerprints and photographs of the dead terrorists had been circulated to European anti-terrorist squads (*not* through Interpol, which shied away from 'political' crime and to which too many Wrong Countries belonged). They had carried no identification papers at all – probably a precaution against one of them being caught or left behind dead, since even a false passport is a clue of sorts. Clothing was inexpensive but new and smart enough to get them into the hotel unchallenged and up to the room of Al-Warid, the assumed fixer.

He was the only live lead they had, except for having no idea of who or where he really was. The hotel receptionist's description of him had been circulated, too, but just being an Arab was a great disguise. People thought: 'Ah, an Arab' and, when asked, described the stereotype dark-haired, dark-eyed, moustached Arab they saw every day in newspapers and magazines. Receptionists were supposed to do better than that, but this one had protected his employers by studying Al-Warid's suit and luggage (both expensive), passport (Egyptian) and money (American Express travellers' cheques).

Agnes lit a cigarette and grinned wryly. In the end, the hotel hadn't even got paid; all it had got was four deaths, a blown-up, shot-up suite, outraged guests – oh, and that expensive, but empty, luggage that must have brought in the weaponry. She hoped the receptionist belonged to a strong union.

The only news in the latest report was that the police had interviewed Mrs Katbah in hospital. The report was signed by a Commander; Agnes rang the Yard to find out who had done the real work – Detective Chief Inspector Charles Redding – and got transferred to him.

175

'Hello, lass, haven't seen you since you went to Washington, how're you keeping?' Redding was a big beefy man with a big beefy voice.

'Middling fair –'

'I was chatting to one of your mob the other day, I mean ex-mob, don't I? Have you really joined the Good Friends?'

'On loan, only on loan.'

A roar of jovial laughter. 'And after what I've heard you say about them!'

'The chickens are home and roosting. Charlie – is it okay with you if I go and interview Mrs Katbah?'

'I dare say . . . if she'll see you. Did you get our report?'

'I've seen it.'

'She just confirmed what happened in the room, nothing more than we knew from the tapes. And she never saw the one that scarpered, Al-Warid. D'you think a girlish chat'll get you something we missed?'

'I'm not trying to tread on your boots, Charlie. It's anything she might have picked up from her husband about the Jordan situation.'

'And what might have happened to our super-tank, hey?'

She froze for a moment, then remembered Redding would have seen the translation of the cleaned-up tape which made it clear what the torture had been about. 'That, too.'

'It's still missing? Bit of bad luck, that. Okay, love, I'll pass the word to our lad outside her door. Who're you going to be?'

'Foreign Office.'

'Right . . . What'd you say to coffee and a wad afterwards? Nothing grand, just for old time's sake.'

Good old Charlie; he knew from experience that it was one thing to send a report to one of the secret mobs but a very different thing to get more than thank-you in return. If Agnes did pick up anything new, a cup of coffee would be well invested.

She let him choose an ex-serviceman's club near Victoria.

Sand dunes aren't tank country, they aren't any sort of fighting country, being oddly like house-to-house combat with its short ranges, slow movement and high casualties. But the sand was there, between them and the motor road to the east, and no matter what strength the 17th Armoured had rushed down here, there would be far greater strength in the north and west.

For a time they stuck to the gulleys, going as fast as possible, and angling if anything to the south. The sand reached far down into Saudia, according to the map, but he thought – or hoped – the Saudi tanks would be wary of venturing into the dunes. Not without supporting infantry to peek round corners for them. Come to think of it, he could have used a platoon of infantry to do that for the MBT90. Come to think further, he was an infantryman himself if it came to that, and it might. But for the moment they just keep going as fast as they could.

He was standing up on the seat again, muffled in the kefiyah, because the PVD screen couldn't anticipate the continuous changes of angle and view. One moment a low steep dune gave him only twenty metres view to one side, the next moment he could see 400 metres down a winding gulley. Behind, he could see nothing; the sand they churned up was thicker and heavier than the dust of the stony desert and it filled the gulleys side to side.

But they were in a maze and the inevitable happened: a dead end where you either turned back or cheated by kicking your way through a hedge. Maxim was all for cheating, but these were sand dunes, not hedges.

Timbrell had slowed; Maxim stopped him, then they backed up against the steep downwind side of a high dune that a Land-Rover might come down but certainly couldn't shoot down. 'I'm getting out for a look-see. Sergeant, keep an eye on me. You won't hear me shout.'

He took the rifle from the stowage rack and started

tramping diagonally up the face of the dune, the kefiyah fluttering against his forehead and the blown sand stinging his eyes. The sun was high now, but the wind blew its warmth away with that strange hissing song he remembered from other deserts: a myriad sand-grains being rubbed together. As his view widened, he slowed until he was walking almost backwards to keep an all-round watch. Just below the skyline, he stopped.

Around half the horizon, the whole skin of the desert seemed to be moving with the wind, rippling away in a creamy mist. There were a few darker, static smudges where low bushes clung with wide roots and the sand had piled up in little pimples, just high enough to hide a man lying down. Something else moved at the corner of his eye, and a small bubble of thicker dust welled up between the dunes and was blown away. He tracked on with his eyes, estimating where it would show next; instead, the top half of a Land-Rover and the long tube of a TOW launcher reared up and vanished, followed briefly by its cloud of sand.

One, he thought. There has to be at least one more. Leapfrogging, probably, as soldiers did (and tanks, too, although nobody had told him that): one stopped ready to give covering fire while the other rushed forward to find a firing position, then the first rushed . . . Not very fast, but fairly safe. And you couldn't fire a TOW from a moving vehicle – or rather, you could fire it but not guide it properly.

He was just beginning to think there was only one, or he had seen the hindmost of them, when a second launcher and the shapes of men huddled round it rolled across the same gap, about 400 metres to the north-west. Two – and as it vanished, bullets spattered the sand just below him.

He hurled himself wildly down the slope, losing the rifle, rolling to a stop, finding the half-buried rifle again, clambering breathless onto the tank and yelling at Al-Hamedi: 'Move off, back the way we came,' before he could scramble in and find his headset.

Not clever, that, he thought grimly. Because I could see only a glimpse of them I didn't think how obvious I would be, a dark man-shape in a wilderness of sand.

'They're north of us, running parallel and a bit behind. Two Land-Rovers with TOW. I'm going to go right, soon.'

He picked a gulley leading north and Timbrell slowed into the turn. 'Driver, keep it as fast as you can.' With such a low centre of gravity, there was no danger of the tank overturning unless it tried to run across a steep slope. The secret of sand driving was always to take slopes – up or down – head-on.

'We can tear a track off,' Timbrell said between clenched and shuddering teeth.

The gulley wriggled, then turned west, with a small slope blocking the way. 'Go over it,' Maxim decided immediately. 'Gunner, traverse right.' He let himself swing with the long barrel to face backwards: the Land-Rovers had to be there somewhere.

The tank actually leaped the top of the slope, most of it clear of the ground, slamming down onto the unknown far side with an explosion of sand and sliding to the bottom where they would have buried the gun muzzle into another upslope if it had been pointing that way.

'Go right!' – he was forgetting the proper commands, but Timbrell managed a grinding turn, pivoting where they stood, and jumped forward again. Another winding gulley, rolling side to side as a bowled ball would have done, and then there was torn sand crossing their path: the Land-Rovers' trail.

'Stop!' Their sand-cloud caught up and blew past – they were facing north again – and the Land-Rovers were to the right. Run away or chase? He might get clear away – no: they would hunt him as long as they lived, soon probably in a bigger pack. He had the advantage of their trails for the moment . . .

'Move off, fast, right stick. Gunner, traverse left.' Gun forward again, down a wider gulley this time, Al-Hamedi swinging the gun slightly to cover each bend before Timbrell

179

could turn it. Maxim put a hand on the commander's machine-gun, checking yet again that it was cocked.

The two sets of trails ran together, then ahead they diverged and one became broken. Somebody had stopped there, to cover around a bend to the right that he couldn't yet see. Would the patrol have turned towards where they saw him, run ahead to try and set an ambush, doubled back? Round the bend . . .

The Land-Rover was coming straight at them, fifty metres ahead. He clenched the trigger of the machine-gun before it was aimed, the turret turned, he saw a distant shape in the boiling sand beyond: the second Land-Rover.

'Charge!'

The Land-Rover tried to dodge, swerving to their own right, its machine-gun sparkled, their own gun blasted and then they struck. The right side of the tank reared over the Land-Rover in a screaming and crunching of metal. Something flared in the distance and Maxim ducked into the hatchway. A huge bang and vivid flash followed him, the tank jerked to the left and stopped as if it had rammed a cliff.

'Target the other Land-Rover!' He hauled himself up to the machine-gun as the turret came round, the co-axial already clattering at the vanishing shape of the Land-Rover at the next corner of the gulley. He saw a figure tumble from it, then ducked again as bullets screeched off the armour around him. The main gun didn't fire.

'No target in sight,' Al-Hamedi reported.

'Driver, ahead fast.'

'Can't. We've lost a track.'

'What?'

'Didn't you hear it? Feel it? We took a hit and we lost a track.'

'We can't move?'

'Jesus! – of *course* we can't!'

Feeling shaken, stupid and above all static, Maxim searched his mind. Then: 'Out, everybody out.'

He stood up and grasped the machine-gun to cover

them. Al-Hamedi came out of his hatchway like a leaping fish and disappeared over the far side. Timbrell hauled himself painfully up, sat down and slithered off the front, then fell over.

'Sergeant – are you armed?'

'Yes.' Al-Hamedi's hand came up, waving his M-16 rifle.

'Up there;' the sand-slope to their right; 'move.' He waited until Al-Hamedi had scrabbled up the dune and was lying flat just below the crest, then climbed down himself. Timbrell was sitting by the front of the tank, head dangling and looking white and exhausted.

Maxim found his own rifle, remembered it was still full of sand, and took one of the submachine-guns instead and cocked it. Then he looked at the Land-Rover and its crew.

He thought there had been four of them, but couldn't be sure. The upper half of one man was complete; the rest of him and the others were now and forever part of what had been the Land-Rover until a 40-ton tank had rolled over it. Nothing now stuck up more than eighteen inches above the sand. The smell, for the moment, was of petrol.

The tank had barely cleared the crushed vehicle when it had stopped, its left track cut through by the TOW. The missile had hit it at an angle, sheering through the very front wheel – the 'idler' set high off the ground – and the broken end of track dangled over its remains down into a heap of sand-crusted metal below. Maxim paused to kick the track, then paused longer to wish he hadn't; the solid steel links didn't budge a millimetre. He came round the front to Timbrell.

'Alec.' He didn't look up. '*Alec*.' This time Timbrell raised his head slowly. 'Are you all right?'

'I think so.' Said very slowly. He shook his head and touched the plaster on his forehead. 'I just feel a million years old.' He sounded it.

'Can we repair the tank?' It looked like a workshop job to Maxim, but tank crews did repair tracks in the field; he'd seen them at it, and it had looked hard grinding work.

Timbrell turned his head slowly towards the piled track. 'I don't know. Take an age.'

'Get back on board and defend it. Use any weapon you like. But stop the engine first.' Maxim dumped the submachine-gun and found the Gimpy, then trudged up the slope to Al-Hamedi. 'Anything?'

'No. I think they are . . .' he waved his hand half-right, over the crest. That was the way the remaining Land-Rover had vanished.

'I'll go forward. Cover me.'

'Shall I take the machine-gun?'

'D'you really want it?'

'Yes, Major.' It seemed he did, so they swapped. Maxim far preferred the M-16, which was less than half the weight of the Gimpy and its cartridge belt, yet could still fire full automatic bursts.

'Any reloads?'

'No. I am sorry.'

So Maxim had only thirty rounds in the rifle. He checked it over, glanced down at Timbrell hauling himself painfully into the commander's hatchway, then ran slanting ahead down the slope.

He followed the visible length of the gulley, right up to where the Land-Rover had gone out of sight and where one of its crew lay crumpled and moaning. Maxim looked cautiously around the bend, then climbed a bit up the slope for a better view. The floor of the gulley was a mess of tyre-tracks: both Land-Rovers had passed that way twice, and the second one yet again. Somewhere it would have turned off, and if he followed the track he'd know where, but didn't want to get out of Al-Hamedi's sight. Or rather, he didn't want to bob suddenly back into Al-Hamedi's sight and get his head shot off. But he might have to risk that.

He ran down and up the other side of the gulley. There was a shoulder there, formed by a bush whose roots had been undercut on one side, so that it already broke the skyline and gave a small patch of shadow below. It was as good cover as he'd find within miles. With Al-Hamedi placed there, covering that end of the stretch of gulley, and Timbrell warned to watch back in the other direction, he could go hunting.

22

The nineteenth-century architect of the hospital had clearly intended that patients should leave it, if not the world as well, with the comforting knowledge that mankind could build something far more permanent than itself. The place might be back-breaking to clean, difficult to heat and impossible to modernise, but by God it wasn't going to fall down.

Mrs Katbah had one of the few remaining private rooms, high up and at the end of a pale green corridor ceilinged with pipes and wires. Agnes knew just which room because of the man and woman on chairs outside it, and the way their blank stares fastened simultaneously on her as she rounded the corner. The man stood up slowly, young, short-haired and sports-jacketed.

'I'm Agnes Algar from the FCO.' Automatically, she passed her big shoulder bag to the policewoman for a search.

'Yes, Miss Algar,' the man said. 'Chief Inspector Redding called us about you.' He glanced through the porthole in the door. 'She's awake, you can go in.'

Agnes retrieved her bag, knocked politely and opened the door.

The woman lay stiffly on the high hospital bed, a shape-less gown up to her neck, her black hair sprawled across the pillow and a drip feed plugged into her left arm. She had a strong, near-beautiful face and her dark bloodshot eyes stared at Agnes angrily, making her feel insipid and awkward.

'I'm Agnes Algar from the Foreign Office. I . . . we wondered if you could spare us a few minutes . . .'

'I'm not going away.' Her voice was low, husky, strained. 'Sit down.'

Agnes pulled a hard chair over to the bed and sat, nursing her big handbag. 'We're very sorry about what happened and –'

'Your soldiers, shooting like mad people.'

'And that we couldn't save your husband.'

'*Insh'Allah.*'

'Is there anything we can send you? Jordanian newspapers or magazines? I'm sure we –'

'My ambassador will bring these things.'

'Good. Have they been to see you?'

'They come yesterday.' On the table facing the foot of the bed there were three hospital vases of flowers: a spray of narcissi and freisias, a bunch of daffodils and a bunch of tulips. Their colours emphasised the bleakness of the little room, and their scent was lost in the century-old atmosphere of antiseptic.

'I would like to ask you a few questions,' Agnes said.

'I tell your police everything.'

'This is about Jordan . . . When did you know you were coming here?'

The dark eyes turned to the ceiling. 'I think . . . three days and then we come.'

'Have you visited Britain before?'

'No.'

'Do you have any friends in Britain?''

'I think no . . . At the embassy perhaps some people I know in Amman before . . .'

'Before you left Jordan, your husband believed there could be trouble with the 17th Armoured Brigade. What did he tell you about it?'

'He said nothing. He does not speak with me of his work.'

'Did he mention the tank, at the Zweiwindburg?'

She turned her head slowly to look at Agnes. 'The Zweiwindburg?'

'The torture was about where he thought the tank would be, we know that.'

'The police tell me you have recording . . . yes, he told them the Zweiwindburg . . . I do not understand it.'

'You hadn't heard the name before? He hadn't mentioned it?'

'He does not speak with me of his work.'

'How long were you married to him?'

The eyes squeezed shut and tears trickled sideways down her cheeks. 'More than two years . . . not three years.'

And what the hell do I ask next? Agnes thought. Certainly not about the rape. Then Mrs Katbah coughed wetly and groped for the Kleenex box on the bedside table with the telephone, her lungs still flooded from the anaesthetic. Coughing obviously hurt her.

'Do you want a nurse?'

'No-o.' A damp croak.

'Then I'll leave you in peace, I'm sorry I . . .' Agnes babbled her way out into the corridor and almost forgot herself by reaching for a cigarette. The policeman and policewoman just looked at her.

'Did you get what you wanted, Miss?' he asked.

'I don't think so . . . Were you on yesterday?'

'Yes, Miss. We had the eight-to-four then, and the day before.'

'And she's only had two visits before this?'

'S'far's I know, Miss. Chief Inspector Redding and a couple of his people, then a man and a woman from their embassy.'

'Who brought the flowers?'

He half smiled. 'Chief Inspector Redding had the big bunch of purple ones –'

'Narcissus and freisias,' the policewoman said scornfully. She was small and dark, in a loose skirt and colourful quilted jacket. 'The Jordanians brought the tulips, and a nurse came up with the daffs.'

'D'you know if anybody's rung her?'

'Can't ring in on that phone,' the policeman said. 'It's outgoing calls only. Standard procedure in hospitals.'

'Oh.' Probably he'd spent more time in hospitals as a guard than most people had as a patient. 'Well . . . thanks.'

Of course, the second Land-Rover might just have run away, radioing in the news and asking what to do next. It wasn't in perfect shape, having lost one of its (probably) four-man crew, maybe with others injured. On the other hand, it knew it had scored a hit with the TOW and that the tank wasn't in perfect shape either. And if whoever was on the far end of the radio – Major Zyadine? – knew his job, there was only one message he could send: stay in contact with the tank.

He moved in short rushes, picking his stops carefully in advance and going into a crouch, head swivelling, at each one. There was no more point in throwing himself flat than there was in crawling through a landscape where there was virtually no cover but the dunes themselves and the enemy could bob up in any direction. Movement was his cover.

Two hundred metres down the gulley, a single set of wheel tracks turned east out of the confusion of ruts, and Maxim followed. The Land-Rover had been going fast, throwing sand outward on its turns and digging deep where it had bounded over a small hillock. Gradually the trail swung around northwards; he came across one place where it had stood in a little bay formed between two slopes – probably to listen for any pursuit, but proving it wasn't scared of pursuit; the TOW launcher must be reloaded and working.

He pulled the kefiyah down off his head and tucked it into his jacket as a scarf; with his head constantly turning, he needed protection against a chafed neck more than sunstroke. He also hoped it would help his hearing, but the wind and its orchestra of sand grains was still singing the desert song.

After a time, the trail turned west, and he paused to

187

think. The Land-Rover had come a half-circle and headed back towards the tank but – he estimated – north of it. Downwind, for one thing, so it would hear the tank's engine if it were running, but still fairly close to it. It daren't get too far away for fear of losing any sense of where the tank was. The Land-Rover crew didn't know these dunes; nobody knew these dunes, since the wind could reshape them completely within weeks.

So the Land-Rover would stay north of the tank, looking south. And he would stay north of the Land-Rover and look south, too. At the next hint of a gap in the dunes, he broke away from the trail and tried to parallel it, staying one dune away.

It wasn't that simple, of course, since the dunes and gulleys weren't city blocks and streets. Twice he crept – and now with at least a guess of where the enemy was, creeping made sense – up the shoulder of a slope to make sure the tracks were still there on the far side. The second time, they weren't.

Go back and pick up the trail again? It would take time, and he was getting uneasy about time. If the Land-Rover planned a second attack, he was giving it the chance it needed, with only two men guarding the tank. He slid carefully down the end of the slope and crept forward from there.

He knew the Land-Rover must have turned off somewhere to his left; now he saw why in the dead-end slope on his right. It must now be somewhere beyond the steeper slope right ahead. He took a careful look, a deep breath, and the dune at a run.

Ten feet up the slope the impetus was gone and he was scrabbling ankle-deep in sand that was already trickling downhill from the wind above. Panting and sometimes falling on his left hand against the slope he went slantwise, skidding six inches down for every foot he made upwards. Ten feet from the crest, then five, then flopping sideways just a foot below the top and the wind-blasted sand flicking his hair like insect-scale gunfire. He checked the rifle again, drew up his knees and pushed himself gently upward until he could peer over the crest into the wind. Immediately he saw a man, his back turned, working his way up the slope on the far side of the gulley below. He was about fifty metres away, carried a rifle, and was doing exactly what Maxim had done: sneaking up for a look south.

The Land-Rover must be in the gulley below, and he raised himself carefully to look down. He was head and shoulders high when he saw it, a little off to the left, with the driver in place and another man standing at the machine-gun mounted by the passenger seat and swinging it suspiciously around the horizon.

Maxim swung the rifle into his shoulder, thumbed the selector to automatic and fired two short bursts into the Land-Rover. He saw the figures crumpling as he lifted the rifle at the man on the far slope, who was turning, losing his footing, sliding downwards. Maxim tracked him with the rifle.

Sand spat up from the crest beside him, he was knocked sideways by a punch in the left ribs and threw himself forward over the crest with no idea where the fire was coming from but desperate not to lose the one enemy he could see.

He came up sitting, ten feet down the slope, snapped off one shot and the rifle jammed. The man had stopped, flat on his back against the slope, feet spread and dug in, rifle coming to his shoulder . . .

Maxim wrenched back the cocking handle, feeling the scrape of sand in the works and almost losing the rifle as the strength drained from his left arm, brought the fore-sight onto the man – who was frantically tugging the handle of his own sand-jammed rifle. My God, the desert'll have us clubbing each other to death with fancy lumps of technology yet – and he squeezed the trigger again.

The burst hammered the man back onto the slope and his rifle slid away. The second burst stopped after two shots, but it was enough.

But there had been another, a machine-gun. It had stopped now, so probably he was out of sight, but he'd be better off even further out of sight and the only cover was the Land-Rover. He tried to stand, but a shark bit him in his left ribs and he sat back in a swirl of cold dizziness and laid his forehead on the metal of the rifle across his knees.

Reaching cautiously under his left armpit he felt blood, but his left hand still worked, he could breathe, and when he dribbled there was no blood there. He carefully unwound the kefiyah from his neck and stuffed it against his ribs, then just sat and waited for Al-Hamedi – who, of course, had shot him.

23

Agnes had first met Charlie Redding when he was an inspector in the Met's Special Branch and in constant touch with the Security Service. Now he had been promoted away and she thought he was ordinary CID these days, though his background made him an obvious choice for an investigation like this one. She didn't know much about him; he seemed a solid, cheery beer-and-chips family man who'd been in the Army for some years before joining the police. This last explained the club. It was for other ranks of all services, with none of the pretensions of the far older officers-only clubs on and off Piccadilly. There was lino instead of marble, paint instead of wood, and the pictures on the walls were poster-size photographs of aeroplanes going woosh and warships going splash.

Redding was waiting, blunt-faced and wrapped in a double-breasted blue suit and a tie with an odd motif denoting a police club or some past operation (will there be a Snowflake Committee tie? she wondered. Of course there would be: that was the only certain outcome).

'You've never been in here before, I'll bet, lass. Not the sort of place your new mates would join.' The Intelligence Service had a reputation, not entirely undeserved, for living well. 'We can get coffee in the cafeteria.'

It was a nostalgic replica of the genteel help-yourself teashops that Agnes remembered from schoolgirl trips to London but which had surrendered to an army of hamburger and pizza bars. They sat down in a stiff leatherette

191

booth around a plastic-topped table with a tray of coffee and cream cakes.

'I'm not eating,' Agnes said.

'Didn't think you were, lass.' He took a mouthful of cake and dropped saccharine into his coffee.

'A balanced diet, I see.'

'If you can balance when you stand up after it, that's right. How's life?'

They swapped small talk – more about colleagues' divorces than security matters – until the siege and Mrs Katbah drifted into the conversation.

'The Anti-Terrorist lads just don't have the manpower,' Redding explained. 'Not for just collecting statements, routine stuff. They're talking to their own contacts, but we're doing most of the legwork.'

'Anything new on the contact man – Al-Warid?'

He wiped his fingers delicately on a paper napkin. 'Nah. We reckon he was resident in London or somewhere near. The others might have been, or come in specially for the kidnapping.'

'They don't have to be Jordanian.'

'S'right, we've thought of that. Could be PLO, Syrian, one of the Lebanese mobs – they all want to get King Hussein, don't they? You know more about it than I do –'

'Not me.'

'– but I'll tell you one thing: they weren't amateurs. They don't send raw recruits on a job like that. They'll have done something before, somewhere. And we'll probably get lucky on them one day; trouble is, so what? – they're dead. Except Al-Warid and he could be out of the country now. The Boss isn't going to let me keep much manpower on this if we don't look like getting anywhere. So if you've got any ideas from Mrs Katbah . . .'

'She's pretty angry at us.'

'Yes. She's frightened as well, I'd say. So'd I be, what she's gone through, and there could be others want to know what her old man said in that room. They tried hard enough with him, why stop now? I don't know if she knows

192

anything, but I'd guess she won't talk, not to us, until she's back among her own kind. If they move her into the embassy or one of those private clinics with mostly Arab patients.'

'That could be days; we want her to talk now.'

'What about?'

'Anything Katbah could have said about the revolt. He may have smelt it coming: he told the tank crew where to hide if they had to.'

'Did he?' He took out a packet of small cigars and lit one, then held the light for Agnes's cigarette.

'It's in the transcript. Thank you. Some Crusader ruin called Zweiwindburg.'

'They went to a lot of trouble about that tank, it must be important to them. I suppose it must be important to us. Are we looking for it?'

'How would I know? Zweiwindburg isn't on the 31 bus route.' And Charlie Redding isn't on the Snowflake Committee.

He nodded without meaning anything and sipped his coffee. The cafeteria was filling up, mostly with older men in sombre sports jackets and open-necked shirts – pensioners and probably ex-sergeants, Agnes guessed. Young men who'd only done a few years in the services and got nowhere wouldn't want to join a military club.

'Funny thing, that,' Redding said. 'The timing of the revolt. Just when the tank was there.'

'I understand it's been there for a month.'

'These trials take time. Suppose they'd got hold of it, not much use to them, just one tank. Wonder where they'd have sent it?'

'North?' she suggested.

'Yes, Damascus, next stop Nizhni-Tagil.'

'*Where?*'

'Just one of those places the Soviets build their tanks.' His years in Special Branch had given Redding a more international outlook than the average London copper; the sly expression was all his own. 'Must be quite a tank, if the Soviets go to all that much trouble. Big risk they're taking – if it was all their idea.'

'D'you ever go fishing, Charlie?'

'Nasty business, all those poor innocent little fishes trying to swallow hooks. Mind, I may find I've got time for it if the Boss decides this Al-Warid business isn't worth the manpower, nothing big behind it.'

'Charlie, I'm the new girl in the whore-house; I don't captain the hockey team yet.'

'But you know who does. And you know my number.'

Agnes finished her coffee and shook her head at the idea of another. 'If Mrs Katbah could remember anything the Colonel said, anything.'

'She's scared. You saw her –'

'Yes, I know. But there might be something, she wouldn't know it was important, if she'd only open up. Or if we can open her up.'

'Ay, ay, lass; we can't get rough with her. I mean, she's foreign and important, she's been raped, shot, seen her old man tortured to death –'

'And things like that can spoil your whole day. But if you don't find Al-Warid – and you've been looking for four days now – who else have you got? I'm not saying you send in your gorilla squad and have her resist a bit of arrest, but do this much for me: get a list of everything that's happened, visitors she's had, messages, calls she's made.'

'Is this an official request?'

'If it helps to say we've asked for it, yes. But it should be stuff you've got anyway. And if anything comes of it, you get the credit anyway.'

'I've heard that before. One thing I've never heard is If there's any shit, you'll be swimming in it alone, Charlie boy.'

Agnes shrugged. 'I thought you wanted something to happen. But be honest if you want to, go and tell your Commander you'd be better off gone fishing . . .'

'All right . . . Have I got your new number?'

* * *

194

Al-Hamedi was briefly and almost formally apologetic, then started to do what he could for Maxim's wound, but giving him quick and almost suspicious glances the while. Maxim tried saying: '*Insh'Allah*,' with a shrug which hurt but didn't help. He wanted to say: 'Look, I took a risk, most of which came off. It was my decision. These things happen in our trade.' But he felt that wouldn't help either, because there was something dark and complicated going on in Al-Hamedi's mind which Maxim could only guess at and Al-Hamedi himself probably didn't want to face.

Maxim had shown military incompetence by getting himself shot by his own side. But worse, he had forced Al-Hamedi into the military incompetence of shooting someone on his own side. So could Al-Hamedi trust Maxim any more, particularly since Maxim obviously wouldn't trust a man who had shot him, which made Maxim not only incompetent and untrustworthy but unjust for not trusting Al-Hamedi any longer?

Or something like that. Whatever it was, it was complicated and had as much to do with Maxim being British as Al-Hamedi being Arab. He shrugged, mentally this time, and just hoped it would work itself out.

There wasn't much Al-Hamedi could do for the wound except ease Maxim out of his combat jacket and tie the kefiyah round his chest, then half-support him down to the Land-Rover. There were a lot of holes in it and blood on it, but once Al-Hamedi had turfed the driver's body out, the engine started first time. He drove carefully back to the tank, stopping to hoot the horn and shout at Timbrell before they came into view.

The tank had a reasonably well-stocked first-aid kit – people get really hurt on trials as well as in wars – and Timbrell more or less took over while Al-Hamedi kept watch.

'Don't bother with looking out for the moment,' Maxim told him. 'Listen on the radio. Check the channel with the one in the Land-Rover.' Al-Hamedi gave a brief expressionless nod and started to do that.

While he was still within hearing, Maxim said to Timbrell: 'I stuck my head up about 200 metres away where he couldn't recognise me; my fault, I should have kept the kefiyah on.'

Timbrell began swabbing Maxim's ribs with near-boiling water, bringing overlapping pains that made Maxim flinch. 'Did you get them all?'

'Yes.'

'How many?'

'Three.'

Timbrell wrung out the cloth and began more swabbing. Maxim said: 'Remember to move some more water into the BV.'

'You went out into the sand to kill those three and you did and you got yourself . . .'

'What's so bloody odd? I'm a soldier.'

'I was eight years in the Army . . . I just never met anybody like you.'

'I bet you did. You just never saw them in action.'

'Could be . . . Do you ever dream about them – the ones you've killed?'

'For God's sake . . . No, I don't. I don't know them. I dream that somebody's got a gun on me and I'm moving like lead trying to cock the action on a jammed weapon.' And why did I say that? – because it had so nearly come true in that other gulley? He had never told anybody, not his dead wife Jenny nor Agnes, though both had seen him wake sweating and gasping from that nightmare. Maybe it was a guilt dream, a civilian subconscious reminding him he owed God more deaths than he could ever repay, but he didn't want to know. He just wanted to forget it – and for Timbrell to stop his own civilianised maundering and treat him as just another piece of damaged but repairable equipment. That was how he wanted to see it himself.

'Just get a bloody dressing on it.'

'You've got torn muscles and maybe a cracked rib. A few inches one way and –'

'It would have missed.'

'If you want to look at it that way.' He began winding bandages tightly around Maxim's chest.

'How's the tank?'

'Repairing you seems to have taken priority; I haven't had a proper look, yet, but I think we can get mobile again if we half-track it.'

'What?'

'You'll see.' He dressed Maxim again and tied the kefi-yah as a sling for his left arm, then fetched him a mug of over-sweet coffee and a packet of glucose tablets. Al-Hamedi came up to make a formal report.

'Major, the radio talk is all a callsign – I think it is a command post, not so very far – to ask what the Land-Rovers did.'

'They'll pretty soon get the idea that the Land-Rovers are knocked out, and they'll know roughly where . . . Look, both of you: it may be time for a bit of democracy. You know the state I'm in; I can ride in the tank and do some jobs with the controls, but in any case it'll take time to repair and it won't be as good as new – right?'

Timbrell nodded. Al-Hamedi stayed impassive.

'All right. The Land-Rover seems to be in running order. We've still got the plastic explosive so we can still blow the gun and get away in the Land-Rover. I want to know what you two think.'

Timbrell and Al-Hamedi looked at each other, unwilling to be the first. Timbrell took off his glasses and wiped them with a carefully selected patch of a handkerchief that was mostly grease and dried blood. At last he asked: 'Can either of you handle the TOW launcher?'

Maxim couldn't: the British Army only used TOW on helicopter launchers. Al-Hamedi said: 'No. I have not been trained.'

'So,' Timbrell said, 'we'll be down to small arms and the machine-gun for defence– and no armour plating. *But* we

197

can move off now and go faster than a half-tracked tank.'
He looked at Al-Hamedi again.

Maxim knew he was being unfair, that he had taken
over command and was now trying to spread its load. But
if they stayed with the tank they had to do it wholeheart-
edly; in particular, he didn't want Al-Hamedi sullen and
doubtful. He might not believe in Maxim again, but he
had to believe in what he himself was doing.

That didn't mean Maxim was above a little cheating to
get his own way, in true democratic fashion. 'With my own
background, I'm naturally a Land-Rover man.'

'I'm a tankie,' Timbrell said instinctively.

'I am also a tank man,' Al-Hamedi said.

'Well . . .' he looked from one to the other. 'Do we
stick with the tank, then?'

Timbrell put his glasses back on. 'I'm damned if I want
to give up now . . . we can always fall back on the Land-
Rover.' Al-Hamedi nodded.

'Okay,' Maxim said. 'Sergeant, d'you feel like getting
on the radio and pretending to be the only survivor from
the Land-Rovers? Say they're both knocked out and the
tank went off heading north, not damaged.'

Al-Hamedi took his time thinking this over. 'You want,
when the tank is repaired, to go on east?'

'Same plan, yes. We can't go south, but if we stay close
to the border we can't be flanked from that side. The
border runs east-west, so we have to go east or west. West,
they've probably got tanks coming up.' Before, Maxim
wouldn't have felt the need to spell it out as fully.

'I will try with the radio, Major.' He went away.

'Alec, you'd better work out what needs doing. Work
out how I can help, too.'

Timbrell went on looking at him. 'You're a tricky
bastard . . . That's a compliment, by the way.'

'Thank you.' He felt exhausted, drained. But until Timbrell came back with a work plan, he could close his
eyes . . .

24

Agnes rang the office from a public phone in the club and was requested – the word was actually used – to get back and talk over an urgent matter with Mr Blake. She didn't know any Blake in Six, so assumed it must be one of Giles's cover names that nobody had got round to telling her about. That turned out to be right, and he apologised nicely for it.

'When somebody already as senior and experienced as yourself joins us,' he flattered her, 'we tend to assume you have a knowledge of the often arbitrary details of our procedures. It must be intensely annoying for you . . . However, I hear you've been hospital visiting?'

'You suggested I should go and see her as soon as she was fit enough.'

'You're quite right, I did. But I've had a slight spasm from the real Foreign Office about it. It appears that they wanted to visit her as well, and were told they already had.'

'What cover should I have used?'

'I know, I know. It's just unfortunate that in this morning's hassle you didn't have a chance to get me to clear it with them first. It's a perennial problem; I've assured Scottie that it won't happen again until next time. Did she have anything to say?'

Agnes eased herself around in her chair and tried to think of a long way of saying 'nothing'. Giles had the dubious privilege of an 'inside' office, a windowless room in the core of the building and as much a basement as any umpteen floors below. For security reasons – probably – the furniture was very modern and simple, without crannies and mouldings to hide listening devices, although quite likely Giles had his own built in somewhere.

'She didn't say much,' she said finally, 'except that she doesn't much like us, which is fair enough, and she's scared, too. I suppose a couple of plainclothes coppers on guard doesn't seem much by Middle Eastern standards. What it boils down to is she says Katbah didn't say anything to her about the revolt. Whether she's just frightened to admit she's got any useful knowledge . . .'

Giles leant his elbows on his desk and delicately touched the sides of his mouth with finger and thumb. 'Not necessarily. The Colonel was in a responsible and sensitive post: he wouldn't have been likely to chatter to his wife (she was a fairly recent wife, wasn't she?) – and you can double that in spades for them being Muslim. They, as your researches will have told you, do not confide in their womenfolk about their work . . . How badly injured is she?'

'The medics aren't sure, but she might end up paralysed from the waist down. In a way, that doesn't really count since she hasn't been told that.'

Even Giles was a little taken aback. 'That seems to be carrying cold blood to a rather low temperature.'

Agnes shrugged. 'If she does know something, I want us to know it – today.'

'I appreciate your personal involvement, which is perhaps unfortunate, but she may simply be being loyal to her late husband. In the broadest sense, her loyalty is due to Jordan, not to us.'

'It would be nice to know what she's told the Jordanian embassy.'

'Yes, I quite agree, but the real Foreign Office won't let us ask the embassy detailed questions, and we have to abide by that. Our national policy on all this' – Giles got to his feet; there was something about the word 'policy' that made people stand up and walk about while they talked of it. Was it just the implication of scale, Agnes wondered, or that they wanted room to shift? – 'is to sympathise with Jordan and pass on any helpful information, such as the radio intercepts, but to avoid as far as possible the subject of the tank. In Jordanian eyes, that remains a very minor matter compared with an attempted revolution.

'Of course, this isn't entirely compatible with the interests of Defence, our other main client in this matter. Frankly, I have no idea how important this new tank is; the military tend to have a schoolboyish faith in any new toy they develop. By the time it actually reaches the front line they're usually reduced to saying "It's the quality of the men manning it that really counts." But continuing good relations with Jordan is vitally important to any Middle Eastern policy we may adopt. And the neutrality of this Service is vital to the maintenance of that relationship.'

'Neutrality?' It was a word Agnes hadn't heard often in her years with the secret world.

'Just that.' Giles perched on the edge of his desk and gave her a fatherly smile. 'Another – slight – disadvantage for you in joining us late, and from the perhaps narrower world of security, is that you haven't had a chance to grow up imbued with our more *international* viewpoint, the contribution we can make to foreign policy in ways you might not fully appreciate. Ways quite apart from the provision of intelligence.

'This may be easier to illustrate by taking a negative example first. Suppose that Jordan were, at this time, to uncover a British espionage operation on their territory. Think of the damage it would cause to the relationship – think of the damage the Israelis caused themselves when they got caught with their fingers in the American till. But now take the positive side, the help we have actually been able to give Jordan. All of it clandestine: the radio intercepts, the tapes from the hotel siege and – in collaboration with our Washington brethren – reconnaissance photographs. And all passed covertly, never openly, to the government in Amman.'

So Harry and I were, in a way, both working for this Service, Agnes thought sourly. Well, he isn't now; he bloody soon got back on his own side of the street.

'Take,' Giles went on, 'an imagined, I hope unimaginable, further instance: a complete rift with Jordan. Diplomatic relations broken off, our military aid kicked out – what would remain? *We* would, and the international bazaar where we would continue to trade titbits of information with our Jordanian equivalents and maintain a channel through which the two governments could work covertly towards a resumption of open relations once tempers have cooled. This is not a fancy; it's happened more times than you might think – intelligence services providing a diplomatic safety net when all else has failed.

'But only, and I stress this, if this Service can maintain a stance of neutrality, unbesmirched by political or military adventures. In practical terms, by avoiding activism. *Activism*,' he repeated, standing up again so that he could smile benignly down on her. 'I'm quite sure you won't commit us to anything that might be so described.'

Agnes felt humble. Daddy had taken her into his own private den, humbling in itself, and told her that she was grown up now, it was time for her to know that the world was not as she thought it was, that she was not halfway up a career ladder but at the very bottom – but now of an unimagined golden ladder stretching infinitely high. And with Daddy's wise counsel, but only with that, she would climb and not put a foot wrong because when Daddy tells you you are a big girl now he usually means you are really still a little one.

'You'd better come along and report a nil return on Mrs Katbah to Snowflake,' Giles said, lifting the phone to call a car. Agnes nodded and kept a humble, thoughtful smile on her face because she fancied Daddy had also been telling her that he was on his way to becoming head of the

202

Service and nobody, but nobody, was going to rock the ladder while he was on its last few rungs.

Maxim woke because they woke him – then realised how long he had slept and what through. They had erected the crane again, and with the auxiliary motor for power had lifted off the bazooka plates protecting the left-side wheels and track. Then they had unbolted and sledge-hammered off the half-melted remains of the idler wheel – all this noise within a few feet of where he had been asleep.

'I don't know how you do it,' Timbrell said. 'A couple of times I checked to see if you'd gone and died on us.'

Maxim croaked a reply; he had slept with his mouth open and his tongue felt like an apprentice sand-dune. The wound was a stiff ache, with scorching pains when he moved; both of them helped him up and more or less propped him against the Land-Rover.

'Now you can be real a commander,' Timbrell said, 'since you can't do anything but talk.'

'Buggery I can't. I can use my eyes and a gun.'

The two of them looked as much in need of sleep as he had been: Timbrell was stripped to the waist, Al-Hamedi with his Arab repugnance at public undressing had his shirt sleeves rolled up, both were camouflaged with a mixture of sweat, grease and sand. But there was no resentment in their faces; perhaps they felt, absurdly but humanly, that their brutal hard work had put them level with him and his wound.

'How did the radio go?' Maxim asked.

Al-Hamedi almost smiled. 'I think I was a good actor. I said what you said and that I was very much hurt and the radio' – he blipped his thumb – 'not working so good. And I said to come and save me quick.' He was pleased with that last touch.

'And?'

'They said I must wait. They could not come.'

'That *is* good. D'you know who you spoke to?'

'Just a callsign.'

203

'Can you guess what rank?' Rank tends to show in voices.

'It . . . perhaps he is a major.'

'Zyadine?'

'I do not hear his voice ever.'

'I've spoken to him, but can't remember . . . Now what?'

'We need to move the tank,' Timbrell said. 'You can't help.'

'Then somebody run me up to where I can see.'

Al-Hamedi drove the Land-Rover almost to the top of a gentle slope back down the gulley, and after some careful parking left Maxim with just his head and the pintle-mounted machine-gun showing over the crest.

He now had a pair of binoculars and some sand goggles, both looted from the dead crew, but still couldn't tell how far he could see across the dunes: the usual problem of judging range in the desert. He thought the wind might be easing as the sun drooped westwards, but it still hissed in his ears and sand crawled into the wheel-ruts around him. Good: it would be doing that to their much older trail on the stony desert and their route into the dunes.

Come to think of it, the trail was probably filled already, since it wouldn't be as deep as that of the Land-Rovers. Where they had only a few square inches of each wheel in contact with the ground, it had two tracks each two feet wide, and almost five metres of each on the ground. Despite its vastly greater weight, its actual ground pressure per square inch was less than that of wheeled vehicles – which was why tanks could cross softer ground than they could.

At, of course, a price: they could have changed a shot-up wheel on a Land-Rover in five minutes. Behind him, the tank engine rumbled as they slaved on to get the track linked up again.

25

The basement room at Defence was almost excited: they had the first real news of the MBT90's whereabouts from satellite photographs that the Squadron-Leader was pinning to the board in front of an attentive audience.

'Remember,' he kept reminding them, 'these are three hours old. Anything can have happened since then.'

'Could they be in Saudia?' Agnes asked.

There was a hush, then Giles said: 'I'm sorry, my dear, I forgot to tell you. Forgot you weren't here when we heard. The Saudis have closed the border, at least we think so. Scottie, have you had any reaction from your Office?'

Agnes stared woodenly at the map. The Squadron-Leader had located the exact position of each photograph and was linking them to the map with coloured wool: the traditional blue for the MBT90 (our forces) and orange for everything else (the enemy). The single 'blue' picture showed a dark rectangle, a smaller dark smudge and two much smaller dots.

'What on earth is that?' Sir Anthony asked.

'It looks like a man on a camel,' the Squadron-Leader said. 'If you look at the shadow.'

'That's a camel, all right,' Scott-Scobie agreed, feeling that the Foreign Office should have the final say on such things. 'But why have they stopped? To ask the way?'

'More likely to ask if he's seen anything and bribe him to keep his mouth shut,' the Brigadier said perceptively. 'They've done about thirty miles in a straight line. Of course, it wouldn't be a straight line, so they've done more.

And just about all eastwards: where did they get the fuel? I thought we were assuming the tank was empty or it would have got away in the first place.'

'We could have been wrong,' George shrugged. 'Or they filled up from the tank they knocked out.'

'Can you see that?' somebody asked, and they clustered closer – just another bunch of little boys eager to see a broken vehicle, Agnes thought. But the Wadi Rum ran north and south, and on one of the orange-wool-linked pictures it came up as just a strip of early morning shadow. At the south end, where it opened into the desert and the sun, there was a group of non-tank vehicles which the Brigadier identified as 17th Armoured's tactical HQ, directing the search.

Another picture showed three shapes – tanks, the Brigadier said – towing streamers of dust across the desert almost due south of the Wadi. Yet another was of two small shapes – Land-Rovers, said the Brigadier – almost due east of the MBT90 and the camel, in among the softer, rounded shadows of sand dunes.

'Don't like that,' the Brigadier said. 'They've got a flanking position and it looks as if they're carrying missile launchers.' He peered closely. 'That could be bad news.'

Watch out, Harry, watch to the *east*. But Agnes's silent shout stood no more chance of getting through than . . . well, than all their modern military radios did. And she was looking at the past, three hours old by now. She narrowed her eyes at the camel photograph, but it was etched in horizontal lines by the television transmission from space and the closer she got the more frustrating it became. One of those two grainy dots must be Harry trying his primitive Arabic on the camel rider, and it could be the last picture she ever saw of him, but it was too remote and official for emotion.

Giles had backed out of the group, waiting for her at the big table. When the first thrill of the photographs had worn off the others, he said: 'Agnes has been to see Mrs Katbah this morning. Perhaps she will : . .'

She could almost have delivered the message as a shrug. Mrs K had said she didn't know anything more and quite possibly didn't. She was angry and frightened. The only hope was if she'd told the Jordanian embassy something; she looked at Scott-Scobie.

'Doubt it. I mean, what could she know anyway?'

'And our boys in blue,' Sprague said, 'still don't seem to be having any luck with the missing Mr Al-Warid.'

Agnes nodded, then had to explain: 'I had coffee with the DCI handling it. He's an old friend.'

'Oh?' Sprague said. 'Did you?'

'It seems a perfectly sensible thing to do,' Giles said. 'If the police do discover anything, we could use an open link.'

'While my Office is not in charge of the Met,' Sprague said, 'it has the ultimate responsibility for –'

'Who they drink coffee with?' Scott-Scobie suggested.

'I was going to say, their lines of communication, particularly in a situation such as this. I accept that it is a small matter, but . . .'

The Signals girl was beckoning Agnes from the room next door, and she slid away unobtrusively.

It was Charlie Redding on the phone, jovially exasperated. 'Where the hell *are* you, lass? I've been transferred all round Whitehall until I could be speaking to myself for all I know.'

'I'm in a bomb-proof fish-and-chip shop half a mile down under the Bank of England. Have you got the hospital timetable?'

'Yes, d'you want it sent round or shall I read it over?'

'Read it, would you, Charlie?'

'All righty, here goes – everything up to twenty minutes ago. She came out of intensive care around two yesterday afternoon. That's when she went into the private room. She asked for a telephone but it wasn't plugged in until about half three. The Jordanian embassy had already been to see her, from 3.05 to 3.25. She made one local call at 3.35. We –'

'Who did she call?'

'No idea. The meter just ticks up how long the call is and it goes on her bill at the end; it doesn't record the number. We came in at 3.55, left at 4.20. That's all for yesterday. Oh – you didn't want all the doctors and nurses popping in and out all the time, did you? – because I can't do 'em.'

'That's okay.'

'Today, you got there at 10.20, stayed just ten minutes. She made a call – local again – at 10.45. And that's all so far.'

'Has she had any letters or messages?'

'Nothing.'

'Who sent the third bunch of flowers?'

'Delivered by a florist's shop. That was actually the day before yesterday, when she was still in intensive care, so she didn't get them until she was in the private room.'

Agnes chewed this over, and it tasted thin. 'I'd like to know who she's been calling. She said she didn't have any London friends.'

'Her husband would have had, probably. Probably one of them sent the other flowers. Or she could have been calling her embassy, telling them to get her out of there soon as possible.'

'Yes, but she'd only just had the embassy visit when she made the first call . . . Who came from them?'

'The ambassador's wife, couple of blokes, one of them the embassy doctor.'

'Umm. Charlie – do you really love me?'

'Course I do, lass – and the answer to the next question is No.'

'All I'm asking is one teensy-weensy little –'

'I'm not touching her phone, lass. I'm not even going to ask for a warrant. I've got to put reasons in writing and I don't *have* any reasons. The good old days are gone – well, for the moment, anyway.'

'Oh, come off it, Charlie.'

'I'm telling you. Your old mob might still cut a few

corners, but for this one I doubt it and I'll tell you why. And it isn't just the story getting out that first we shoot her, then we tap her phone. It's the hospital: they have to be in on it. We can't go to the exchange and intercept every call coming out of that place, it has to be done at the hospital switchboard or the actual phone in her room and the hospital's going to want the paperwork double *perfect*. You know how they protect their patients – unless it gets in the way of teatime.'

It wasn't much worse than she'd expected, although perhaps she'd been spoiled by the buccaneering attitude of Security. And perhaps she still was.

'All right. But I want to go back and ask her a few more questions. No thumbscrews, just questions. Will you tip off your guard dogs?'

He couldn't refuse that; all he could do was ask: 'What's in it for us?'

'You don't really love me, Charlie.'

'I don't really know if you can cook.'

Back in the main office, the Brigadier was reading back a signal to be sent to the *Alamein* for onward transmission to Maxim in the MBT90. The fact that none of the other signals had been acknowledged and the MBT90 was getting even further out of range – as the Squadron-Leader had pointed out – was irrelevant. He was too inexperienced in such affairs to realise how responsible and aware the signal would look in the committee report and minutes.

'. . . two missile armed Land-Rovers ten kilometres east your position 0803 Zulu stop Saudi border may be closed stop urgent advise Harpoon.'

'I suggest "probably closed",' Giles said.

'I think we have to say something about avoiding contact with Saudi forces.' Scott-Scobie was staring grumpily at the tabletop.

'Isn't that incompatible with saying that the border "may be" or "probably" is closed?' Sprague chipped in. 'They, to my mind, amount to an invitation to go and see whether it is closed or not, in which case contact with Saudi forces seems more than likely.'

'I concur,' Sir Anthony said.

'With what?' Scott-Scobie demanded.

'You. But that of course brings up the question as to whether we as a committee can actually give orders to an officer in the field.'

'I think we can make clear,' the Brigadier said, 'that the whole signal is advisory.'

'The whole signal will be at least four hours out of date,' said the Squadron-Leader, who had been writing it down and crossing it out. 'But it isn't as if they're going to get it, anyway.'

He had known they would all glare at him, so he had his head down over the signal pad.

'What,' Agnes asked, 'would you really like Harry to do now, if you could get through to him and lay on whatever you wanted?'

'D'you mean an ideal fairy-tale ending?' The Brigadier, Agnes sensed, was a bit wary of her, unable to pigeon-hole her either as a member of the Secret Service or The Little Woman. 'Well, if the Americans had a task force in the area and would lend us one of their big helicopters, then get clearance from Saudi Arabia or Jordan itself, and then fly in and pick them up, they could blow up the tank as originally intended.'

'What would you tell Harry to do?'

'Ahh . . . ' he stared across the room at the map. 'Make a break for it north-east, they won't be expecting them to go north at all. Then rendezvous with the helicopter at the Batn el Ghul station on the road and rail to Ma'an. Good landmark, I imagine.'

'This is just daydreaming,' Scott-Scobie said impatiently.

'Is there any chance of it happening?' Agnes persisted.

The Brigadier looked sad but manly. 'Absolutely none, I'm afraid. There isn't an American carrier within a thousand miles.'

'*Now* can we get back to the signal?' Scott-Scobie said, glowering at Agnes.

'Should we suggest,' Sir Anthony wondered, 'that they act at discretion?'

'Having met Major Maxim,' Sprague said, 'I would prefer *with* discretion.'

Only Giles bothered to notice Agnes tiptoeing out; she pointed at her open mouth, indicating an early lunch.

26

A track link is sometimes called a track shoe and is more fundamental to any tank, from the first ones built in 1915, than a horseshoe is to a horse. Without a shoe, a horse can limp along; without a link, a tank can only sit there and squirm – and anyway, the horse came before the shoe, but the tank could never have been invented without the link.

Seventy-four links made up the left track of the MBT90, running in a conventional layout from the drive sprocket high at the rear to the idler wheel high at the front, then back under the row of road wheels; an endless belt that now had two broken and melted ends. With the idler wrecked, Timbrell's plan was to 'half-track' that side: take out other links besides the two shot-through ones so that when the track was joined up again it would be shorter, not reaching the idler at all.

The only thing to be said for the plan was that it was the only possible one. It was strictly get-you-home: the tank would steer like a car with a flat front tyre and not go much faster; moreover, he would never get the track tension right: the endless belt would be too tight or too loose, always likely to snap link pins and leave them with another rejoining job. But link pins are a tank's horseshoe nails and any tank carries plenty of spares.

In principle, it was a simple matter of bringing the two broken ends of track – now at different ends of the tank – together again. Reversing the tank carefully onto the rear end, road wheel by road wheel, effectively brought that

212

end to the front (though the tank had moved back, not that end forward). Now both broken ends were at the front. Hammering out link pins got rid of the broken and unnecessary links – eight in all, Timbrell estimated – and the track was the right, shorter, length to be joined up. Unfortunately you can never make links join properly on the ground; still, all it needed was to lift the lower end up over the front road wheel until it met the other end, whack in new pins, and the track was endless again.

Just a routine task for any tank crew, though not the one they most miss in retirement. And they would have preferred not to do it short-handed on soft ground among blowing sand. But the biggest problem was the normal one: each track link weighed 70 pounds. Seventy-four sculptured pieces of steel each about two feet by seven inches added up to nearly two-and-a-half tons. The end that had to be lifted up over the road wheel in the final stage – a dozen links – would be 840 pounds. Of course, they'd never have managed it without the crane, but even the crane couldn't reach everywhere. Just think of weights such as those involved at every stage of the operation, think of manoeuvring a 40-ton tank by inches when what it really wants to do is bog itself down for good in the trench its backing-and-forthing is digging in the sand. And then think of what tankies think of infantrymen like Maxim saying they go to war sitting down.

Even from 150 metres away, Maxim had begun to revise his infantry viewpoint. He heard the tank roaring and screaming like a mating dinosaur, Al-Hamedi driving and Timbrell doing a mad-conductor act in front to guide him. He saw Al-Hamedi, youngest and fittest of them all, finish one task and then kneel in a prayer attitude, except in the wrong direction, totally exhausted for several minutes. And at last he saw the tank drive clear of the torn area of sand and Al-Hamedi walking slowly up to drive him back.

Maxim said a few words of praise and sympathy, but they looted the Land-Rover and climbed back into the rumbling tank almost in silence. Maxim took a last look

213

around the battlefield – that was what it had been and that was what it looked. Sand had already softened the outline of the crushed Land-Rover and its ghastly crew, soon it would fill the ruts and sift over the abandoned track links and bazooka plates; only the second Land-Rover, bullet-holed and blood-stained, would remain to be salvaged. God alone knew how many patches of how many deserts had swallowed such military junk – and men – in the last fifty years.

When he slid painfully down into the commander's seat again he realised how much the tank had begun to smell, now not of machinery and its fluids but of men and theirs. How on earth did you clean such a mixture of solid metal and delicate electronics? Well, not their most urgent problem. He checked that the PVD was on video, looked across at Al-Hamedi, then couldn't get himself to give the proper crisp military order.

'Okay, Alec,' he said, and they moved off.

The same policeman and policewoman were outside Mrs Katbah's door, and Agnes had to chat to them for a few minutes whilst a nurse tidied up inside. They weren't surprised to see her, but by now they were pretty sure she wasn't as pure as the driven Diplomatic Service. Still, theirs not to reason why with a chief inspector's seal of approval.

Mrs Katbah's dark eyes were no more welcoming than they had been that morning, although the drip feed to her arm had gone and she was sitting more upright in the bed.

'I'm terribly sorry to barge in on you again like this,' Agnes babbled, 'but there were just a couple more questions and I've got some good news as well. Can you tell me: on the aeroplane from Jordan, did you talk to any of the other passengers – about where you were going to stay in London?'

'No. I did not talk with anybody except the lady with the food.'

'I see. Fine. And had you told anybody in Jordan, before you came?'

'No. I think no . . . the Colonel did not tell me what hotel we are going to until we are on the aeroplane already.'

'Good, thank you. That clears up the point. May I make a quick phone call?' Agnes snatched up the whole apparatus, dumped it in her lap along with her big shoulder bag, opened the bag, found her diary, consulted it, dropped it, got in a mixup with the phone and finally punched her own home number.

She let it ring half a dozen times, then smiled apologetically. 'Everybody's always out at lunch. I'm sorry. It doesn't matter.'

'You said there was good news.'

'Er, yes. I shouldn't really tell you this, I mean it's supposed to be a secret, we aren't even going to tell your embassy until it's all over, some time tonight . . . but since you've been involved, well . . . you remember the terrorists forced your husband to tell them where the British tank was hidden? – at Zweiwindburg?'

'I think I . . . yes, I think he told them . . .'

'So you see, last night we sent in a British crew to get the tank and we've just heard it's safe. By radio.'

'It is safe now?'

'Well, not yet, no. But they're going to go up the road to Ma'an and there's going to be an American helicopter waiting to rescue them at Batn el Ghul, when it's dark. So it'll be safe soon. But please don't tell your embassy or I shall get into trouble for telling you. Thank you very much, once more, and now I'll let you get some rest. I do hope you'll be out of here soon.'

Out in the corridor, she asked the woman PC where the nearest lavatory was – at the stairs end of the corridor – and headed there at top speed.

'Hope she makes it in time,' the policeman observed.

Agnes did, too. She slammed the door of the cubicle and switched on the receiver in her bag before sitting down. Then she extended the aerial, plugged the earpiece

215

in and turned on the little tape recorder. And then waited. And waited.

Somebody used the cubicle next to her and went out again. Somebody else was helped in by a solicitous nurse, who paced around outside, murmuring deconstipating spells. And Agnes waited.

The earpiece gave a rattle, the purr of the dialling tone, then a series of clicks; Agnes couldn't translate them immediately, but all the Jordanian embassy numbers began 937, and this hadn't been that. The other phone rang three times and a man's voice said: 'Yes?'

Mrs Katbah said: 'Salem?' and then it was a fast, anxious dialogue in Arabic; all Agnes could interpret was the anxiety. Next door, the constipation ended in triumph and little groans of relief and almost a cheer from the nurse who, now relieved of care, knocked on Agnes's door and asked if she were all right.

'Oh yes, I just felt a little faint when my friend started talking about her operation . . . I'll be all right, I'm just not very good at medical things . . .'

'Can I get you anything?' A slight hint of superiority at anybody 'not good at medical things'.

'No, no, I'll be all right in a moment.'

The dialogue ended in a final click. Agnes waited, in case there was another call immediately, then shut down the aerial and whizzed out as fast as she'd come in.

27

Only after a kilometre or more did Maxim stop wincing before the pain whenever they lurched or hit a bump. And it wasn't just his own side, it was the tank's. Perhaps Timbrell had been too thorough and gloomy in warning him of the weakness in the rejoined track; gradually he began to assume that if it broke again, it could be fixed again, and his trust returned. He now sensed in the tank not an inflexible strength but an animal strength in depth, that could be injured without being destroyed, work well without having to work perfectly.

Like myself, he thought wryly.

But they moved at no more than jogging speed, Timbrell picking his way and making every turn as gentle as possible. After a few kilometres, the puffy dunes began to deflate, the horizon expanded and they ran out onto hard stony desert. It was only a patch some kilometres wide and with dunes all round, but while it lasted they could go straighter and slightly faster than on sand.

'Alec, keep close to the dunes in case we need cover in a hurry.'

Al-Hamedi stayed standing up, head out, although driving commands were no longer necessary. Below, Maxim set the PVD to a slow all-round scan and practised reaching for the controls with just his right hand. The electronic switches and knobs were easy, being compactly grouped on his 'dashboard', but if those failed he would have trouble with the stiff and wide-spaced hand levers and wheels.

Had that been a dot on the screen? He swung back to it and zoomed in.

'Aircraft west!' Al-Hamedi dropped into his own seat, swinging the hatch shut overhead. The dot on the screen bulged quickly, sprouting wings to the edge of the frame and then rushed past, its thunderclap muted by the armour. He spun the camera to follow, then tilted it as the Phantom began to climb in a turn to the north. They watched it pass back, perhaps slower now and some thousands of feet up, then curl round again.

'Alec, turn right around.' This could be an attacking pass. 'Shut your hatch if you haven't already.' There was no point in standing up to reach the commander's machine-gun: it would be no more use than a water-pistol against a fast aircraft. Maxim growled with resentment at the intrusion – and their helplessness.

But the Phantom kept its height, passing overhead beyond reach of the camera.

'Commander, another thing – to the west. Please . . . ?'

Maxim nodded and Al-Hamedi spun the camera to another dot, coming low and slower. After a moment, they both decided: 'Helicopter.'

'Alec, stop. Sergeant, stand up, please. Keep an eye on the Phantom.'

The helicopter was veering to their right, slightly north of them. As it got closer and more side-on, he realised how big it was, with a sagging stomach like a pregnant fish and a six-bladed rotor twirling on top.

'Israeli Super Frelon,' Al-Hamedi called down.

'Is it armed?'

'I think no, but it carries many troops.'

'*If* we want to shoot at it, what do we use?'

A pause, then: 'Shell, at the engines. But it is very difficult in the air.'

'If it stays in the air, fine. Alec, can you turn to stay head-on? Traversing right.' He grasped the pistol grip and turned the turret until he had the helicopter in the sight, then tracked it. But he couldn't reach the safety lever, the one control Timbrell hadn't trusted to electronics.

'Sergeant, come down and take the gun.' Maxim opened his own hatch and painfully hauled himself up. The helicopter, huge now, tilted back in a slowing descent – another zero-zero landing, Maxim supposed. Dust flared out, flattened by the downwash of the rotor and then boiling up around a wide circle. Pale behind the dust, the Super Frelon gave a soggy bounce and settled heavily about 150 metres away.

Without any orders, the tank and gun twitched into perfect position, staring blankly at the helicopter. And just in case anybody watching from it thought they'd still got the right address for a jolly party, Maxim ostentatiously cocked the free-mounted machine-gun. He was feeling a cold and confident anger at this intrusion; he realised they all felt it, the tank felt it. They had run and hidden and worked and fought and bled to keep the tank alive, and now it *was* alive, in a way he had never thought possible, a live and viciously dangerous multi-brained beast.

Maybe some of it was the light-headedness and tunnel-thinking of exhaustion, but the beast they had become wasn't tired. If he said *Kill*, the beast would kill without hesitation. And with an Israeli helicopter and crew spattered across the desert, the fury of three governments would come down on them like an avalanche. But two other people would know, in a way those governments could never know, why he had said Kill.

'Commander to crew: I don't know what the hell they want, but if they do anything unfriendly I'll fire one burst as a warning, then order fire on the helicopter itself.' Then, more formally: 'Shell. 150, helicopter. On.'

'Loaded. On,' Al-Hamedi said crisply, and the beast needed only one more word.

The helicopter's rotor had almost stopped, though he could hear the whine of the turbines above the tank's own low muttering. A square door just behind the cockpit slid open and two men, baggy-bodied with tapering legs like all soldiers in modern combat dress, jumped down. They wore red airborne berets and carried submachine-guns slung from their shoulders. The first one raised a hand in the universal 'peace' sign and they walked forward. Maxim saw others at the doorway and faces at the windows along the helicopter's side.

He let the two get to twenty-five metres and held out his own hand: stop. They stopped and the leading one called in Arabic.

'Do you speak English?' Maxim called back.

That confused them. The leader didn't, the other knew enough to ask if they really meant English.

'Yes. English tank, English crew.' Except for Al-Hamedi, but he wanted to keep the issues simple. The leader hurried back to the helicopter. While he was conferring at the doorway, Maxim saw a big ramp door start to lower like a drawbridge from under the helicopter's tail boom.

'Co-ax,' he ordered. 'Tail door of helicopter – just miss it. Short burst. Fire.'

The turret jerked left and the soldier in front turned to see what it was aiming at, then the co-axial machine-gun snapped off a quick burst. The soldier swept his sub-machine-gun off his shoulder and into the aim – and saw Maxim's machine-gun pointing at his chest. He stayed frozen in an aggressive stance, but around the helicopter doorway there was arm-waving and silent shouting. The ramp door slowly lifted shut again.

Maxim hadn't even realised the door was there: it stretched the full width of the helicopter and could have loosed a dozen men in a couple of seconds.

'Sergeant, target the engines again.' The leader was galloping back towards them followed by a bare-headed man in flying overalls. When they reached the twenty-five-metre mark, the aircrewman called: 'What were you shooting about?'

'Because I'm not going to get myself surrounded. You

keep everybody else on board or you'll find yourself waiting for the next bus to Tel Aviv.'

'Okay, calm down. We want to talk.'

'Just two of you, then.'

As Maxim expected, the one dismissed was the one still holding his submachine-gun; he slung it reluctantly and trailed back towards the helicopter.

'I'm Major Maxim, British Army.' He didn't expect, or get, any names in return: the Israeli military tends to stay anonymous. 'And what are you doing here?'

That wasn't easy to answer. After some consultation, the airman said: 'You could say we've come to help. Like stopping the tank getting caught by 17th Armoured Brigade.' His English was faintly American and he had a loose-limbed American stance contrasting with the compact wide-shouldered paratrooper – a captain, Maxim thought. 'We knew you were on the loose but didn't know it was an English crew. How did you –?'

'Never mind. The point is, we're here and in charge. So if you'll just flutter off, we'll get on with it.'

The airman translated this but didn't wait for an answer. 'You'll never make it. You got yourself surrounded and the Saudi border's guarded – did you know that?'

'We know it. And what's your idea of help?'

'Look, you can't believe we're out to harm an English crew, right? We'll lift you out."

'The idea is to save the tank.'

'I'd say the idea is to stop it getting snitched and ending up in Moscow. We'll haul out any secret bits you can unscrew and blow the rest. We've got a demolition team.'

'Thoughtful of you.' And it was a believable offer, far more realistic than switching to the Land-Rover had been. 'We've got enough explosive ourselves to wreck anything secret. With your two penn'orth, we could rip it all apart.' He was interested to see what they'd say to that.

The two of them swapped quick, low comments in Hebrew; the captain didn't seem happy.

'No need,' the airman said cheerfully. 'We'll take the bits of the breech and fire control out for you.'

'For *us*?'

'Sure. They belong to you.' And we'd get them back, Maxim knew, after a few little delays (you know what red tape and paperwork these desk wallahs go in for, old boy) while Israeli experts photographed and measured and analysed every square millimetre of those bits. It wasn't his job to hand over the tank's secrets to *anybody*.

'No thanks. We'll press on ourselves. Sorry to have troubled you.'

The captain didn't need that translated; he said something quickly to the airman, who lost his cheerfulness.

'Sorry about this, but . . . our task's to stop the tank getting into the wrong hands. I don't want to sound unfriendly, but we're going to do just that. You've done a great job so far, but you're running out of luck – I mean, just look at yourself.' He waved a hand at the tank.

Maxim said nothing.

The captain spoke to the airman, who shook his head sadly. 'I don't want it to come to this, but we can stop you. We've got anti-tank weapons on board, too.'

'And *we've* got an anti-helicopter weapon staring down your throat. So far we've taken hits from a 105 and a TOW and they haven't stopped us, so you'd better be feeling lucky because we only have to *breathe* on you and what's left'll be as surrounded as anybody. Tell him that and then I'll tell you *my* conditions for not opening fire. Get on with it.'

Maxim's anger was real, not just the anger of the beast. Or so he hoped. And the anger of the paratroop captain was clear even at that distance.

The airman finished translating. 'What d'you want to say?'

'You – and him,' he jerked his head at the circling Phantom above, 'have done a great job in giving away our position. That's all the help you've been so far. So how about telling us something about 17th Armoured's positions?'

That needed more consultation. Then: 'There's three tanks on the edge of the sand about twenty kilometres north-west, and a clutch more spread out over the open ground to the west, further away. And there's something on the track due north of here, but we didn't get a close look at them.'

'All right. And when you get back, pass the situation to the British embassy.'

'You know I can't promise that.'

'And give us a packet of cigarettes.'

The airman stared, then grinned. In disgusted fury, the captain handed him a packet and the airman came close to throw them up.

'There you go. Would you really have shot us up?'

'Would you really have fired at us?'

'Just to immobilise you, maybe. We had orders.'

'I know. And *I* was thinking: however much the 17th Armoured wants to catch *us*, they'd divert a fair bit of force to capture a stranded Israeli unit. And I'm sure you'd keep them busy for some time.'

The airman looked thoughtful, then shook his head. 'But I still say you're wrong.'

'No. We just belong to different armies.'

28

The Snowflake Committee was lunching in situ. Somebody (Agnes had no doubt it was the girl from the communications office next door) had brought in a deep-sided wooden tray of sandwiches, sausage rolls and cans of soft drinks. Instinctively reacting as if it were a diplomatic buffet, they were eating standing up and chatting, skilfully balancing drooping paper plates and squashy plastic mugs.

'Libya,' Scott-Scobie was telling Sir Anthony, 'used to have something called Kitty-Cola.'

'What did it taste like?'

'God knows. I may have been young and adventurous in those days, but there are limits.'

George was missing, but there was a middle-aged woman whom Agnes recognised but couldn't place in that context. She was stoutish, wrapped in a dark blue silk dress that kept her bosom marginally above her waist, had a ruddy face and a strong splay of top teeth. She looked like an organiser, and seeing that she was shadowed by a polite-faced young man with a briefcase recalled to Agnes that she did in fact do her bit in trying to organise the Foreign Office.

'I don't know if you've met Miss Agnes Algar from my Service,' Giles introduced them. 'Dame Winifred Finn, Secretary of State at the Foreign Office *of course*.'

Agnes's file-card memory had already caught up: Number Two to Lord Purslane, having to explain foreign affairs in the Commons, before that at Trade, a Midlands constituency, husband in the construction business, hint of scandal over some contract but that was the construction business for you, blown over now, no apparent security risk . . .

They shook hands. 'Glad to see the Service hiring more women. Do they let you *do* anything there? Don't worry, Mr Giles, I'm not prying – well, not into your Service's affairs. I'm trying to find out what this Committee is *doing*. I hope you realise that, with Lord Purslane still at Chevening, I've had to field the Jordanian ambassador this morning and he's getting jolly agitated at the news coming out of Jordan – what little he's getting. How much more do we know?'

The Brigadier, as host, said: 'Very little, I'm afraid, Minister – although we don't know how much the Jordanian government knows.'

Scott-Scobie hitched his trousers and stepped into the breach. 'Apart from some outdated satellite photographs, I doubt we know any more than you do, Minister. Our prototype tank is on the run in south Jordan being chased by 17th Armoured Brigade, and we can't get in touch with it. That's all.'

'*All?* Why isn't this being handled by a Cabinet Committee?'

Sir Anthony, who saw his own job on the Committee (and the Committee knew it) as being to judge the moment when it started to achieve something and only then have the Cabinet Office hijack it, tried to point this out in anything but those words. Dame Winifred listened, frowning in the effort to interpret.

'I think what it amounts to,' Norman Sprague added, 'is that this Committee's function is essentially the collection of information and the establishment of a communications link. And so far, alas . . .' He saw his job as being the frank admission of failure by others.

Dame Winifred looked around them. 'There is an important policy issue here. For a start, who is actually making our policy? My Office or Defence? Who's here for Defence? Is it you, Brigadier?'

'Actually,' the Brigadier said, 'it's Mr George Harbinger, I don't know if you know him . . .'

'I've met him. Where is he?'

Sprague made an elaborate gesture of unveiling his wristwatch from his gold-linked white cuff. 'I'm afraid the pubs won't be shut for some little time yet, Minister.'

Sir Anthony smiled wanly, the Brigadier frowned, Agnes felt furious – at Sprague and George both.

Scott-Scobie just shook his head. 'Right now it doesn't matter where any of us are. Our policy in Jordan is being made by Major Harry Maxim. And we can't reach him to tell him to stop it.'

'Maxim? A Major Maxim? Who's he?'

There was a pause, then the Brigadier said: 'He's – probably – in command of the tank.'

'He broke the hotel siege the other day,' Scott-Scobie said. 'He's a useful man in a trouble spot.'

'And if it isn't a trouble spot already,' Sprague observed, 'it will be within five minutes.'

'Whereas it often takes Mr Sprague a full ten minutes,' Agnes said. 'But then, he doesn't risk anything in the service of his country except his manicure.'

There were several grins, and Sprague was quick enough to produce one of them. Dame Winifred glanced at Agnes, then said: 'Well, I'm glad to see you're one big happy family. But this revolt has been going on for the best part of a week now. The rest of the world has managed to keep out of it, except Syria, as usual, and us. *We* appear deliberately to have got involved. What earthly chance do we have to align our policy with the US or NATO or anybody else when that policy – and you said it – is being made by one man in a tank?'

Scott-Scobie asked promptly: 'What do you suggest we do, Minister?'

Dame Winifred suddenly realised they were all watching her with deferential, expectant smiles. 'Well – you've obviously tried radio . . . isn't there any other way?'

'None that we've been able to think of.' He waited, then

added: 'We *may* be able to relay a message through an American Stealth reconnaissance flight some time this evening, but only maybe. You've seen their ambassador: did he drop any hint that Jordan might move to put down the revolt? That would be a great help if it got 17th Armoured to pull back to defend Aqaba.'

'He said nothing about that and I can't see us proposing it to him; it would be yet more interference in Jordan's affairs.'

'It would still help us. You might put it to him that having the secrets of the tank in SovBloc hands, including Syria's, isn't in Jordan's interests.'

'How important is this Very Important Tank?'

George should have been there to field that one; instead, the Brigadier found himself saying: 'Well – we – I – don't know how far advanced the Soviets are with liquid propellant research . . . they could be four of five years behind the West . . .They'd make up those years in one jump . . .'

'In one small field of military technology. If they got it they wouldn't suddenly be able to hold the West to ransom or start World War Three with impunity?'

'We'd still prefer that they didn't get it,' the Brigadier said feebly.

'I'm sure, but we – I include Lord Purslane – don't believe the tank could be the main reason for the revolt; at best, a supplementary benefit. You can't really be thinking that Russia would take such a risk just for a piece of more-or-less conventional military equipment.'

'The timing of the revolt, Minister,' Scott-Scobie said doggedly. 'Nobody's yet come up with a better reason for that.'

'Scottie, are you still playing on our team or have you accepted a transfer fee from Defence?'

He clamped his mouth shut. Dame Winifred, somewhat appeased if no more informed, decided to make that her exit line, collecting her private secretary on the way.

Scott-Scobie slumped into a chair and slammed the flat

of his hand on the table. 'Where the *hell* is George? How do I come to be defending his Department, which got us into this ghastly mess, against one of my own ministers?'

There was a murmur of sympathy, then the members turned to root about in the lunch tray. Agnes tried to draw Giles aside. 'I've got something I'd like to tell you about before I tell the rest.'

'Oh? Something from your police friends or something you've done yourself?'

'Mostly I did it myself.'

Giles sighed. 'I seem to recall a little talk we had earlier today –'

'Yes, but it's still something they have to know.'

'You aren't actually an *ex officio* member of this Committee, you realise? I invited you along as one of my Department; I take the responsibility.'

'You may not want to. But they have to know.'

Giles took only a moment to decide. 'Very well: go ahead and tell them. I'll support you . . . as far as I can.'

'I know, Edwin. Right –' she turned to the table; 'Gentlemen, I wonder if I could . . . We've established that Mrs Katbah is a traitor, to her husband and Jordan, and we think we've found the contact man, Al-Warid.'

She saw the shock on their faces, heard Giles's quick intake of breath behind her. She ploughed on. 'I saw Mrs Katbah again and gave her some confidential and inaccurate information. The moment I'd gone she rang a number in St John's Wood and passed it on. The police have traced the number – it's in a block of flats – and are setting up some sort of surveillance.'

'Was her telephone tapped?' Sprague pounced.

'I did that myself, stuck a radio bug on the base and then recorded the intercept.'

'Is it still there?' Giles asked quickly.

'No. The policewoman on guard got in and removed it.' Charlie Redding had been absolutely furious about being forced to order that.

'Did you authorise this, Edwin?' Sprague asked.

'No, that was Miss Algar's own remarkable initiative.'
Giles had warned her how short-lived his support might
be, and she didn't blame him. If a subordinate of hers had
acted as she had done, she would have gone volcanic.

'So we have a totally unauthorised interception,'
Sprague began, relishing such an early revenge for her
manicure comment. 'Indeed, a criminal offence –'

'Let's leave the crucifixions until Easter, shall we,
Norman?' Scott-Scobie cut in. 'What does this give us?
Go on, Agnes, you've had time to think.'

'Mostly assumptions. Going back a bit, she was Katbah's
second wife, married less than three years. He was already
an influential soldier by then so an obvious target for
seduction, probably with no immediate aim in mind. When
they needed her, he hadn't talked to her – about where
the tank was – as they'd hoped. So they set up the kidnap
and torture instead, her rape was presumably faked to add
to the pressure – it didn't happen in front of him, remember
– and then when our people broke in, she survived and
the rest didn't.'

'Only *just* survived,' Sprague reminded them.

'Yes. She'd only learned about Zweiwindburg the same
time that the others did – but then she was in intensive
care for three days and couldn't pass it on. She only got a
telephone when she went into a private room yesterday
afternoon. She made her first call at 3.35. We assume it
was to the same contact she called just now, who may be
the man who called himself Al-Warid at the hotel. I'm just
calling him that for convenience.'

The Squadron-Leader had been doing some quick calculations at his own table. 'He only got the call at half past
five Jordan time. The 17th Armoured must have been
moving towards Zweiwindburg by midnight. That signal
couldn't have gone through Moscow and Damascus with
all the encoding and –'

'Why should it?' Agnes asked. 'Every now and then
somebody in espionage actually does something *simple*.
He gets on the phone and dials direct – usually to Moscow

or East Berlin, in this case I'd think Amman – and he tells them something. And all our surveillance and electronic bugs and computerised decryption machines can't do a damn thing about it. We may track him back in the end and it wouldn't work as a system, but in an emergency – and that's what the Zweiwindburg news was for them – you can't beat it. *We* can't beat it.'

'So you joined it instead,' Scott-Scobie said. They had listened to her quietly; now she wasn't the new girl in Intelligence, but somebody with nearly fifteen years experience in counter-intelligence. 'And we assume he's done the same with your new bit of news by now – incidentally, what was that?'

'I told Mrs Katbah we were in touch with the tank and had ordered it to Batn el Ghul station where a big American helicopter would meet it.'

Every head turned towards the map.

'Oh Lord,' the Brigadier muttered.

'Why Oh Lord? You said it was the best thing that could happen but certainly couldn't.'

'Yes, but I don't know about announcing that the Americans are helping us –'

'Forget it,' Scott-Scobie said briskly. 'If the 17th Armoured want to announce it, it's just a silly propaganda lie – and perfect proof that this Al-Warid is in touch with them. What are the police doing about him? Have they got a tap on his phone yet?'

'No,' Agnes said. 'They need a good reason to apply for an intercept warrant and the only reason they've got is evidence from my illegal tap.'

'Ah,' said Sprague with false sympathy, 'that does rather handicap us.'

'No it doesn't.' Scott-Scobie was still being brisk. 'It's your job to see your Minister signs that warrant. Tell him we all want it – the Cabinet Office, my Office, Defence, Giles's Service.'

'I still have to offer him some acceptable evidence –'

'*Fake* it, man. You and the police dream up some other

way they could have traced Al-Warid – Agnes'll tell you who the coppers are. And both of you get *on* with it. Good God, I never thought to see the day when I'd be telling the Home Office how to bypass the law.

'I'm sorry, Edwin,' he turned to Giles; 'I seem to have kidnapped your Girl Friday. But the greater good . . .'

'Not at all,' Giles murmured. 'She seems to be something of a free agent at the moment.'

Wearing a fixed smile, Sprague followed Agnes into the side room to find a less public telephone. The Brigadier, recalling that he was the nominal chairman of this Committee, sat down at his table and shuffled papers so as at least to look busy.

Sir Anthony dragged his chair up beside Scott-Scobie and Giles. 'Forgive me asking – and it's only a very small matter – but if you didn't authorise Agnes to plant that, ah, bug, then how did she get hold of it? Do your people sort of carry around such things as a normal . . . ?'

Giles gave a tight little smile. 'All agents collect such things. Stuff they've been issued with and pretend they've lost, or Russian kit they've found and not handed in – or they get it made up for them in the back room of some little electronics shop. We don't like it, but what can we do?'

'And if you looked in the back of your socks drawer,' Scott-Scobie grinned, 'you might even find some mementos of your own days in the field?'

'I'm afraid that's conceivable.'

'Just like soldiers,' Sir Anthony said reminiscently. 'Well, it's a rather ironic development.'

'How so?' Scott-Scobie asked.

'That if all Agnes says is true, we have a line of communication to 17th Armoured but still not one to our own, ah, force. The tank.'

'Oh yes. Is there anything we can do to exploit that further, Edwin? Feed this Al-Warid another load of bull?' Scott-Scobie asked.

'I've been thinking about that,' Giles said judiciously,

'and it seems to me rather risky. It depends on two un-knowns: whether, and how soon, 17th Armoured gets this information from Al-Warid – and the actual situation out there. If they all go galloping off to this Batn el Ghul station hoping to capture the tank and an American helicopter into the bargain, well and good.' He waved a hand at the map. 'It's a good thirty miles from the tank's last known position, and I imagine there's no reason why our Major Maxim would go that way at all. But if they know where our tank is now, they aren't going to charge off somewhere else, no matter what Al-Warid tells them.'

'Yes,' agreed Scott-Scobie sombrely; the flurry of news and activity was wearing off. 'And we're only guessing that the tank's still in one piece.'

Once Agnes had put Sprague in touch with Charlie Redding, there wasn't much more she could contribute. The old yen to be on the spot made her think of going over to St John's Wood and nosing in on the surveillance, but that would just get Redding even more annoyed. It was a difficult enough location anyway: one of the new blocks of flats near the Regent's Park mosque, mostly inhabited by rich Arabs and tricky for a Western face to penetrate, and on a main road where parked cars and vans would be illegal and obvious. The flat was in the name of an Egyptian family, hitherto regarded as respectable; perhaps Al-Warid (or whoever he really was) was a sub-tenant or flat-sitter.

While Sprague was still on the phone to the Yard, George came in carrying a handful of paper and wearing a comfortable expression. He gave a couple of signal flimsies to the girl, then smiled enquiringly at Agnes.

'What news on the Rialto and points east?'

'Some. Nothing from Jordan.'

'Ah, have I been missing something?'

'Yes.'

He frowned, puzzled. 'Do I sense a monosyllabic – isn't it absurd to have a five-syllable word to describe one syllable? – antagonism to your old guide and mentor?'

'You do.'

'And may I enquire –'

'Come outside, George.'

In the empty corridor, she looked at him coldly. 'Where have you been?'

'Mainly in touch with US Third Air Force and RAF Akrotiri about the Stealth overflight. God and mechanical gremlins willing, it should take off at 1650 our time.'

'George, Harry is out there in that tank.'

'My dear Agnes, I know that as well as you do. And you know I did try not to get him involved.'

'You could have got him ordered *not* to get involved.'

'Harry is *a soldier*; in the right circumstances, his *job* is to get involved. If he's the best man for the job then it's his duty –'

Agnes felt the fury gripping inside her, partly because she knew she was wrong about this, but so right about . . . She exploded. 'Then why can't you fucking well stay sober enough to be some use in keeping him alive?'

George gave a startled jerk, then slid easily into a weary, misunderstood tone. 'Oh really, I've had a couple of lunch-time snorts, but that doesn't mean –'

'A couple now and how many before that? A big neat one to get you normal in the morning? And a few more to see you through to lunch? When are you going to need another?'

Like a man tugging the wrinkles out of his waistcoat, George took a self-conscious grasp on his dignity. 'You may have seen me go over the top a few times, but I honestly don't think it's as bad as –'

'*Honestly?* – bollocks! I've seen it happen to others, you aren't the first or last, you're just another Whitehall drunk.'

George flinched; a uniformed messenger wheeled a cart of folding chairs around a corner, ignored them, and trundled on down the corridor.

'D'you think everybody in there doesn't *know*?' Agnes opened fire again. 'They're making jokes about it. D'you think Annette doesn't know? You talk differently, make different gestures, by this time of day. Every damn day I see you.'

'I'm sorry, but Annette does not come into this discussion.'

'That's up to you and her, she can stay with you until you melt for all I care. And I'm not trying to cure you. I'm just begging you, begging you, not to touch another drop until Snowflake is over. No longer than that . . . I used to admire you, George. You can still be good, when you let yourself be.'

She went around the corner with her sheepskin jacket swinging like a cape.

George walked slowly to the toilet at the other end of the corridor and washed his face in cold water, then drank some. Then he looked at himself in the mirror – something he rarely did. Could they tell? He was a bit fatter in the face than he should be, his eyes a bit puffy and watery, but he always looked like that, and he certainly wasn't always . . . Damn it, he was *not* drunk. He'd had a few, yes, and had needed them – he had long since admitted that to himself. And everybody knew he drank, but they didn't know how much, that was something he didn't admit even to himself. But he could carry it, or at least hide it . . . couldn't he?

He felt shy of going directly into the Snowflake office, so went back through the communications room and drank a cup of coffee. That, at least, should make the difference. He went on through.

'Hello, George,' Scott-Scobie said cheerfully. 'Things have been happening while you've been pub-crawling.'

29

When the air filters clogged this time, the symptoms came on quicker and fiercer; as Timbrell had said, they were throwaway items that should have been replaced already. They kept going just long enough to get back into the dunes to the south, out of sight. Another round of coffee while they waited for the engine to cool, then the crane to lift the engine covers and Timbrell and Al-Hamedi began the monotonous banging.

Maxim stood in the hatchway keeping watch. With the tank still, it was a welcome change of position once the pain of making the move had worn off. The sun was low enough to dazzle him from the south-west, and the sides of the steeper dunes were in shadow; the wind was only a breeze, not enough to ruffle the sand or affect his hearing. He heard the helicopter before he saw it.

'Stop!' he shouted. Then: 'Helicopter, west. Get closed up.'

He brought the binoculars onto it, flaring against the sun: if it was that damned Super-Frelon again with another unrefuseable offer . . . But it was smaller, weaving above the dunes and obviously without benefit of high reconnaissance to guide it. The Alouette of the morning? – he had wondered why that hadn't turned up again.

The air filters were slammed into place and Timbrell scrambled up to trip the crane and let the first engine cover down with a rattle and crash. Not bothering to start the auxiliary engine, he hand-cranked the chain back up and Al-Hamedi hooked it to the second. Rattle, crash – and they were ready to move. But was there any point to moving?

'Alec, don't start up.' Their camouflage might just work, there was no need to throw up a puff of dark smoke against the bright sand. Al-Hamedi, denied the engine power to swing the main gun and co-axial, leaned out of his hatchway, hauled the Gimpy from the rack and balanced it across the turret. No need to ask him if he was prepared to fire at the supposedly loyal but hijacked pilot. Maxim swung the mounted machine-gun.

Not that rifle-calibre machine-guns brought down many helicopters. They were fleeting and the range was pure guesswork: you needed missiles or radar-aimed cannon. But you can't get lucky unless you fire.

The Alouette straightened over the stony desert, probably seeing at least snatches of their trail etched with shadow by the low sun. It was almost level with them when it twisted in flight and they had been seen.

No need to give fire orders, either. They both squeezed off short bursts, echoed by the clatter of cartridge cases on the armour. Incredibly, the helicopter reared, seemed to spin around its own rotor and swooped out of sight behind a dune.

'Alec, start up! Move off! Left – never mind, just get into the open.'

They ground ponderously out of the dunes and the helicopter sat maybe 400 metres away, bubble cockpit shining and blades winking in slow rotation. Two figures jumped out; the tank charged – slowly – towards them.

Maxim fired a burst that ripped dust behind the helicopter's tail. Now with power, Al-Hamedi brought the turret round and the co-axial added a burst near its nose. Bracketed, the two figures stopped and raised their hands. Two others climbed out slowly and put their hands up, too. Nobody seemed to be injured.

What the hell do we do with prisoners? Maxim wondered. Well, first we interrogate them, then . . . well, we interrogate them, anyway.

He had the tank stopped about a hundred metres away. 'Sergeant, I think you'd better deal with this helicopter crew.'

Al-Hamedi found a submachine-gun and walked forward, staying clear of Maxim's line of fire. Two of the crew wore drab overalls and no headgear – presumably the airmen – one of the others wore a red beret and a combat jacket, the second a black beret and a pullover. Al-Hamedi made those two drop their pistol belts, then searched them; the aircrew seemed unarmed.

After a few moments, he made three of them lie down and brought one of the aircrew back to the tank.

'He is Lieutenant Masri, the pilot. He says that he and the other are loyal to the King. He says also the helicopter is not properly damaged, not much. It will fly.'

'Oh?' Maxim looked at Masri.

'You hit us somewhere on the tail boom, I think. We felt it and I made it an excuse to pretend we were out of control and landed. So here we are.' He was young, small-built and eager to please but nervous with it. Maxim wasn't surprised at his English: it was the language of aeroplanes, even French-built ones.

'One other,' Al-Hamedi said, 'is Major Zyadine.' He hadn't lost any of his normal suspicious expression.

'Is he? Good.' Then, to Masri: 'Have you reported seeing us – our position?'

The answer wasn't quite that simple, but Masri was anxious to talk, and did. It seemed that five minutes ago they had reported they were following a trail eastwards. Yes, they had seen the Land-Rovers, bodies and debris, but hadn't landed: the sand dunes made that tricky, and Zyadine had been in a hurry. No, they hadn't known the tank was damaged. Yes, they had originally thought it would be heading north – Maxim nodded appreciatively to Al-Hamedi – and had wasted twenty minutes searching up that way.

'What have you been doing all day? We saw you early this morning . . .'

'We flew a big search then, and I put down Major Zyadine at the command post on the track from Wadi Rum. They have several vehicles there now, about ten kilometres north of here –'

'Any tanks?'

'There are none there, but they have three Centurions at the edge of the sand about twenty kilometres away. The Major told them to wait there until he had found you and then he would guide them. Yes, I had put the Major down there this morning, then we had to go back to Aqaba to refuel. While we were there I managed to make an electrical fault – they thought we had sabotaged it but the ground crew said it was normal, they are also loyal, so we could not fly again, and Lieutenant Asfar was wanting to shoot me' – he glanced viciously back towards the others – 'but you can see God was merciful. We got back to the command post an hour ago.'

'How much fuel have you got left?'

'I think nearly two hours.'

'Okay. Take a seat over there.' He waited until Masri was out of hearing. 'Well, do we believe him?'

Al-Hamedi's whole lifetime had been in a Kingdom of plots and revolts. 'He maybe is tricking us.'

'What do they gain by landing? They could have stayed in the air and reported everything about us: position, battle damage, direction. And what he says about 17th Armoured's positions tallies with what the Israelis said.'

Timbrell had crawled out of his hatch to join in the conversation. 'I'd want to be sure the helicopter really is okay. If we did shoot it down, they could have concocted a line of bull to feed us.'

'Take a look at it, see if you can tell. Sergeant, you interrogate the observer and see if he tells the same story, particularly about 17th Armoured's positions. But if it's all true, we've got ourselves a helicopter and two hours' fuel; what do we do with it?'

They looked at each other. 'One thing,' Maxim added,

and called to the pilot: 'Oi! Lieutenant – how many people does your helicopter carry?'

'Five. That is with the pilot, me.' He had taken Maxim literally and was sitting in the desert off to their right.

'Thank you . . . Yes, I'd been thinking, but it doesn't quite work.'

'He could get all of us except Zyadine and the other one up to Ma'an,' Timbrell said, watching Maxim carefully.

'Yes, but I don't want to let go of Zyadine: he's right at the heart of this revolt. Without him . . . well, it'll be that much weaker.' He had no wild dream of collapsing the revolt by capturing its keystone personality – yet a revolt did depend on personalities, far more than any army unit does. Take a major out of a brigade and it would literally close ranks and carry on, being designed to take casualties – overmanned, if you like. But take a leader out of a revolt, one of the handful who have invented that revolt and persuaded others to break their oath and follow . . .

'At least it'll weaken the hunt for us,' Maxim went on. 'This tank can't be the central purpose of the revolt and maybe not all his chums are as keen on it as he is. Or on spreading so much of their force over a hundred kilometres of desert to try and find us. No: I don't want to let Zyadine go.'

Al-Hamedi, who took a more simplistic view of revolts, said helpfully: 'I will shoot him if you wish, Major.'

'No, thanks. Your government wouldn't thank you, either. They'd probably like him for a trial. And I wouldn't mind us getting the credit for capturing him: we've been running up a bill in Jordanian kit knocked out.'

'What it boils down to,' Timbrell said flatly, 'is we can't leave the helicopter observer alone here with the other 17th Armoured character. And we can't split the three of us; we all go or we all stay. It's the fox and the goose and the bag of corn.'

'Except the helicopter won't be coming back; I don't think it can refuel at Ma'an, there isn't an airfield there.'

'D'you want to send Zyadine to Ma'an, then?'

'Not much. We don't know what units are there and they may not react quick enough to be much help. I want to keep Zyadine here and exploit him ourselves – by radio.'

'How the hell do you fit a prisoner in the tank?'

'The speed we're going, he can walk. And if he can't keep up, he can run. And if we break down again, he can bloody well work. Right, here's my Thought For The Day: we send the other character, Lieutenant Whatsit, with the helicopter crew to Ma'an. But first they do a proper recce of the area and give us a sitrep on 17th Armoured positions. After that . . . well, Ma'an'll know the situation and have our radio channel. I don't think the helicopter'll be much more use unless it can refuel. But it'll be dark soon, anyway.'

'That's okay by me,' Timbrell said, looking at Al-Hamedi. The Sergeant said: 'Yes, Major. I will talk with the helicopter observer now.'

Timbrell watched him go. 'I don't really know why I'm going along with this. That helicopter's the best chance we've had to blow the tank and get out, the original mission. But we've come so far – I'd just like to finish the course.'

Maxim nodded, but it sounded phoney to him. It was the sort of thing people said, not what they did.

'And maybe I'm confident that you'll get us through,' Timbrell went on. 'You're a good commander, Harry, even of a tank. I don't know if it's training or what, but I know I never had it; I was always having to act it. You've got it. Mind – if you were a major in the Armoured Corps you'd have to command about sixteen tanks, not just one. That might stretch you a bit. I'll go and see if this helicopter really is damaged. If it is, you'll have to have a new Strategic Thought.'

'Thank you,' Maxim murmured, but not until Timbrell couldn't hear.

30

The Squadron-Leader was pinning up a new set of satellite pictures – when he could get them away from the Committee members – being meticulous with his map references and coloured wool. But the only photograph showing the MBT90 was in the Brigadier's hands and he was in the middle of a Committee scrum. It had been taken soon after the last shots had been fired in the dunes and showed Al-Hamedi walking past the second Land-Rover towards Maxim, sitting wounded on the dune above, with the immobilised tank 200 metres south. Only it didn't show that to them: nobody knew what to make of it, although everybody except Agnes and Sir Anthony Sladen had an opinion.

Agnes knew nothing about war; Sir Anthony was old enough to have fought in one. 'If you'd taken a picture in the middle of any great battle – Waterloo, the Somme, D-Day – you'd see people just standing around, sitting down for a smoke, lying down for a bit of shut-eye. History doesn't photograph well.'

'*Something* must have happened,' Agnes muttered, wondering which of the blurred little figures – upright, sitting or lying down – could be Maxim. She wanted to turn the page, see what had happened next – but there was no next page. And the picture was hours old, he could be dead now if he hadn't been then. I've been in love before this, she thought defensively, I can be in love again. *He* was in love with somebody who's dead, so I can do it, too. Stupid bloody soldier.

'*Can* I have it now?' appealed the Squadron-Leader. 'You can see it just as well up on the board, that's what it's *for*.'

Nobody took any notice. It was George's turn to squint myopically at the fuzzy rectangle of the tank, with Scott-Scobie waiting for his opinion; George had been in the (peacetime) Armoured Corps.

'They must have *run over* one of the Land-Rovers; the wreckage can't be from the tank . . . but you can't tell if they're stopped or not. I think they've been hit . . .' But that was the bright scratch left by the Saudi tank's gunfire; the pile of broken track links was at the tank's north-east corner, in its own shadow. 'You just can't tell.'

The girl from next door came in with a new signal and while they were distracted, the Squadron-Leader pounced on the photograph.

'Another signal from the *Alamein*,' the Brigadier read out. 'Just half an hour old. Still no contact, but they've picked up what they think must be Israeli aircraft on radar, passing into Jordan just north of the Saudi border. Heading east when they lost them. One is probably a helicopter. That's it.'

'Israel getting into the act,' Sir Anthony said. 'Everybody seems to be focused on that tank. Us, the Jordanians, Americans, Saudis, Syrians and Russians by proxy and now the Israelis. The poor buggers are getting to be a what's-its-name. You know what I mean.'

'Sorry, I don't,' George said politely.

'You know, what you used to call on the artillery net when you spotted an important target of opportunity. No, you wouldn't know,' he continued in his church-lesson-reading voice, 'you spent your time messing about in inflammable tin cans, too. You could bring every gun in a division, hundred or more, down on a single target inside five minutes. They've changed the phrase now, call it something else since NATO. Means the same thing, though: everybody concentrating on some unfortunate bunch who've stuck their noses out of cover.'

'It sounds right, whatever it is,' the Brigadier said.

'Uncle Target,' Sir Anthony remembered. 'That was it: Uncle Target.'

In the end, it was easier to tie a greasy piece of rope from Zyadine's waist to a ring-bolt at the back of the tank and perch him on the engine decking. The turret was swung to the left, which put the barrel aiming north, and Maxim had changed hatchways with Al-Hamedi, so the Sergeant could look forward and Maxim back – at Zyadine among other sights.

'Nice day for a revolution,' Maxim called. 'I mean, as days and revolutions go.' Zyadine just sat there, the shapeless combat jacket shaping itself around him, the way uniform does to a serious soldier. He wore the British paratroop badge, though in the Jordanian position on the left breast, so he must have done a British course and come out proud of passing it. Useful to know these things. Maxim had no badges on his borrowed jacket and was glad of it, hoping Zyadine didn't remember they had ever met. He wanted to be blank, an unknown.

'Harpoon,' the headset said, and began reporting nothing closer than the command post, fifteen kilometres north, although the three Centurions were closing up to it from the west. Roughly paralleling their own course, Maxim judged, and probably faster.

'Helicopter, take a look further west to locate vehicles, including tanks, reported south of the Jebel umm Sahm area. After that, hop off home.'

He thought he saw a distant bumblebee heading for the setting sun; there was no point in guarding the PVD screen, not in this territory and with a helicopter watching far further.

'Your Centurion troop is heading for the CP,' he told Zyadine. 'Presumably obeying your orders.' No reaction. 'I tell you what, why don't you give one of them to your Russian friends? They're just peasants, they wouldn't notice the difference.' The Centurion was forty years older in design than the MBT90, older than Maxim himself. But some military designs lasted: the pistol he had tucked into his arm sling was a Browning P35, which stood for 1935.

'I don't understand,' he went on, 'why an Arab should sell himself to the Russians. I think of Arabs as a proud people who believe in God, but I suppose . . .'

'I am not sold to the Americans, like you.' That was a reaction.

Maxim grinned. 'So you are sold to the Russians, then? Pity.'

'You think my revolution is because of some Russians?'

'*Your* revolution? You're only a major. You do what you're told, like me. People who make revolts are far more important. Like Russians.'

'I am a leader –' then Zyadine stopped.

'Just camel-shit turned up by a Russian ploughboy,' Maxim said soothingly. When you stuck a bayonet in somebody – he never had, yet – the training said you twisted it to make it easier to pull out. But he didn't want to pull it out, just keep twisting it.

'Major Maxim' – so Zyadine had remembered him, which was a pity – 'our revolution is for God. You do not understand that. You can kill me, but that is God's will. I know your country, I know your Army and I ask, what do you fight for? It is not to get rich; I know British officers are not rich. It is not for your rich leaders, I have heard you speak of them and you despise them. And you do not fight for God: I never hear you British soldiers speak of God. You fight because you are a soldier, that is all, and you know soldiers must fight like a gun knows it must shoot. But when it stops shooting, when it is broken, it is nothing. Like you, Major Maxim, when you stop shooting, when you die, what will God see then? Nothing.'

Twisting the bayonet hadn't had quite the effect intended. Maxim kept a calm smile on his face and asked: 'And who ordered you to capture this tank? God – or the Russians?'

'It is God's will,' Zyadine said firmly.

'No, I think it was Major Zyadine's will. You didn't trust God enough – you decided to have the revolt at this time so you could capture this tank and buy Russian support with it. And because of that you've probably made a mess of your revolution.'

The left earpiece said: 'Harpoon, this is helicopter. We have located force approximately thirty kilometres west of you, moving towards you. Identify two Khalids, two Centurions, two personnel carriers, three Land-Rovers. Over.'

'Thank you, helicopter. Head for Ma'an now. Good luck. Harpoon out.'

'Good luck, Harpoon.'

He needed to look at the map. 'Sergeant, there's no enemy closer than fifteen kilometres. Traverse right so you can watch the prisoner. I'm going down to look at the map.'

'I will look at the map, Major. I understood the helicopter.'

'Okay, carry on.'

The stony desert petered out and they began swaying gently between more sand dunes. The higher ones threw long dark brown shadows now, and their south-western slopes were becoming blood-orange as the sun touched the high horizon of dust. Desert afternoons usually ended like this, itchy and grubby; it took the night to lay the dust and restore peace and distance.

He found one of the Israeli cigarettes and got it alight one-handed. Zyadine wasn't going to try and jump him; he was too busy clinging to the engine grilles, not wanting to fall off and be towed through the sand.

The description they'd been using of him as 'Chinese' wasn't so far wrong, less because of the high cheekbones than the wide face. Not one of the desert tribes, probably Palestinian; probably why he'd had to prove himself by going in for the pointless paratroop training (Maxim had done it himself, but knew that no army was going to risk mass parachute drops from slow transport aircraft ever

245

again). Just a way of proving you're something special – and Zyadine had done that.

And then helped organise the revolt of a whole brigade. Now *that* was something Maxim had never tried, and Zyadine knew he had already made a mark on history that Maxim never would. And would now die content; if Maxim took the Browning and pointed it between Zyadine's eyes, he wouldn't flinch, and would end up a happy corpse towed behind the tank.

But given a choice, his corpse would be happier if it could have done a little more first. Have actually captured the tank, used it to bribe the Russians into – what? Pushing the Syrians to tear down the Jordanian monarchy, boot the King's severed head in the dust? – there were precedents in Jordan for that. But he'd probably settle for anything less, just a little extra stretch of his life to achieve a little more . . . It might be useful that he had classified Maxim as a simple I-am-a-gun soldier.

Timbrell said: 'I don't know if anybody's noticed, but we have to make a decision; do we go north or south of this?'

Stretching up to look over the turret that lay crosswise to his view forward, Maxim could see a scarred heap of rock poking up ahead, with a little ring of grey-green bushes that fed off the rainwater spilling down it and a long sand slope on every side.

Go south of it, not that it mattered much.

'Driver,' Al-Hamedi said, 'left stick . . . go to north of the hill.'

It didn't matter much. 'Sergeant, can I see the map?'

Al-Hamedi stretched across the turret to pass it. It was still horribly small-scale, drawn for whoosh-zoom aeroplane warfare, but perhaps nobody had bothered to map this part of the world for anything else. He located the heap of rock as the only spot height within twenty kilometres: that put them less than ten kilometres from the Ma'an road and railway. Then a few kilometres south on the road to the border control post. Probably Alec would like to run on a road, however poor, for the sake of the repaired track.

And three Centurions, still about fifteen kilometres away at least to the north-west, then the clutch from the west which couldn't be closer than twenty-five kilometres. They were boxed north and west, their bluff of heading north had worn off, and Zyadine's earlier reports of the fight in the dunes and so on had given away their position fairly accurately. But nothing could catch up with them for . . . for what?

'Anybody,' he said on the intercom, 'what speed can a Centurion do?'

'Bloody slow,' Timbrell said, 'but it was a bit before my time.'

'It's chasing you now. Sergeant?'

'I think thirty-five kilometres on the road, perhaps twenty-five on sand like here. I do not command a Centurion for a long time.'

A bit before all their times. A real old soldier of a tank – hadn't he heard a story about the first prototypes being rushed across Europe in April 1945 in the vain hope of getting themselves shot at before the war ended? Yet despite missing that Seal of Approval, the Centurion had become an export success, sold around the world and still, much-modified and up-gunned, in service with armies like Jordan's . . .

Good God, *that* was why Timbrell hadn't wanted to leave this tank and take the helicopter out! All that bull about wanting to 'finish the course' – but he wanted to finish it in his own tank and *Then will he strip his sleeve and show his scars, and say you too can have an arm as tough as mine, just a million quid apiece, only ten per cent down, sign here* . . . Starting with the British Army, but tomorrow – the world.

'Are you all right, Harry?' Timbrell was asking, and Maxim realised his choked laughter had carried through the intercom.

'Sorry, Alec, sand in the throat.' Timbrell the company

man – yet why not? He'd been a company man far longer than an Army man, and did it matter? Well, yes, understanding a man's motivation was vital to predicting when that motivation might run out. But he knew where Timbrell stood – or wanted to: right next to this very tank at the next British Army Equipment Exhibition.

But he wasn't at all sure why Al-Hamedi was still here. Not for Timbrell's reasons, nor Maxim's – whatever *they* were – and he wasn't on Zyadine's holy warpath. But if they kept moving, in not much more than an hour motivations would have stopped mattering. They were doing about ten kilometres an hour, the Centurions catching up at about fifteen – if they were heading in the right direction. They were out of touch, and every minute, every metre, got more so. That was just fine.

31

The satellite photographs were now safely pinned to the board, their coloured wool connections to precise map points giving them a spurious significance, but their brief importance had soaked away like a shower in the desert. Still parched of hard news and communication, the Committee had drifted away and sat down. Even the Squadron-Leader had stopped making deductions, even to himself.

'Agnes,' Scott-Scobie called, 'get onto your rozzer chums and see if they've learnt anything from their surveillance. Oh all right, you too, Norman,' – as Sprague began to look hurt at being bypassed. But it was a futile time-filling exercise, as they all knew.

'If they captured the tank,' Scott-Scobie pondered, 'would they broadcast it – to show they'd revenged their losses? Or just tell the Syrians quietly and let them tell the Russians?'

Nobody knew. 'I suppose,' Sir Anthony said, 'the Russians *are* behind it all? It may be just wishful thinking that for once they mightn't be, but . . .'

'Who else wants the tank? It has to be a serious industrial power.'

'Oh, I'm not saying they don't *want* it,' Sir Anthony placated quickly, 'just questioning whether they'd take all the risks inherent in starting a revolt mainly for that purpose.'

'You're sounding like the Pantomime Dame.'

'Out of the mouths of babes and Ministers,' Giles said. 'They do sometimes get things right. My Service hasn't turned up any trace of Russian involvement, not in the revolt itself nor in the Katbah kidnapping and torture. Not even in communications, if Agnes is right about Al-Warid calling Jordan direct.'

Scott-Scobie grunted; the fact that the Secret Intelligence Service *hadn't* discovered something proved nothing to him. Nothing new, anyway.

But Sir Anthony had been encouraged by Giles's support. 'Wouldn't one have expected the Russian approach to be more along the lines of suborning the tank designers at Coventry? Or has the KGB over here gone native and called a strike?'

'They'll be suborning away as well,' Scott-Scobie said crossly, looking round for allies. 'George, you've been remarkably quiet since the pubs shut.'

In fact it had been since Agnes's denunciation, and George was still reluctant to draw attention to himself. 'Does it matter if Moscow's involved or not?' he mumbled. 'They'll be involved as soon as 17th Armoured gets its hands on the tank. And we can do bugger-all; did you want us to do a different sort of bugger-all?'

'Coming from the Department which decided to invade Jordan without even bothering to tell the Foreign Office . . .' Scott-Scobie began, but since he wasn't sure how to finish, he welcomed Agnes back into the room instead. 'Anything new?'

'Just the phone calls made from the St John's Wood flat in the last few days.' She held a piece of paper. 'Two to Jordan, both the same number in Amman; one about this time yesterday, the other two hours ago. That isn't evidence you can take into court, but . . .'

'It's good enough for us,' Scott-Scobie said. 'How's the surveillance going?'

'It's set up, what they can of it. They haven't got into the block yet, but the telephone intercept's on line. Al-Warid's still there, all right.'

'Presumably sticking by the phone *and* keeping his face off the streets,' Giles observed.

'We haven't got enough evidence for a conviction yet,' said Sprague, who had come back with Agnes, 'but we can arrest him without charge and see what turns up in the next three days.'

Agnes turned on him. 'Norman, for *God's sake* don't let Charlie Redding do anything like that. And don't let your Minister start wanting quick returns for the intercept warrant and police man-hours either.'

A bit taken aback, Sprague said: 'I would have thought you, of all people, would want to see him and Mrs Katbah brought to justice or, if we can't achieve that, at least, injustice. But for them, your Major would probably have got clean away by now.'

'I know, and I'd like to have her raped with red-hot pokers. But not yet.'

'What do you see happening to them in the long run?' Giles asked quietly.

Agnes was wary of any invitation from Giles to stick her neck out, but she was still the only one of them whose job had involved collecting evidence for prosecutions. 'If the hotel receptionist identifies Al-Warid and there's some corroboration from fingerprints on the luggage he left there, we might tie him into the murder of Katbah. But it'll be thin stuff to give a jury. And we'd have to arrest him and put him in an identification parade – and suppose the receptionist didn't identify him? As for helping the revolt, that's no crime in Britain.'

'It would certainly be enough to make him an undesirable and deport him,' Sprague said.

'That's not much when we started with murder. And we couldn't send him specifically to Jordan. Syria would take him happily.'

Giles nodded. 'Then what do you suggest?'

'Keep him on ice, keep surveillance going. When this is over, he'll be working for somebody else. Let's see who his contacts are.'

'And Mrs Katbah?'

'Much the same, except let Jordan do it; she'll be going

back there when she's fit. The only evidence we've got against her is her tie-up with Al-Warid, and if we don't charge him . . .'

'To say nothing of your illegal tap,' Sprague said. 'Of which, I agree, we say nothing.'

Agnes smiled dismissively.

Scott-Scobie looked around. 'Well, it sounds good sense, but it doesn't do much to slake our thirst for vengeance.'

Giles said gently: 'Of course, there may always be another approach.'

Agnes nodded: the others looked puzzled.

Giles said: 'It depends on the outcome. If we have a happy ending, we could always circulate – quietly – how grateful we are to Al-Warid and Mrs Katbah for their co-operation. That would bring them enemies I would not, myself, care to have. But we are not going to do that, are we, Agnes? Because that would use them up, destroy them as potential sources of information merely for the brief thrill of revenge. And that's why we aren't going to try and feed more disinformation down this Al-Warid's throat. As Agnes herself says, he is money in the bank – whilst unspent.'

Al-Hamedi said: 'Driver, stop.' Then: 'Major, there is a building in front.'

Standing high and using the binoculars, Maxim could just make out a flat-topped shape, probably built of sandstone since only the shape identified it among the dunes. As usual, its range and therefore size were pure guesswork, but it must be on the road or railway.

'Driver, advance,' Al-Hamedi said.

'I should go right a bit, come at it with the sun dead behind us,' Maxim suggested, and Al-Hamedi gave more orders, taking them out of sight again, then stopped. He got Zyadine down, tied his hands behind his back and then on a fifteen-foot leash to a hook on the tank's front. Zyadine would be light on his feet with the tank snuffling at his collar: Maxim remembered walking ahead in the dark, last night.

Al-Hamedi climbed back, still in the commander's position, and slid down to watch the PVD screen and swing the gun forward. 'Major, will you be gunner? Load shot, target the building, take the range.'

It made a change, and Al-Hamedi was an experienced tank commander, but Maxim wondered a little at his own demotion. Being effectively one-handed, he made a poorer gunner than he did a commander, but he didn't think there was anything nasty at that building anyway. Dutifully, he punched the right buttons, pressed his forehead on the periscope sight and triggered the laser as the building came back into view. 845 metres.

Of course, they could have bypassed the building altogether and joined the road further south. But there was just a chance it might be the border post itself: the map marked the frontier hereabouts as 'approximate' and that applied to his estimate of their own position, too. Range 720. He pressed the button to transfer that to the gun.

Range 650. 580. 530.

'Stop, gunner, dust left of building, fire!' The heavy gun jiggled with absurd coquettishness as Maxim swerved it left, saw a smear of dust in the narrow-angled sight, tracked to the front of it – and a dune filled the sight.

'Target not seen,' he reported.

Al-Hamedi glared at him from under the breech.

'Did you see what it was?' Maxim asked, now looking at the wider angle of the PVD screen.

'I saw only dust, but –'

'It looks like the road runs higher than the desert, around here. The building's probably at the highest point, and he took off along the other side of the road, out of sight.' A watcher in a wheeled vehicle, probably with a radio. Zyadine would have ordered him down from the command post – only about 25 kilometres away – just as a backstop. Maxim would have done the same: from the roof of the building you could probably see the road a good way north and south.

So 17th Armoured were in contact with them again. A pity, but the frontier couldn't be more than a few kilometres south of here. 'Should we move off again?' he suggested.

Timbrell had the tank moving before Al-Hamedi gave the order. Naughty, Alec, but Maxim knew he should have made it clear he had passed command to Al-Hamedi. Oh well, just a few kilometres.

Now Al-Hamedi was standing up, saying: 'Driver, slow – there is a railway line in front. Driver, find your own place to cross.'

This would be the old pilgrim railway built by the Turks from Damascus right down to Medina, site of Mohammed's tomb, and which Lawrence and the Bedouin tribes had spent so many happy hours blowing up in 1917–18. It had stayed that way for nearly seventy years, and even now the repaired section only reached a few miles into Saudia. And in that time, the camel track had become a paved road and the huge five-axle trucks had taken over from the wood-burning railway engines that had stripped Jordan of its forests. But they still had to cross the line to reach the road.

Keeping the gun-sight on the building – just over 200 metres now and, he was sure, unoccupied – with an impression of some grey concrete structures beyond it, Maxim felt Timbrell position the tank for the crossing.

He hadn't really thought of railway lines being awkward for tanks. But they are unyielding narrow strips of steel, unnatural to a beast built to tackle mostly natural obstacles, and he heard the extra clatter as the tracks rolled over the lines – and the gunshot snaps as track pins in the repaired and now over-tensioned left track parted. And there they were, blocking the line quite as effectively as any of El Lawrence's demolitions could have done.

32

'Say again,' the Brigadier shouted at the telephone, 'this is a terrible line . . . I SAID THIS IS A TERRIBLE LINE! Now I'm getting you . . . Good God, is that really noduff? . . . Why did they do that? . . . How badly? . . . Have you got a map reference? . . .'

It gradually dawned on the Committee that this wasn't another routine query from the Brigadier's normal office or his wife asking if they were free for dinner with the Mathiesons on the 16th. But even then they did nothing so gauche as to cluster round asking 'What's happening?' and 'Who is that?' They had both personal and official dignity to maintain, so they just sat or stood where they were, stopped breathing, and did their damndest to overhear.

At last he put down the phone, stared disbelievingly at his notes and looked up at their silent faces. 'That was Colonel Jeffreys, our man in Amman. The Jordanian Army's been onto him, they've got a helicopter crew, loyalists who'd been forced to fly for the rebels, who say they made a phoney forced landing by the tank – about two hours ago. And they had a Major Zyadine – he was Brigade Major to the 17th Armoured and probably one of the ring-leaders – with them. And . . . well, Major Maxim took Zyadine prisoner and sent the helicopter back with the news to Ma'an.'

After a moment of digestive silence, they forgot their dignity and exploded with questions. The Brigadier stalked through them to the map and planted a finger on it. 'There, just about there, ten miles west of the road and railway. Two hours ago.'

He's alive, Agnes thought, *alive*. Or was two hours ago. Wait a minute: why hadn't the helicopter brought them out? But somebody had already asked that.

'It seems the helicopter couldn't carry the tank crew and Zyadine, and Maxim wanted to hang onto him.'

'Is the helicopter going back?'

'Jeffreys said the Jordanian government was thinking about it, but probably wouldn't do anything until tomorrow morning. It's about dark out there now. Oh' – he glanced at Agnes – 'he said Maxim had his arm in a sling but the helicopter crew said he seemed okay. The tank was a bit knocked about but rolling all right.'

Wild thoughts were churning in Agnes's mind. If Harry was just a bit wounded then that was all right because it was now somebody else's turn to get hurt . . . And if he was wounded badly enough he'd be out of the Army and nothing like this would ever happen again . . . She shut her eyes for a moment and told herself not to be such a silly illogical little schoolgirl. Nothing, really, had changed – however much the rest of the Committee was having orgasms about it.

'He confirmed the tank was guarding the original radio channel, the one the *Alamein*'s been using, so we know how to contact him if we get the recce plane overhead.'

'Can the Jordanian Army get in touch with him?' Agnes asked.

'Very much doubt it. Ma'an's about a hundred kilometres away.'

George asked: 'Did Jeffreys say anything about the Jordanian Army making any move?'

'No. I didn't want to ask him, bearing in mind it was an open line going through an Amman switchboard, but he'd have dropped a hint if he'd heard anything like that.'

'They don't actually *have* to move,' George muttered. 'They only have to say they're *going* to move. That'd scare the rebels back to Aqaba.'

'Think on, old boy,' Scott-Scobie said. 'The Jordanians aren't going to lose face by saying they'll do something then deliberately not. Probably a better chance of the revolt collapsing if it *is* spread out across the desert. They've already lost one of their leaders – I wonder what Harry wants with him? Has he got his Special Air Service pocket torture kit on him?'

'Oh for Christ's sake!' George snapped, then heaved himself up and lumbered over to the map. It showed nothing that wasn't already printed on his mind: he just wanted to stare at something that he didn't suspect of looking slyly back and wondering if old George was being irritable because he'd had a jar too many or one too few. A few hours without a drink wasn't the problem, it was not knowing when he would be able to have one, since he'd promised Agnes –

I didn't promise her *anything*, he remembered. And if I had just one now and then waited a few more hours and had another I'd be drinking at the same rate as anybody in this room. So I can have one now, from the bottle in my desk upstairs. Reassured, he turned cheerfully from the map to see what the goings-on at the doorway were about.

It was Ministry workmen wiring up a loudspeaker and special telephone to link with the reconnaissance flight that should be taking off from Cyprus in about an hour's time. George needed to make a final check with the US Third Air Force, the British-based parent body through which he had wheedled the flight, and all the room's phones were now busy.

'I'm popping upstairs to call Uxbridge,' he told the Brigadier, and slipped out through the busy doorway, hoping Agnes hadn't noticed.

Timbrell was staring at the broken track, and even his long nose managed to look weary. Al-Hamedi bounced down, carrying the M-16 rifle – now reloaded from the loot of the Land-Rover. 'I will search the village: you will give me cover fire.'

257

'Don't bother,' Maxim said, 'there's nobody there. I'll go up myself if there's nothing I can do here. Tie up Zyadine's ankles and stick him somewhere we can see.'

Al-Hamedi looked like a slapped child. 'There is perhaps a machine-gun there . . .'

'If we had more men, more time, it's the first thing to do, yes. But our big problem's here. Please, Sergeant.'

And really, Al-Hamedi was only being the perfect soldier; less perfect ones were always getting shot by people they *knew* weren't there. Like Len the helicopter pilot – maybe like Maxim himself.

But he handed the rifle to Timbrell and trailed off to Zyadine.

'Thank God for that,' Timbrell muttered, opening the tool-boxes built onto the tank's rear. 'I thought you were letting him take over completely.'

'He's an experienced tank commander – and he seemed to want to have a go.'

'And you know why, don't you?'

'It doesn't seem as if I do.'

Timbrell bent to peer at one end of the track and its shattered pins. 'Of course, I've known him since these trials began and in less hurried circumstances. He's a first class tank man, one of their best – and still a sergeant. He doesn't come from one of the best Bedouin tribes and his father was mixed up in the failed coup of 1957 and . . . well, I expect you know the Jordanian Army better than I do.'

'I know that being an officer is one of the most secure and best-paid jobs in the country.'

'If you can get it. But had you thought they're going to need a whole new batch of tank officers once this revolt's over and they've purged the ones from 17th Armoured? He's proved his loyalty, now he wouldn't mind being the man who brought the tank *and* a rebel leader across the border. He may think you don't need the glory.'

'Bugger the glory. Can I help at all here?'

'No, you go and keep watch again.'

'Alec – thank you for telling me that. Tell him I was saying great things about him.'

'Wilco. But not so much that he thinks you really want him to take command?'

'If you get that track fixed in time, it won't matter.'

Using the binoculars from the roof of the sandstone building, Maxim could cover most of the road both north and south for about three kilometres, and the desert on either side for an unknown distance. Ages away to the west, the sun rested on the tops of a cloud bank over the coastal range, the mountains they had weaved through in the helicopter. Below, on the edge of a tide of shadow creeping up from the dunes, the tank's gun and crane stuck out at awkward angles as Timbrell and Al-Hamedi tugged and hammered at an end of track.

Maxim had been prepared to try and bully Zyadine into helping, but the other two had decided it would be too much effort to make sure the help didn't become sabotage, so the Brigade Major was a trussed bundle beside the railway line. More humiliation was probably better conditioning than any physical torture anyway, Maxim believed.

The 'village' was no more than they had seen from the dunes: three concrete shells on the far side of the road intended, until the money had run out, as a filling-station, a café and probably a police post. You found half-finished projects like that all over Jordan. The sandstone building was far older, a rest-house/trading-post/fort from the days when the road was a camel track and the Turks maintained a garrison to keep an eye on the wandering tribes. It was a single room about twelve metres deep and half as long again on the side where a doorless gap, high enough to take a camel, opened onto the road. Inside, the only light came from rifle slits chiselled through the two-foot-thick walls and a hatchway in the wooden roof fifteen feet above. Climbing the shallow but uneven ladder one-handed with a rifle slung from his shoulder had been interesting.

It had been climbed before, that day. The watcher who had vanished up the road northwards in a cloud of dust had left fresh cigarette ends and food wrappers by the western parapet. He could have seen the tank – or its dust – coming a long way off; once Maxim thought he saw dust to the south, presumably around the control post at the 'approximate' border. This certainly wasn't it.

The last direct light of the sun went like a slow blink, a softening of shadow and enrichment of colour. He waited until the brightness in the west had faded a few moments further, then swept the horizon through the binoculars. He kept on going, although he thought he had seen dust to the north, to complete the circle before concentrating on one point.

At his desk, George didn't pour a drink, he picked up the phone and called the Uxbridge HQ. Now the drink was at hand, there was pleasure, even serenity, in waiting for it. George *enjoyed* secret drinking; perhaps a good spy had to enjoy the daily mechanics of deception and betrayal, quite irrespective of the value of his spying. George had come to like the first twenty minutes at his desk when his hand was too shaky to write his own signature, anticipating the small miracle that half a glass of vodka would bring. That was the best drink of the day, when he could almost stand back and watch its effect on himself, and he often wished it could stop there, that every drink could be the first. Long droughts caused by long committee meetings brought a hint of the same effect, but never quite the same. For that, he had to wait until tomorrow.

The Colonel at 3rd Air Force confirmed that the mission, callsign Cactus, was on line for take-off from Akrotiri at 1600 Zulu: anybody dealing with aeroplanes and time zones had to think in Greenwich Mean – 'Zulu' – time. Yes, they would be able to communicate with the pilot in flight, but only via an Air Force officer who would reach them shortly. They didn't want, if George would forgive him, amateurs cluttering up the airwaves. Was there anything more they could tell the pilot in advance?

'The last we heard,' George said, 'suggests they'll be close to the railway and road south of Mudawarah. D'you want a map reference?'

'No, it couldn't be precise, right?'

'Correct. I've got the frequency they'll be guarding and we've warned our ship – that's callsign Blackbird – to stay off the air, but if your man has any long-distance problems, he can use them as a relay . . .'

They rambled on, metaphorically prodding and kicking the mission to make sure no bits were likely to fall off. Once, then twice, George opened his deep file drawer where the vodka was, because he could enjoy a secret drink on the telephone, too, although he decided against it this time. And would it be impossible when TV telephones became a fashion? Not that they would become a Whitehall fashion: there were enough civil servants who thought the ordinary telephone gave the public too much opportunity to trespass. But even then, he could take a mouthful from a glass of vodka, watered so that he could gulp it and posing as pure water. He had done that in front of people already, and they had never suspected.

Or had they?

There couldn't be much fun in being a spy if everybody knew and was politely concealing that they knew and *making allowances* for your little weakness. It wasn't just 'a little weakness', it was a Great Weakness, he was a Big Sinner.

Who cared?

Agnes had said 'just another Whitehall drunk'. But the hell with Miss Agnes Algar, he'd have a drink right now without her knowing and that would show her.

Then he realised the door was open and she was looking at him. How on earth had she got up . . . ? But of course she had been in his office often before and been issued a Defence pass to attend Snowflake. She came in and sat down across the desk from him.

261

'Thank you again, Colonel,' he finished up, 'and we'll be in touch when the mission's complete.'

'Well,' Agnes asked, 'have you had one?'

'Not yet.'

'Going to?'

'Probably.'

She nodded. 'Well, pour one for me when you do. It isn't as if you could do anything. None of us can do anything. Harry's as much on his own as he was twelve, more than twelve, hours ago.'

'Oh come on, we'll have the reconnaissance flight up soon; we could be in touch with him in . . . an hour and a half.'

'Oh yes, if he's alive, and if he is – what then? When you'd gone, they sat down and said: "Right, what do we tell Major Maxim when we get through?" *And they couldn't think of a bloody thing!*'

'Well . . . it depends on what he tells us.'

'They said that, too. I asked them what he could tell us that would let us do something useful. They didn't know.'

'If we could have got the Saudi border re-opened,' George mused; 'Scottie did try on that . . . or if we could get the Jordanian army to move in . . .'

'It's a bit much to expect them to start a civil war just to pick up our mistake.'

'We didn't invade Jordan, the tank was there by arrangement with them, and it was their army that revolted. And I didn't expect it to spin out like this, I just wanted a helicopter insertion to blow the tank up and out again. A quick in and out.'

'Like Suez. Vietnam. Nicaragua. Northern Ireland.'

George looked at her, then gave one long shrug. 'I didn't think it through, not of all the things that could go wrong. I'm sorry. I haven't been doing the job as well as I should.'

Agnes looked back bleakly. She didn't mind George dabbling in self-recrimination, it was a step – in some direction or other. 'Let me have that drink, anyway.'

'It's just plain vodka.'

'I know.' Desk-drawer drinkers usually ended up with tasteless, odourless vodka, just the pure shot in the vein. 'Give me some water in it, would you?' There was a carafe by the glasses on a side table.

George poured her drink, then, after the briefest hesitation, his own. She pulled her chair closer to the desk to use it as a table, and for a few minutes they sat opposite each other and sipped, Agnes's gaze wandering over the mementoes of George's life: the framed photograph of Annette and the daughters, the ghastly onyx pen-and-ballpoint set from a retiring prime minister, a small silver horse, probably from George's Dragoon Guards service, a letter-opener shaped like a bayonet for a man who never opened his own letters . . .

'Are you in love with him?' George asked.

'I don't know. Or don't want to know.'

'Is he with you?'

'He says so.'

George raised his eyebrows. 'He's a straight shooter, our Harry.'

'Ha! *That's* the story of his life. D'you see me as an Army Wife?'

Almost irrelevantly, because he had only just thought of it, George said: 'Of course, you could try getting word to this Al-Warid that the Jordanian army is going in to break the revolt.'

Agnes stared. 'But I . . . It'd look damned odd if I went round to Mrs Katbah again and spilled more state secrets . . .'

'No, bypass her. You've got Al-Warid's phone number, haven't you? Pretend you're a nurse, say Mrs Katbah's gone back for another operation, and she asked you to pass on a message. Something she'd got from an embassy visitor: the Jordanian army is going south tonight.'

Agnes sat silent for a moment, fingering her lips. 'One thing it would do: Edwin Giles will make me change sex just so he can castrate me. It'll all go straight onto a police tape, you know.'

'So? They won't ring up Al-Warid and say "Cancel that last message." At least we'll be doing something.'

'Suppose he . . . no,' Agnes flicked through a sequence of objections and solutions. This was the sort of thing she was good at.

George stood up, instinctively reaching to finish his drink, then didn't. He smiled wanly at the glass. One mouthful not drunk; it might be a step. 'I'm going downstairs. You can use my phone. And you can always become an Army Wife.'

33

In the still twilight, the dust on the northern horizon just hung there, a tiny blur as if somebody had touched a finger across the fresh paint of the dunes. Maxim hadn't warned the tank, there was no point in taking their minds off the repair yet, but now there was dust in the south also, bubbling up quickly and definitely on the road itself.

He shouted at Timbrell and Al-Hamedi, but the closer mutter of the auxiliary engine drowned him. He fired a shot from the M-16 and that whipped them upright.

He pointed. Even head-on, he could see it was coming fast, and when he got the binoculars back on it could see two pinpricks of light in the dark point of the dust. Some vehicle, clearly not a tank, charging along with headlights full on, well before they were needed, and coming from the border.

'Don't – fire – before – I – do!' he shouted down, and Timbrell waved back. Al-Hamedi was up beside the commander's machine-gun.

Somebody – the Turkish garrison? – had carved rifle slits in the parapets, too, now weathered to deep thin V's. Maxim laid the rifle in one facing south, took a quick glance north through the binoculars and crouched awkwardly behind the slit.

The building had been sited so that it was on the highest local point and the road either side of it weaved gently along the top of a slight ridge, with the ground sloping away on both sides. The Land-Rover – it was yet another military one painted the usual desert ochre – suddenly slowed when it saw the tank down to its left and the lone driver waved. Then it stopped and the driver got out: big, in drab overalls, and Piers.

'How did they find you?" Maxim asked. He had first had to explain his damaged side and the state of the tank, learnt that the border was open again – at least at that point – and had moved the party back to the tank so that work could continue. The crane was gradually hoisting one end of the track up to catch on the teeth of the driving sprocket; the sprocket would haul it up and over for rejoining.

'I tell you, it didn't last long only it took ten years off my life.' Piers' blond hair was aged by grey dust and his overalls would have disgraced the sort of garage Maxim avoided, but his face was just tanned; he had been a month in this climate already. 'I waited while you moved off – boy, I thought they had you with that missile coming from the dunes, I was glad I'd bailed out then. But when you went out of sight, the Saudi tanks moved off and I started walking. I went south-east and I must have crossed the border when I heard you start up a new battle. That brought the Saudis back like fleas to a dog, four tanks in all and armoured cars and tracked infantry vehicles and all they could see was me, boy, every gun looking my way and me walking along with my hands so high I was hanging onto God's bootlaces and not feeling like John Wayne, not one bit of it.

'But they saw I wasn't a superior invading force and then they saw my badges and thought I must be a pilot and crashed an aeroplane somewhere and I had a real time until they found someone who spoke English and then it was all right. I told them the story about twenty times in all and they *communicated* on the radio, I think they must have got the British telephone system by mistake, it would have been quicker to teach a camel to speak and send him, but then they brought me along to the frontier post and . . . here we are.'

266

The tank roared and made a brief jolt forward. Timbrell climbed out of the driver's hatchway. Maxim called: 'How long, Alec?'

'Ten minutes, quarter of an hour.'

'Keep it coming. There's been movement up north.'

Everybody looked, but from below even road level nothing showed against the deepening blue.

'Do they know you're here?' Piers asked.

'Well, they do now.'

'Oh God. Oh Jesus,' as Piers realised his own tearing dust trail and its stop at the village had passed the message. 'Look, just pile aboard the Land-Rover and set a charge on the tank like we planned –'

'It'll take ten minutes to set the charge and no longer to fix the tank – Alec?'

Timbrell nodded, blank-faced, and turned to the track-work. Al-Hamedi was hooking the crane to the other track end. Maxim headed for the village and, after a moment, Piers followed.

From the roof, the first look through the binoculars showed no dust cloud up the road; then, scanning wider, Maxim realised it had moved nearer and eastward, well out on the far side of the road. He knelt, propping the binoculars to watch the dust swing degree by degree round from north to east. If that was one of the Centurions, then probably the two others were hidden by some fold of ground up the road to the north.

'I suppose there's no chance of the Saudis coming up and giving a hand?'

'Not them, boy.' Piers shook his head firmly. 'Half a bloody army just one inch inside their border at the control post and that's where they stay.'

'Can't blame them, it isn't their fight. How did you get the Land-Rover out of them?'

'Not theirs, it belongs to the Jordan frontier guard. A patrol came down the road some time this afternoon and the guards hopped over into Saudia and asked for asylum or something. The Saudi colonel didn't think it would compromise his neutrality if I took a Jordanian vehicle to come and look for you . . . There.'

South in the dusk, a light glittered shakily through the hot air rising off the road: the frontier post, just five kilometres, maybe half an hour at their speed, a whole world away.

The auxiliary engine had stopped, replaced by measured sledgehammer clangs that echoed off the wall below them. Everything a tank did, everything you did to a tank, was loud. And between clangs, they could hear the distant, surging *whoooar-whoooar* as the Centurion worked round their flank. Already it was too dark in the east to see the dust trails, but the half moon hanging over Saudia was waiting for the glow of the sun to fade before switching to full brightness; they were in the eye's blind spot between sun and moonlight, and outlined against the lemon-yellow western sky as well.

'Better get your head down,' Maxim said, sitting below the parapet.

Piers crouched slowly beside him. 'You're going to get yourself surrounded, boy.'

Maxim jerked his head towards the clanging tank. 'I'm ready when it is. Why don't you get on your bike and head back? You can't do anything more here, and you're a softer target.'

'No, I'll go out with you.'

'Why?'

Piers took his time answering. 'I bailed out once before . . .'

'There wasn't really room for you and you hadn't got anything to do. I wouldn't have let you go if you'd been essential. You still aren't.'

'If they're staying . . .'

'Alec's staying because he wants to get the tank home and show how well it does in battle and win an Army contract for it. Al-Hamedi's staying because it proves his loyalty and heroism and he hopes he'll get a commission out of it. Good sensible reasons. Now why you?'

Piers said: 'Misplaced pride, I suppose.'

'Oh no. That's why *I'm* here, thinking I could drag this tank home by leadership qualities and my bare teeth, and I've probably brought them a desert too far. That motive's full up round here: find yourself a better one or go and misplace your pride somewhere else.'

Piers said nothing. A light winked at the corner of Maxim's eye, and he looked south-west to see a red comet gliding slowly down. From that direction, it could be a Saudi signal flare. But another red comet burst and curled down due west. Answering, a white flare popped silently in the eastern sky.

'Now where else would you suggest?' Piers said softly. 'I think you really have got yourself surrounded.'

But for the installation of the loudspeaker and special telephone the whole Snowflake operation would, George reckoned, have been hijacked physically across the road to the more refined setting of the Cabinet Office. Now something was actually going to Happen and everybody wanted, if not a part in decision-taking, then certainly in decision-taking-watching, and the room was full of new faces; the civil service members of the original Committee huddled around a corner of the main table, well away from the loudspeaker over the Brigadier's chair.

'We'd have a far better legal argument,' Scott-Scobie was saying, 'if there had been a British crew stranded with the tank in the first place and they were merely trying to escape. Our title to the tank can't be disputed; we have a clearcut right to it, or compensation if we don't get it. Instead –'

'But if we'd just sat on our fingers,' George said, 'and hadn't got it back, then your Office would have had to get Officially Upset with Jordan. And you don't know how they'd have reacted to that. As it is, they'll have to get upset with us, put their cards on the table first and you can see what you've got to play against. Don't tell me your Office wouldn't rather react than act, any day of the week.'

'We'd rather not have to do *anything* in the Near East at the moment. It was the Ministry of Defence – or is it Attack, these days? – who ordered a deliberate violation of Jordan's –'

'Goalpost,' the loudspeaker said, 'Cactus is in flower.'

Everybody went very quiet and a ripple of satisfied smiles ran through the room. Now a thousand miles of electronic knitting that the Squadron-Leader wanted to explain but nobody wanted to understand joined them to the cockpit of a Stealth aircraft climbing south out of Cyprus.

'Cactus, this is Goalpost,' said the controller at Mildenhall, just a few dozen miles away but no louder. 'Copy in flower.'

'Gentlemen,' the uniformed USAF Lieutenant-Colonel said, 'the flight is airborne and on course and should be in radio range of your tank in approximately forty minutes. Thank you.'

'I just don't want anybody to think,' Scott-Scobie whispered fiercely, 'that we have anything like a strong case in international law.'

'Isn't there a doctrine of "Hot Pursuit"?' asked Agnes, materialising quietly and slipping into a seat among them. 'You could try invoking one of "Hot Retreat".'

Scott-Scobie scowled. George said: 'Just give them money,' in the smug knowledge that the entire Foreign Office budget wouldn't buy his own Ministry one new nuclear submarine.

'And what are you going to tell Harry?' Agnes asked quickly.

Sir Anthony, who had stayed loyally with the Committee rather than join his Cabinet Office colleagues around the loudspeaker, waved his hand. 'As you can see, my dear, a number of new fingers have joined the pie. So far, the consensus is to advise him to try and negotiate a crossing at the border on the Ma'an road – since he seems to be heading that way in any case.'

'That's probably what he's planning to do already,' George said. 'If the tank holds out.'

'There's no news from Saudia, I presume?' Sir Anthony asked.

Scott-Scobie made a gesture that was half a shake of the head, half a shrug, and came out as an irritated wriggle.

'Can we tell him,' Agnes said, 'that if he can't get across, just to hang on?'

'For what?' Norman Sprague wanted to know.

Agnes gave him a brave little smile; he didn't know how angry, and how soon, he was going to be with her. 'Oh, just if anything turns up.'

34

When Maxim and Piers reached the tank, Timbrell was folding the crane back along the turret. 'We're as ready as we'll ever be,' he said in a flat voice. 'Only we're not going to go any faster than we have been – still ten kilometres an hour and *them* on our flanks.'

Another scatter of signal flares had gone up around the horizon. 'What are they doing?' Maxim asked.

'Sorting out their positions so they can shoot at us without the overs hitting each other.'

Yes, that made sense. 'Sergeant!' Al-Hamedi raised his head from the hatchway. 'D'you know what radio channels they're using?'

In the dark, Al-Hamedi's stillness showed the bland hopeless look he was giving Maxim. 'No, Major, I do not –'

'Find a command channel for me, please.'

The head vanished slowly, but he heard the radio come alive. Timbrell said: 'In case you wanted it, the plastic explosive and the fuses and so on are in the stowage behind the turret.'

'Thank you.' He climbed awkwardly up onto the tank and found a headset. The radio was alive but deserted – in Europe every channel would be chattering away – until Al-Hamedi clicked into a short crackle of Arabic.

'That is the tanks in the west, Major. Aisrak. Ahmar is in the east.' British-built tanks out there, British callsigns: blue to the west, red to the east.

'It'll do. I'm going to put Zyadine on the radio to tell

272

them not to fire. Then to pull back and let us out to the border. We'll let him go free then.'

'He will not do it.' Al-Hamedi needed no time to think that one out. Then, having thought it out a little further, he added: 'He will betray us. He will say the tank is damaged, that it cannot go fast.'

'They must have an idea we're damaged – we wouldn't still be here otherwise. And yes, he'll say that; that's why he'll go on the radio. But he'll say what we want him to say as well. He'll prove he's here.'

The first shell exploded up in the village, a flick of light somewhere in the concrete buildings, brief as a blink. Real high-explosive is like that; the stuff they use in war movies is low, slow explosive and probably mixed with jellied petrol as well, because the real thing doesn't look impressive enough.

'Anyway,' Maxim said, 'I'm putting him on the radio. You handle the set, but don't cut him off too quickly. Get Zyadine up here!' he called into the darkness. Another shell, from the west this time, flashed against the fort wall. In between the higher road and the dunes, Maxim guessed they were invisible to both east and west. The danger lay up the open road to the north, and a flare had gone up from there, too.

Zyadine came forward, hunched and gasping from the just-released ropes, herded by Piers and a submachine-gun. Another shell – from the east – exploded in the sand fifty yards south. The gunfire was very slow, allowing each tank gunner time to spot the burst of his shell so that he could correct his aim from that.

'We're tuned to your command net,' Maxim told Zyadine. 'I want you to tell them to stop firing and let us go south on the road. Or you die. We'll release you at the Saudi border. Tell them that and nothing more – all right?' Zyadine's hands were still tied behind him; Maxim put his own headset over Zyadine's ears, adjusted the microphone for him, then leant forward to say: 'Major Zyadine is ready to broadcast, Sergeant.'

It was just possible that Zyadine had been fooled, because Zyadine believed Maxim was a simple I-am-a-gun soldier. Yes, every army had such soldiers, just as there are doctors and lawyers and writers prepared to live and die on their shooting record. Maxim believed – or hoped – he was something more, but the answer wasn't easy because it was diffuse, fragmented. He was a father to Chris and a lover to Agnes and not bad at either, he could talk about Count Basie and a few other musicians, he was kind to cats and some of Agnes's television friends . . . it didn't add up to a crusade; that might be his weakness.

He could tell just when Zyadine started passing forbidden information: his voice became a loud gabble, too fast to interpret, ending in a deep breath as Al-Hamedi cut him off. Maxim took back the headset. 'Did he say what we expected?'

Al-Hamedi lifted from the hatchway. 'Yes, but also he said to keep firing, that he wanted to die.'

'And that is one hell of a big help,' Piers said from behind Zyadine.

'They're firing now. They can either go on or stop. What have we lost? Stay on the radio, please.'

'What happens if they do stop firing?' Timbrell asked.

'We move up to the fort, there's more solid cover there. What's the doctrine on using tanks in street-fighting?'

'Put simply – don't.'

'That's fine, if they've read the same book and we're there first.'

'Can we fit the tank into the fort?'

That idea hadn't occurred to Maxim. He knew in theory that tanks could simply back into houses, crunching brick walls, and sit in the front parlour invisible from three sides, but it wasn't tried on exercises: they paid enough to British and German farmers for flattened crops and shattered fences as it was. Yet, he realised, at the back of any true tankie's mind must be the thought that if Der Tag ever arrives, there will be drawbacks – such as a very short life expectancy – but at least I can now start knocking down people's homes.

Al-Hamedi reported: 'They say they have stopped firing. They let us go to the border. But, Major –'

'Tell them to pull out to the north and we want to see them do that.'

Piers said sourly: 'Do you believe them?'

'No, but they'll probably lay off for long enough to make us believe them. Alec – the fort doorway isn't wide enough and the stone's two foot thick. Can your tank –?'

'No, but you're the one who understands explosives and you've got two kilos of it, haven't you?'

Although the radio link was 'discrete' which presumably meant some version of secure or untappable, the Cactus pilot obviously felt no need for chatter. Agnes tried to imagine him – and fancied she could; she had once had an affair with a test pilot. She saw a quiet unhurried man sitting in his high lonely faintly-humming, faintly-glowing cockpit, watching dials and making tiny precise adjustments, carefully arranging the parts of a puzzle he knows he is going to solve.

Funny: she hadn't tried imagining Maxim in the tank. Or maybe she didn't want to; it wouldn't be organised and unhurried.

'Cactus,' the loudspeaker said, 'Charlie at this time.'

That was overdoing it, Cactus: 'at this time' was unnecessary verbosity. Was the loneliness getting to you? Or the tension? 'Charlie' would be, literally, a turning point, the third on the flight and probably somewhere in Egypt, beginning the run-in east. Condemned to subsonic flight by the rounded, blended shape built for radar invisibility rather than aerodynamic efficiency, Cactus was moving no faster than an airliner. Forty-three minutes from Cyprus to the Ma'an road.

Sprague had been called out to the communications office next door; now he was back, leaning over Giles and asking: 'Edwin, I wonder if I could have just a little word with you?' He didn't look at Agnes as he said it, and she didn't look at him except for fifteen years experience of looking at people when they didn't think she was. Giles stood up, smiling politely, and followed Sprague into a corner. He doesn't know what's going to hit him, she thought.

But George did. 'Ten seconds and counting.'

'I beg your pardon?' Sir Anthony broke out of an escapist conversation about international law with Scott-Scobie.

'A certain amount of ground zero is about to set in,' George said. 'I think young Agnes is going to need our moral support.'

Sir Anthony looked puzzled. George went on watching his hand tremble on the table, the way it did in the morning but never at this time of day. He should have finished that vodka upstairs, that would have staved it off for another half hour. He didn't know what came after the trembling, he had always cured it quickly. He didn't want to know. But he had to stay and see Agnes through.

And there was Giles, still smiling but making a firm gesture towards the communications office. George followed Agnes and, not knowing why, Sir Anthony and Scott-Scobie followed him.

'Close the door, please,' Giles said, 'and I don't think you've met – it's Detective Chief Inspector, isn't it? – Redding.'

Agnes said: 'Hello, Charlie,' and the others murmured something. Redding was the only other person there; the teleprinter girl had been eased out.

'Norman . . . ?' Giles offered him the floor.

'I have here a tape of telephone intercepts,' Sprague said, holding up a cassette, 'which I think will convince you that . . . ' He couldn't think quite what.

'They shall be the terrors of the earth,' suggested Scott-Scobie cheerfully. 'Yes, but there's something good coming up on the channel next door in a few minutes. Speed it up, Norman.'

'This was done at my suggestion,' George said flatly.

'Really?' Sprague deftly fitted the cassette into a small player and said, right on cue: 'May I introduce you to Nurse Barrett?'

After a minute of Nurse Barrett and Al-Warid, Scott-Scobie said to Agnes: 'This sounds remarkably like you, me darling.'

'I could have done a whole load of accents, but I wanted the bastard to understand me.'

'Yes, I see that. When derailing the wheels of government, one wants to come across loud and clear. And you do. All right, Norman, she's convinced our revolutionary correspondent that the Jordanian army's coming down like the wolf on the fold, what does *he* do next?'

Reluctantly, Sprague switched off the tape. 'He first rang the hospital to try and contact Nurse Barrett again – and there *is* a Nurse Barret, and she *had* just gone off duty in Mrs Katbah's wing' – he stared at Agnes as if her efficiency in establishing this background made her doubly guilty – 'and they told him they couldn't give nurses' private numbers under *any* circumstances . . . And then he rang Amman.'

'The usual number?' Agnes demanded. 'And passed on the message?'

'The message was in Arabic.'

Pause. Then Charlie Redding said: 'We had an Arabic interpreter listening to the intercepts, sir, just in case . . . Yes, he passed on the message just as Miss – Nurse Barrett – gave it to him.'

Another pause, then Scott-Scobie said: 'Well, it may be progress of a sort, certainly it's proof of Al-Warid's complicity.'

'If there's any blame,' George said, staring at the floor and clenching his hands in his pockets, 'it was all my idea.'

Giles put his fingertips together as in prayer, lifted them to his lips and said softly through them: 'I will have you shot for this, Agnes.'

Turning back to the main room, Scott-Scobie – who hadn't heard but had a good idea of what Giles's prayerful fingers indicated – said: 'All Edwin means is that his Service is so full of weirdos doing things for personal reasons he's glad to find you're one of them. George, you look as if you need a drink.'

The sandstone blocks were cracked, and the mortar between them old and tired. With his survival knife, Piers was able to gouge out deep crevices where they didn't exist already. Maxim plugged them with the plastic explosive, joining the detonators to fingers of det cord that knotted into a hand and then a short wrist of safety cord.

'More likely bring down the whole building,' Piers observed.

'Anything would be an improvement,' Maxim didn't really think the whole structure would collapse: it rested on the sheer size of the blocks, not on the binding effect of the mortar. The roof might crack and sag, but it was made of dozens of wooden beams – from Jordan's forest days – and it could lose a few without risk.

'Ready. Step around the side, south.' He flicked his lighter at the fuse and followed. He was just reaching the usual moment of doubt about the fuse when the wall beside them gave a loud grunt and covered them with dust, mortar and fragments of stone. The brief street between the fort and the concrete buildings was full of dust, too, bright in the moonlight and settling slowly in the windless night. He looked at the rubble; there wasn't anything he didn't think the tank could overcome.

'Flash them an OK.' And out there in the desert, there would be confusion, suspicion and a lot of radio chatter about the inexplicable bang.

He let Al-Hamedi guide the tank in, walking beside it with a headset on a long lead. It curved ponderously backwards, crushing lumps of sandstone back to sand, filling the doorway and more than filling it, its right rear end gouging a notch, just fifty pounds of stone, from the untouched side. And then, except for three metres of barrel, it was inside.

'Silent watch?' Timbrell called.

'Yes, you can get down. I want the radios left on. Piers, tie Major Zyadine's feet again, would you? I'm going up to the roof for a look-see. And somebody turn on the BV, we've got time for a cup of coffee now.'

For a moment, nobody moved nor said anything. Then Piers said coldly: 'It should be a cup of tea, of course, this being what I would call a crisis. What are we hoping for now, Major?'

So he was 'Major' to Piers now. 'Time. It's on our side for once, though I agree not much else is. We're wearing Major Zyadine's little revolution down. He didn't plan it this way, not spread across a hundred kilometres of desert from their base at Aqaba. But he wasn't confident enough of his revolution: he had to sell off a bit of it to the Syrians and Russians – or thought he had – and then he couldn't ignore us taking the tank away and *now* he's got a dozen and more vehicles out there running their fuel tanks empty and their batteries flat and getting punctures and blocked filters and track problems, those things don't only happen to us – and did you remember to order refuelling bowsers and workshop vehicles as well, Major?'

He could see only a one-sided outline of Zyadine in the moonlight that slanted brightly through the thin rifle slits and cracks in the roof but reflected poorly off a floor that was probably a hundred years' of camel dung. But Zyadine made a useful target for a speech aimed at all of them – and all, in their way, soldiers.

'And did you remember rations and water trucks? There's at least a hundred men out there, including the command post, knowing whatever happens here *they've* got to get back a hundred kilometres to Aqaba. Some of them have been awake as long as we have.'

'They have enough ammunition,' Zyadine said. Maxim heard the little sigh of agreement from the others in the darkness.

'Yes, if they obey you. But they may not be sure who was giving that order: an army major or a revolutionary.

279

You want to die, become a martyr – but they're not going to die, not all of them. They're thinking about food and fuel and tomorrow and getting back to Aqaba. And some of them could be thinking about going on trial for this revolt and saying "We just did what Major Zyadine told us" – but Major Zyadine got himself promoted to Paradise and isn't around to speak for his men any more. It isn't always a commander's job to get himself killed first, Major, it's sometimes his job to stick around and see what he can rescue from his mistakes – somebody, something – up to the bloody end.'

As Al-Hamedi climbed into the tank to turn on the BV, Maxim said quietly: 'D'you want to take command?'

'No, Major.'

'It'll happen to you, one day. You'll get some people into something and – if it's you – you'll get them out again. I'll say that in my report – Christ, I'll have a thousand reports to write – and see your army gets a copy *if* you want it. But until then, I'm running things.'

'Yes, Major.'

That was probably the best Maxim could do.

35

'Cactus, bingo,' the loudspeaker said. 'Concentration of vehicles at point November. Buildings five kilometres north, designate that point Tango. Do you copy?'

'Cactus, we copy.'

A fizzling silence. The Lieutenant-Colonel said quickly: 'Point November is the border crossing.'

'Cactus, reference point Tango, niner repeat niner vehicles west in arc from three one zero to two two zero approx distance two kilometres one vehicle three five zero approx two kilometres two vehicles . . .'

Just a weather forecast, Agnes thought, just figures that say sit in the garden with a drink or tie yourself to the mainmast until the hurricane passes, but she still saw the man unhurriedly counting the points of light on his radar or infra-red screen and knew he was getting it right. She tried for a moment to assemble the pattern in her mind, but the Squadron-Leader was scribbling ecstatically, the first real-time you-are-there information that whole day. He'd know.

'Going channel Delta. Do you copy?'

'Copy channel Delta.'

'Gentlemen,' the Lieutenant-Colonel said, then noticed Agnes, 'and lady – the pilot has switched over to the radio channel that you informed us was the one your tank would be guarding. That channel does not broadcast on this link-up.'

In the silence, the Squadron-Leader plunged through the crowd to the map-board and began stabbing pins into it. They built into a strong half-circle to the west of Point Tango, a far weaker one east.

'Is that – I mean that Point Tango – where our people are?' asked a voice from the Cabinet Office crowd.

'Well, the implications from the enemy dispositions suggest –'

'Should we be calling them *enemy*?'

The Squadron-Leader opened and closed his mouth.

'I think "opposition" sounds less emotive,' the Cabinet Office voice went on. 'Or possibly "dissidents".'

'Oh, don't let's hurt their feelings,' Scott-Scobie said, trying not to giggle; 'just call them "good friends who have a bloody funny way of showing it".'

The Squadron-Leader put his finger on the map, which showed no symbols except the road and railway. 'I think . . . our people must be there, yes.'

From the roof, which had a lot more cracks in it but wasn't falling down, Maxim could see almost nothing; just an occasional moonlit blur of dust as a tank or other vehicle changed position. And he couldn't hear much, either: a surge of noise as a vehicle moved, the steady mutter of some tank's auxiliary engine charging its batteries. There certainly wasn't a general pullout to the north; on the other hand, there wasn't any general movement to close in on them. A force that was supposed to be attacking yet was just sitting, not even shooting, sounded like a force that hadn't made up its mind.

Meanwhile, his crew had had a tin of hot food each and a tin – they still had only one mug – of weak coffee. The survival manual on desert living had forgotten that one: bring enough instant coffee.

A distant voice below said: 'Harpoon, do you copy?'

They had left both radio sets on and both fed through a loudspeaker that, although Maxim didn't realise it, was another of Timbrell's innovations, saving the crew from having to wear headsets when they dozed or ate.

He staggered down the dark ladder, wrenching a sharp

pain into his side, but Timbrell was already aboard the tank and answering.

'Harpoon,' said the metallic American voice from the belly of the tank, 'please identify yourself. Over.'

'Hold on.' Timbrell stuck up his head and waited until Maxim found a headset, then switched to transmit.

'This is Mike Bravo Tango Niner Zero, Major Maxim commanding. Over.'

A wait, then: 'Harpoon, who played piano on "L'il Darling"? Over.'

Maxim gaped, then wanted to laugh aloud. 'This is Harpoon. It was Count Basie, it was his band. Over.' It made sense: if the tank had been captured, it was unlikely to be by a Jordanian Count Basie fan. They had talked to somebody – Agnes, probably.

'Harpoon, this is Cactus overhead. Please report situation for relay to your friends.'

The Lieutenant-Colonel said: 'The delay is probably Cactus talking to your tank on channel Delta. It may be your tank wasn't expecting any calls this late, as it is out there . . .'

Don't try to be *funny*, Agnes glared at him, this is –

'Cactus, I have contact with Harpoon on Delta. He is at point Tango, holed up in a fort. Reports tank still active but short ammo and capable of only ten kilometres per hour. Do you copy?'

'Copy, Cactus.'

The telephone in the Lieutenant-Colonel's hand obviously came alive. He listened, nodding, then bent to a piece of paper and his voice came through the loud-speaker.

'Cactus, this is Goalpost Bravo. Message for Harpoon reads Believe Saudi border now open . . .'

And that, in the end, was all we could say, Agnes thought. That if he can go another five kilometres south – half an hour at his reduced speed – past all the pins on the map, those 'opposition' or 'dissident' pins which weren't short of ammunition, then we can pat ourselves on the back for a job well done.

Well, it took a lot of pins to corner my man, and even then he found himself a fort. A desert fort, for God's sake, did he just dream that into existence from his boyhood reading?

Maxim wasn't any more impressed by the message. 'Big deal. Cactus, forget London. Just give me the position of all units in my area and any movement.'

'Roj, Harpoon, hold.'

Piers had pushed Zyadine up beside the tank, guarding him but wanting to eavesdrop himself. 'Who is it up there?'

'Some American reconnaissance aircraft.'

'Probably one of their Stealth types. It is nice to know somebody cares.'

'That's about all he's been able to tell us, so far. What radar and so on would he have?'

'Nothing but the best. It is a compliment, them sending one of those aircraft over.'

'I'd have chosen a squadron of ground-attack aircraft myself, or at least an airdrop of coffee and cigarettes.'

Cactus cut in on them, starting a detailed situation report, adding that movement of tanks was difficult to detect unless they were going at speed.

The loudspeaker had been silent for some minutes, but the Lieutenant-Colonel had been talking to Goalpost at Mildenhall on the phone. 'It seems your Harpoon has hijacked Cactus on the other channel to use him for local tactical reconnaissance.'

'Best thing to do,' Sir Anthony said, and the Brigadier nodded. Agnes looked round to get George's opinion – he always had one, on military matters – but he had vanished. The poor bastard, she thought. But it doesn't matter now.

'Goalpost, Cactus. Relay from Harpoon. He estimates enemy is repositioning for an infantry attack. Estimates two personnel carriers among forces to west. Over.'

Sir Anthony and the Brigadier were both nodding now, as if the enemy had done the proper, correct thing.

'Cactus, what is your fuel state? Over.'

'Goalpost, Cactus estimates can remain bingo area ten more – Goalpost, hold.' An abrupt cutoff, that. The room looked instinctively at the loudspeaker.

Then: 'Goalpost, Cactus observes and Harpoon confirms enemy has opened fire. Over.'

36

The first shell had hit the north wall of the fort with a smack and shudder that brought dust pouring from the roof. It had startled Maxim as much as anybody, although he had expected a bombardment once he had deduced an infantry attack from Cactus's report.

'It would appear that they have broken their promise,' Piers said sourly.

'We got a lull out of it; we got up here without being shot at. They let us strengthen our position.' He was going to say more, then realised Zyadine would be overhearing him. 'Sergeant, get on the radio and ask them why they broke the agreement and what do they want from us to re-impose it?'

Even in the dark, he could feel the laser look Al-Hamedi was giving him. 'Get on the radio, Sergeant!' Al-Hamedi's shadow swarmed up onto the tank. Maxim continued with the bit he didn't mind Zyadine hearing: 'There are two callsigns, probably Centurion tanks, up the road to the north, and I think they're ranging on us now.'

A shell obligingly whacked into one of the concrete buildings across the street, sending a flick of light through the doorway. 'They'll be able to provide enfilading fire until the last moment, with infantry coming in at 90 degrees from the west. Out *there*, there's probably four tanks and two armoured personnel carriers full of troops. Oh, and there's one tank to the east, but I don't think he'll fire unless we make a break for it, east or south. He's just a backstop.'

'It sounds as if our position,' Piers said, 'would be over-rated if it were termed "hopeless".' There probably wasn't really a hundred years of Welsh bitterness about mine disasters and poverty imposed by casual English owners distilled into Piers' tone; probably Maxim's tiredness made him imagine that. But welcome it, too.

An explosion on the north parapet above them sent lumps of stone rumbling across the roof and dust pouring down the hatchway, creating brief shafts of moonlight from the rifle slits. Al-Hamedi lifted his head from the tank hatch.

'Major, they say they will stop firing and go north if we release Major Zyadine now, here.'

'Say I agree. That's fine. If they stop firing before they kill the Land-Rover outside, he can take that. *Tell* them that.'

'Why are you doing this, Harry?' Piers asked. So he was 'Harry' again.

'Because it's the only chance we've got. We *have* to trust them – and I'd rather die in ten minutes' time than right now. Untie Major Zyadine.'

They could do nothing but obey him: go to lonely unstructured deaths or a communal command-guided one. They all had military backgrounds, they would all prefer to die in company – and commanded.

Al-Hamedi raised his head again. 'They say they do not trust us unless they speak to Major Zyadine again.'

'Let him talk to them. Where's a headset?'

'He will tell them –'

'Find him a headset!'

Perhaps the firing had stopped; it hadn't been intensive enough to tell. Zyadine was brought forward by Piers and Timbrell and fitted with a headset; when he launched into Arabic, Piers said to Maxim: 'He *will* tell them our situation. And when he is gone –'

'And I keep telling you that they *know* our situation. Let's just see if we can get him to go.'

'*Get* him to go?'

'The script's been changed. We don't want prisoners cluttering up the place now.'

Al-Hamedi rose again from the hatch, just as Zyadine took off the headset. 'Major, he has said he will go in the Land-Rover. They will go away, back, when he reaches there.' His voice showed how little he believed it.

'Good. I thought Major Zyadine might want to live a little longer if he got the chance. Which way are you heading, Major?'

Al-Hamedi answered for him. 'The road, to the north, with lights on.'

'Fine. We'll wait about ten minutes, and then move out south. Remember, Major, we're trusting you and your friends.'

He thought he saw Zyadine's eyes glitter in the moonlight, but all the Major said was: 'I am not going because I wish to live for ever, like you, Major.'

'Of course you aren't. You're going because *we* want to live for ever. But you are going to let us live, aren't you?' he added.

'Yes, Major Maxim, I will let you live.'

'Good. Piers, give him the keys to the Land-Rover. It's parked between the buildings across the street.'

Zyadine hesitated in the jagged, moonlit doorway, but not because he was afraid of incoming shells; the tank firing really had stopped. He just didn't trust Maxim, particularly not the Maxim who seemed to be trusting him. Was he going to be shot in the back, by the Maxim now ostentatiously taking a pistol from his kefiyah sling, slipping the safety catch and cocking it and saying: 'Go on, get moving, I don't want you hanging around here when you could be saving our lives.'

Zyadine probably did want 'martyrdom', as far as Maxim could understand the concept, but that in itself was tunnelling his thinking into his own life and death, not his units out in the desert. And that was what Maxim was thinking about; he had no interest in shooting Zyadine – a commander without a command – in the back. But he was very interested in shooting that command in the back while it sat thought-locked, waiting to see if it got its commander back.

Zyadine took his first steps across the moonlit street towards the Land-Rover and Maxim said quietly: 'Alec, we'll be moving out about a minute after he moves off. Get on board but don't start up until I tell you. Ahmed' – the first time he'd called Al-Hamedi that; it might help, with the mistrust he'd been radiating just now – 'we'll be firing at two Centurions, probable range 1,000 metres, you choose what ammunition. The ones to the north, then we'll swing round in cover of the fort and shoot west. There's two armoured personnel carriers out there, probably closer than 1,000 metres, ten men in each one, only twenty men in all for God's sake, if we hit one we've halved the infantry attack.'

Across the street, the Land-Rover whined and roared. Its headlights came on.

Standing instinctively back from its light, Maxim went on: 'Piers will stay here with the Gimpy. It's got a hundred rounds and he can take the belt from the commander's machine-gun as well. Find a rifle slit facing west and pick off any of the infantry that de-bus from a personnel carrier we don't hit. That's all we have to do. Now *move*.'

Timbrell and Al-Hamedi did, Piers didn't. With swaying headlight beams, Zyadine pulled the Land-Rover out into the street and steered carefully through the scattered lumps of sandstone and, by now, concrete. He didn't wave good-bye, but kept going north, accelerating as he cleared the rubble.

'Start up!' Maxim called.

'It is as simple as that,' Piers said beside him. 'Shoot here, shoot there, against a force six or eight times superior, and we go home for tea. It breaks my heart to think of all the philosophers down the ages trying to make gold out of expensive stuff like lead and all the time . . .' The tank engine came alive with a noise that was explosive in the little fort. Maxim hauled himself onto it, one-handed.

'. . . And all the time,' Piers yelled up at him, 'the Army has known how to make it out of simple bullshit. Don't worry, I will hold the fort for you. It touches my poetic soul to say that.'

'Not if you don't take the cartridge belt off this gun, you won't.' Piers scrambled up to unlock it. 'And,' Maxim shouted in his ear, 'watch your *front*. Don't start worrying about your flanks and rear until you've seen nothing for five minutes. It'll take them that long. And you'll get a bit of bombardment before they de-bus, if they do. Don't worry about it. Just keep your head down and your eyes up.'

Piers dropped to the crackly camel-dung floor. 'Thank you, boy.' Maxim didn't hear it, it was whispered as from the bottom of a doomed Welsh mine-shaft; but in fact Piers was feeling quite cheerful as he rigged the machine-gun to fire from the chosen slit and laid the spare belt of ammunition carefully across lumps of stone and wood that should keep it off the dung floor. Maybe not cheerful, just a light-headedness, a total forgetfulness of past and any future beyond the next minutes in which people might come to shoot at him and he would be able to shoot back. It was all so simple and not at all lonely, as the tank crashed out of the doorway and left him alone, because nobody could be lonely with a machine-gun.

There were three dots on the PVD's infra-red screen and Al-Hamedi was centring on one of them as the tank swung left and stopped in the middle of the street, protected from the west by the bulk of the fort.

'Fire when ready,' Maxim said. He saw the laser ranging figures stabilise in his own sight, the breech grunted down fractionally.

'Firing n –' the tank jumped back on its heels and another dot moved on the screen, diminished, hovered and flashed.

'Target!' Al-Hamedi shouted exuberantly.

'Engage second target.' The autoloader was already

290

cranking up a fresh round. The breech slammed shut and almost immediately slapped backward. A new dot appeared on the screen (of course, solid shot would carry a tracer in its backside so the gunner could see where a miss went). And that was a miss: the dot bounced off the road to die among the stars.

But now there was only one dot on the screen.

'No tank target in sight,' Al-Hamedi said with careful emphasis. 'Do you want to shoot Major Zyadine?' He – the Land-Rover – was the last dot. The other Centurion had backed out of sight.

'Don't bother. Alec, reverse hard . . . Stop! Left stick, advance . . . Stop! Gunner, targets at about a thousand. Take the nearest.' With a live tank still up north, he had shunted the tank round the corner of the fort, facing west and safe from the north. And the nearest targets to the west would be the personnel carriers.

The tank jumped and a dot on the screen flashed and dwindled as its engine – and its men – cooled. He had no need to give another fire order, the turret had already jerked around, the autoloader rammed in a new round, *the beast was working!* Put as many dots on the screen as you like, send the four corners of the world in arms and we'll just pick them off like tin ducks in a shooting gallery.

Jump, dot on screen, but no flash. Then a ragged series of flashes as the tanks out there opened fire, and Maxim realised he didn't want to get into a four-against-one tank battle. They'd killed one personnel carrier, halved the infantry attack as promised.

'Alec, hard reverse. St –' But they'd already rammed the concrete building across the street, obviously knocked it flat because all the impact did was sway Maxim's head back.

'Advance, right stick, get us up beside the fort doorway.' They jumped forward, swivelling right, then Maxim's seat was whipped around as the gun muzzle – sticking out a good eleven feet ahead of the tank – caught the corner of the fort and flicked the turret and its basket left.

It dazed Maxim and Al-Hamedi, but Timbrell was unaffected and shouting: 'Traverse left, give me some *room*!'

While Maxim was trying to find the controls and while they were still side-on to the second tank, the world seemed to explode.

37

Agnes found George in his room upstairs. He didn't try to hide the glass on his desk, just asked: 'Would you like one?'

'No thanks.'

'I'm sorry, I just couldn't hold –'

'I know.' She sat down. 'Cactus is still orbiting the area. He's lost contact with Harry but says he's seen a lot of explosions on his radar.'

'It couldn't have been radar, explosions wouldn't show on that, it must be infra-red. And Harry's radio's probably gone on the blink, it happens all the time in tanks.'

'Especially tanks that are being shot at by half a dozen other tanks.'

'Yes . . . the radios are probably in the turret bustle –'

'The *what*?'

'Back end of the turret, it turns with the turret, simplifies the wiring, makes it easy to get at, but it's vulnerable.'

'George, are you trying to reassure me? Because if so, stop it.'

'Why did you come up here?'

Agnes lit a cigarette – something she hadn't dared do in the Snowflake office, nobody else there smoked (or dared to). 'They're not trying to *do* anything, just making sure no blame attaches to them. All the Cabinet Office crowd, and Edwin Giles himself – he doesn't care if the Service doesn't *do* anything, just that it doesn't make a mistake. I always thought the Service was full of –'

'I know what you thought it was full of.'

'– but at least I thought it was trying to do something apart from telling itself where it got its shirts made.'

'The trouble is, we haven't had a good war for so long.'

'I beg your pardon?'

'In a war, you can win victories. In peace, you avoid making mistakes. If there's no victories to be won, how d'you judge a man? Then you get a war and somebody orders the charge of the Light Brigade.' George was speaking with the deliberate one-foot-in-front-of-the-other diction of somebody proving he wasn't touched by drink. But his thinking *isn't* touched, Agnes realised; he wouldn't still have this office if it were – and probably he won't really stop drinking while his thoughts stay sober. .

'Harry's a bit of an exception,' George went on. 'That's why his future isn't so certain – his career, I mean.'

'His future could be over now. It's just not *knowing*.'

'You've joined a long line of waiting women, probably headed by Penelope, wife to a certain Odysseus, believed also to have used the name Ulysses on occasion, who toddled off to the Trojan war and stayed unheard of for –'

'George, shut up.'

Talking to the remnants swilling in his glass, George said: 'We tried – you, and Nurse Barret, and me, and Scottie did what he could – and we may yet have won. *We* did something. Now all we have to do is wait.'

'I've remembered why I came up here: it was to have a quiet place to cry; your ladies' loos are . . . And when I've done that, you can give me a drink.'

38

The tank had been moving but was now stopped. It was very dark – the PVD screen and most of the lights on the control panel were out – and smelt of fire. Only when Maxim fumbled aside the hatch above him and a mixture of moonlight, dust and smoke poured in did he realise his eyesight had been knocked double, like once in a football game, like once or twice in deep drunkenness. But even double vision couldn't account for the shape of the turret's rear end and the smoke sagging out of it.

They were alongside the fort again – two slightly overlapping forts – facing north. The hit had spun the turret again, probably dizzying him more than Al-Hamedi, who seemed to be moving in the opposite seat, testing controls, and Timbrell who was calling: 'Are you all right? Can we fire? Or d'you want to get out of here?'

'Hang on, Alec,' Maxim mumbled. 'Can we fire?'

The turret creaked hideously overhead, metal tearing at metal, obviously damaged and with the hydraulics or electrics shot out, since Al-Hamedi was grinding a hand-wheel and gasping with the effort. Maxim rammed his forehead against the sight, to see if it were working.

It was – double, of course. He shut one eye, glaring and blinking as the landscape creaked round with the traversing gun, grasped the pistol grip – now useless except for the rangefinder button and perhaps the trigger – and there was a dot to the right, coming towards the centre. The Centurion up north.

'On! Are we loaded?'

'No.'

'Shot, d'you think?'

But it wasn't that easy, because the autoloader had failed, too. Al-Hamedi was hauling a shell from the magazine below the breech and levering it over his right shoulder into the gun. Maxim had found the elevating wheel and was grinding it up to match the laser-designated spark on the sight . . . Then the world had to end again.

The padded eyepiece of the sight became a boxing-glove on the end of a punch coming in at over a thousand miles an hour. He thought it had broken his neck; it had certainly blinded him with tears.

'Ahmed, take the sight and fire. I can't see anything!'

He felt the elevating wheel move as Al-Hamedi took over, just remembered to lift his head back – and that hurt – for the whack of the recoil.

'Target,' Al-Hamedi said.

Piers had kept his eyes westward despite the explosions in the street behind him – some the tank's gun, some incoming shells – that lit the fort briefly and then sent slow drifts of dust down from the roof. Everything that happened near this damned fort made the roof leak dust. He had seen one personnel carrier, a dim scorpion crawling out of the dunes in the moonlight, 'brew up' – that Army phrase that could mean making tea or turning an armoured vehicle and its crew into a shower of white-hot metal. The shells had started just after that, slamming into the wall and not penetrating but shivering scabs of sandstone off the inside – and dust, of course.

And then men, sprawling like disturbed ants from the last dunes, visible in the moonlight only because they were moving, and he set the sights for 600 and squeezed off a burst, wishing he had tracer to see where the bullets were landing, not worrying it would give away his position since they knew his position – and hadn't that Maxim already said something like that? – and then, at the third burst, some of the figures had fallen down. Or just lain down.

But the others were running back into the dunes. He fired at the running ones and two of them fell down, too. They hadn't meant to do that while running away. So it works. I squeeze the trigger and people fall down dead. God, I think I belong on Your board of directors now. But it was only that bastard of an English major who . . . then he heard the shells bursting again, the rattle of machine-gun fire (it must be hitting the fort, but made no noise soaking into the soft sandstone) and realised how many fingers on how many triggers and how big a board of directors it would be.

He suddenly knew there was somebody behind him – not heard: his ears were singing from the explosions – and knew a moment of utter terror because he had just killed people and so it was *right* that somebody should creep up and kill him. He was wrenching the heavy machine-gun from its slit to swing it around when Maxim said: 'What's been happening here?'

In breathless bursts but trying to be strictly military and unemotional, Piers told him.

'How many?' Maxim asked, moving to the slit to peer out.

'I think I hit four. It could be five.'

'Out of ten. They won't mount another attack. They should have lobbed shells on the roof, they should have had mortars, then fired smoke to blind you.'

'And that is your professional fully-adjusted-for-seasonal-averages opinion of what they should have done to kill us all?'

'It's what they were there for.'

At some point Maxim had pulled his left arm out of the kefiyah sling which now draped around his shoulders like an old lady's shawl. There was fresh blood glinting on the dried stain on his combat jacket, and his right hand was black with blood. *Right* hand?

'How is the tank?' Piers asked.

'It moves, the gun fires . . . Alec's dead. I want you to –'

297

'How did . . . ?'

'He opened his hatch and stuck his head out and got it shot off. Maybe he didn't trust his own design, maybe his periscope got hit first, it's all a mess now, I don't know. I want you to guide Al-Hamedi back in here. We've got Alec out.' So it was Timbrell's blood on that right hand.

'And what happens now?'

'We sit in the toughest tank in the world inside a stone fort until their ammunition runs out. All I said to Zyadine was true: they're wearing themselves down out there. And now they've got casualties to take care of, too. You didn't kill all the ones you hit, the normal ratio's about five to one, injured to dead. Lot easier for an army if everybody who got hit died automatically; when you've got a mate screaming in pain you have to detach a couple more to look after him. Much more simple if he was dead. Just press on regardless. You may not have killed anybody. Lucky to do so at that range, in this light.'

Piers managed to feel both affronted and relieved at the same time, then realised that Maxim might have intended that – the relief, anyway. He looked at the hunched figure, wrapped in such a mixture of blood-stained clothing, leaning against the wall and holding the binoculars to his eyes with a blood-blackened hand. What sort of man *are* you? he wondered.

'They're moving,' Maxim said. There was a distant surging noise of engines from the west. 'Moving north. I don't get it. Sergeant! Fire a round at something. Anything.'

At the siege of Carcassonne – or somewhere, it was pure legend but pure tactics too – they had thrown their last goose to the besiegers to show how much food they had to spare, and the besiegers had given up and gone home. Now he would throw one of their last shells, just to show the gun was still working.

Piers covered his ears against the noise but there was nothing he could do to stop the inevitable dust.

*　　*　　*

George put the phone down. 'Cactus is just leaving the area. He reports hostile units moving north, concentrating on the road about three kilometres up.'

'North?' Agnes had been delicately mopping her eyes and sipping the vodka George had poured.

'North is what he said. They can't be mounting an attack from there. They're pulling out.'

'You mean they've done what they –'

'No. They've failed. Nobody got into Point Tango. It worked. We've won.'

Agnes started crying again. He'll be coming home, she thought. Safe. But wounded, hideously crippled and not Harry any more. Or his airliner will crash in the Mediterranean or hit an Alp. Oh God, I really must be in love with him.

What in *hell* good does that do me?

'They *are* going north,' Piers called down from roof. 'Seem to be converging on the road, out of sight. Maybe your friend Zyadine –'

'No,' Maxim said. 'I don't think they'll be listening to him – if he got through okay. Not since they realised we used him as cover for our sortie. But north's no place to mount an attack.'

'Then perhaps they are pulling back to Aqaba; you said yourself they would have to go soon. But if you think it is unprofessional of them, get on the radio and –'

'The radios are shot out.' Maxim sat down on the steps to the roof, then had to move over as Piers came down. 'Did your pilot, Len, have a wife?'

'Margaret, – yes, I know her.'

'And Alec Timbrell? – I didn't get to talk to him, not in that way.'

'He was married, but I never . . . Oh, I see: you are thinking you must be writing letters to them. But you don't –'

'I was in command.'

Despite a Welsh love of hearing his own voice, Piers

299

suddenly decided not to say it was lucky Maxim did not have to write letters to the families of everybody he had got killed in the last sixteen hours, only those on his own side. Then he thought of being in Maxim's place – a huddled lump of foul clothing on the steps to the hatchway – and clamped his mouth tighter.

Al-Hamedi came across from the tank, now backed into the fort again, and began a technical report of what systems were dead, half-dead or working.

'And the BV?' Maxim asked.

'It is boiling.'

'Good. We'll have a cup of hot something . . .'

'Water.' Piers could hear, not see, Al-Hamedi's grin.

'Better than nothing. Then we'll move south if we're sure they've pulled out. You'll have to teach Piers about loading the gun, first, I can handle the firing. Just in case. Oh, and we should have got any papers off Alec, I know he had a notebook about the tank . . .'

No, I do not want to be this man, Piers thought, but I think – just think – we have to have such men around. God help this world, but until He does . . . I have to drink a cup of hot water and learn how to load a tank gun.

GAVIN LYALL

BLAME THE DEAD

'There was just the one shot, and maybe I heard the thud as it went into his body. Then I was on my face in the roadway, gun held straight in front . . .'

Just one shot on a snowy Sunday in France, but it spoilt James Card's professional reputation as a bodyguard – as well as leaving him with a body he hardly knew and a pistol he didn't want to explain.

That was when he knew the time had come to take a look into the ex-life and times of Martin Fenwick, sometime Lloyd's underwriter and deceased man of many parts . . .

'First rate . . . the writing, like a Hitchcock movie, instantly transmits the flavour of each new face, each new scene'

The Guardian

Post·A·Book

A Royal Mail service in association with the Book Marketing Council & The Booksellers Association.

Post·A·Book is a Post Office trademark.

GAVIN LYALL

SHOOTING SCRIPT

'I don't know if you're working for Jiminez or not. But either way, the general made a mistake. You should've been in jail. Now you're loose, and that worries me. Because you're still a killer . . .'

Flying charter around the Caribbean wasn't quite the same as flying high cover against Migs in Korea. But it was a living. A flying living.

Carr had been careful, kept his hands clean, built up a solid reputation. In this part of the world you couldn't be too careful. So why, all of a sudden, did everyone look at him as though he was working for the rebels?

Maybe it was the film company who'd hired him. And the plane. Why did the plane have to be a B-25, an old World War Two bomber . . .?

'Caribbean politics made even more turbulent by one of the most compelling of contemporary storytellers'
The New York Times

HODDER AND STOUGHTON PAPERBACKS

CLIVE EGLETON

PICTURE OF THE YEAR

Seven Moslem peasants killed on the Soviet side of the Iran border. A woman drowned in her bath in Yorkshire, while in Switzerland her husband is shot at point blank range. In Germany, an American soldier inexplicably goes missing. Four totally unrelated incidents. Or are they?

Michael Radford of the Department of Subversive Warfare is the man who starts to make some crucial connections and suspects a major intelligence operation is underway. But first, in a race against time and the enemy, he has to decipher a satellite photograph that, at first sight routine, is set to become the Picture of the Year.

'Rooted somewhere in that territory staked out by Ambler and le Carré'
The Literary Review

'Sweeps gustily along to a brutal near-comedy of defection'
The Sunday Times

HODDER AND STOUGHTON PAPERBACKS

MORE TITLES AVAILABLE FROM
HODDER AND STOUGHTON PAPERBACKS

GAVIN LYALL

☐	42976 3	Blame the Dead	£2.95
☐	42975 5	Shooting Script	£2.95

CLIVE EGLETON

☐	42151 7	Picture of the Year	£2.95

Charles 372

12:30

All these books are available at your local bookshop or news-agent, or can be ordered direct from the publisher. Just tick the titles you want and fill in the form below.

Prices and availability subject to change without notice.

Hodder and Stoughton Paperbacks, P.O. Box 11, Falmouth, Cornwall.

Please send cheque or postal order, and allow the following for postage and packing:

U.K. – 55p for one book, plus 22p for the second book, and 14p for each additional book ordered up to a £1.75 maximum.

B.F.P.O. and EIRE – 55p for the first book, plus 22p for the second book, and 14p per copy for the next 7 books, 8p per book thereafter.

OTHER OVERSEAS CUSTOMERS – £1.00 for the first book, plus 25p per copy for each additional book.

Name ....

Address ....

....